I0735137

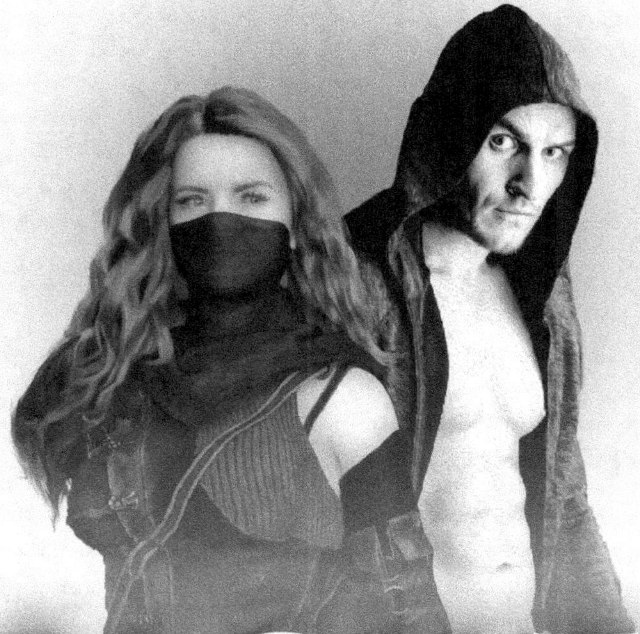

FIGHT

for

DARKNESS

Susan Stradiotto & S. Johnson

Eden Prairie, MN

Fight for Darkness

Published by
Bronzewood Books
14920 Ironwood Ct.
Eden Prairie, MN 55346

Cover Design: Bronzewood Books

Interior Design: Bronzewood Books

Edited by: Purple Rose Editing, LLC

Paperback ISBN-13: 978-1-949357-47-9

eBook ISBN-13: 978-1-949357-48-6

Printed in the USA

CHAPTER 1

Pain exploded in Kane Macleod's jaw. He shook off the blow, sweat flinging from his ear, but a dark curtain still narrowed his sight toward an all-too-familiar pinhole. Another punch landed, and blood flew from his mouth. The sweet twinge of agony zinged across his cheekbone. The cage bit into his back. He raised his gloved hands to block the next blow.

Almost.

He was almost to the point. The dark cloud limited his sight; heat built inside.

Kane threw an uppercut into Ramm's jaw, and the fighter stumbled backward. The blow put distance between them. Reprieve. Kane's vision narrowed further—a tunnel surrounded in black, a rifle's sight—the crystal-clear image of Ramm at the center. Kane lurched off the fence, his muscles coiled. He reared back to—

DING!

The ref jumped in Kane's path. Kane dodged, still intent on Ramm, but an arm across his chest said, *Cool off for a hot minute.*

"To your corner, Kane," growled the ref.

Somewhere far away, a squeal and rattle sounded. The cage

opening? Hands on Kane's arms pulled him backward. His trainer, Broc. And the cut man. What was his name? It wasn't important in the heat of the moment.

The dark cloud receded, and Kane backed into his corner, feeling like an animal trapped in barbwire. He spat the mouthguard into Broc's open hand, blood and all. Eyes closed, he opened his mouth. Water flooded inside and then flowed pink into the sickly yellow pan.

"Shocked you haven't Raged yet." Broc forcibly turned Kane's head one way then the other, examining the damage. "You're usually there by two. Seal that one up, Tim."

Oh yeah, Tim. That was the cut man's name.

Kane asked, "What"—hiss—"round?" He winced as Tim swiped a Q-tip over the cut above his eye.

"That was four. One more." Broc pushed away the cut man and mopped Kane's face with a rag.

Kane pushed away the towel and took the deepest breath he could manage. Ribs still felt good. No blood dripping into his eye. He zeroed in on his opponent, the reigning UFC Heavyweight champion. For another minute anyway. With Kane's laser focus, the crowd, his team, the announcers—all the commotion around him—went mute.

A toll bell resounded in his head, ringing like angels' voices, and an odd form of comfort settled over him. He knew what he needed to do. Muscle memory. Thought process. A well-oiled machine.

Fingers snapped in front of his eyes. "Kane!"

Kane blinked at his trainer. "Yeah, what?"

"You got this?"

"Fucking bell brought me back. Next one, he's on the mat."

Broc gave a single nod, held up a fresh mouthguard, and left the cage when Kane grabbed it.

Kane leaned forward, gripping the chain link fence to hold him in place against his coiling leg muscles. He was ready to pounce like a tiger on prey. His tongue ran over his rubber mouthguard, and he tasted blood. It landed on his tongue and fueled him like fire.

Behind him, amid the rumble of the crowd, someone asked, "He gonna pull it off?"

Was that Tim? If so, he's fired after the match. Wait, did Kane get that choice? It didn't matter. *Stay focused, Kane.*

"Two more punches, and he'll earn his name," said Broc.

That's my man!

Kane bounced on the balls of his feet, ready. He punched one gloved hand into the other, eyes locked on to Ian Ramm. And Ian glared back, black pupils taking up the whole of his irises, and his lips pulled back in a sneer, revealing his neon green mouthguard.

This title was Kane's, and he would fight to his death.

DING!

The fifth and final round was on.

Kane rushed out of the corner faster than a cheetah's attack, eyeing his opponent like a slab of meat. He sneered at Ramm but refused to lift his fists. Defense? He didn't need any fucking defense. No, he needed to punch.

To fight.

Not act like a coward.

Kane wasn't a coward, and in front of the hundreds of people watching, he refused to be.

He needed to wake the Raging beast inside, so he lowered his fists.

Ramm answered the invitation, rearing back and letting his red-gloved fist fly. It happened as if in slo-mo, and Kane turned slightly to let the punch blow off his jaw. He danced back a step, feeling the jostle through his calf, thigh, glute, abs, and into his shoulders. A ripple crossed his body like a tidal wave on the shore. A rushing, crashing sound in his ears, deafening along with the hollers around him. Another wave of noise ready to collapse him.

Ramm closed in and went for the clench around Kane's

neck. Kane ducked and wove under his opponent's arm, spun, and turned back to face Ramm. A smile cracked Kane's face.

His opponent came in for another strike. Hook, jab, hook, jab. Kane braced his core and took them all. Not an ounce of pain. Not a push of air. Kane was a stone statue.

Then, Ramm stepped back, drawing his brows down as he sized up Kane. But Kane remained utterly still, his fists at his sides. The curtain closed in around a central point in his vision again. Here it was. The beast.

The Rage.

Red.

Hot.

Blinding.

Ian Ramm blurred in Kane's sight. Then the image came back in high-res. Suddenly, the bastard across the ring wasn't Ian Ramm; he was morphing into the *monster*. He was someone from long, long ago. And that fucker's voice: *Just you and me here, kid.* The last word echoed as if Kane's ears were the deepest, coldest caverns. That man couldn't come close to Ramm's 270 or even Kane's 265. That fucker—the coach, as Kane remembered him—was a buck-eighty at most with a receding hairline and horn-rimmed glasses.

Kane's remaining pinpoint of vision hazed over in red. The slimy voice said again, *Just you and me here, kid.* Kane tucked his chin and gave in to The Rage.

His fists flew, knees punched upward, feet kicked. Meanwhile, *the coach's* nose and ribs crunched. The coach fell to the mat. Kane's feet found the soft spots between ribs and hips, then he dove on top of his opponent. Left-right-left-right. Over and over. Kane would beat away the demon if it was the last thing he did.

It would be the last thing he would ever do.

DING! DING!

Hands pulled him away, but Kane's arms kept flying.

The coach wasn't dead yet. Eyes bugging out, pupils rolled up into the back of his head, but not enough blood. Never enough blood.

Somewhere in the dark, the timbre of Broc's bass grounded Kane, and he sucked in a cool breath. Red receded like the riptide pulling back out to sea, but he still heard the pounding in his ears. Louder than his thundering heartbeat or the stomping on the concrete floor. An earthquake. Blood gushed in his ears, and he blinked the redness from his vision.

"Kane, man. I gotchu," said Broc. "Slow down. Slowly now."

The bass drum silenced, and the cheering blasted against his ears. Some boos too. Then, over the mic, "Kane 'The Rage' Macleod beats The Ramm with a TKO!" Another emcee said, "That's right, Joe, technical knock-outs are our local hero's trademark. And after that one, Kane will be heading to Vegas for the UFC Heavyweight title match!"

The dark haze was receding now, inking back into his peripheral vision, and Kane squinted against the spotlights. Someone thrust a belt into his hands, cool to the touch and moist with humidity, and Kane scanned the ring. The medics were helping Ian Ramm out of the cage. Not the demon The Rage had showed him. Ramm—not Coach Robbins. Fuck!

Ramm stumbled, but walked mostly, blood dribbling in his wake.

Good, Kane thought, *he's alive.*

Something dark in him added, *For now.*

Broc's hands landed on Kane's shoulders. "You good, man? Come back to me."

"I'm here, Broc." Kane hefted the belt to another round of cheers, and a smile broke across his face. He spat his mouthguard onto the floor and watched groupies scramble for a piece of him. Turning to his trainer, he commanded, "Locker room, pronto."

He had come back from the darkness, but he was done with the limelight. He needed a shower and to hit the street, disappear somewhere in Wickney's concrete jungle before he went to his apartment to crash. Kane looked into the aisle at Ian Ramm, who waved to the crowd before disappearing into his own locker room. He would be fine. And Ramm had the UFC to thank for that.

Damn good thing Kane found this outlet for his Rage. If it wasn't for the bell, the refs, and the trainers, he'd probably have . . . well, he tamped down that possibility. That time had passed, and he had survived another day.

Kane's voice was as distant as his mind when he asked Broc, "We won, though?"

"You bet. Three-point-five mil, man. Some take for a fighter not even on the boards a year ago."

Smiling again at the crowd, Kane beat a path toward the locker room. He picked up speed, relishing the sound of his feet on the floor, and jogged toward solitude. Before ducking through the door, he held the belt high and gave a final roar. And the crowd roared back, albeit sounded like squealing piglets rather than a boar.

"There he goes," the emcee wailed over the PA system from the arena beyond the now-closed door. "Kane 'The Rage' Macleod."

"He showed us his name tonight," added the other emcee, "and the rookie is on his way!"

Kane stopped at the shower door and put a fist to Broc's chest. "Need some time." Something deep clawed to the surface, like it had in the ring, and he didn't want it to lash out against his trainer.

Broc lowered his gaze and gave a nod. "We'll be in the room there."

Kane slammed the door to the showers closed, stripped his gloves and clothes, and turned on the hot water. The hiss of the pipes echoed, louder than the splatter of water against cold tile. The room steamed up, and he stepped under the faucet. Scalding water bit his skin, but it washed away the blood and sweat along with the memories. The pain told him he was still alive and everything would be okay. He could tuck the coach away again for a time.

Kane let the water run over his face for minutes, then turned and slumped against the cold white tile. The contrast in temperature shocked him into reality again as he slid to the floor, head in his hands. Maybe one day, someway, somehow, he'd banish his demon.

Showered and dressed, Kane slung his duffel over one shoulder. He opened the locker room door and winced when the hinges gave a low whine. To Kane's ears, it sounded like trumpets announcing his departure. Go figure, no one was in the hall. He sure as shit expected Broc to be waiting when he emerged. Damn good thing he wasn't because Kane needed to GTFO—get the fuck out. Club Infinity sounded superb. Thumping music, dark spaces where he could fade into the shadows and enjoy his one and only after-the-big-fight drink. Sazerac—shaken, not stirred.

The humid night slapped him in the face, but he'd take July's stickiness over January's icy bite any day. The heat on his skin felt good. Hood up, he turned west away from the Wickney Convention Center entrance and toward the West End, a darker section of the city where more people than not would ignore him. After the dazzling lights on him during the fight and the crowd roaring his name, he wanted to slip through a few cracks and be anonymous. Even if it was only short-lived. One day, though. One day, he would find his way out of the accursed spotlight.

"Kane!" a voice he'd known all his life yelled.

The Rage, still so close to the surface after the fight, coursed through Kane's veins again, but he took a deep, stabilizing breath. He kept his eyes wide and focused on the concrete scene around him. He was no longer in a cage.

"Kane, wait!"

An overinflated sense of guilt grabbed him and held him in place. *Put on a happy face, man.* Kane raised his brows, took another deep breath, smiled, and turned. "Hi, Kiera." His sister found him without fail after every fight.

She stopped running as she reached him. "Where are you headed?"

"Home," Kane lied.

"We should go to Mom's."

"I'm beat, Kiera, literally." He ran a thumb over his split lip.

Kiera reached toward his face, her forehead puckering with

her standard nurse's concern.

He turned his head and pulled the hood closer to shadow the bruises. "I'm fine. Better than fine. That fight just set me in the black permanently."

His sister folded her arms over her chest and put out one hip. He looked her almost in the eye, and her scowl said she wasn't letting it go tonight. "Kane, you know Mom doesn't give a shit about the money. She just wants to touch you and feel that you're safe."

"Really?" Kane snapped, but Kiera just quirked a brow, so he added, "You know good and well she listened to the fight and knows I'm safe."

Their mom couldn't see, but she would have had the TV on regardless, listening to the fight blow by blow, grasping the arms of her chair every time the crowd gasped, and pacing her tiny living room for sixty seconds between every round.

"She wants her hands on you. *You* know good and well that she doesn't rest until she can feel how bad your injuries are."

"Not happening, Kiera."

They faced off on the street beside the convention center for what Kane would have sworn was five minutes. Standing there with her lips pinched, his sister was just as stubborn . . . well, almost. But something eased between Kane's shoulders. His sister and mom were all he had, so he'd give her what she asked. Only not right now. He reached for Kiera, pulled her close, and hugged her around the shoulders.

Quieter, he said, "I need space tonight. Go home. Tell Mom you saw and touched me and that I'm fine. I'll come over first thing in the morning."

Kiera squeezed him gently around the waist. "Promise?"

He let her go and stepped back. "Promise."

Her eyes flitted away and back to meet his, then she nodded. "Make it before noon?"

Kane nodded. *Though no promises,* he thought but didn't say.

"Just be safe."

"Always."

CHAPTER 2

MALIN LURKED ON A BROAD window ledge four stories above the street, her boots securing her foothold while her cloak puddled around her and flowed over the rim. Wickney at night had the best of the best shadows, the places where dark witches like her thrived. The streetlights were tinted amber and left pools of golden light along the sidewalks below, but the city's old masonry absorbed most of the glow. This made the city perfect for the war against the Light-wielding Semaphors.

A gentle night's breeze rustled the feathers at her collar, itching her skin. Nothing was unusual about the night in Wickney's West End. Not many cars frequented the narrow streets, and people favored walking in the few warm months available. Horns blared and sirens sounded from the freeways in the distance, but they barely disrupted the buzz and thump coming from Club Infinity across the street. She felt the buzz across skin, hair rising, and the thump against her rib cage.

Two warriors from her coven were inside the club, but Malin preferred this vantage point. Here, she could see and catalog every human, faerie, and other creature who frequented the club, and there were many. More came each day. She'd yet to see the group of Semaphors that Morgana had described. The monotony grated on her nerves. She checked her watch for what seemed the hundredth time since Conrí and Tierney had entered Infinity.

Nothing.

Beneath her cloak, Malin's bonded dragan slid around her waist and vibrated as he rested his head over her shoulder near that hollow just below the collarbone. "Soon, Breyze," Malin said to soothe her familiar. He was thirsting for a fight as well. "Be ready."

Malin startled when a laughing couple stumbled out of the club under the neon sign. But they were only human, and by the weave in their steps, they were incredibly drunk. A shriek of laughter cut the tension, and she eased her back against the stone, sat on her heels, and moved her hand to her belt. Weapons still at the ready. She weighed them in her hands. Malin knew the weapons of Darkness well after years of training.

She sighed. It *had* to be soon, right?

Her watch buzzed, and she looked down at the screen.

TIERNEY: "GOT 4 ON THE MOVE. 30 SEC."

Malin hit a button on the side, and the countdown started. She popped upright in the tall opening. "Breyze, now."

When the bite pierced at her collarbone, she waited for the flood of . . . ah, yes, there it was. Magical venom coursed through her veins. Malin took a split second to let it permeate her senses then called the wind: "*Gaoth*." The dark magic answered, and she levitated, easing her body downward to the street. She moved a hand and steered her descent toward the shadows beyond the streetlights outside of Club Infinity.

When her boots touched the ground, she smirked. "And they said witches ride brooms."

Malin checked her watch again. *Ten seconds. Nine, eight, seven . . .*

When the first two men—not that they deserved the honor of being called "men"—emerged, she put on her tinted glasses. As a witch of Darkness, one of the Cailleach, Malin had to protect herself against the Semaphor auras. Light was her proverbial Achilles heel, and the putrid green surrounding the Light-wielders would be enough to blind her. Two more Semaphor slime-balls exited the club, each also glowing with a putrid greenish-yellow toxicity. She hunkered down, far enough in the shadows that she could stalk her prey like the hunter she was. They gathered in the spotlight, chatting. Then, the obvious leader of the four whirled in her direction. All of them scanned the street as they strutted toward her.

"Ready, Breyze?" Malin whispered and felt a vibration from the dragan wrapped about her shoulders. She curled her fingers around the handle of her weapon.

Tierney and Conrí exited Club Infinity in the next second. Like Malin, they could slide by almost any human unnoticed, but if an onlooker knew what to look for, their shades and cloaks would give them away. Her friends and fellow dark witches would see into the shadows and find her, so Malin gave them a nod.

Palming an S-blade handle in each hand, she moved to the alley's mouth. And waited. When the Semaphors came close enough, she whispered, "*Lanna*," and the S-blades zinged into existence, a long S snaking out from both ends of each handle. The blades, forged by the All Mother's darklings from *Dorcha*—the Darkness itself—made the distinctive sound of a sword being unsheathed.

The sound drew the passing Semaphors' attention.

Perfect.

"Are you on Godric's mission?" she whispered to the slime. She needn't raise her voice; where she had sensitivity to light, they had sensitivity to sound, and they tilted their heads to listen.

The four marched in unison, their attention square on Malin. Good.

Tierney and Conrí skipped into a run as they came up behind the Semaphors. Malin backed into the alley, and the Semaphors tracked only her movements, using whatever powers their Maker had granted them. In a readied crouch, Malin stepped back deeper into the alley and commanded to Breyze,

"Venom."

Breyze struck his teeth into the skin on her neck, and more dark magic flooded through her body.

"*Dubh*," Malin said, freeing the magic granted by her familiar to do its work.

Any light in the area evaporated, leaving her, her friends, and the Semaphors in heavy blackness. Malin removed her shades; she'd paid a pretty penny for those and didn't want to sacrifice them to the fight. She continued to ease backward step by step until Tierney and Conrí closed in behind her foes.

The air felt heavy around her suddenly—the calming effect Conrí's dragan, Rezei, emanated. Malin tried to jerk out of it, but it pressed hard on her shoulders until they began to slouch.

Malin groaned, fighting her heavy eyelids. "Breyze, tell Rezei to focus his calm on the slime only."

After a few chatters, the heaviness lifted from Malin, but the Semaphors still shook their heads under a dazed effect. She shook her shoulders and lifted her head, eyes focusing on the slime.

Zhing-zhing. Zhing. Tierney and Conrí called their S-blades forth.

Two of the Semaphors turned so the four stood back to back. All four held their hands out low and to the sides, palms up, and started to chant. Their words were hefty but gravel-like, so low that the concrete grew dense.

"Now!" Malin lunged forward before their Light could counter her spell. She swung her blade high toward the first Semaphor. Yes, number one was definitely distracted. He extended his weapon—a Maker's staff, they called them—and batted away her blade. Malin whirled low and cut at the second's stance. He leaped into the air, and Malin's blade swiped beneath his feet. When number two landed, he called forth an identical staff, growled, and aimed the end at Malin.

She turned her head and pinched her eyes. "Light!" she called in warning to Tierney and Conrí.

Just in time too, because she heard the ray of Light sizzle as it flew behind her. Next, a blow struck her upside the head. She opened her eyes to number one, rearing back for a second strike, and crossed her blades above her head.

Beyond her two opponents, numbers three and four engaged with her covenmates, but with two to fight, Malin didn't have time to focus on them. She put a boot in number two's chest and whirled to counter another attack from the first.

"Coming," Conrí yelled.

"Got it!" Malin called back, slashed one of her S-blades at number two, whirled, and slid a blade between number one's solar plexus and his ribs. She felt the blade hesitate, then with a grunt and more pressure, it sank into the cartilage. A gurgle of flesh and blood tore through the grunts. She angled her head to look into his terror-filled eyes as he misted into nothingness. Her blade came away clean. She'd never understand what their Maker did to eliminate the blood, but when vanquished, Semaphors simply evaporated into thin air. Better for cleanup, she supposed.

Another lash landed on Malin's back. Standing with her legs wide and feet staggered to give more leverage, she faced number two and twirled the blades. She stopped with one blade poised to slash and the other ready to stab. Conrí dispatched number four and slid up behind number two. Conrí's S-blade wrapped around his throat and paused.

Malin heard the distinctive hiss of number three evaporate. One left . . . only one.

"No!" ordered Malin. "Don't vanquish him yet."

She needed him to find Godric, the sole reason she had come on this hunt.

True to form, the Semaphors hadn't said a single word to them during the fight.

She sauntered over to the bald man, his staff lying on the ground at his side. His hand reached for it, fingers inches away. "Hold him," Malin told Conrí.

He obeyed. No question. Following her orders. Malin was his superior whether she would admit it or not.

Malin released her concentration on her S-blades, and they

vanished. She took a step, then another. "Breyze, let's have a little fun."

Her dragan, the eldest bonded dragan in her coven, slithered out. Breyze's black-out goggles remained tightly in place, and he felt his way with his forked tongue. The small dragans were concealed under the witches' cloaks and would die on contact if the Light reached their sensitive eyes. But Malin and her team had this situation under control. Conrí held the Semaphor beneath the arms, the slime's hands splayed wide so he couldn't call for the Light he needed to harm them.

Breyze slithered toward number two, pausing mere inches from his face with venom dripping onto the ground. He hissed.

"Now," Malin started, "you will tell me where I can find Godric."

She couldn't count how many semaphors she'd asked this very question before killing them. She knew they *could* speak because Godric did. But they never talked to her. Maybe one day, she'd get lucky, and Godric would be the one she and Breyze faced off against. But, for the time being, she would just have to try with each and every one until she had some luck. This had been going on for a decade. Or more? But she wouldn't stop until she'd avenged her sister's death.

Number two squirmed and worked his jaw as if he were chewing.

Malin grabbed his chin and opened his mouth. Her fingers dug into his skin. "Oh no you don't! Answer my fucking question, bastard!" Not again!

But it was too late. His open mouth filled with white froth. He convulsed, then he poofed into mist along with his Maker's staff that had fallen to the ground.

"Bastard!" Malin tossed back her head and roared into the night. When finished, she uttered in a deadly tone, "Godric, you will answer to me and to the All Mother. One day. Somewhere. Somehow. I will have you on your knees before my blades and Breyze's venom."

They wouldn't kill him outright. No, Godric didn't deserve such mercy. What she could do to him flooded her mind.

Malin rotated in a slow circle, hands out with palms upward, and spoke into the ether as if her words would ring in Godric's ears like a clarion bell. "By the All Mother and all she granted you, you will suffer for eternity for what you've done to my family and my coven."

A can tinkled near the alley's mouth.

Tierney tucked away her S-blade handles. "We have company." She waved her hand and erased the dark sphere spell Malin had cast. "*Saor.*"

Ommi, Tierney's dragan, chittered.

Breyze moved back inside Malin's cloak, out of view. The blackness faded until it seemed a normal amber-lit night in Wickney. A man stood at the alley's mouth, wearing a hoodie and sweats, his fists clenched at his sides and his brows drawn tightly together.

"Let's go," Malin said to her friends and started marching. She had just enough venom coursing through her blood to call a cloaking spell. "*Clúdach,*" she said on the first step.

Conrí and Tierney moved to her forward flanks—standard formation, the leader following two warriors. The two witches passed the man on either side. Malin walked straight toward him.

Look away, asshole.

Why did it seem like he could see her? Most of the time, they thought it was a rat in the alley, shook their addled heads, and kept right on moving. But this one didn't. At the last second, Malin moved to her left to avoid plowing straight into him. The interloper was tall, probably outweighed her by a hundred pounds, and despite the baggy clothes, clearly had a torso that tapered enticingly from shoulder to waist.

Keep walking, Malin, her inner warrior reminded her. *Not a Semaphor, so why are you even taking notice?* She tucked her chin and stretched out her stride. She made it past him only a step when a hand hooked into her elbow.

KANE HAD WAITED IN THE mouth of the alley, his feet wide and hands ready at his sides in loose fists, as the trio had approached. He couldn't shake the image of the strange fight and flashes he'd stumbled upon. As the woman clearly in charge of the group passed him, the strange feathers on her cloak brushed his shoulder with a *swoosh*. Like a tickle of a breeze. Her companions were several steps away by the time Kane grasped on to her arm and felt her toned muscle. An electric jolt rushed over his skin.

"Hey, what's doin' back there?" Kane tipped his head toward the alley's depths. He kept his tone friendly, but it was all forced. The Rage was seeping back into his gaze, and he couldn't get away fast enough. He stared at her like he had stared at Ramm.

The woman blinked up at him—surprise or confusion or . . . ? He couldn't name it, but there was an otherworldly and deadly stillness about her. Her eyes trailed down to where Kane held her elbow then back into his face. He had never seen irises that color. Black, dancing with violet streaks. His mouth went dry, and his throat bobbed. It had to be a trick of the streetlight's glow.

"Release me." Her voice was low, husky, almost a purr of a sound. A hiss sounded, her cloak moved, and something slithered over Kane's hand.

He pulled back, hand in the air. "What the fuck?" His eyes tried to focus but couldn't pierce the blackness. Did the woman have a snake on her? No fucking way.

The other woman who had passed whipped around. "Malin? Coming?" The voice wasn't friendly, the same deathly stillness about it.

Malin stepped back. She pulled the cloak around herself and what appeared to be a large snake. "Who are you? And how . . . ?" Her brows lowered in a deep furrow.

Did she live under a rock? Everyone in Wickney seemed to know Kane's face since he—and his inner beast—had started climbing in the rankings in the UFC. He was the local hero and villain. His face was on posters and all over the news. He was famous, although infamous would be a better term.

The other woman whispered something Kane didn't understand. It sounded foreign and musical, and Kane's breath-of-fresh-air thought vanished. He suddenly had an urge to shake off a chilling and thick sensation as if he were moving through mud. His thoughts came slower momentarily, and then, with a deep breath, the feeling passed. He examined the two women closer.

Who the hell wears cloaks in the city? In July? "Going to a costume party?" Kane curled a brow upward.

The man wearing a trench coat and shades rushed over, tapping his glasses. "Yeah, man. That's it. We're on our way to . . ." He inhaled sharply. "Hey, aren't you that fighter?"

Kane swallowed, blinking long and slow to match his steadying breath. There it was: the dreaded recognition that took too long to settle in. Kane preferred when it happened outright instead of someone scrutinizing him like a lab rat. If the man's eyes had been visible, Kane was certain he'd have that glazed-as-hell, starry-eyed BS expression in them. He missed his anonymity.

The other woman pulled at Malin's cloak and swiped her blonde braid over her shoulder. "Yep. We're late as it is. Let's go." She wore glasses too, but hers were cat-eyed.

Trench coat hesitated, still gaping, but the woman added, "You too."

Malin joined them, and they slipped away with only a brief glance backward, leaving Kane alone and gaping. A hole had opened in him, and he felt his beast moving in it.

Chapter 3

MALIN HAD TROUBLE TEARING HER eyes away from the man and fought with all her will to keep her eyes trained forward, toward the adjacent alley where they could disappear. She had things to do, and Godric weighed on her mind. Breyze touched her shoulders and back, hiding further under her cloak. But . . .

Her steps slowed. "Conrí, who was that man?"

"Cowan." Conrí gave the slang for *human* as he leaned forward. "He's a cowan, Mal. An MMA fighter. Big name in Wickney, and the fastest rising amateur in the UFC today. You'll probably see him everywhere tomorrow."

Tierney shot Conrí a warning glare. "Doesn't matter. Keep moving."

Malin felt a pull, a rolling in her gut, and turned. The fighter still stood in the alley watching them go. A statue caught in the shadows. He had clearly been in a brawl recently; fresh bruises bloomed around one eye and he had a split lip. But he appeared to be hiding from something with that hoodie and sweats. Didn't seem to matter to him that no one else wore sweats near Infinity at the clubbing hour. Furthermore, it was ninety degrees at midnight. Too mother-damned hot to wear a hood. Even hers was down at the moment, and sweat trickled down her hairline onto her neck.

With his feet in a wide stance and the left slightly forward, his arms angled away from his sides—a clear indication of muscle protruding from his deltoid area. Fighter for sure. Had to be nearing 300 pounds. But there was something more there. If he was only a cowan, he wouldn't have seen through her cloaking spell or Tierney's effort to muddle his thoughts.

"No." Malin stopped. "You two go. I'm staying to find out more about him."

"Mal—"

"Tierney, it's an order." Malin loved Tierney, but she had decided. Also, after they had lost yet another lead toward Godric, she needed some space.

Conrí and Tierney both bowed their heads, deferring to her command. Conrí turned away first.

Tierney's soldier attitude faded. "Be safe." She touched Malin's arm then followed Conrí into the alley where they could enter the window between realms and travel through the Fold to get to the All Mother's realm—the Penumbra.

Malin waited for them to trace the Awen and pass from this world into the Penumbra, then slowly turned to find the man in sweats—Kane—still watching her. His eyes bored into her. The cloaking spell remained active, so none of the other cowans could see her. This man, however, stood out, his eyes trained on her as if she were his prey. A group, probably students from Wickney University bent on a good drunk at Club Infinity, approached him. How could they not notice someone so much larger than everyone around? Kane averted his gaze from the oncoming people, allowing his hood to obscure his face. His shoulders slouched forward to make himself smaller—as if that was possible. He hid in the shadows, his moments as quick as a cat's.

Yes, thought Malin, *he's definitely hiding.* Famous, but didn't desire fame. Couldn't be a cowan in truth or he wouldn't see her. One explanation remained. He had the nimh, a gland that tied him to Darkness and allowed him into the world of witches. *Her* world.

Effin-A, that made her responsible. But she didn't have that kind of time or the desire to foster someone into Darkness.

As soon as the college kids passed, Kane squared his shoulders to her again. He stepped into the street without looking for oncoming cars. Then again, cars were infrequent in the West End. He moved in her direction. Yeah, absolutely *not* a cowan.

Malin's heart thumped into motion as he came closer. He stood a full head taller than her, so she had to crane her neck to look at his face.

Breyze chittered beneath her cloak, but Malin stroked his underbelly to calm him. To calm herself.

"Who are you, and why can you see me?" she asked Kane.

He laughed once. "Better question: why wouldn't I be able to see you?"

Malin wasn't about to answer that particular query. She pursed her lips. Not yet. Probably—no, *hopefully* not ever.

Kane lifted a hand and stroked a feather adorning her cloak. "This must be some kind of—whadda they call it?—cosplay? Isn't that usually saved for comic con fans?"

Having no clue what a comic con was, Malin shrugged. "My friend told you we're on our way to a costume party."

"In July?" Kane eyed her sideways.

She let her gaze drift down his body and back up, then smirked. "Sweats? *In July*? At a nightclub?" Malin crossed her arms. "You'll get more questions than me."

He glanced to the entrance of Club Infinity, where people waited to enter. Everyone in line wore anything from rubber suits to tank tops and dog collars to a miniskirt-and-bra combo. Both of them were out of costume and stuck out from the crowd.

"Where did your friends disappear to?" he asked.

Yeah, not answering that one. If he didn't know why he could see her and didn't understand that others could not, maybe she could get out of this unscathed. It would be a load off her shoulders if he could wait for the next Cailleach to find him and bring him into Darkness.

"Oh, yeah. Speaking of my friends. I should go." Yes, she really should, but when she tried to turn away, something held her in suspense. *Stop it, Malin. You know better than this. Wipe him and get back to the Dark.*

Would wiping him work? Surely it would if he was still functioning in the Daylight Realm. She couldn't drag another person into the Penumbra and have him tied to her coven and the danger that entailed. After all she'd experienced with her sister, it was a simple decision.

Leave, she commanded her legs to move.

Nothing.

A muscle ticked in Kane's jaw. "Well, Malin . . ."

Her stomach flipped at the way he drawled her name. She swallowed the saliva that had built in her mouth. Maybe she needed food.

He continued, "Since we're both nighttime oddities"—he tipped his head toward the club—"join me inside for a drink?"

Wipe his memory now. He won't remember, Malin told herself.

Breyze vibrated around her waist again, seconding her thoughts.

Preparing the spell, Malin drew in the Darkness and a breath—

"Kane!" a squealing voice called from a block away. "It's Kane Macleod!"

The squeals multiplied. The single peal turned into six, sounding like a group of whining puppies. Six girls in platform heels and skirts so short there would be six full moons if they bent halfway over ran up to Kane and nudged their way between them. Malin tried to hold her ground, but the cowans were strong when together. She was pushed out of the way, and her hand steadied Breyze on her back. The girls mauled Kane.

"Can I get your autograph?"

"Oh my God, I can't believe . . ."

"I don't have paper."

"Oh, just sign my boob."

"Can I get a selfie?"

"That fight tonight was . . ."

Malin tried to listen, but she didn't understand what they said. Cowans were . . . interesting creatures. None of their voices had a unique sound. With teased hair and too much makeup, these girls looked like photocopies from those kinky magazines sold in the corner stand down the street. But these girls were prettier, more lifelike and alive, than the thin sheets and even thinner bodies.

Malin backed up and gave a pencil-thin smile. *"Dearmad."* She waved and turned into the alley.

Kane had started tending to his gaggle, so hopefully the wiping spell would work on his not-entirely-human mind.

She slunk into the alley and found the mark, an Awen, symbolizing the window between realms, the entrance to the Fold. As she traced it with her finger, the symbol darkened in the stone and the wall wavered like black silk. Malin cut her gaze back toward the street once, chided herself, and stepped into the Penumbra.

Kane Macleod, cowan or otherwise, would be fine. He had time before the nimh's effects would begin, so maybe another witch would find him and take pity. Whether he became a witch or pháirtí, he would need someone to bring him into Darkness before it was too late.

K ANE'S VISION BLURRED AND THEN started to clear again, as if he were coming to consciousness after a knockout. And he knew about being knocked out—from his younger days. He noticed girls crowding him.

Fans.

He needed to tend to his fans. The same way one tended to poison ivy or a termite infestation.

Having fans meant his MMA career moved forward. Broc had always said, "They're the reason you're here. They pay your prize money." Yes, that's what he needed to do. Give them the attention they wanted. He was nothing without his fans.

Kane's hand felt heavy as he accepted the marker from the one. She pulled her bra to the side, and he averted his gaze as he scribbled his name on her milky white breast. Her nipple was perked, even in the heat.

Then he paused with the marker in midair. He didn't want this. He wanted to talk to that other wom—

He glanced around. Where had she gone? Who was she? Mary? No. Marin? No.

Why did he feel so fuzzy? His mind. His skin. His clothes. He shifted in his sweatshirt and pants, suddenly too constricted in them.

One of the fangirls pulled him down by the collar for a selfie. He leaned close to her but subtly searched the street for that woman.

Malin! Her name was Malin.

The selfie looked like shit. The girl resembled a raccoon wearing bright red lipstick. She grinned, but he looked puzzled and drugged as he stared off into the distance. Sweat made his skin slimy-looking. It seemed to satisfy her, and he couldn't care less.

Kane blinked, tried to smile, and shook his head. Maybe he needed sleep instead of a drink.

He pushed out of the crowd, hunched his head toward the ground, and started jogging. If the girls followed, he was prepared to sprint.

CHAPTER 4

Godric Laferty floated in his saltwater pool within the sanctuary. The water and light, both blessed by the Maker, washed him clean of filth and all that was dark, gave him extended life, and offered strength to his soul. The saltwater tasted good too. When he stepped out of the pool, his skin cooled with the air in the converted warehouse where he had established his sanctuary and Semaphor training center.

Before he dressed, Godric knelt at the altar and said a quick prayer of thanks. "Thank you, my Maker, for saving me from the Dark. Thank you for showing me the path of Light and teaching me to wield it in your name. I vow to you, I will bring Light into the Darkness and persecute those who call upon the dark magic. In your blessed name."

A shiver racked his spine when he stood. The scorching hot water and the underwater UV lamps within the blessed pool left his skin red, but that would turn bronze over the next day. He wrapped himself in a lush terrycloth towel and padded down the hall to his private rooms. There, he dressed in loose-fitting shorts and a tank before he went to the command center.

He'd been floating for an hour while the night was upon the city, not something he usually did. But that night, he was running behind. Godric preferred to perform his cleansing just before dark so he could monitor his units throughout the dark hours—the times when they waged war against Darkness. However, he felt confident his newest right-hand man, Daniel, would have things well under control.

Before Godric had been saved, the disorganized band of Light-wielders had been in chaos. Now, they were a well-oiled machine. With every step he took through the well-lit halls, he relished the progress he had made in rebuilding the Semaphors. Godric had found this abandoned warehouse and had it renovated specifically for their purposes. Thank the Maker for his talents with the stock market. He had plenty of money to ensure their headquarters were crafted as an homage to the Maker of Light himself. He'd had all the windows in the place sealed off and soundproofed—to hide what went on inside and not to block out the daylight. In place of the sun's warmth, they'd installed a plethora of light sources so that every room, every nook, every cranny, would all be bathed in bright daylight around the clock. Now, it was home, and a better home than he'd ever had. Constantly warm and so different from the years he'd spent with the coven in the Penumbra with the . . . He shook his head. He wasn't going there. The memories were too wrong and tempted his desires too much. He needed to keep his focus on the Maker's work. Hopefully, Daniel had had some success with the nightly patrol.

In his private rooms, Godric dressed in athletic gear, and then he made his way to the center of the warehouse. Command central, he called it. On one side, the room had a wall of computer monitors and multiple stations to observe the city and his teams' progress throughout the nights. To the other side, there were several punching bags, three treadmills, and a large mat where he could train his soldiers to fight. Along the wall, a stash of training staffs stood in a neat line.

Godric looked longingly at the training center and vowed he'd get in a few punches after dawn. First, he needed to check on his units around Wickney.

He wiggled a mouse, waited for the computer system to fire up, then typed in a few commands. Before long, through his network that bounced off multiple data centers around the world, he hacked into the cameras from the Local, a downtown club where the preppy college kids gathered. Godric didn't think twice about watching the unsuspecting human crowds around Wickney because he had employed the best of the best computer gurus to make sure the Semaphors' electronic activity was untraceable. Sally—though that surely was just a cover name— down at the college computer fix-it shop had hooked him into her hacker network.

That was just an added layer of protection because Godric's activity was harmless to the everyday average Joe. He couldn't care less about what the humans did; he was checking in on his units and searching the night for any dark witches who'd come out from the Penumbra. They were the plague of the Earth.

On another screen, he pulled up the tracking program for his soldiers. A little circle with the number six showed up on the map in downtown Wickney at the Local. Godric returned his search to the cameras until he found Daniel and another five Light-wielders wandering the club amid the college crowd and the Fae who hung out in the downstairs bar. The Local, or the Local U, as the underground part of the establishment was commonly called in Wickney. He didn't care about the Fae. They were born of the goddess Danu's Light, and the Maker had charged him with eradicating Darkness—or Dorcha, as the sinners of the Penumbra called it. Godric had other things to deal with. More important things.

Things looked calm in the club downtown with his first unit, so he returned to the map. Another three of his Light-wielding soldiers were at the theater down the street from the Local toward Wickney University. There weren't any cameras inside the theater, so he couldn't see those soldiers with his own eyes, but when he zoomed in on the map, the signals for each were unmoving. Alive, then, but probably just watching the show with the rest of the crowd.

He panned the map westward toward the other popular nightclub in Wickney: Club Infinity. Thrumming his fingers, he waited while the map refreshed. It sometimes took a second for the blips to appear, so meanwhile, he tapped into the cameras at the grungier club.

Bodies writhed on the dance floor, people—humans, that is—playing with darkness and not knowing the danger they courted. Despite their leather clothing and often solid black attire, they would all enter the daylight tomorrow, so they were of little concern. In this crowd, however, the men Godric missed were his soldiers who should be circulating among the crowds or lurking in the corners and watching. Other than the humans standing around waiting for their drinks at the bar, the barstools were empty too.

Damn, he usually found a Semaphor trying miserably to blend in at the bar. But nothing. Godric turned back to the map, panned, zoomed. Still nothing from their trackers. He refreshed to make sure the network connection was solid and waited. He'd sent four soldiers there, but no signal from their microchips could be found.

"Aarrrrgh!" Godric roared to the wall of monitors. He dropped a hand to the scar on his upper left abdomen. The skin there remained numb from where the Maker had removed the cursed extra organ he'd been born with—a nimh, the witches had called it. A tumor would have been a better description.

The surgery had nearly killed him and left an angry black scar, cold and numb to the touch. It followed the line of his rib cage. The only drawback to having the accursed thing removed was that he could no longer see or find the Awens that marked entrances into the Fold. When his fingers strayed to the skin adjacent to the scar, he once again felt his own warmth and closed his hand in a fist.

If those dark witches took another four of his men, he would . . . what would he do? He was already hunting them down like beasts. He'd have to double down on his mission to eradicate them and their dragans. He had lost four soldiers, so he would create eight new Light-bringers. He would add two more every time one went missing.

He picked up the phone and pressed the listing for Daniel in his contacts, then waited for the answer. He commanded, "Get over to Infinity, now. Take someone with you. West team is missing." Godric ran a hand over his skull cut.

"Sure thing, boss. You sure they're not just out on the street?

Maybe they're tracking."

Godric dropped a fist on the desk. "I can't find their signals in a three-mile radius. If they were going further, they'd have dropped a message."

"On our way, boss." Click.

Godric tossed the phone onto the desk hard enough it slid off the other end. He paced behind the computer desks and glanced at the door. Maybe he should go himself. He was probably closer. No, he decided. Then there would be no one here to monitor progress. He marched back and forth, getting closer to the punching bags with each pass. When he passed within touching distance, he glanced back at his phone on the floor, then fell into a fighting stance. He punched once, lightly. That felt good, so he let his fists fly into the bag until he dripped with sweat.

When he finally took a break and looked back at the huge monitors, there were two blips near Club Infinity. He rushed over to take a closer look.

The red dots weren't inside the club but in the alley to the north. He looked at the clock. Dawn was coming soon. The witches wouldn't be out there this close to the daylight, so—

Ding-ding. Ding-ding.

Godric scrambled under the desks to grab his phone. He swiped, barked, "Talk," and looked at the digital clock on the computer screen. 5:19. Sunrise.

Daniel's voice sounded hesitant. "Boss?"

"I. Said. Talk!" he spat through his teeth.

Daniel answered, "Alley north of Club Infinity. Scorch marks. Four of them."

Training more recruits wasn't the next thing Godric wanted to tackle. He squeezed the phone so hard it cracked in his hand, turned, hurled it at the punching bags, then rotated back around and put his fist straight through a monitor on the desk.

He stepped back, stared at it in horror, then took more deep breaths to calm himself. "Maker, deliver me from this anger." He shook his hand, deciding the pain was penance as he appraised the smashed screen. "Guess I'll have to pay Sally another visit."

STRADIOTTO & JOHNSON

CHAPTER 5

Safely inside the Penumbra, Malin retracted her cloak and removed Breyze's goggles. Her small dragan uncoiled from around her waist and flew at her side, his serpentine body slithering through the air at shoulder height. Breyze's wings pumped effortlessly then spread to hold him aloft. The Penumbra, named by the All Mother for the ultimate Darkness, seemed bright to Malin's eyes. The Daylight Realm stung her retinas even at night, but here, the dark streets and buildings cast in a deep violet hue soothed the beginnings of a blinding headache. Though she had been born on the other side, she had been through the dragan promise ritual and now thrived in Darkness.

Cowans who possessed the nimh but hadn't yet been welcomed by the All Mother would see nothing but black in the Penumbra, but she had been walking in Darkness for hundreds of human years. Every muscle in her body eased now that she had returned home.

First stop would be the caves, the entrance to the aerie, where Breyze could nest, eat, and commune with the other dragans while Malin returned to the coven house and the few remaining dark witches who made up her coven. Although, she hoped not to meet any of them this morning and to take her meal in solitude. Breyze chittered happily along the way, as if he relished every step and wing-stroke of progress they made. Simply being in the Daylight Realm taxed her dragan, but he was her means to access the power of Darkness. Venturing across the Fold without him would be too dangerous. Unless Malin called upon him, he lay dormant under her cloak while they were away from the Penumbra, so upon their return, he always vibrated with renewed energy and flew circles around her as they neared the cavern's entrance.

Malin opened a palm, and Breyze touched it lightly with his snout: a kiss.

"Do you think Ommi and Rezei will already be home?" Malin asked, her heart aching as it always did with the knowledge Breyze wouldn't be able to see his brother Aemro, who had been Myla's bonded dragan. They'd once been a team, the four of them, but no more.

Chip-chip. Chit-chit-chirp, answered Breyze.

Witches and their dragans didn't speak the same language; their mouths couldn't form the other species' words. However, she had been bonded to Breyze long enough to know his anxious sounds, and he understood the inflections in her voice.

When they reached the aerie, Malin held out her arm and waited for him to wrap around her and pierce the skin at her wrist, filling her with dark magic again. Breyze kissed her palm again and flew away to visit with his kind. Smiling, she left him there, faced north, closed her eyes, focused on the facade of her townhouse, and said, "*Bhaile.*"

The air shimmered around her; she felt weightless for seconds before her feet touched the ground again. When she opened her eyes, a dozen steps climbed toward her coven's front door before her. The Penumbra resembled Wickney's residential areas, townhouses and flats lining cobbled streets. Her coven's townhouse spanned a full block. Farther up and down the way, the residences to her left and right were quiet, as everyone who lived in the Penumbra would have retired by the time daylight came on Earth. For one of the Cailleach, the hour was well beyond bedtime.

Her stomach rumbled, but she needed to wash away the stench of the Semaphors before she could tolerate food.

When she entered, sounds from the kitchen to her right clattered. She pinched her eyes tightly, sighed over the company she had wished to avoid, and stepped gently toward the grand staircase. She'd go upstairs and clean up first. Perhaps then, she wouldn't disturb her coven's last meal.

After a quick shower, she braided her wet hair and dressed in a soft one-piece dress that fell just below the knees. It felt more like a long, over-sized T-shirt than anything presentable. Comfort. She slipped her feet into a pair of canvas shoes and returned downstairs. Her plan hadn't worked, so she quietly joined the commotion in the kitchen.

Malin had taken a seat at the long table before anyone noticed she had entered. The routine felt calm and normal. Conrí rinsed a huge colander of noodles while another of her covenmates, Brogan, tested the spaghetti sauce with a hunk of bread, and Tierney tossed a salad.

When Conrí turned around from the sink with the bowl, his eyes and mouth opened wide. "Heya, Malin."

Brogan looked over his shoulder through a veil of hair. "Yo." Verbose as always.

Malin waved and gave a tired smile.

Tierney scurried over with the salad and a basket of bread and plopped into the chair next to her. She leaned in a bit too close. "So?"

"So what?" Malin asked, knowing exactly what information Tierney wanted and trying not to make eye contact with her eager friend.

Although Tierney had warned her back in the Daylight Realm, she must have simply been worried about exposure. She had been pushing Malin toward anyone and everyone who seemed to have potential for a few years now, not that she'd found herself a pháirtí either. Though she knew it would be coy, Malin sometimes had the urge to throw Tierney's lack of partner right back at her friend.

Malin said, "I got nothing. You?"

Conrí barked a deep laugh. "Cut the shit, Mal. What happened with the human, not-so-human fighter?"

"Yeah, Mal." Tierney wiggled her eyebrows. "What happened with Kane Macleod?"

Brogan startled at that and hefted the pot of sauce from the stove. "Macleod? UFC Macleod?"

How did everyone know this man? "It's nothing." Her stomach growled again, so she reached for the bread. "Last meal smells fantastic, Brogan."

"Bullshit, Mal!" Conrí said, placing the noodles on the table. "Macleod saw through the cloaking spell. He's got it. And that draw you had toward the man? Dayum!"

Malin rolled her eyes and reached for another hunk of bread. The bread was just as good as any man.

Tierney regarded her sideways. "The question is: What are you doing about it, Malin?"

Malin chewed. "And the answer is: I'm not doing a damn thing about it. Can we just eat so I can get some effin shut-eye?"

That shut 'em up. Malin just hoped it was the end of the conversation. The four witches sat in blissful silence for several minutes, passing the food and digging in. The quietness was thick enough that Malin had time to calm her rumbling stomach before Conrí grunted and said, "No."

Malin, Tierney, and Brogan all stopped chewing and gave him wide-eyed attention. Malin and Tierney exchanged a glance. Which one was going to ask?

"No." Conrí set his jaw, dropped his fork, and folded his thick arms on the table. "We can't 'just eat.' Insubordination be damned. It's about time you thought about the health of this coven. We're not at our strongest until we're thirteen, and right now, we have four, Malin." He held up four fingers as if she didn't know how to count. "Five if we count your mother, but she's retired. Your coven needs new blood."

"Damn right," Tierney added around a mouthful. "Whether he's fit to be a witch or a pháirtí, if he's got the gland, we need him."

Mother-forbid Kane Macleod be fit to be a pháirtí. In that alley and on the street, he only had eyes for Malin. Despite the fact that Tierney was there, he picked *her* out of the trio, and Malin was used to people choosing Tierney. But after what had happened the last time, she couldn't fathom taking on another pháirtí. Just not in the effin stars.

Through gritted teeth, Malin said, "If Macleod is indeed one of us, another coven will find him. He'll be fine—better even—with a stronger group of witches and a leader who has a grain of desire to strengthen the coven bonds."

Conrí pressed the point. "Our duties to the dragan and the All Mother depend on *you* making *our* coven strong."

No longer hungry, Malin dropped her fork onto the plate with a clatter. "We have been through this too many times. Once Godric is captured and is at the mercy of Aodh, I am more than happy—"

"You gotta let your demons go," Conrí murmured almost into the table.

Malin flattened both hands on the table, ready to launch from the chair, and fixed her eyes on the warrior. "*Excuse* me?"

He sat back, crossing a booted foot over one knee. "You have us. You need to trust us to do that bidding for you. We've trained together for a century. And like I said, we need *you* to rebuild this coven. Hell, you ticked Morgana off so bad she chose to live in"—Conrí shuddered—"the Daylight Realm. Yet Pysae remains here in the Penumbra, spending his days alone in the aerie without his bonded witch. How long has it been since Morgana used dark magic or nourished the bond?"

Conrí left unsaid the bigger worry: that the bond might be too weak to allow Morgana to return in her full capacity.

"That was Morgana's choice," said Malin.

Who was she to command a witch otherwise? She was no dictator, and she needed no allegiance. In truth, Malin felt certain the other three remained in the coven house only for the sake of friendship and their own familiar bonds.

Brogan kept his head down, hair hanging to the side of his face and plate. He didn't utter a word but glanced at Conrí and

Tierney from time to time, as if they shared some sort of silent bond.

"You in on this too, Brogan?" Malin pointed her fork at him.

The man gulped from a large mug of beer. He lowered it slowly, then wiped a hefty hand across his lips and goatee. "Can't argue."

Tierney placed a hand over Malin's on the table. "C'mon, sweetie. We need you."

The touch sent fire through her blood, heat tickling her cheeks, and Malin pushed herself to standing. She swiped her half-eaten plate from the table and dumped it into the sink. Standing there, leaning on the counter, she felt three gazes boring into her back. These three were her closest friends. They had been there when she had received that dreaded package and discovered what happened to Myla. They had witnessed how much it broke her. That situation had been her fault for choosing the wrong human with an effin nimh. She couldn't do it again. Why didn't they get it? If it had happened to any one of them, they'd understand.

Apparently, she couldn't expect that much because none of them had siblings.

She turned around, ready to put a nail in the coffin for a good day's sleep, and sucked in air when she noticed her mother. Minerva, former leader of Malin's coven, stood in the doorway, her eyes warm and glazed over. The simple presence of her mother reminded her the coven was supposed to be led by twins: Malin and Myla. She was only half of that—and not even that much thanks to the need for revenge that simmered in her blood. She didn't have time to worry about Kane Macleod or any other human who was damned with a nimh. She needed nothing but Godric's suffering.

She and her mother stared at each other for long moments. Malin steeled herself as tears threatened to spill from her mother's eyes.

The sight lodged a lump in Malin's throat, but she would not give in, would not cry. She wrapped her arms around herself. "I can't right now. Good morn." She wove around her mother, bound for the stairs and her private rooms.

Before Malin reached the first steps, her mother stood before her, blocking the way. She almost caught Malin in a hug, but at the last minute, Malin backed off with her hands in the air.

"Mathair," she breathed the formal greeting.

Her mother remained quiet, searching Malin's face for—what? Answers?

Malin asked, "How much of that did you hear?"

"Enough to know you've met a charge you should follow." Minerva's voice was warm but firm.

"I will. After Godric. I promise."

"Your coven is right to challenge you, Daughter. Your vengeance has gone on for far too long."

"Mama." Malin choked, tears burning their way up from her throat. She inhaled through her nose to staunch them. "We're close. I can taste it. If I lose focus now, we may never find him. And how many other covens are in danger while he breeds the Maker's army?"

The elder witch reached out and traced Malin's hairline. "How many times have I told you? Neither Myla nor Aemro were your fault. But if you let this continue, you are responsible for every brick that crumbles around this place. If you know of a young one, you must try."

Malin turned away from her mother, folding her arms and closing her eyes. Kane Macleod's face flashed in her mind. His gaze on her had been so intent. If what she suspected was true, how could she risk anyone else she cared about by being that greedy? How could she entertain the idea of another mate when the last one had betrayed her so? It simply wouldn't work.

She put her chin on her shoulder, half-turned to her mother. "I need more time."

Then, regardless of her simple attire and canvas shoes, she stormed out the front door and down the steps. Malin ran. Her braid thumped on her back with every step. Where she would end up, she didn't care as long as it was safe and solitary. Away from prying eyes and voices who thought they knew better and those who wanted her to do something she couldn't. When her feet finally slowed and stopped, she fell to her knees, out of breath and heavy with sweat. The thicker dark magic in the air at the All Mother's house welcomed, embraced, and comforted. She bent forward until her forehead touched the stone. And wept.

CHAPTER 6

Soft, demanding lips trailed up Malin's arm from the inside of her wrist to her shoulder. At her collarbone, he ran a tongue up the side of her neck and nipped her earlobe. Malin groaned and writhed, pleasure tingling down her spine and into each limb. Warmth throbbed in her core. She reached for him, desperate to have her mouth on his, to taste the man who tortured her. Her fingers brushed through the soft hair at the back of his head, but he wouldn't give her what she needed.

He chuckled and brushed a finger over her lips. "Patience, my warrior."

The voice. She'd never believed a voice alone could light such a fire in her, but it made her yearn and rub her thighs together to try to satisfy herself. Strong hands pushed her knees apart. Malin whimpered, whispered, "Yes," and sighed as he settled between her legs.

So much better.

He kissed her inner things. Then his velvet tongue caressed her lips, teasing before he found her core. He sucked her into him once.

"Mmm." Malin arched into him.

But teasing was indeed the game. He released her.

"No," she complained, reaching for him, but she also relished the feel of his naked weight brushing her body as he crawled upward. He kissed her jawline, then stilled.

Malin opened her eyes at last and looked into desire-filled eyes the color of the ocean under moonlight. She reached her head up to capture his mouth with hers, but he pulled back with a wicked smile. His teeth gleamed like pearls.

"Kane, please." She no longer cared that he had reduced her to begging.

The weight of him, his smooth chest brushing her nipples, and his cock positioned to enter her in a single drive.

Kane thrust a hand into the back of her hair, wrapped the strands around his fingers, and pulled gently.

Malin moaned, and her eyes fluttered shut. Such sweet torture. She ran her hands up his back, over his broad shoulders, and reached for his hair. But it prickled against her fingers.

Pain lanced through her chest. Every muscle in her body tensed. Malin's eyes flew open, and she stared into all-too-familiar olive-green eyes and a perverse, self-satisfied smirk.

Malin bolted upright in bed and leaned over to reach for her S-blade on the table. *Kill*, her only thought for several heartbeats. Then, she realized she was alone and safe in her room within the Penumbra—where Godric could no longer enter. She dropped the handle of the weapon and sagged, sweat pouring from her body. The satin sheet tangled around her limbs. Her breathing came heavy, and she could feel the remnants of the pleasure countered by the stabbing sensation. She rubbed her chest with one hand and combed through her hair with the other.

"Effin-A," she breathed, considering the desire that still coursed through her blood and the dampness between her legs.

Why, in the name of the All Mother, couldn't she put Kane Macleod out of her mind? It'd been a week since she met him on the street, and she was *dreaming* about him. *You need to effin check yourself, Malin!* Even Conrí and Tierney had stopped pressing her on the topic, but her mother still eyed her with a mix of sorrow and disapproval every time they met.

Malin pulled at the sheets and rolled to get free from the entanglement. Naked, she moved to the bathroom, turned on the shower, and took account of herself in the mirror while the water heated. Her hair was a hot mess, and her cheeks flushed. Geez. She stepped under the hot water, allowing it to scald away the remnants of Godric and Kane. She needed to fight, to find the slime who haunted her. Hopefully, it was nightfall or after in the Daylight Realm, so she and Breyze could hunt.

*D*ING!

Round two. Kane danced toward The Viper on the balls of his feet. His hands were raised. His body coiled for an attack.

V.J. Valez had fifty pounds on him and would be fighting in the super heavyweight division at the UFC title match, one class above Kane. But Macleod liked to fight the larger ones; it prepped him to handle opponents in the heavyweight division, who were closer to his 265 pounds. The small-time money fight at Endure Muay Thai, EMT for short, was one Broc had arranged in a long series of matches to train him for the championship a little more than a month away.

The Viper threw the first punch. Kane ducked and came up with a hook to his ribs. The two danced apart and circled the ring. Fists raised, Kane locked eyes with his rival and waited. Then, in three, two, one . . . he charged. The Viper met him center ring. Kane threw a left jab. It connected, but The Viper came back. Damn, the man hit hard, and air whooshed from his lungs. Kane dodged the next blow but then eased off his defense. He needed the punches and the pain to trigger The Rage.

The Viper hammered him, right on cue.

"C'mon, Kane," Broc called from the side, "let the beast out!"

He was trying. The hits his opponent landed fucking hurt, but the dark veil that foreshadowed his Rage wasn't coming. He ducked under the next swing, threw several more punches, and danced away.

Ready for his retreat, The Viper stepped to the side and rounded with a Tae Kod, the hook kick catching Kane in the chest. Kane stumbled and righted himself, but the lights shining on the ring were at the perfect angle to blind him. Spots littered his vision, then the face of that woman on the street came into clear focus. *What the fuck?* He moved sideways to avoid the light, but the image wouldn't go away. A halo of light surrounded her head, but shadows lurked in her eyes.

Before he could see again, his jaw sizzled, pain exploded through the left side of his head, and Kane plummeted to the mat. The Viper dove on top of him—punching, kneeing, and pinning. The weight of the large man lying on him sucked the air from his lungs. Kane jerked and fought, but he was trapped. Caught like an animal in a cage—in this case, a cage of strong arms and a hefty body that felt like a hundred bricks.

Suddenly, the fighter's weight was gone, but the pressure didn't leave Kane's chest. The mat bounced like The Viper moved away. Kane rolled to his side, palms pressed to the mat and chest moving rapidly. The ref counted. Kane blinked hard, but all he could see was that woman.

"Four. Five."

She was the last thing he needed to be thinking about. But the vision wouldn't go away. She just stared back at him. Into him.

"Six. Seven."

He put his elbows and knees to the mat and tried to push himself up. He called to the beast, but no one answered.

"Nine. Ten. Valez takes the match!"

Kane pounded a fist onto the mat and went limp.

Defeat.

In the locker room, Broc examined Kane's nose and jaw by tilting his head back. "Open your mouth." Kane did, and Broc peered inside. "Nothing broken. What gives?" The trainer sat on the bench across from Kane, elbows on his knees and leaning forward.

Kane lifted one shoulder in a halfhearted shrug, gritting his teeth. "Got distracted. Fluke." He stood and opened his locker. He wasn't about to tell his trainer that he'd been thinking about a chick he'd met on the street a week ago.

Kane couldn't even figure out why she'd crept into his mind. He wasn't fit to be thinking about a woman. Like he'd be any kind of man for her. With how damaged he was, he wasn't even close to friend material.

"Horseshit, Kane. You never get distracted. What *gives?*"

"Damnit, Broc. Nothing. The lights hit my eyes. I saw spots. Valez took advantage. End of fucking story." Kane grabbed a towel and beat a path toward the shower. He couldn't answer questions he didn't have an answer to himself.

Broc called after him, "You can't let that happen in Vegas next month!"

Kane rolled his eyes and turned on the water. He wouldn't. But Vegas would likely be his last fight. Hell, with enough money from the semi-finals to keep him comfortable, he wasn't sure Vegas was really *his* ambition anymore. Enough money for Broc and he would be free. The only thing was . . . he needed an outlet for The Rage.

He needed to free The Rage before it came out on its own and hurt someone around him.

Though, he couldn't figure out why it hadn't come forward in the match against Valez. Even now, he couldn't call it up.

$\mathcal{A}$N HOUR LATER, SIDLED UP to the bar inside Club Infinity, Kane rolled the whiskey and black licorice spirit around his mouth. He savored the strong taste of the Sazerac because he only allowed himself the one. The club was quiet on a Wednesday, so he also relished sitting at the dimly lit bar, the music a bit more low-key than normal, and the bartender, Quinn, minding his own business—for the most part. But just as Kane had the thought, Quinn started in his direction, a second Sazerac in hand.

Kane gulped the last of his drink, stood, and tossed a fifty on the bar. "You drink that. One is my limit." *And only after a match,* he reminded himself. He wouldn't go down the drunken, drugged-up road again.

Quinn swiped the fifty. "Let me grab change."

"No bother," said Kane, "'s yours." The liquor made his tongue heavy.

The bartender tapped his fist on the rail twice. "Next one's on me then. You win tonight?"

"Nah. Got the shit kicked outta me."

"Not like *The Rage.*" Quinn tilted his head.

Kane swallowed but recovered with a wave. "Laters, man."

A groupie stopped him at the door, begging for a selfie. Would that shit ever stop? If he won his next big fight, the answer was probably no. He posed with a fist up and a fake smile, then sent her on her way. She planted a red-lipped kiss on his cheek before departing. Worse had been done.

Outside, Kane gulped in the still-hot night air, loving the heat. He unzipped his hoodie halfway and turned toward his apartment. The couple-a-mil he made on the last prizefight made the future seem like easy sailing. He would drop that in a good interest-bearing account and live off the proceeds for the rest of his life. But if he won the match in Vegas, he would set Broc up for life too. His trainer deserved that much for sticking with Kane's sorry ass, not to mention pulling him off the streets back when The Rage was fresh. So, yeah, he would go through with the fight. Maybe once he had won the UFC Heavyweight title, he would get the hell out of Wickney and out of Wisconsin altogether. He hated the damn cold, so maybe he'd buy a nice place on the beach somewhere. The South Pacific sounded good. Not Tahiti or Bora Bora though—too many tourists. Too many faces that might recognize him. He did prefer to hide in the shadows.

Fifty or so paces down the street, Kane came to an intersection, looked both ways, and pressed forward. Suddenly, a strobe-like flash pulsed from the mouth of an alley ahead then died. He halted and tensed. His hands balled into fists, and his heartbeat sped up. Maybe he got a concussion in the fight earlier?

Another flash and flicker came from the alley, then complete blackness swallowed it again. Kane ran forward.

He stopped just before the mouth of the alleyway. A grunt, and a groan. A swish through the air. A scuffle of feet on the concrete. He looked around the corner.

A fight.

Three men against three others—two women and a man.

Was that . . . ? He squinted. *Fuck yeah*, that was the woman who'd messed with his match tonight. He lurched toward the fray at the same time someone called his name.

"Oh, thank God! I've been looking for you since the fight," Kiera said. "You gotta come."

He groaned, shoulders tensing, and looked back at her. "Not now, Kiera!"

She didn't seem to see what was happening in the alley. Apparently, didn't hear it either, though he was also starting to lose the sound under the blood rushing past his ears.

"Go home. I'll come straight there. Gimme an hour."

"Kane!" she yelled, reaching for him.

"Go home!" The Rage suddenly clawed at his throat. "Now!" He couldn't look at her stricken face any longer. He turned back to the fight, a moth drawn to the flame.

One of the men held a staff toward the woman who had haunted Kane, and light beamed from the staff's end. *What the hell?* Malin wore dark glasses but still raised an arm, shielding her eyes. His stomach flopped when she stumbled backward. Kane crouched, in his trademark style. He might have lost a match earlier, but civilians would be an easy takedown. He wasn't about to tolerate someone beating up on women like that.

A hand landed on his forearm. Kane pivoted, throwing an

instinctive punch.

Kiera squealed and dropped to the ground, her body crumpling.

"Shit!" roared Kane.

Just the thing he was trying to stop. He was the culprit now. To his own damn sister. And she was sprawled out on the ground.

He looked at the fight in the alley. Only two men now faced the three in dark cloaks.

He looked back at his sister's crumpled form. This was why he wasn't fit for anything. Too impulsive. All he did was react and destroy. He crouched at Kiera's side, hands shakily hovering around her face. "Damnit, Kiera, I told you to go."

A bruise was spreading around his sister's eye, and Kiera wasn't moving. What the hell should he do now? If he touched her, he'd probably do more damage.

Kane pulled out his phone and unlocked it, ready to hit the Emergency Call icon at the bottom. Two poofs, like the release of trapped steam, burst behind him, and he turned. Three figures rushed toward him, cloaks billowing like comic book superheroes. Where had their enemies gone?

The man, same one he'd met a week ago—what was his name again?—crouched on the other side of Kiera. "Hell, man, why'd you drop her like that?"

Kane growled deep in his chest, heart rattling in his rib cage, but didn't have an answer. The man seemed to know something about tending wounded, and he turned Kiera's face to examine it. A familiar motion, like Broc did when Kane had been bloodied in the ring. He put a hand under her nose, then felt at her neck.

Malin trotted to a stop, eyeing Kane. "She alive?"

Conrí. That's it, Kane finally recalled the guy's name. Why did details about them seem so fuzzy? Even looking at them seemed fuzzy, and he blinked quickly. So he focused on Kiera again, who was clear in his bleary gaze. The person who *should* have his focus.

Conrí answered, "Looks like it, but she's out cold." He glared across Kiera's body at Kane, who still sat on his heels and held his cell phone like an idiot.

"Didn't mean to." Kane fumbled with the phone again. "Calling an ambulance." He managed to unlock the thing, mumbling, "I told her not to follow. To leave—"

The other woman, the one with blonde hair, snatched the phone from his hand with lightning fastness and said to Conrí, "Get her to the darklings."

"No," barked Malin, making Kane rock back on his heels, but after shooting her angry and disapproving glances, the other two ignored her.

"The darklings will know what to do," the blonde woman insisted, nodding to Conrí, who began to slide his arms under Kiera.

Kane faced off with the blonde woman. "What the fuck is a darkling?" He stood, nose and eyes above her, but she glared up at him with all the malice of the Viper from the fight he had lost earlier.

Malin stepped between them, one hand on the other woman's shoulder and a hand on Kane's chest. "Tierney, I've got it." Her voice was strained, and she seemed hesitant to turn around or look at him.

Strangely, her touch made him believe everything would be fine and hunky-dory for about two seconds before he started getting twitchy again. He curled his hand into a fist, The Rage circling in his gut.

Malin lifted her face to his. "You. Relax and come with us."

Conrí hefted Kiera into his arms, cradling her like a baby.

Guilt stabbed Kane's chest over how fragile she looked. Her arms were limp branches, head lolling to one side, legs spindly and hanging at odd angles. "Don't move her!" Kane reached forward to stop Conrí. "We need a medic first. We need to call an ambulance. What if something's—"

"*Socair*," Malin whispered, her hand growing warmer on Kane's chest and a shadow surrounding it.

"What," he started, but the muscles in his back and shoulders relaxed. Belief washed over him that they would be the better option for his sister—but that was stupid. He didn't know these people, the ones who claimed to be going to a costume party in July, who were fighting with strangers who were now missing. They were fighters, like him. He started for Conrí, intent on helping his sister.

"We'll get her help," Malin insisted, pushing him backward with more strength than fathomable from someone so tiny. He could've lifted her with his pinky.

"How . . . ?" Kane stared at her, not knowing which question to ask: *How will you get her help? How did you do that?* He looked down the alley toward the stone wall at the opposite end. *How did you make those men disappear? Where are they? What happened? What the fuck is going on?* More questions piled up in his head like a car wreck in winter, but he had to focus on what was important. He had to weave through and find the end.

Conrí grunted at him with a sideways scowl then trotted off, carrying Kiera. The two women followed. It all seemed as natural as breathing and fighting. An everyday occurrence. Yet Kane's feet wouldn't budge. They had her, and everything would be fine. Right? *C'mon, motherfucker. Kiera's your sister, your responsibility. Move your ass. This is your fault anyway. All of this is your fault.*

At the street, Malin turned back. She pursed her lips, her brows drawn together. What did that look mean? Anger? Resistance? That she didn't want to speak to him? Disapproval? Hell. He would sure-as-shit disapprove if he saw someone else coldcock a woman, so how could he blame her? Surely, she was about to tell him to get lost. Or she would punch him herself?

Destruction. All I'm good for. Reason 853 why I should take my sorry ass somewhere where I can't hurt anyone else. Kane clenched, unclenched, reclenched his fists at his sides. Sweat made his skin slick.

But Malin tilted her head and hooked a thumb over her shoulder, pointing after the others. "You coming?"

Kane followed.

Across the eerily quiet street, they entered another alley, Conrí leading the way. About halfway to the dumpsters at the end, Tierney skidded to a stop at his side. Then Malin slowed her jog, her eyes raking across the street and around, her hands at her sides, and then she stepped up to the stone wall. Malin began searching the wall for something. He was about to ask when she seemed to find it. With her index finger, she drew on the stone.

A symbol lit up. No, it didn't precisely light up; it darkened, if that was possible when in the shadows at night. Shadows deeper than the night formed a circle around three lines and three dots on the dark gray brick.

Kane hissed in a breath. "This is bat-shit insa—"

"Shh," Tierney hissed.

The wall moved, stones dissolving into an inky black pool.

Kane blinked, certain Quinn had spiked his Sazerac with something more than whiskey and absinthe. Acid? Nah, Quinn wouldn't do that. Would he?

The stonework swayed like it was blown by a wind. But the night was still, hot, and humid. And nothing would make a stone wall move that way. Kane scrubbed both hands over his face, his two-day-old beard rasping.

Conrí smirked and walked right through the wall with Kane's sister in his arms.

Kane jumped back a step, his stomach lurching into his throat. Acid coated his tongue. His hands trembled, and his heart pounded in his chest like a high-school drum corps at halftime. His arms flailed sideways to try to get a grip on himself, on something. On reality.

This was impossible.

Tierney giggled and winked at Malin. "See ya on the flip side."

Malin reached for him, determination in her eyes and the set of her jaw. At his chest, she fisted his hoodie in both hands and turned him. Even if he wasn't stunned to shaking, he probably would have let her have her way—*any* way she wanted—with him. She fixed her jaw and pushed with all her weight into his chest. He stepped backward three times, driven by her force . . . into the blackest of black.

Malin released him, and he reached out for her.

Somewhere in the dark, he heard her low, velvety chuckle. "Welcome to the Penumbra, Kane Macleod."

Chapter 7

STANDING BACK, MALIN WATCHED THE fighter, judging whether he could see anything within the Penumbra. Exactly how strong was his nimh? Was he actually supposed to be here? If not, she could throw him out. Damn her coven, damn her mother, but most of all, damn Kane Macleod for laying out someone, another cowan, during one of Malin's battles.

Kane was already tied to the witch world in some way, but that didn't mean the woman he knocked out was too. Before they could let her go, they would have to determine how much she had seen and wipe her memory if necessary. Geez, who was she kidding? They would have to wipe her memory regardless of the battle now that she was inside the Penumbra.

If it was only one cowan, that would be one thing. But the situation was way more complicated. She and her covenmates would have to ease this fighter, standing blind before her, into their world. At least, he already had some skills in combat, so it wasn't the worst thing that could've happened. Malin pursed her lips. Perhaps he would be useful, but damn him also for forcing them to vanquish the slime before she could ask about Godric. Maybe she had been going about it all wrong.

The individual battles were getting old, and they were

certainly unproductive—aside from ridding the world of the unnatural beings. The Fae were naturally Light-bearing creatures. The Semaphors, on the other hand, were bastardizations of the Light. Malin pulled her hair over one shoulder, still watching Kane, but with ideas brewing. Would it be possible to track one of them back to wherever Godric was hiding? That idea had potential; she'd have to drop in on Morgana when she went back to the Daylight Realm. But for now, she had other pressing matters.

"That woman you punched, Macleod. Who is she?" Malin asked, waiting some distance away with her arms crossed and observing the man's tapered physique along with his reactions. Her crossed arms gave her some protection.

After that dream, she could almost feel the rippled muscles along his abs. She dug her nails into her palms. *Do not go there*, she scolded herself. *In fact, All Mother, please let his eyes adjust on their own—witch, not a potential pháirtí.*

Kane held both arms out as if they might touch something to give him a clue where he was. *Ha! As if.* He rotated in a slow circle. "She's m-my sister." His eyes stretched to their limits—a reflex, an attempt to welcome the nonexistent light in through his pupils.

Malin sighed. He couldn't see here. At least not yet. Damn. They'd have to feed him the tonic, but she didn't want to admit what that indicated.

Conrí had already left for Dark Haven carrying the unconscious woman. Tierney leaned on a building nearby, keeping her trap shut but wearing a self-satisfied smile. Malin bit the inside of her cheek so she wouldn't yell at Tierney. Both Ommi and Conrí's dragan Rezei circled overhead.

Malin opened her cloak. "Join them," she said to Breyze. Then to Tierney, "Take them to the aerie."

Free from the dangers of light, Breyze flew upward, intertwining his long body with Ommi's and Rezei's. The three dragans collectively chittered and chattered. Tierney folded her arms, raised a brow at Malin, then the four of them left her with Kane.

"What was that noise?" Kane turned his head to either side, peering upward.

Wiping a smile off her face, Malin grasped him, stopped his spinning. "Here." She took one of his hands and inhaled sharply when a current raced up her arm. *No effin way. Still not going there!* She breathed in deeply through her nose. "Okay, focus on the feel of my hand."

"How could I focus on anything else?" Kane's voice rumbled with a dangerous tone, but he had stilled, stopped his searching.

Was she supposed to read his meaning as thankful? Sarcastic? Or maybe . . . no. He couldn't have felt the buzz between them too.

Malin swallowed to ease the tightness in her throat. "We need to go to Dark Haven so you can see. Can't have you frenetic while I do this, so stay calm."

Kane squeezed her hand in silent agreement, then relaxed.

At least one of them was relaxed.

Malin focused on the stone archway and courtyard in the All Mother's castle, the holy place where Aodh's darklings worked her dark healing magic on those in need. "*Bhaile,*" she said.

The air shimmered.

"Whoa," said Kane and flailed when the solid ground beneath his feet was gone.

"Easy. Easy," she reassured him, seconds later adding, "Brace your legs like you just jumped and are about to land."

He did, and they both touched down with a soft bend of the knees.

"This way." Malin pulled Kane along, leading her new charge begrudgingly.

K ANE'S MIND SWAM. *I SHOULD be running for home, for safety, for something. But here I go, fucking following this woman like a puppy. Home wouldn't have done much for Kiera either, but I should have gotten her to a doctor, owned up to whatever damage I did, and accepted my punishment. At least my sister would have been in good hands. But . . . Malin. Her touch. And that man said Kiera would be better off with them. What the hell have I gotten us into?*

He tried not to drown in the sea of questions threatening to push him under. Too many to grab on to one and hold, and too much confusion with Malin still touching him. What had she—or was she doing to him? What were these weird words she whispered? Why did the ground disappear beneath his feet? Were they floating? Ten minutes, maybe more, passed. The Penumbra? What the hell was that? Where was Kiera? Why couldn't he see? He needed to get away, and fast. Running wasn't an option because he had no connection to the ground. He couldn't leave Kiera here.

There was one thought blaring louder than the rest in his head: *Why does it feel like I will suffocate if I let go of this woman's hand?*

Suddenly, he felt pressure under the soles of his tennis shoes and a tug at their conjoined hands. Kane walked behind her still, now unafraid of the oppressive blackness, uncaring that he couldn't see, trusting someone for the first time since he'd decided high school wasn't his cup o' tea. He stepped confidently over hard ground—cobblestone likely, with the uneven ridges. Then the air around him changed. It stilled, indicating they'd moved from outside to within a building. The smell changed too. Instead of fresh night air, it smelled sterile, hospital-like, and burned his nostrils. Yeah, perhaps the man, Conrí, hadn't been full of shit. It seemed they were going somewhere where Kiera could be cared for, so they must be in a hospital. But the feeling of the stone beneath his feet didn't jive. Still, he had Malin's soft but strong hand in his, so all would be well.

Was that assurance real or imagined?

Real. Had to be for both his sister's and his sakes.

Malin stopped leading Kane forward and urged him sideways until his shoulder met a wall. "Wait here. I'll be right back."

He tightened his grip on her hand and started after her. She couldn't leave him alone with no sight. The blackness surrounded him like a void, swallowed him up whole like he was in a whale's belly. If she did leave him alone, he certainly wouldn't be so sure of himself. She placed her free hand on his abs. Another sizzling current shot through his blood and his heart hammered.

She said, "Promise. Everything's going to be fine."

Her voice, her touch—what kind of spell had she cast on him? This certainly wasn't normal. He'd never had this reaction to anyone.

Ever.

He believed her. How utterly strange. This gave a whole new meaning to blindly following someone.

Then her hands were gone with a change in the wind. He reached after her, but he only grasped empty air. Kane sensed only a void. Where had she gone? Why hadn't he heard her walk away?

Somewhere in the dark distance, a door swooshed open and closed. Kane's chest constricted; breathing came hard. He turned back where they'd come from—not that he could discern one damn thing. Then he spun to face where he'd heard the door.

Questions screamed at him in his mind, echoed in his ears, and made him see stars. He lifted both palms to cover his ears, but he couldn't block out the sound. Lost, falling, alone, a loser, worthless, a destroyer, not worthy. *Kiera's paying for my Rage now.* Kane balled his fists, as if creeping toward fight time. No sight.

A ghoulish voice whispered in his ear: *Just you and me here, kid.*

No.

Fucking.

Way.

He didn't even get the vision this time, but he knew the image in the blackest part of his heart: receding hairline, horn-rimmed glasses, beady eyes. Kane dropped into his fighting stance.

Then there was nothing else, no sense of a presence and no escalating Rage. Alone, in a quiet more silent than hospitals with their fluorescent lights buzzing overhead. His heartbeat slowed, and his mind reeled again. He must have finally arrived in hell. And the angel who brought him here must have been Lucifer's twin.

Kane slumped against the wall, his hoodie hiking up his back as he slid down. On the floor, he dropped his fists to his sides and released them. His eyelids sagged closed as he leaned his head back. *Kiera, I am so sorry. I'll get you out of this if it's the last thing I do.* Kane breathed in through his nose and counted to twenty—pushing enough air out of his body that he gulped in the next breath on a reflex. It was a technique his therapist had taught him as a teen. Thing was, it worked like a gem. It was the *only* thing that shrink told him that *did* work. He focused on Malin, pushing all other thoughts away with another long exhale.

"Yo!" a new voice barked, deep but clipped.

Kane scrambled to stand, bracing a hand on the wall.

"Heya, Brogan," Malin's voice called from where the door swoosh had sounded.

Brogan? Someone new? Kane crouched, facing the voice with fists raised to block whatever came his way. He felt like a child having to learn how to fight again.

Malin's soft yet strong hand touched his forearm. "He's a friend," she said, then waited until Kane dropped his block and straightened. "And I have another here with us. His name is Emrys."

Brogan grunted. Or was that a laugh?

Emrys, with a higher pitched, lilting voice, said, "It is a pleasure to meet you, Master Kane."

Between a silent Brogan and this new man, Kane recoiled. *Master?* His tongue felt the size of a blimp and dry. He was the furthest thing from a master. And a master of what?

Emrys continued, "I've brought you something to drink. It should be quite refreshing." He chuckled, the high-pitched tone grating across Kane's skin. "Though, perhaps not in the way of taste."

"Drink?" asked Kane, shaking his head. "Nah. Thanks. I'm good. Just need to get my sister and get her back to a hospital." Yeah, that was what he needed to do.

Malin's hand on his arm squeezed, and he instinctively moved closer to her. Looking down, he sensed her face inches in front of his and heard a hitch in her breath. Yeah, that made his lower abs clench.

She said, "This will make things much easier for you, Kane."

Damn that breathy sound she made when saying his name. Angel or devil, he didn't care at the moment. He wanted to grab her and hold on for dear life. Among other things.

Malin added, "You will *see* after drinking this. Promise." She fell quiet.

The expectant silence begged him to take the cup, but he couldn't. Not only could he not see the thing, but he wondered, *What if it's poison?* Wouldn't be the strangest thing to happen to him that day, but if that meant he'd never see his sister again . . .

He opened his mouth to refuse.

"Kane, please. Don't make me force you." Malin's hot breath hit his face, and that did it.

He would do anything this woman asked. Like he was jelly in her hand. He would even consider dancing for her. Abso-fucking-lutely anything. Kane jutted out his hand in the direction of Emrys's voice. Something changed in the other stranger now behind him. As a trained fighter, Kane sensed how the air shifted just before his opponents attacked, and he perceived that in Brogan.

Kane wanted to roar his frustration over not being able to see. If he needed to fight, he couldn't do it blind. Instead, he bit down and said through clenched teeth, "You say this'll let me see?"

"It will," Malin and Emrys replied in unison. Kane only needed to hear Malin's voice.

"Then hand it over."

A small cup, cool to the touch and heavy as if it was crafted from stone, landed in his right hand. Kane counted to three and then tossed it back, swallowing the whole thing in one gulp. The liquid fizzed on his tongue and tasted syrupy-sweet.

Emrys started, "Wai—"

Kane coughed on the sugar—not something he normally allowed to enter his body. He thought he would've missed it. It tasted horrid, but the deed was done. Medicine down the hatch.

Emrys's voice lowered to a resigned murmur. "I was going to say sip it slowly."

Kane's eyes felt *heavy*. Not truly heavy, but he didn't have a better way to describe the pulling sensation. A headache bloomed behind his eyes, then stabbed. He blinked several times, trying to alleviate the discomfort, but it grew sharper, more intense until pain filled his skull like hot needles were being driven through each pupil. He swiped at his eyes with the heels of his hands, but that only intensified the feeling. He pressed fingertips to his temples. No relief.

Someone wailed in pain.

Wait, that was him.

A moan vibrated through his chest. He stumbled into the wall. Malin steadied him from the front. He latched on to her, and other hands were on him too, keeping him upright. He squeezed his eyes tightly shut. Maybe blindness was better. He groaned. His eyes burned. He sucked in breath after breath, trying to exhale slowly, but his body sped his breathing more and more. Drums pounded in his ears; his heart tried to gallop from his chest.

"Oh . . . argh!" he complained.

Finally, he got a good breath and blew it out on a ten-count. Couldn't manage twenty. He kept his eyes closed. That seemed to ease the pain.

"Almost there," Emrys said softly in his ear.

A hand rubbed down the back of his shoulder and arm. Like a medic. His sister was a nurse, and she had that kind of touch. So, Emrys had to be either that or a doctor, right? And that liquid had to be medicine. Weren't they supposed to warn him of any side effects before letting him shoot it like tequila?

Another wave of pain. Kane felt certain his head would explode. He growled. He'd had concussions before, but nothing made him want to crumple like this. "Fuck!" he roared.

Then—nothing. The pain evaporated.

He stood up straight, eyes still shut. He removed his hands from the sides of his head, and the pain blessedly stayed away.

Kane opened his left eye. Blackness. He waited. And Malin's figure before him—uncloaked and wearing dark clothes, leather if he had to guess—appeared in the dark. He opened his other eye. The man, Emrys, wore a robe, looking like a freaking monk. Kane peered over his right shoulder. Brogan stood with his feet apart and arms folded over his broad chest. That man had to be every bit of Kane's weight or more. His black hair, straight, hung over one shoulder just about to his waist. The man pursed his lips and nodded.

Kane blinked several times. The lights were off. Though he could see everyone in crystal-clear detail, it was still dim, and everything was highlighted in a blue hue.

"Good," Malin barked with a nod, then grabbed Emrys's sleeve, said, "The woman, you said she'll be well," and started down the hall.

Brogan clapped a ham-sized hand on Kane's shoulder. "C'mon. Here for the girl, true?"

CHAPTER 8

Malin breezed into the treatment room, the Penumbra's version of a hospital room. Kane's sister lay on the bed with her head raised, appearing to sleep peacefully. Conrí sat at her side with a worried expression, seeming like a troubled family member more than a stranger. Malin narrowed her eyes at her friend but didn't ask. Bruises mottled the left side of the woman's face, and her eye was swollen shut. Kane had definitely done some damage. How someone could do that to their own sister didn't make sense, and it was a good enough reason for Malin to keep Kane away.

Emrys asked, "What did you say was her name, mistress?"

Malin sighed. She couldn't keep a darkling from addressing her with the prescribed respect to any coven member, even though it made her itch. He was, after all, her brother by marriage. "Kiera," she answered. "That one's sister." She hooked a thumb toward the hallway, where Kane was. "How fast can we get her well and out of here?" She had hunting to do, and she hadn't counted on dealing with this tonight.

Emrys didn't get the chance to answer before the door swung inward. Kane and Brogan walked inside, filling the remaining space in the small room.

Emrys said, "She has a concussion. We need to wake her, bu—"

"Then wake her the fuck up!" Kane barked, sounding like a rabid hound more than a man.

Conrí stood, staring down Kane, and his fingers wound into tight fists. Malin could almost hear her covenmate growl at the fighter. What in the Light? That action was so unlike Conrí's normal, easy-going attitude.

Malin stepped between them. Amid all the male posturing to protect the wounded woman in the bed, she had this strange urge to protect the man who'd put her there. Effin insane, but having no time to think on that, she straightened until her back was like a board. "Conrí, sit. You, just stand there and"—she waved a hand up and down Kane's body—"look pretty. Please continue, Darkling Emrys." Heat flooded her cheeks because, truly, couldn't she have come up with anything better to say? She couldn't even look at Kane.

Emrys folded his hands at his chest and bowed to her. "Yes, Mistress Malin. The woman—*Kiera*, you said—would do best if we can wake her. But do you wish her to wake and open her eyes to darkness?"

Kiera moaned, quickly flipped her head to the other side, and mewled. Kane went to her other side, opposite Conrí, but Malin didn't stop it. No one was throwing any punches. Yet.

Malin stood face to face with Emrys and lowered her voice. "Can you tell without waking her if she has a nimh?"

"A what?" barked Kane.

Malin sighed. There was something wrong with the fighter's hearing, and it was starting to annoy her. Could he speak at a normal level?

Conrí laughed singularly, humorlessly. "You have one, asshole. Why wouldn't she?"

"Have what, asshole?" Kane threw back.

Malin rolled her eyes. "Conrí, hush! Kane, I'll explain later."

Her covenmate peered over, regret showing in his eyes, and nodded. At least, that was one of them silenced.

"I'm sorry, Emrys." She waved a hand, encouraging him to continue.

Emrys slipped his hands into the opposite sleeves of his tunic. "We can run a scan to look for the fifth cardiac chamber, but the nimh blends with the spleen on the images. It would be best to wake her now though. We do not want to risk her slipping into a coma."

"Then wake her up. Now," Kane demanded. "Whatever's best for my sister. Do it."

"Does he know?" Emrys asked.

Malin started, "We don't th—"

"Know what?" the fighter interrupted. Again. Damn it, he was only asking the natural questions, but it wasn't helping the situation at all.

"If I may, mistress," Emrys said, "it would be best for the patient if we kept the outbursts to a minimum." His eyes darted to Kane, who was huddled at his sister's bedside. A hand touched the non-bruised side of her face.

Malin caught Brogan's eyes and pointed to the door, then did the same with Conrí.

Emrys added to the men, "Yes, sirs, we need it quiet for the patient."

Conrí and Brogan gave her a single nod, marched to each of Kane's sides, and looped his arms. Kane started to thrash, looking more like a fish out of water than a prizefighter.

Malin checked the venom left within her body, waved a hand, and breathed, "*Socair.*"

Visibly, the fighter relaxed.

She took two steps and touched Kane's chest again—the current rushing up her arm be damned—and said, "I will join you in the hall momentarily." She exchanged glances with her coven's warriors, assuring herself that they would keep him calm while she finished up here.

If Kane didn't stay calm, Malin was sure Conrí could handle it, though maybe in not such a peaceful way.

After the three men returned to the hallway, Malin breathed her relief. "Now. What are our options?" she asked Emrys.

"Well, we must wake her periodically to ensure she doesn't slip into a deep coma. She is responsive to pain, as you saw when she moved." Emrys walked over to Kiera's bedside. "Is there a reason you do not want them to know? Her brother clearly belongs here, so it is possible she does too."

Malin glanced toward where she'd last seen Kane being dragged from the room. "I'm not loving that prospect. Let's keep her in the dark for now." She winced at the unintended pun, but Emrys didn't seem to notice. "Once we know if she has a nimh, it might be easier to explain. I've already got one neophyte on my hands, and that's more than I bargained for."

Emrys gave her a warning glare.

She didn't need, or have the capacity, to deal with two at once. She stared at the door. Especially if the man out there had the potential to be pháirtí rather than a witch, a notion she was still trying to wrap her head around.

The healer opened Kiera's good eye, looking inside with an eyepiece. He was silent for a minute. "With cowans, sometimes the light in the human hospitals is harsh after a concussion. We could wrap her eyes and tell her that it's to protect her while she recovers."

"Do it." Malin nodded. "Wrap her eyes. That way we don't have to explain the dark yet."

"I will put a salve on the bruised eye to speed the healing. That'll be another good excuse to wrap her head. I should scan her still, correct, mistress?"

"Yes. But if she has the extra chamber, don't tell her. Let her believe she's in a hospital and you are Doctor Emrys. How long before the tonic wears off for Kane?"

"Eight to twelve hours."

Malin checked her watch. Still the wee morning hours in the Daylight Realm. Time to get the fighter to the other side—she'd push him there if she had to. She laid a gentle hand on Emrys's shoulder. "Thank you."

KANE PACED THE HALLWAY. THE cool, calming sensation Malin had created between his shoulders when she spoke that strange word had started to fade. His head still felt fuzzy, no matter how many times he shook it, though he should've been happy that he could see clearly. Kinda.

"Socair?" he whispered, too quietly for the others to hear and still uncertain if it was correct. He rolled the word around on his tongue, but it sounded like he didn't say it right. Not when compared to the silky smoothness of Malin's tone. Just the thought made the fuzziness return in his head like he was the one with a concussion.

Tension continued to gather in his muscles, gripping him the tightest when Malin emerged from the room. The familiar swooshing of the door behind her sounded quieter now that he could see. Everything was tinged with blue, but he would take it over the pure black nothingness any day. When he made a move to face Malin, both men squared off on each of his sides, their shoulders seeming wider in their fight-ready stances. Two—technically three—could've played at that game, so he matched the stance.

Malin held up her hands and said, "It's fine." She waited for them to stand down, then crossed her arms and looked up at Kane. She hesitated before asking her next question; it was a choice she didn't want to offer. "Do you want to stay here for Kiera or go back to your world?"

Something twisted in the pit of his stomach, and he suppressed the urge to touch Malin. *Damn, what is it about her? Quit with the mush; focus on doin' right by Kiera. What did she say? Go back to my world?* The twisting in his gut turned to a stab. "Hell fucking no." How could she suggest he leave his sister alone in this dark place? She might wake up blind, like he'd been, and scared. He threw a hand out toward the door. "Not with my sister unconscious in there."

Malin raised her chin a notch higher. "Emrys is going to treat the swelling in her cheek and wrap her eyes. He said people—*humans*, that is—can be sensitive to light when they have a concussion."

"How—" Kane bit the question off. His muddled thoughts were probably clearer to everyone except him. And that pissed him off. He thought about the last time he'd had a concussion and how the light had pierced through the back of his eyes like a hot fire poker. It felt similar to what he had experienced after drinking that sickly-sweet thing the doctor had given him. Although, based on his firsthand experience, the monk-looking doctor in there probably had a point.

Malin continued, "He will wake her up once that's done and keep waking her every hour to make sure she's recovering and comfortable. If he needs it, he'll use the Dar . . ."—she swallowed—"magic to help her recover. Emrys will take better care of her than your white-coats, you can be sure of that."

Kane crossed his arms. "Don't think there's anything I can be sure of after tonight." His voice was softer than he intended. In fact, he sounded like a scared little kid, so he puffed out his chest and raised his head. He looked down on the petite Malin.

Malin reached out a hand and touched his upper arm. "If it was my sister in there"—she cleared her throat—"I would be just as concerned as you."

He hoped that meant she understood and would be gentle with him. He didn't mean to hurt Kiera, and she had to know that.

"If you go," she continued, "we will come get you as soon as she no longer needs observation, and you can take her home."

He looked down at her hand, long fingers resting softly on his bicep. He flexed, wished he didn't have the sweatshirt on so he could feel the heat from her touch. He needed to feel her touch him again. No! He *had* to stop thinking these thoughts.

With a deep breath, Kane insisted, "I can't get to her if you take me back, so I'm staying." He didn't add that he wasn't too keen on leaving Malin either. He took one step toward her, answering the magnetic pull. Was the static crackling between them real? Imagined? More of her magic? Didn't matter. Going back was definitely a no-go. "Why *can't* I stay? I deserve answers too." Now that he could see and he'd had a few minutes to settle himself, the questions that had been deafening him before clarified to a point he would be able to ask them in some kind of logical manner.

The two men behind him came closer, a warning in his peripheral vision. It made Kane's gut clench, his hands ball into his fists, his stance square.

Malin lifted her hair, slipped a band from her wrist, and tied it off her neck in some kind of messy knot. Her eyes, appearing more violet here in this strange light, flicked between him and the men at his sides. She shot another warning glance at them, and a flash of pride heated Kane's blood. She had just taken *his* side over her own friends'.

Kane ground his teeth, slowly exhaling, waiting. He wanted Conrí and Brogan to vanish, hoped she would tell them to get lost. And also, how dare she deprive him of the vision of her long waves? He wanted to rip the band in half to see her hair falling back over her shoulders. Better yet, over a pillow. He balled his fists, still pushing air number by number from his lungs. Despite his desire, he commanded his body to remain in place. *Don't reach out. Don't tell the men to take a hike. Don't touch her. Don't pull her hair free. Forget this. Focus on Kiera. There's a reason you stay away from connections like that. Remember?*

Kane exhaled harder and cursed the coach for coloring every goddamn possibility in life with shit. He'd never be free of the impulse to maim, and he just couldn't risk anyone else that way. That's why Kiera was here, hurt, needing someone to wake her every so often. His impulses. His fault. And he wouldn't do that to another woman. He didn't think he could've done it to any woman in the first place, let alone his own sister. Kane rolled his shoulders back and expanded his chest, sucking in the air he'd been pushing away.

The wait for Malin's answer was torture. The smell of her, warm like cinnamon and sugar and happiness from his mom's kitchen before they had moved into Wickney, was torment. He didn't need these mixed reminders. He needed to erase what he'd done to Kiera, but the best he could do was to wait for her to get well.

If he took her to the "white-coats," as Malin called them, he would have to explain himself. Maybe this was a better option? Once Kiera was better, he needed to take care of his trainer and disappear. Once and for all. Make that destination a *private* island in the South Pacific.

Malin tapped her foot, seemingly debating. "All right. Follow me." She marched past him, bumping her shoulder into his arm.

Kane couldn't move. Did she just give in? He didn't know her well enough to judge, but she hadn't seemed like someone who would give up so easily. His eyebrows knitted together, not trusting how easy this was. Had she already known he would stay and planned her next move? He looked questioningly at Conrí and Brogan, both of whom shrugged and tilted their heads in Malin's direction.

"You two comin'?" Kane asked, trying to keep his tone light and friendly. He was anything but in the moment.

Conrí cocked a half smile. "Nah, man. She only told you to follow."

Good! Wait, no, not good. But he didn't care.

Kane pivoted and jogged to catch up to her.

Silently, she walked outside. They were in another alleyway, but Malin trekked toward the corner and turned left. Following, Kane got his first good look at the place. The building they'd just exited overlooked Wickney Square and should have been the courthouse. Yet it wasn't the same facade. It was a castle with a hulking stone face and pointed arches between the columns. He scrubbed both hands over his face, making sure he wasn't imagining it. The front of the building would make one think the ceilings within should have been grandiosely vaulted, but inside, it had seemed more like a modern hospital.

Kane's jaw hung open as he took in the vision to his left then to the right. The rest of the scene looked like downtown Wickney under a black light, except there were no neon store signs on the shops around the square and there were no towering lights in the park. No cars decorated the streets in the most congested sector of Wickney. In fact, there were no painted lines indicating where to park, only the cobblestone streets. And across the way at Wickney Police Department, the building appeared as he recalled, but there were no black-and-whites.

"What the fuck?" Kane uttered as questions piled into his already cluttered brain.

"You're in the Penumbra, Kane." Malin pressed on at a pace that surprisingly challenged his own natural stride. How did she move so fast on those shorter legs?

She'd said that before. *Penumbra.* He still had no clue what it meant. "I'm in the what?"

She didn't face him and didn't slow. "The Penumbra. The Dark Realm. One of the many realms. Quit gawking."

The Wickney Square he remembered had spotlights on the statues, but those were absent here too. With his eyes, he traced one stone sculpture from base to top. "Whoa. What's that?" He pointed to the curved and winding animal at the top. Those were supposed to be Wickney's politicians throughout the years. He turned to another. "And that?" His feet stopped moving as he took in the snakelike stone figures, each with two sets of wings spread as if in flight.

Malin sighed. "Those are the ancient ones, dragankind. The ancestors of the dragan we now protect." She sounded bored— no, more than that. Annoyed by him, like he asked the stupidest questions possible. But how was he supposed to know?

"You're shitting me, right?" He barked a laugh. "Dragons?"

"Dragans," she corrected.

"Dragons"—he still mispronounced it—"are for fairy tales and gaming geeks."

She huffed and stretched out her step.

"Wait," Kane said. "If dragons are real, they certainly don't look like that."

Malin trained her gaze forward. "Not only are *dragans* real, but they are also the reason the All Mother created the Penumbra. They are the reason the Dragan Gardaí—that's me, the others you've met tonight, and many, many others—exist.

Our dragans needed a home away from the daylight and away from the Light Realm created by Danu, the Fae world. Now, move along. I'd like some tea before bed."

Tea? That sounded too normal, something tonight had been anything but. A stiff drink would've been more appropriate. Although, he needed to keep his head clear; alcohol would only make this mess so much worse. He'd gone down that road before—the reason he only allowed himself one to celebrate his wins.

At the next corner, Malin walked into the street without glancing in either direction.

"No cars?" Kane hopped off the curb, gaping at the scenery. If this was the same layout as Wickney, they had entered on the West Side earlier, then she had done something where his feet hadn't touched the ground to get them miles away to downtown.

"No. No cars in the Penumbra," Malin said over her shoulder. She'd put more distance between them.

Kane skipped after her. "Where are we going?"

"My house."

His heartbeat quickened, and his mouth went dry.

Kane reached forward and grabbed her by the elbow, spinning her to face him. They stood looking at one another, alone, on the quiet street, in the blue-hued night, air sizzling around them. Kane had to force his dry mouth open. It smacked when he finally pried his tongue from the roof of his mouth, but at least he could spit out his question. "You moved us five or six miles in an instant before. Why are we walking now?"

Malin's mouth opened, closed, opened again. "I, uh." Her eyes dropped to his lips then lifted to meet his gaze; her sweet scent accosted him again.

The combination of all that and her being so damn close to him lit his blood on fire. *Fucker, no. Don't. Not yours. Never yours.* He let her go and took a deliberate step away—a weak effort to keep from pulling her up against his body, to keep from seizing her mouth with his, and to hide the tent-action going on in his sweatpants. Jeans would have concealed his hard-on better, but he only owned a few pairs of anything but sweats or gym shorts.

The soft pants were betraying him this time.

He groaned, refocusing. He wasn't going there. "Well?"

"It's only a few blocks, and I don't have the magic right now."

Kane narrowed his eyes at her. "You only have it sometimes?" He thought she was called a witch or something. Didn't witches have powers? Magic within them?

She folded her arms and jutted a hip. "It's triggered by venom, so yeah, only sometimes."

"Uh, by what?" Other questions ghosted away. Did she say *venom*? Like from snakes or scorpions? Couldn't be what he thought of as venom if it came from the dragans. He pointed back toward the square and the statues. "The . . . ?"

"Yeah, the . . ." Malin flipped a hand toward the dragan statues, then cracked her neck. "Look. I'm done. No more effin questions until I'm inside and off my feet."

Kane set his jaw, took a step closer, and lowered his voice. "You brought me to this strange whatever you called it. And my sister's in trouble. I think I have a right to some goddamn answers."

Malin sucked in a breath and blew it out through O-shaped lips. He nearly crumbled when he thought about what she could do with those lips. What she could do to him. What she could make him do.

"You're right."

"But?" He narrowed his eyes. Why the hell was she so hesitant?

"I will explain but not here." She looked around at the empty downtown street, and he looked around too. "Not where others might hear."

"Others?" Kane raised his arms to indicate the general area, scanning for others. "There is no one else around."

"And you're so effin sure? With your plethora of experience in this realm?"

He shut his trap and ground his teeth. Heat flamed in his cheeks. Realm? Who talked like this?

They stared off.

Finally, Malin rolled her eyes and started walking. "I'm not hiding, but there's a lot to unpack. I'm going to the house. Follow, or don't. Doesn't effin matter to me." She started into the distance before he followed her.

Chapter 9

MALIN PULLED OUT THE CORK-SEALED jar with loose-leaf tea as Kane Macleod sat behind her at the coven's kitchen table. She felt his eyes boring holes into her back as she warmed the teapot, and he still watched her as she brought two cups to the table. When the kettle whistled, she returned to the table and poured steaming water over the mixture of dried lemon balm, chamomile, and valerian.

"Now what?" Kane looked into his empty cup. His fingers thrummed impatiently against the sides, but she couldn't blame him, no matter how annoying he was. She would've done the same thing if it was her sister.

"We wait for it to brew."

"I'm not much of a tea drinker." His big hands with scarred knuckles looked awkward handling the small cup.

Other than Tierney, she couldn't get her other covenmates to try her favorite evening tradition either. "It's relaxing. I drink it every day before bed." Bed sounded so nice at this moment.

Kane's blue eyes flashed at her. "It's not going to do some weird shit to me like that stuff I drank back in the hospital?"

This wasn't any kind of potion, but she really didn't feel like explaining more than she had to. So Malin smiled and checked her watch. Let him think what he wanted as long as he shut up.

"You should do that more often," Kane said, the sharpness in his voice softening, putting her at ease.

"What's that?" she asked by reflex.

"Smile." He put down the cup and leaned onto the table. "It shows your dimple."

She lifted a hand to cover it, smile fading. Even the asshole she'd thought would be her pháirtí had never mentioned her dimple. The only person who had ever noticed had been her sister, Myla. They'd had mirror-image dimples.

She blinked several times, gripping the cup in front of her. *Banish those memories, Mal. Focus on what's in front of you for now. Come back to your purpose later.* She reached for the teapot. "Tea's ready."

Malin poured Kane's cup first, steam curling from the surface, then hers. Simply the smell made her yearn to fall into bed. *Hrm, bed.* The thought combined with Kane's proximity made her heart skip. *Absolutely not!*

But he wouldn't take his eyes off her until after she sipped the sweet-bitter brew and returned her cup to the saucer. And the heat in his gaze scorched her skin.

"Try it." She nodded toward his cup.

His brows pulled together, but he lifted his tea, smelled it, and tasted. He sighed, then squinted. Was he waiting for the same reaction he'd had at Dark Haven? At least, he had learned his lesson the first time.

"It won't hurt you. No magic. Just a few sleep-enhancing herbs."

His shoulders dropped with her reassurance. "Sweet, but much better than the sugary shit." Sitting back with the cup and crossing his feet at the ankles, he said, "Q and A time."

"You have thirty minutes at most before I'll be good for nothing but bed." Malin held out her hand for him to proceed.

Kane cleared his throat, but blue fire blazed in his eyes at her mention of bed.

"Sleep," she corrected herself. "I meant sleep." Her cheeks blazed. She didn't need to correct herself, but she had, and it made her look like a blathering fool.

He lifted one corner of his mouth, eyes now shifting as if he was sorting through something. "Let's start with magic. How's that real?"

She swallowed the tea in her mouth and sighed at the comfort of the herbal goodness wrapping around her like a warm, familiar blanket. Bed was sounding even better. "In the modern tongue, we call it the Darkness. The Dorcha, in the ancient language." Malin waited for a reaction, but he only pinched his lips, so she continued, "Conrí, Brogan, Tierney, and I are Cailleach, dark witches. We are also the Dragan Gardaí, which means dragan guard. Cailleach have true magic through the venomous bite of the dragan combined with an ancient word that releases the power of the All Mother."

"That means . . ."—Kane scratched at the stubble on his chin—"*I* am also one of these dark witches?"

"No."

Kane recoiled. Perhaps she'd been too quick with spouting that answer, but she was still trying to come to terms with what he might *actually* become. His lack of darkvision in the Penumbra meant he wouldn't be suited to using magic. He would, however, be suited to other things.

The bed creeped back into her mind, and she took another sip of her tea, focusing on that hotness instead of Kane's.

Not wanting to voice the implication, even to herself, she swallowed. He waited with his brows pulled together, so she continued as best she could. "You have a gland called a nimh, so you are meant to be here. But you aren't intended to be a witch, and you aren't capable of wielding the Darkness." Malin ran a thumbnail along the woodgrain in the table. "If that were the case, you would have been able to see without the drink Emrys gave you at Dark Haven."

"Dark Haven? Not the courthouse? Okay. How did I get this gland? Some kind of disease? A cold?"

"You were born with it."

"You have one?"

Malin nodded, the sweet herbs beginning to weigh her muscles down. It wouldn't be long before she would be in a deep and hopefully dreamless sleep. She certainly didn't need a replay of the dream about Kane she'd had before.

"Does my sister have one?" he spouted.

"We don't know. Emrys will be testing her to see."

"What is it? Some sort of mutation?"

"Damn that bastard, Stan Lee." Malin rolled her eyes. "We aren't X-Men."

"How do you know I have it? No one tested me."

"We can if you want. There isn't a definitive test that can be done—aside from cutting you open. Whether it's magic or just the placement of the gland, the nimh doesn't show on any scans. The best we can do is a heart scan to see if you have the extra chamber that feeds blood to the gland." She lifted a shoulder in a half shrug. This was no big deal to her.

Kane narrowed his eyes at her. "Uh, extra what?"

Malin remained silent, allowing the news to tumble around in his mind. All the new information could definitely muddle someone's thought processes. It was understandable if he needed a few minutes to digest it.

Suddenly, his eyes narrowed suspiciously. "If you can't test, then you can't be sure of anything." Another logical conclusion.

She swirled her tea. "Well, since you could see through my spells in the Daylight Realm, I'm certain you have it." She yawned, then motioned to Kane's mostly untouched cup. "Don't you like the tea?"

He tilted it toward himself. "It's fine, but I'm not much of a tea or coffee—or really anything—drinker. 'Cept water."

Malin's eyes drifted down to Kane's biceps stretching the seams of the otherwise loose-fitting hooded sweatshirt. *Prizefighter*, she reminded herself, but it wasn't something she forgot easily. He must keep to a strict diet and exercise routine.

Her mouth watered when she imagined his arms, chest, and abs free of the material. No. She couldn't go there.

Clearing her throat, she asked, "Other topics, Kane? I'm sleepy."

He apparently ignored her suggestion. "I've seen you fighting twice now in that alley beside Club Infinity. Who were those men you were fighting?"

Malin halted with her tea halfway to her mouth, and she stared at the caramel-colored liquid for what seemed an eternity until it blurred before her eyes. "You give the Semaphors too much credit by calling them that." She lowered the cup, trying and failing to keep her hand from trembling. "A man has honor, or at least a moral system."

Although she was safely in her coven's kitchen, Malin's mind placed her in the church where she'd confronted the traitor who had sold his soul to the fallen god Semar, the one they called the Maker. In that vision, and for the first time in her life, her sister wasn't fighting by her side.

Malin's voice sounded a million miles away when she commented to Kane, "All the slime do is hunt, maim, and kill. They are not worthy of being called *men*."

Kane blinked at her. Yeah, he had probably never heard anyone talk like that before.

Time to get off the topic.

"No matter. They have nothing to do with you or your sister. Finish your tea. It'll help you sleep," she said and downed the rest of her own lukewarm liquid.

When he finished too, Malin reached for his cup and saucer. She stood, taking both cups to the sink and leaving them on the counter. Malin braced herself with her arms for a few seconds as she gathered her thoughts and blinked tears from her eyes.

"Let's find you an empty room." When she turned, she ran straight into the wall of Kane's chest.

He grasped both her upper arms in his strong hands, and Malin forgot to breathe. Recalling her dream, her fingers itched to touch his sides, but she balled them into fists instead. Her height, compared to his, had her looking at the little hollow in the center of his collarbone. She licked her lips and lifted her gaze to meet his. The temperature in the room must have spiked by fifteen degrees.

A rumbling sound rolled from his chest, and he clenched his jaw, a vein popping out of the side of his neck. He pushed her away a hair's breadth, nostrils flaring as he pulled in air. "It does matter. I don't fucking know the details, but I'll be damned if I'm going to stand by while a bunch of—what'd you call them? Simpers?"

"Semaphors," Malin breathed, knees weak with how he touched her. Held her. She was ready to fall, only to be picked up by him. What else could those arms do?

"Sema*phors*," Kane echoed, stressing the wrong syllable, then pursed his lips in thought. After another split second, he said, "They were larger than you, and they had you outnumbered." His eyes were fixed on hers, but his pupils were dilated. Clearly, he saw something else too. "I couldn't let them hurt you. Or your friends." A strange expression ghosted over his face, as if he couldn't reconcile his own words with whatever he saw in his mind.

Did he really think he could save them? Insane! Malin slid to the side, freeing herself, and she felt bare without his touch. "We had it in hand."

And if he hadn't been there, they might have found the information she needed to find Godric at last. *Kane* had distracted her. *Kane* might have prevented her from getting the revenge she so desperately needed. Malin's heart hardened.

"You had no idea what you were walking into. We had everything under control." She marched for the door. Before exiting, she looked over one shoulder. "Come on. We have free rooms where you can sleep."

MINERVA, MALIN'S MOTHER, STOOD WITH her back to the wall outside the kitchen, listening. The man in the kitchen with her daughter—*Kane*, Tierney had said—hadn't said much within the conversation, but the hairs on Minerva's arms raised when he spoke about defending the coven from the Semaphors. He had the right instincts to become pháirtí if he hadn't already started that transformation. Given that he was a fighter and that he couldn't see immediately in the dark, he would make a good ally for them in the Daylight Realm. Then, in the way Malin had breathed through her words, she had felt something too.

Of course, Minerva's stubborn daughter would take a long time to admit such things. Minerva only hoped it wasn't *too* long. They didn't have the time.

When Malin's boots hit the floor in a rapid beat toward the door, Minerva ducked under the stairs.

Her daughter came to the door and paused, inviting Kane to stay in the coven house for the night, then she headed toward the stairs. It was a start. Kane came to the door after her, looking suspiciously to the right near where Minerva hid before following Malin to the stairs. He definitely had the sense, unlike the last man Malin had believed her mate.

Minerva waited to hear sounds on the second floor before she emerged from behind the stairs and went into the kitchen. Immediately, she noticed the two empty cups on the counter. She backed up and looked toward the front door, the stairs, then down the back hallway to make sure she was alone. Then she gathered her robes and crossed to the cups.

The first one she lifted had a familiar pattern of tea leaves at the bottom: a man holding an ivy leaf and a large hawk flying in the clouds over the man's head. The signs that there would be love and happiness in her daughter's future, but there would be a great foe in the mix. Minerva replaced Malin's cup and reached for the other one. She stared at the leaves for a long time before the images became clear. The ring of leaves around the edge made her grin, but that faded when she made out an ivy leaf divided by a line. And when she saw the serpent within the ring, the cup fell from her hand, went tumbling to the floor, and shattered.

CHAPTER 10

THERE IT IS!

Finally, in the oppressive blackness, Kane found the doorknob. He'd awoken from a strange dream with disembodied faces floating before him. Kiera's, Conrí's, Brogan's, and all the others he'd met since the alley fight he had interrupted. Malin had been the most prominent and haunting though, and he had woken with a rock-solid cockstand and his hands balled into fists. He'd never encountered a woman like her. She hadn't giggled or swooned, didn't ask him for a selfie, and hadn't asked him to sign a random body part. She'd been feisty and almost combative, and he couldn't shake the feel of her body close to his or her hand on his chest and arm. Even though his dream had only included faces, his body reacted.

Chagrined, he remembered Kiera and her concussion and leaped from the bed. After knocking his knee on the four-poster corner and the chest at the foot, he cursed, "Fuck!" and rubbed his eyes in a hopeless effort to get them to see again. Nothing. He fumbled for his clothes on the floor, felt his way to the adjoining bathroom, finally got his cock to agree to let him take a piss, and dressed. Afterward, he felt every wall of the room for a light switch and swore again when he settled on the fact that his efforts were useless.

Once in the hall, he tried to recall how to get out of the house and back to the courthouse. The place Malin had called "Dark Haven." Whatever that meant.

"Cowan alert!" A deep voice called from his lower left, some distance away, familiar, but he couldn't be certain which of the men from the night before it was. The term "cowan" irked him, and he balled his hands into fists.

Stairs must be that direction though, so Kane took a couple of tentative steps.

"Can't see again, huh?" Another deep voice said behind him, this one close enough to touch.

Kane spun, closed his useless eyes, and crouched. Perhaps if his Rage took over, he could sense where his fists and feet needed to fly.

"Whoa there, easy. Not a threat. Malin left us here to help."

"Who are you?" Kane asked. A totally stupid question, but he'd met three males yesterday and could only tell that neither of these were the doctor.

"Conrí. And Brogan's sitting on the steps."

"Yo," called the other. His voice was like an echo.

Conrí added, "I'm going to grab your wrist and put a bottle in your hand. No punchy business, 'kay?"

Kane eased out of his crouch and dropped his fists. His thundering heart didn't stop though, and adrenaline pumped hotly through his veins. "A bottle of . . . oh, that sweet seeing shit?"

"Yup," Brogan answered with a chuckle.

Kane groaned. "It tastes like sugary gin and sweaty socks."

"And you've tasted such things before?" Conrí drawled.

"Smelled plenty." He accepted the bottle. "And drinking this hurts."

"Of course it does. It's activating all the cells that'll allow you to see in the Penumbra, since you don't have that natural ability." A pause. "Yet."

What the hell did that mean? Before he thought about it too much, Kane felt the small bottle for a cap, but there was none. Was that a cork? He grabbed on to it. *Pop.* Yep, a cork. "Where is your leader anyway?"

Brogan chuckled. "You mean Malin?"

Conrí echoed his friend's laugh. "Yeah, you better not let her hear you call her a leader. Those are fighting words."

"Hmmm?" Kane mused. Seemed odd because everyone clearly deferred to her.

"Uh-uh, not my story to tell," said Conrí.

Even though Kane couldn't use his eyes to see the man's reaction, he had the sense Conrí shook his head.

"Mal's down at the training center. Same place she goes every evening when she wakes up."

Kane tossed the liquid back. Despite how it tasted or what he felt like after, he needed his vision. He pinched his eyes shut, waiting for the pain to accost him. He could handle more pain now that he knew what to expect. He had been handling pain for most of his life—physically and mentally. When the stabbing started, he breathed in deeply and exhaled while counting. He continued to breathe while the syrupy shit did its work, and pretty soon, the upstairs hall materialized in blue hues, the same spot where Malin had left him the night before. The house almost seemed familiar, like he was meant to be here, but that was stupid, or at least the stupidest thing he'd ever imagined. He'd certainly remember more about this place if he'd ever been here.

"Wait, did you say evening?"

Conrí came into clear view, nodding. One of those snake things was wrapped around his waist and resting a head on the man's shoulder. Kane recoiled. The animal's blue scales glimmered, and his vertical-pupiled eyes were trained predator-like on Kane. It almost looked like a prop they might use at the local Renaissance Festival, but the tail waved at Conrí's side. How did the man stand that? The mere thought of a snake wrapped around him made Kane shiver.

Stepping back, Kane lifted his fists again by instinct. He wasn't sure how to fight a dragan, even one so small, but the only way he knew how to fight was bodily.

"Oh, this is just Rezei." Conrí stroked the dragan's head. "He won't hurt you as long as I don't ask him to."

The small, snakelike dragan chittered. Agreement with Conrí? A greeting? Sounded friendly enough. Even so, Kane was keeping his distance. He specifically stayed away from the reptile building at the zoo.

Conrí continued, "And yeppers, our schedules are opposite your world. It's always dark here, but we sleep by human day, fight by night. Since it's summer back in Wickney, it's probably about 8:00."

"Ah, hell, I need to call Broc." His trainer would have been expecting him at the gym by 6:00 p.m. for their daily training sessions, and he was never late. Broc had to be freaking out, especially after the loss yesterday. Kane reached into his pocket for his phone.

"Not happening, man." Brogan laughed again, the low rumble grinding Kane's last nerve, but he obviously didn't care to explain.

To Conrí, Kane asked, "Is he capable of more than three words at a time?"

Conrí chucked him on the shoulder, then pursed his lips and looked at the ceiling. "Ya know, I'm not certain he is." He seemed far more friendly today, so what had been his deal in the hospital last night?

"Heeyyy!" Brogan complained from the stairs.

"We haven't figured out the inter-realm communications just yet." Conrí motioned to Kane's useless cell phone. "Or any tech here in the Penumbra, for that matter. Theory is it can't co-exist with Darkness. Maybe one day"—he shrugged—"but it no workey at the moment. Your sister's awake though. Wanna go?" Conrí sidestepped and jogged down the stairs.

Kane stayed, pressing the button on the phone to try to get it to wake up. Something didn't jive. Malin mentioned a heart scan to see if he had that gland. That was tech, right? He pivoted, took the stairs two at a time, and stopped in the foyer, where he met the other two. He wanted to say they were "brothers" for some reason, even though they looked nothing alike.

"I don't get it," Kane complained to Conrí. "Malin said something about a medical test that sounded a hella lot like technology."

Brogan chuckled, and Conrí answered, "Magic, bruh. Magic."

*M*ALIN RAN THROUGH THE SQUARE and back to the training center across the street from her coven's townhouse. Push, pull, one foot forward, then the other. She stopped in the middle of the street looking at the door to her home on her right and the double doors to the training center on her left. Her chest heaved. Her legs burned. Sweat ran down her back and dripped from her brow. But it didn't seem to matter how hard she pushed herself, everywhere she looked, the image of Kane Macleod materialized before her eyes. And she was back before she started on this run, her core throbbing and mind distracted.

Damn, why couldn't Conrí have left him there with his sister to find help at the human hospitals? Kane had been getting ready to call for help. It would have been just as easy to let him do that as it was to bring him to the darklings, and it would have made things so much simpler. Now, she needed to find a way to return him and Kiera to the Daylight Realm without their memories. That worried her because her spells didn't work to their maximum potential on Kane, and they seemed to wear off faster. *Frustrating man.*

Conrí and Brogan had him now, so Malin turned to her left for some more exercise therapy. She had to get over this so she could focus on her work. But more than that . . . her mission. It was more than revenge. Her purpose was about ensuring what happened to Myla and Aemro would never, ever happen to another witch and dragan. Her work, mission, purpose, revenge, or whatever anyone wanted to call it was about the survival of their kind. Why couldn't her covenmates or her mother understand?

Inside, Malin grabbed a towel from the shelves and mopped the sweat from her face and neck. She considered lifting but thought better of it and walked past the free weights. She circled around the row of Darkness-powered treadmills too; she'd just pounded out about ten miles. Breyze was back at the aerie, so she had no way to reach the magic necessary to power the machines anyway. At the range, she appraised the rack of weapons and settled on a set of small daggers to hone her throwing skills.

She held one up by the tip of the blade, using the hilt as a sight on the person-shaped target. Pulling back, she flicked her wrist in a forward motion and . . . *thunk*. The first dagger stuck and wobbled between where the shadow's eyes would be if it were a Semaphor. Or any other creature, for that matter, but she only focused on one.

Malin aimed again.

Thunk.

"There you are." Tierney's voice interrupted before she could tell exactly where she had landed that throw.

"Hi, Tierney. What's up?" Malin aimed the third dagger at the target, pulled back, and loosed the weapon.

Thunk-zhing. It landed in almost the exact same hole as the second, ringing against the other blade. The shadow target now had one knife protruding from the head and two from the center of the body, slightly to the right as she looked at it—the heart.

"Three beautiful shots," Tierney said, "as always."

Malin cut her eyes sideways to glance at the witch who'd been almost as close to her as her twin sister, Myla. Tierney had a look about her Malin dreaded, so she strode away quickly and pulled the daggers from her target. Tierney leaned up against a treadmill with her arms folded and one ankle crossed over the other. Malin didn't ask because she could guess exactly what was on Tierney's mind.

And she wasn't in the mood. "I already know what you wanna talk about, and I'm just not interested." What she was in the mood for was stabbing something, but the training course would do. For now.

"Yes, you are." Tierney smoothed out her long, blonde ponytail and picked at a split end. "You're just bent on lying to yourself for some reason, and none of the rest of us can figure it out."

Malin trekked back to her starting point, glared at her friend, and faced the target again. She aimed.

"What are you going to do about him?" asked Tierney.

The dagger sailed to heart center. Another perfect shot. Maybe they needed to upgrade to moving targets? Malin closed her eyes, pictured the outline in her mind, aimed, and threw. *Thunk-zhing.*

Without opening her eyes, she said, "He's not Cailleach. At best, he could become pháirtí. Maybe it's time you took a mate, Tierney." The mere thought of that sent a piercing pain through Malin's chest. No effin way. There wasn't a chance the thought of Tierney with Kane would cause her physical pain. She opened her eyes and rubbed the spot just above her left breast where she'd imagined the sting.

Tierney twisted her ponytail over and over again. The way she looked at Malin shouted a snark-loaded, *Yeah. Right. I'll get right on that.* What she said though was exactly what Malin feared.

Tierney said, "He saw you. Not me. He responds to *you,* Malin, like you're the center of the world."

Malin tossed the third dagger into the air, catching it by the hilt. "It just can't be." Sideways, she tossed the weapon. *Thunk—*into the head of the target. "And you know why."

"How long has that been? A decade?"

Malin grabbed a spear from the weapons rack. She held it across her thighs, squeezing the grip so tight she might have broken it if it had been one of the old wooden ones they had once used to train. "Twelve years."

It had been twelve years since she had held Aemro's dried husk. Twelve years since Myla's heart had spilled its blood over her hands and fingers when she'd lifted it from that box.

"It's been twelve years, Tierney, and it can be another twelve or twelve hundred for all I care." Malin's words sounded quiet, flat, dead, and she kept her eyes trained on the spear's handle. "For all of our sakes, I will not take another mate until Godric and all the Semaphors are vanquished from the realms." Only then would she be free. Only then would it be safe to love.

Tierney's feet entered her field of vision, and her friend grasped on to the spear between Malin's hands. Tears stung Malin's eyes, and one dripped onto the rubber mats beside her foot. Tierney waited for Malin to look up before she said, "Mal, if not for the sake of your coven, then you must try to heal and find your old self for your own sake and for Breyze's, and now, probably for Kane's. Your vengeance is stale."

Malin stared into Tierney's bright, concerned eyes. Tears, still born of anger, confusion, and devastation, streamed down her own face, and she didn't trust herself to speak.

Tierney swallowed visibly. "I talked to Minerva this morning."

Malin flared her nostrils. What did her mother have to say this time? Malin was an adult and had been an adult for a while.

Tierney lifted her chin higher—no hesitation. "She saw something coming. You *and* Kane are tangled at its center."

CHAPTER 11

*A*FTER HER WORKOUT, MALIN SHOWERED, dressed, and beat a path toward Dark Haven. Kane, along with Conrí and Brogan, should have already been there, and it saved her the time of having to deal with Kane. But her own thoughts of Kane were just as bad.

In the Penumbra's version of Wickney, the square did not hustle and bustle like the one in the Daylight Realm, yet Malin passed a couple she'd known for years on her way to Dark Haven. The witch Kai, one of Malin's mother's generation, rolled his eyes when his pháirtí tugged at his jacket and moved in her direction.

Hester smiled broadly, and a bit too eagerly, as she approached. "Malin, so good to see you. How is Minerva?"

"Mother is well enough and up to mischief as always." Malin forced a smile, which was an effort considering what Tierney said her mother read in Kane's tea leaves. She reminded herself to remain pleasant with her elders, just as she would wish to be treated. "So good to see you again, Hester. And Kai." She nodded to the silver-haired man.

Kai dressed in a long coat and wore a wictam hat in the old tradition—not a pointy thing, but one that resembled a bowler with a flatter brim dipping to shade the eyes in the front. It was a leftover from when witches walked more readily in the Daylight Realm, before the All Mother reshaped reality to create the Penumbra. He tipped his head and lifted the wictam but held his tongue. Though powerful, he always had been the quiet type.

Kai turned to his mate with loving eyes as Hester rambled, "I see your mother every other week for cards, but I haven't seen you since . . ." The woman's lips turned downward at the corners, regret forming on her face before she could remind Malin of the last time they'd spoken at Myla's funeral.

Malin bit her lip and looked away. "I've been, um, working." It wasn't a lie, but it also didn't convey the complete truth either.

Hester straightened the shoulder cloak she wore and smoothed her dress at the waist. "Well, dear. Litha approaches. Will you and Minerva join us to celebrate the coming of the darker months?" The woman grasped Malin's hands and squeezed.

Malin hadn't celebrated the eight Sabbats or any of the Esbats—the minor festivals of the moon—since before Godric's betrayal. She'd vowed not to until after the culprit was brought to justice. She answered Hester noncommittally, "I will speak with Mama about it." Now, she needed to extract herself from the pleasantries. "You'll both forgive me, but I'm expected at Dark Haven."

At that, Kai wrapped a hand around Hester's shoulders. "Dorcha bless you and your coven until we meet again."

"And you and yours," Malin answered with the traditional farewell, already backing away.

She passed by the front arches of Dark Haven, not wanting to deal with the prescribed rituals for entering through the front doors. They were almost as bad as the human Catholics. She turned down the alley and entered through the side door instead. The hall toward the room where they'd left Kane's sister the morning before stood empty, and when she arrived at her destination, she stopped to look through the window. Kane sat at Kiera's bedside, holding her hand to his forehead in both of his. Kiera, eyes wrapped, appeared to sleep peacefully with her head still elevated and wrapped in bandages.

"Mistress," Emrys said, "how are you?"

She turned to the darkling. "Well enough. Have you tested her yet?"

"We have." Emrys lowered his gaze to where he had his hands hidden in the opposite wide sleeves of his tunic. The way the material lay without a gap, it appeared to create a single circular tunnel for his arms. She wanted to reach out to him though, as she always did when they were alone. But he had retreated into medicine and his darkling rituals, whereas she'd become a stone-cold warrior. Or perhaps a hunter was a better term.

Malin shucked the thoughts. "And the results?"

"She has the fifth chamber, mistress." And therefore, the nimh, he didn't say, and he didn't need to say it.

Malin sucked her cheeks in and nodded. "Of course she does. If only to complicate the matter more. Have you removed her bandages to learn if she can see?"

"I have not. Would you like me to?"

"No." Malin pinched her lips, then sighed. "The only reason she is in the Penumbra is because of her brother. She may not be ready for whatever the All Mother has intended for her yet."

Emrys glanced into the room. "Do you plan to tell him?"

Malin bit her lip. She refused to look at Kane, but she was painfully aware how close he was. How he sat there. How his shirt was tight against his muscles.

The darkling continued, "You know we cannot keep giving him the elixir, mistress?"

"I'm not sure what I'll do. I don't know if I can tell him about his sister, and I'm well aware that he needs to go back to the daylight. How long before it's safe to move her?"

"I'd feel most comfortable if she remained here for another seventy-two hours. Forty-eight hours at minimum."

"What if we brought her to a human hospital?" asked Malin.

Emrys fidgeted within his sleeves. "That would be acceptable, but we would need to communicate the extent of her injuries. And we would need some kind of credentials to do that. That means . . .”

Malin knew what that meant. She would need to find Morgana. She gave Emrys a thank-you nod and pushed the door open quietly. Inside, she eased it shut so as not to jar Kane out of his concentrated state. Perhaps it was a prayer. Did he believe in a god or goddess? Would he come to believe in the All Mother in time? She stood there for several moments watching the brother and sister and remembering the twin's bond she had with her own sister. She could imagine how torturous it would be to sit at her bedside helpless. But she hadn't gotten the chance.

“I am so, so sorry, Kiera,” Kane whispered, his head still bowed and just millimeters from touching his sister's. “I will get you out of this. You have my word.”

Malin shoved her hands into her pants pockets and whispered his name. His name was thick on her tongue, pouring out like syrup.

With a shiver across his body, the fighter looked up, his eyes glassy, his eyelashes formed in wet spikes.

I wouldn't want to leave either, but . . . she had his safety to worry about. “Can we talk in the hall?”

Kane eased his sister's hand down to her side. Kiera moaned and rolled her head toward her brother, but Malin doubted Kiera knew what was happening around her. Kane whispered, “It's all right, K. I'll be right back.”

Malin felt sick that she needed to keep him from returning. When outside the room, she turned to face Kane. “I need to take you out of the Penumbra,” she blurted out.

No need to stall, though her heart thundered like a drum in her chest, rumbling in her rib cage, and it resounded in her ears.

He looked through the window for a moment, then back into Malin's eyes. His gaze seared her somewhere deep within. “So, my sister can go home?”

Malin shook her head. “That isn't recommended yet.”

“Then I stay.” Kane set his jaw, crossing his arms over his broad chest. He'd left his sweatshirt hanging on the end of Kiera's bed, and he only wore a T-shirt with his sweatpants now, those muscles stretching the cotton to the limits.

Malin swallowed the flood of saliva in her mouth. She laid a hand on Kane's bare arm, and the hair on her arm raised when he flinched. "You trusted me yesterday, yes?"

Kane furrowed his brow. "I did, but—"

"No buts." She held up her other hand, stopping him. "You cannot continue to drink the elixir that allows you to see here."

He growled. "Why? It tastes like shit, but it works like a gem."

"It has side effects." She didn't want to tell him that it could drive him insane with continued use, and she certainly wasn't ready to explore the other option. "Emrys says she can go to a human hospital, but I need to do a little work to arrange that in the Daylight Realm. You'll go with me to do that."

Kane dropped his arms and took a step closer. "Look, I'm grateful for all you and Emrys have done for Kiera, but this is my fault. My responsibility. So whatever the risks, I'll take 'em and wait here with Kiera until you return."

Hesitantly, Malin took Kane's hand, an electric zing running through her as she did. She wished for the Darkness at the moment, so she could cast a spell that'd make him more compliant, but she hadn't had Breyze near since before the end of the prior night. Even though her magic didn't last with Kane, even a small casting would work long enough to convince him. Now, she had to hope her touch was enough. The way his eyes widened as their fingers intertwined was a good sign.

"Conrí said you mentioned missing something. An appointment?" she ventured.

Kane gripped her hand and ran his free hand over his head. "Yeah. I haven't missed a night of training at the gym since I turned seventeen. Broc probably called the Wickney police to put out a missing person report."

That was good. Not that anyone would go to the cops, but that he'd started considering the impact of his absence. She wondered if he had any fights coming up.

She pressed further. "What about Kiera? Who will miss

her? Work? Friends? Family?"

"No—oohhh, hell." His eyes shifted and then closed, but he still gripped Malin's hand. It felt better than she wanted to admit. Then, he added, "I can't believe I didn't think about Mom."

Malin tensed. Another family member? She didn't know how many more she could deal with. "What about your mother?"

"Kiera lives with her. And I lost a fight last night. Kiera usually goes home afterward to assure Mom I'm okay. Mom was probably up all night worrying about both of us this time. Fuck." He ran his hand over his head again.

Malin leaned closer to Kane. Warnings went off like beacons in her mind, but her heart and body pressed onward. Maybe it was a familiarity about his family situation that urged her on? She couldn't be sure, but she softened her voice. "Then we should go. You should visit your mother and assure her that Kiera is okay. Emrys will take good care of her here until I can arrange for her to be transferred." Although, Malin started to rethink the wisdom of making that particular transfer. She would deal with it later.

Kane searched Malin's face, his brows drawn together and the hand that wasn't holding hers fisted at his side like he was ready to fight. They stood in silence, breathing the same air for several minutes. She wished she could read his mind, wondering if he was trying to read hers in the same way. Would he give in? Would he dare to believe she would make sure his sister recovered? He couldn't know her reasons, but she would never willfully harm another person's family. The pain she lived with every day was too much to share with another and almost unbearable for her. She only had one enemy, and when the Semaphors claimed another fanatic from the human population, the convert abandoned all family values in the name of their Mother-forsaken mission. They lived for nothing but to extinguish the Darkness. The worried look on Kane's face shifted, and the time seemed right.

"Trust me, Kane," Malin pleaded, her voice breathy like a feather in the wind.

His jaw clenched. "I suck at trust," he growled through gritted teeth.

Malin almost laughed, knowing that feeling all too well. She pulled their joined hands up between them—strange how he didn't resist, how he seemed perfectly comfortable holding her smaller hand. She examined his knuckles, scars crossing each of them. She ran a finger over the white marks on his tanned skin. "By telling you all I have, I've trusted you with the very survival of my people. And also the survival of another entire species." She looked up into the blue depths of his eyes.

"The dragans?" he asked.

"Yes." A sour tang flooded her mouth. *All Mother, please don't let this be a mistake.* "I know what it feels like to lose a sister, and I'll be damned to hell if I let yours suffer any more than she already has. I promise you can trust me."

Malin held her breath.

Kane's free hand caressed her cheek, gentler than she would have imagined. Malin held herself utterly still while waiting for his next words. She didn't want to admit to herself or to him how his strong fingers melted her from the outside in. This wasn't meant to be. She should stop it before anything else happens. Kane scoured her face. Did he still question if he could trust her? Or if he could trust at all? Or did he look for answers to a deeper question?

Then Kane captured her lips, tangling his tongue with hers. There was nothing gentle about it. His body and lips demanded she respond, and damn her, she devoured what he was giving her. The kiss tasted like warm spices and was feral, mind-numbing, body-melting. And in an instant, it seemed to hold more truth than anything else in her existence.

CHAPTER 12

Fter a kiss Kane should never have stolen, he walked along beside Malin in awkward silence. His lips still tingled, and he could still taste her on his tongue. He could've tasted her all day. What was he supposed to say after that kind of scorching connection? He couldn't put his finger on what drove him to kiss this unusual and literally magical woman. She was strong, filled the room with her presence if not her tiny body. She commanded his attention and would linger in his mind long after they left each other, but he never wanted to leave her. He wasn't sure if he could stay away from her, and the kiss confirmed it.

Conrí said not to call her a leader, and Kane wondered why. She acted like one in every single way, in everything she'd said and done since he'd met her. Kane was definitely not a good romantic match for any kind of leader, but he would've followed her. All there was to him was broken remnants of a teenage boy, someone who didn't really know how to become a man and couldn't rely on anyone but himself. He was little more than a husk of a person who used his fists to work out his Rage.

Despite himself, Malin's words about knowing loss had convinced his inner cynic that people can care. And he believed she would do everything in her power to ensure Kiera healed. All this was more than he could say for any other person he had known, save for his mom and Kiera. Not even Broc showed him as much.

Teachers, they were supposed to care. Ha! After the thing with the coach, Kane believed they didn't give a shit about him. They watched from their desks with their blood-red pens, marking F after F in some little, green-ruled book that was supposed to matter to a high school student. But it didn't mean shit to him at the time. When he just didn't show for school, did one of them call? Nah. Kane had turned to the streets, drugs, and alcohol at night. During school hours, he had started training at Endure Muay Thai. The sounds of the fight had drowned out the echo of the coach's grating voice. With Broc's help, Kane had won his first prizefight before he would have earned his diploma. That was all that happened and all that had mattered over the last few years.

Along the way, he had tried out the relationship thing. That had satisfied some base need, but it never lasted. Either he had gotten up in the morning and left them, or they had gotten up in the morning and left him. Sometimes, he autographed one of his professional photos when he slept with a groupie. And they could all go and gossip about it to their friends; it made no difference to him.

There were never breakfasts or leisurely mornings to get to know one another. The girls around didn't want to speak to him either, really. They used his body as much as he used them. As a result, he'd grown to think of women as faceless figures because they'd all started to blend together. He'd let one, and only one, woman stay overnight. And the next morning, it had made him sick to look at her in his bed. But he had never tasted anything as sweet and sensual as Malin's lips. Something about them. About her. She smelled sweet, but on his tongue . . . He wanted more. So. Much. More. The way her mouth had molded to his and how their bodies fit like a key and lock. Those sensations, real freakin' new!

Somewhere inside her violet eyes, he had found whatever answer he had been looking for. Could he think of it now? Hell no, but he'd seen it in her in the moment. The thought roaring in his mind when he had seized her lips had been, *Thank you!* But taking that kiss was selfish—wrong at best—but it tasted so goddamn right. Not going anywhere, though. Regardless of how she'd gained his trust, he just wasn't right in the head.

They finally stopped, and she looked at him, biting her bottom lip. He found it hard to look at her, scared of what her face might express. What if she didn't like the kiss? He had all these thoughts running in his head that made him want to be sick, but what if it was all for nothing? Malin seemed blunt, but romance was a different kind of territory. An awkwardness about it that made his mouth go dry and caused him to shy away from her. Or any woman who remotely showed him more interest than his body and what he could do in the ring.

After an uncomfortable few heartbeats, Malin said, "Wait for me here." Her voice was softer than usual; her own lips were pursed—perhaps puffy—from the kiss. She moved toward what looked like the entrance to a cave.

A cave? Strange sight in a city. Kane hadn't been watching where they were walking. Everything else in the Penumbra had been a near mirror image of Wickney in positioning, but he had to remind himself that this wasn't Wickney. He still wasn't sure what it was, but then again, magic logically didn't make sense.

Malin didn't leave him immediately, only watched and waited for his response.

He'd taken her words as an order, not a question. "Oh. Yeah, ah, no problem."

She touched his hand again. "I'll be right back."

Kane shivered as she disappeared beneath the stone arch. With her by his side, the air had thrummed, but alone, it felt still and almost stale. They'd passed a few people in the square after they had left the hospital, though he hadn't known if they were like him or her or something else entirely, but as they drew closer to where he now waited, it seemed like a ghost town. As they had neared this cave only a handful of blocks off the square, everything around seemed devoid of life. The quiet was too much, the streets empty, buildings too abandoned. Something or someone had to be lurking nearby. Damn, he sounded paranoid.

No matter how many crevices he scanned—nothing.

And then a hiss reached his ears. He whirled around, blood thrumming through his veins as his heart raced. Malin stood before him with her hands raised in a calm-down gesture. She now wore the cloak he'd seen her in the first time they had met. One of the snake-like dragans floated through the air at her side. Its scales were mostly the color and sheen of amethysts, but around the wings, spine, and horns, there were hints of orange and yellow. The dragan eyed him suspiciously, lips peeling back and baring fangs like it meant to attack. Kane took a step back. He'd always lived in the city and didn't have experience with snakes, but he remembered the mention of venom. He might not have his high-school diploma, but he knew smart people kept their distance from venomous snakes.

Malin chuckled. "Breyze will not harm you."

The dragan chattered and slithered around Malin's arm. When she nodded, it beat its wings against the air once and flew toward him. He locked his knees, held his breath, and widened his eyes. *Don't move. Don't shake. She said he won't hurt me.* Breyze circled him. Kane tried to follow the dragan's movements with his eyes alone.

Behind him, it chittered and chattered some more, then circled him quicker than Kane could blink, creating a breeze in the dead air around him. Next, Kane felt the dragan's body sliding down his back and around his waist until he encircled Kane twice like a karate belt. Still hugging Kane about the waist, Breyze crept upward and reared his head back to look Kane in the eyes. When Kane flicked his gaze toward Malin, noticing her smirk, the dragan let out a peal. Kane jerked his attention back to the small beast, his heart hammering. At length, the dragan nodded and blinked, then released him. Kane's breath left him, and his body slumped heavily. Still alive. Barely.

The dragan flew to Malin, sliding under her cloak with a few more chattering sounds. She touched its head like one would pet a dog.

Kane heaved another breath and sighed loudly.

Malin laughed. "He approves."

That wasn't what Kane got out of the interaction. "That's . . . good?"

"Very." Malin's eyes fluttered shut. She hissed in a breath through her teeth, blew it out slowly, and stepped closer. Her eyes opened, and Kane could swear a purple light flickered through her irises before she asked, "Ready?" and offered him her hands, palms up.

Kane stared at them, trying to make sense of how he felt when he touched her. He had been blind when she had moved them from the West End to Wickney Square, so he had no clue how that worked. "You can take us back to the real Wickney through that floaty thing you did before?"

"No. It's only a flight spell, but it will get us to the Awen much quicker than walking, and we'll cross there."

"Ah." For some reason, that made him feel a little more at ease, not that he trusted what she meant by flight. Maybe it was a word that didn't translate well? "So, you can't just cross anywhere?" He lowered his hands toward hers.

"The All Mother placed the Awen when she created this realm. Many cities around the world have windows into the Fold. We can open them with Darkness, but we don't have the goddess's power to create them."

As their hands touched, Malin moved hers up, so her palms were below his wrists. She wrapped her fingers tightly around his. The brush of skin to skin and then her grip sent a buzz and hum through him. Kane stopped worrying about anything else. He held on, allowing Malin to do whatever she wanted with him.

She whispered, "*Gaoth.*"

Kane couldn't take his eyes off hers, but in his peripheral vision, the city fell away. Pressure released from his heels then the balls of his feet. Gravity no longer existed. They were flying, soaring, or maybe floating over the buildings, but all he focused on was Malin's touch. Whatever she was doing, he wished she would never stop. And he didn't have to be worried about crashing to the earth when she held him up.

"Bend your knees," she said after several minutes, breaking

the trance that he had been in, and he suddenly looked down.

They were a hundred feet off the ground, if not more, and he could've died from a fall up this high. And then what? What about Kiera? And his mom? He couldn't leave either of them ever again.

"Easy there," she said, voice intoxicatingly calm. "Everything is all right."

They landed softly. Malin let go of his hands, leaving his palms and wrists cold and missing her touch. She opened her cloak, and Breyze slid out. Malin strapped a small pair of goggles over his eyes and behind his two horns. He issued a short chirp and returned to his hiding place. Kane watched with wide eyes. He never would have believed he'd have such a thought, but Malin's dragan wasn't the weirdest thing about of this experience. Apparently, he just had to get used to it, but it seemed like no one wanted him getting used to it, maybe him included.

When Malin turned away and started toward a wall, guilt returned to rack Kane. He reached out and grabbed her arm gently until she peered back at him. "Hey. I'm sorry about"— he swallowed—"about kissing you like that back there. It was totally out of line." He let go, then shuffled his feet on the dusty pavement beneath his feet.

She squared off and crossed her arms. The look in her eyes turned to stone. "If I knew you were going to get all regretful, I wouldn't have *let* you kiss me like that." She turned and walked away.

What the actual fuck? Kane blinked several times, struggling to understand her reply. Anger? Disbelief? Stone-cold terror? Once at her side again, he started, "Are you—"

"Here." She held out a pair of glasses. "You'll need these, or the light will be torture." Clearly, she meant to close off the conversation over the matter, even though he wasn't sure he was done. Not that he knew what he wanted to say next. Geez, his thoughts were jumbled, and his tongue felt like lead.

He examined the useless dark lenses. "I can't wear these at night."

Malin pursed her lips. "Have you ever worn contacts?"

"Never had the need. Perfect vision." He smiled, but she didn't smile back.

She put a pair of glasses over her own eyes. "Glasses or contacts, you choose. But you'll be blind again if you choose neither." Malin lifted her arm and extended her pointer finger toward the wall.

Kane flashed back on the shadowy symbol she'd drawn on the gray brick before they had entered the dark place. She did it again: a circle, three lines, and three dots appeared. This time, they vibrated with the blue hue that shadowed everything in the Penumbra. Looking closer and having this strange and magical darkvision at the moment, he made out three concentric circles surrounding the lines and dots, whereas he'd only noticed one before. The wall before him wavered like a curtain.

"What is the symbol?" Kane asked, his voice thin and sounding distant to his own ears like his words were caught underwater.

"An Awen. The All Mother Aodh's symbol representing her, a dragan, and a Cailleach. If you check your Celtic history, you'll find many other meanings behind the symbol. Mind, body, spirit. Earth, sea, sky. Regardless, it allows us to open the windows and travel across the Fold between realms."

"You mean between the real Wickney and this dark mirror image?" He smiled again, hoping to coax one out of her when showing her how much he had learned. How much he had been listening to her.

"That and more. You wearin' the glasses or going blind?" She gave him one last look then stepped through the wall.

Kane dropped his head back and counted while pushing out a breath. People would look at him weirdly, but visiting his mother would be okay in glasses. With her blindness, she wouldn't be able to tell the difference. He put on the glasses and stepped through after Malin. A shiver ran over him, and he found himself in the alley near Club Infinity, sounds of distant car horns blaring. It felt normal, like what he'd known since moving to the city as a boy.

"How long does the juice last anyway?" he asked.

"The elixir?" Malin non-answered.

Kane winced, scanning the alley for other people. "I'll call it juice, if you don't mind." The thought of someone overhearing something that sounded magic-y made his skin itch, and he tried to be conscious of what he put in his body. Elixir didn't have the connotation that he would like.

She harrumphed. "How long it will last is not entirely predictable with you."

He furrowed his brow, wondering if that was a jab at him or at the kiss. Along with the normality of the cars, he felt closer to his Rage here. Kane tried to bite back the sudden irritation, but he snipped anyway, "This is all about your world. Why the fuck don't you have answers?"

She placed a hand on his chest, and he stilled. He wondered if she felt his racing heart below. "*Socair*," Malin snapped back.

Damn her. That cool calm flooded through his shoulders. Or maybe he shouldn't be angry. Perhaps he should be grateful that, when she said that word or touched him, his temper ebbed. The Rage seemed to relax, and it suddenly wasn't a beast.

She stepped square into his space, filling it with an overwhelming presence that didn't fit her small frame. "You are not as predictable as the cowans or other neophytes. My other magic has worn off quicker with you than with others, so I can't give you the straight answer you're looking for." She had definitely changed from the soft, coaxing demeanor she'd had when they were on the dark side, but Kane liked this snarky, angry side too.

As he looked out at his surroundings, he wondered what had brought this side of her out. Was it just being back in this realm? If so, why? Or had he done it by apologizing and questioning the legitimacy of the kiss? He was just trying to be polite, something he rarely thought about. There was a lot about the other world he didn't know, but the thoughts of the kiss brought other things to his mind. And he couldn't seem to shake himself free.

He fisted his hands at his sides, wondering how feisty she would be in bed. His nails dug into his palms but it would not be enough of a deterrent to keep him from grabbing her, kissing her, owning her mouth once again. Perhaps owning her right there in the alley. *No, Kane, not fucking nice.* Propriety halted him momentarily.

Although, he also had to admit, the venomous dragan beneath her cloak might have had a role in staunching his desire.

Malin took a breath and eased her stance. "Less than eight hours, I'd guess, since you slept it off during the first part of the day."

The implication of him being unpredictable was nothing new. It was why he'd been labeled "The Rage" long ago.

Kane glanced toward the street again, taking in the scenery through the glasses. Lights shone a soft blue. What if . . . ? He pulled the glasses down the bridge of his nose and peeked over them. Burning pain seared the backs of his eyes, drawing his lids closed, and he bit back a hiss so Malin couldn't tell how much of an idiot he was. He replaced the glasses, considering. He would go to his mother's townhouse first and hope the juice wore off before he went to EMT to train. That was the best he could do.

He lowered his voice as he said to Malin, "Can we keep the m-word on the down low? It'll draw attention."

She crossed her arms and smirked. "Not as much as you talking to an invisible person."

"Wh—?"

"Truth. Humans can't see or hear me unless I allow it." She pursed her lips, and her eyebrows drew down. "Except you." She seemed not to like the taste of the words in her mouth.

Kane stood straighter and tried to act like she wasn't there. *Except him? Interesting.* If rumors of him talking to an imaginary friend leaked on social, he might not be able to fight in Vegas per the UFC's new mental health rules. The rules were for the best because he had seen some really messed up people in his fighting career, him included.

He studied her petite figure. The ends of her cloak and the feathers on the shoulders swayed gently in the wind, and he could still smell her scent. She was as clear to him as his own hand and as real as the stench of urine in the alley. "That's impossible," he whispered and started walking toward the street.

Malin fell in at his side. "Like everything else you've experienced over the last couple days, right?" At the street, she peered over her shoulder. "Go take care of your mother and your trainer." She started to turn back into the alley and leave him.

Kane grabbed her by the wrist. "Oh no you don't. You're not slipping out of my sight just yet." It was a threat and a promise.

Malin stared at him, then let her eyes drift down to where he held her hand. Something about their contact set him on fire, even if it was angry contact. Did she feel it too?

Beneath her cloak, Breyze chattered. A slither rumbled under her cloak as the dragan-y snake unwound from her body, its skin dragging over her leather.

Fuck fear, Kane decided. He wasn't letting her go. He'd faced worse. Something in her over-the-shoulder look and the energy thrumming between them told him she didn't want him to let go either.

"You said you'd see Kiera got into a hospital here," he said, but the demand in his voice faded to a point he almost sounded like he was begging. And the excuse was weak.

The peal of schoolgirl giggles alerted them from the mouth of the alley. Malin turned her head sharply. "*Dubh*," she said, removing her own glasses and squinting toward the sound. "Good. Just passing. You can take the glasses off for a moment."

Kane hesitated, still refusing to let go of her wrist.

"It's fine," she assured him and placed her free hand in his other hand. "I pulled the Darkness around us, so it won't burn."

Without the glasses, it seemed like he was still in the mirror place—the Penumbra. He had better start using the words she gave him, because it didn't seem like he was breaking ties with her in the immediate future. Nor did he want to. He asked, "How do you do that?"

"I told you. The Darkness. Dorcha. The All Mother's magic." Her voice was soft, coaxing again.

She hadn't said any of the strange words, and he didn't feel the cool calm settle into his shoulders. So this was only *her*, and her touch burned so sweetly. She looked up at him with sincerity and no signs of the hard Malin she'd been projecting.

"I will arrange it," she said, "if that's what you truly believe is the best course of action. But I am inclined to agree with Emrys that she would be better off under his care."

Kane should be angry; he should feel deceived or manipulated. He wondered if she'd planned this all along just to get him out of her world. But the notion scuttled away before it could take root. Instead, he grew more determined to keep her at his side.

"Then you come with me to take care of it." They could both go talk to his mother and trainer, then make an excuse to Kiera's boss at the clinic. Yes. That would be the best plan to stay with Malin *and* to get back to his sister. Simple. "After that, I am going back with you."

Malin stared up at him, questions he couldn't read darting back and forth in her eyes. He didn't dare to ask for her thoughts, only slipped his hand from her wrist downward to intertwine his fingers with hers. Her touch had worked to calm his anxiety before. Would his work the same on her?

Her brows drew together as she started, "I . . ."

Kane squeezed both her hands, swallowed the sour taste in his mouth, and choked out a word he hardly thought he would be able to speak. "P-please."

CHAPTER 13

*M*ALIN SUDDENLY FELT ANCHORED AND steady on her feet in the Daylight Realm. Kane's tentative *please* melted her and gave her purpose. His hands seemed impossibly like home in an alley on the West End of Wickney near Club Infinity, the last place they'd vanquished another one of the Semaphor slime. Malin closed her eyes.

Myla's face, disembodied on a sea of black, floated before her mind's eye. Her sister smiled as if it were just another day, as if her heart were still beating steadily within her chest and she was heading off on a date with her pháirtí, Emrys. The vision also took Malin back to when they, as twins, were preparing to inherit their mother's role in the coven. Minerva had once been High Priestess, and every witch knew the prophecies—Malin and Myla's destiny, she'd once believed—by heart: *The twin-blooded will rise. Inheritance will be claimed. Wielders of cursed Light will perish. Peace will fall upon dragankind, the Cailleach, and creatures from all realms.*

She and her sister were supposed to bring together the fractured worlds, but all she could do now was avenge her twin's death. Before Malin's eyes, Myla's face aged. Her hair turned a silvery shade. The rapid aging the Cailleach experienced in their last decade of life was something Myla never lived to experience. The vision of her looked identical to their mother, a stark reminder of how little time Minerva likely had remaining before her return to the All Mother.

The vision shimmered, her sister making a full transformation into their mother, and Minerva reached for Malin. "Daughter, making the choice that may lead to your peace and happiness is not selfish. The embers within you will warm you when your actions are right. You feel that now. Trust the feeling. Trust yourself." Her mother misted away.

Malin opened her eyes. Kane's gaze regarded her patiently, but lines of worry formed the number eleven between his brows. Considering this seemed insane, but . . .

She recalled the message Tierney had conveyed, the one Minerva had read in the tea leaves. Although, Malin cursed her carelessness for leaving the mugs unwashed on the counter, she couldn't argue with what her mother had seen using her dark gift. "You and Kane are tangled at its center," Tierney had said in a priceless imitation of Minerva. Could that be true? And the center of what? If the vision had been sent from the All Mother, it meant fate. Regardless of how much she resisted, whatever it was *would* come to pass. Malin knew that to be certain.

Malin sucked in the deepest breath she could, unable to believe she was relenting. "Okay." She released one of Kane's hands. "Put on the glasses," she added, and when he had them securely in place, she waved her hand in the air. "Breyze, I need the Darkness." She waited for the venom to take hold, replaced her glasses, then released the Darkness. "*Saor. Chumasci.*"

The cloud that had settled over the two of them before lifted.

"*Féach.*"

Still gripping her hand, Kane pulled back, confusion clear on his face.

"Do you not like me this way?" Malin asked.

He wrinkled his nose. "Not as much."

Malin fought a smile pulling at her lips. "It's just a disguise to hide the parts that are of Darkness. Feel here." Malin lifted his hand to her shoulder where his fingers threaded through the dark feathers of her cloak. "But the spell will make others see a mousy semblance of me, wearing an everyday T-shirt and jeans."

"Damn. What about me?"

She chuckled, scanning the length of his body. "You can stay as you are. You look cowan enough to blend in." *Although, a very well-made cowan,* she added in thought, and her eyes flickered away.

"*What* enough? You've said that word before. What the fuck is it?"

Malin gritted her teeth, not wanting to explain that it could be a derogatory term. "Means *human.*" She waved a hand dismissively. "Where does your mother live?"

"A mile north of Wickney Square, near the university. We can hop the rail a few blocks from here." Still holding her hand, Kane tilted his head and pulled up his hood. Seemingly, he planned on playing up the glasses thing. Kane took a step toward the street. "Let's go."

She supposed the hood and shades would be common for a famous person trying to hide but not for someone who now looked as plain-Jane as she did. "Wait," she said. Might as well get them both into contacts. "Let's step into the club. If we're mingling with cowans on public transit, we *should* ditch the glasses."

He smirked. "Isn't that what I said before?"

It needled at her to concede, so she nodded.

"And doesn't your magic disguise hide yours?" Kane arched a brow.

"No." Malin sighed. "These are cheap sunglasses, not something of Darkness. The magic will only hide my cloak, Breyze, and my weapons."

"Weapons? You aren't carrying weapons."

It was her turn to lift one brow, challenging him but also hoping he would call her out. He would want to search her body for proof. "Whatever you say, fighter." She didn't need to give away her secrets just yet, and she had many.

"THESE ITCH," KANE COMPLAINED AS the tram slowed and approached the North Metro Station near his mother's townhouse. He scrubbed at one of his eyes, trying in vain to rub away the annoying little disk Malin had put inside. If he didn't need one eye to see, walk, and monitor unfamiliar surroundings, he would have both fists in his eye sockets. The contacts shielded the light in the same manner as the glasses, but they were much, much more annoying. "Gimme the glasses back."

Malin grabbed his arm at the elbow and forcibly pulled his hand from his face. "You'll never get accustomed to them if you keep rubbing your eyes." She sounded like his mother.

Through his bleary and fist-filled gaze, Kane saw an elderly lady sitting in the seat nearby smile at them.

From the corner of his eye, he saw Malin return the smile, which looked a little forced with her tight lips, and she said, "He just got contacts for an astigmatism."

Kane snorted—*yeah, right*—and blinked furiously. The contacts moved like suction cups across his gaze.

Malin looked up at him with amusement on her face. "*Honey*, you know what the doctor said."

Did she have to enjoy his discomfort so much? But then again, damn, her little act was fucking hot! Having this little secret between them, each time she played at something, his body reacted in all sorts of public-inappropriate ways. He blinked harder, half because of the contact and half to know if she was real.

The lady laughed. "They can be stubborn, can't they, dear?"

Thankfully, the train slowed to a halt, and the door opened. Malin hopped off. As Kane moved to follow, the lady's painful wince caught his eye. She grabbed on to the rail next to her seat and winced again, placing an arthritis-warped hand on her hip. Kane reached over to help her up and off the train. "Do you need help getting somewhere?" he asked.

She extended a trekking pole, leaning her weight onto it, and pointed down the platform. "No, sir. My daughter is just there, but I appreciate your concern." She patted his arm and winked at Malin. "You've got a good one here. Hang on, dearie."

Kane hid his growing grin under his hoodie. Malin tucked her chin as a young, dark-haired woman jogged toward them, hopping to a halt and kissing the elderly woman on the cheek. "Thank you, sir. I've got her from here. How was the trip, Gram?" She took the woman's bag and led her to the elevator.

Malin moved to the side, waiting with her arms crossed over her chest and wearing a small and amused smile.

Kane didn't miss the suggestion in her look and dropped his head back to stare up to the ceiling. "Let's just go." He headed for the exit.

A few blocks north of the station on Little Sarsfield Street, Kane stopped in front of the stairs into the brick building where he had spent his teenage years. The good times and the bad, and then the ugliest of them all just before he'd found EMT and Broc. His body coiled like the snakish dragan on Malin's back, and his heart pounded so loudly in his ears that it sounded like a rush of waves. He came back here often to check on his mother, especially after every fight so she knew he would survive another day, but having Malin here felt different. Not wrong but not quite right either. Malin seemed like she had everything figured out, minus a few passing details, and Kane would prefer it if she kept believing she had him figured out. It was easier than the alternative.

Stuffing his hands into his pockets, he declared, "This is it."

They climbed up together, but when he reached across Malin for the doorbell, her scent overwhelmed him. Suddenly, he was in his early childhood home. He was eight, maybe nine. It was before his mother went blind, and his dad, unable to handle caring for her and two kids, left the three of them alone in the lake house. Shortly afterward, they moved to Wickney from the small town of Shawano, so his mother could access more state services necessary to help a young, single, and disabled woman with two children. She had been a business owner, an independent baker who provided pastries to the local coffee shop, deli, and market. Every night, she would roll out cinnamon rolls, set them aside to rise, then melt down some butter, sugar, and cinnamon to make them ooey-gooey-yummy the next morning. And when she finished, she sat down to read with him and Kiera. Those weren't simple times, but they were simpler. Something, at least, that had been good in his life.

"Are you going to ring or just hold your hand there?" Malin asked, extracting him from the happy memory. He wished that she hadn't.

He turned his head to look at her, stared at her for a long moment trying to reconcile the sensation thrumming through his blood. This woman smelled exactly like the happiest memory he had. *How?* he wondered. She was about the furthest thing from a baker he could imagine, and he imagined many things about her and what she did when he wasn't around. The problem was *not* imagining her.

"Well?" she prompted again.

"Ah, yeah. I'm just wondering what Mom will think about me bringing a woman here." And that was the truth too.

Kane had never brought anyone home who might resemble dating material—not even a friend. He'd been fairly popular in his early high-school years, but that all went to shit after the coach incident.

He blinked. *No—not thinking about that.*

Most teens brought dates home at some point before they left home. In Kane's thirty years, he hadn't. Bringing Malin here, yeah, that was a hundred and ten percent new territory. But nothing could be done about it now, no call to his mom to prepare her for their arrival, no easing into it. They were on her doorstep, and he had to face it. Whatever his mother's reaction, he would have to assure her this wasn't something to get hopeful over. He was here to let her know both he and Kiera were well. That was it.

He punched the bell and chimes rang from within. They waited and waited. Eventually, the sound of the squeaky first step told him Mom was close to the door. "She was upstairs," he explained to Malin. He hadn't prepared Malin for what they were walking into—out of what? Shame? Concern that Malin would find him unworthy? Fear that she would turn away? When his mother's hands patted at the other side of the door searching for the lock, he raised his voice: "Mom, it's me, Kane." He couldn't be concerned about Malin's thoughts when his mother was struggling so much.

The patting quickened. Two locks clicked, and the door opened inward.

$\mathcal{M}$ALIN HAD BEEN STUDYING KANE intently, the way he hesitated slightly before ringing the bell and the way he explained meaningless things to her. *How odd,* it struck her, that he would be so nervous to return to his home. Walking back into her coven house always soothed her, but for Kane, that clearly wasn't the case. Perhaps he feared how his mother would react? Whatever the case, the opening door brought her back to the here and now, and she blinked, shifting her gaze forward.

The woman looked like Kiera but twenty years or so older. She stretched her hands forward. "Kane? Kane? Where are you?" Her voice sounded oily with panic.

Frozen and forgetting herself, Malin let her mouth and eyes gape. A milky film covered the woman's eyes, her cloudy irises and pupils wandering, searching, but never finding a target. A different kind of darkness afflicted the woman.

Kane stepped forward, taking her hand and placing it on his face. "Here, Mama."

The woman eased visibly to have her hands on her son. Kane peeked over to Malin, who slowly raised a shaking hand to cover her mouth. She tried to turn her head away, but she couldn't tear her attention away from the woman.

Blind. Kane's mother. Is blind. That meant she carried a dominant gene in her line. *She* had the nimh too, so of course Kane and Kiera would both have a nimh. *By Dorcha! How did his mother go this long without being called upon by Darkness? How could we not have learned of her before her children showed signs? How had the Semaphors not discovered her in this realm? Shit . . . shit-shit . . . shit-shit!* Malin tried to recover, especially with Kane still looking at her and his face drooping by the second, but she was stuck. Frozen. Her mind ran through possibilities, but none of them seemed plausible. Around and around her mind went like dragans at play, chasing each other's tails.

The woman smiled and pulled him into an embrace. "Who is with you?" The woman's fidgety, wandering eyes fixed on Malin like they hadn't done with Kane. Her brows dipped into a V.

Malin couldn't breathe, much less speak. Did the blind woman see her or sense the dark witch in her? She waited, hoping to learn the answer.

"Mama." Kane shrugged a little, his mouth quirked on one side, but his brows frowned with concern. "This is Malin. Malin, my mother, Beatha."

A pang of guilty bile gurgled in Malin's stomach, and she stood as far away as the porch would allow. She didn't understand. How couldn't she have known? How couldn't her own mother have known this family existed here in the Daylight Realm? Kane being one of them was a lot to process. Kiera made two—not terribly out of the question for siblings. But a third? Impossible. Especially to find someone with the gland so advanced in age she had lost her sight.

Beatha would still have many years of youth before her if she'd been brought into Darkness at the right time. The stab of duty and guilt almost sent Malin running from the porch.

Beatha held out her trembling hand and waited, but Malin didn't even have the control for common cowan pleasantries. "It is a pleasure." Her irises began moving again—jerky, non-seeing, and aimless. Perhaps it'd been Malin's imagination and Beatha didn't see her frozen in the dim pool of porchlight. "How do you two know each other?" she asked.

Kane widened his eyes and nodded, prompting Malin to finally accept Beatha's hand. It felt frail to the touch, like crepe paper wrapped around bones. Kane's voice sounded pinched as he answered, "She's a friend"—a smile started on the woman's face, but Kane quickly added, "of Kiera's."

What? Of Kiera's? Great, now she was a part of whatever lie they had to tell Beatha to ease her mind. She didn't know anything about Kiera, and she preemptively tried to string details together based on what Kane had said. And Kane had said very little about his sister. Or himself.

Beatha gasped and lifted her face to her son. "Kiera? Wh-where is she?" She twined her crooked fingers—premature arthritis, yet another sign of Beatha's missed calling—into Kane's zippered lapels, latching on to him as if she might lose him too. Fear and pain and nothingness ruled this woman's world, and it sliced into Malin's soul. Without receiving her answers, the worried mother pulled on her son and continued, "Is she hurt? She must be . . . I always worry about you. Never Kiera because she always comes home at night, but last—"

Kane gently took his mother by the shoulders and urged her inside. "Kiera is well, Mama." His voice sounded so soft and loving. Malin flushed with warmth at hearing him and seeing him with his mother, much like when he had helped the lady from the train. How could she stay irritated with someone who showed so much kindness?

With a *follow me* look at Malin, he continued, "Let's go in, out of this humidity, and we'll tell you all about it."

Momentarily, Malin considered rekindling her anger at Kane for putting her in the middle of whatever lie they needed to tell, but the thought warred with her duty to the Darkness, the All Mother, and dragankind. A horrid thought ate at Malin: *We—all of the Cailleach—have failed Beatha Macleod and her family.* Malin had to do better for Beatha . . . and for Kane.

Kane and his mother walked inside and down a hall, turning at a door on the left. Malin couldn't coax her feet into motion. Every part of her remained preoccupied with the fact that entangling herself with Kane and Kiera, and now their mother, was no longer a choice. But why, in all the realms, did it feel so much like a betrayal?

Mother and son out of sight, Malin finally budged. The street behind her was sleepy, and the clouds in the sky blocked out the moon's face. "Forgive me, Myla," she whispered. "I have not abandoned my vows. You and Aemro will have justice one day, but this is necessary now." She stepped inside and eased the door closed, blocking out the rest of the world.

She took slow steps down the hallway, thankful not that Beatha was blind, but that she didn't have the need to reach for the lights in the house. That benefited Kane tonight too, though he probably wouldn't think of such things.

The hall was lined with candid photos in mismatched frames. Looking closer, Malin noticed braille dots on the bottom of each frame. There were two of the same size with matching frames at the center. One showed Kane hefting a title belt for his prizefighting. "Heavyweight Champion, Northern Region," the belt read. The second showed Kiera in scrubs holding a diploma. Malin squinted to read the diploma: "Bachelor of Nursing, Wickney University," then the words on the pocket of Kiera's scrubs: "WC North" in big lettering with "Wickney Clinic North" below. Moving on, a smaller photo—maybe a four-by-six or three-by-five—caught her eye. The frame had once been painted bronze, but the paint had worn off near the braille. The picture inside had yellowed with the passing years. That mattered little, Malin realized, because the woman who "saw" it certainly envisioned it as the actual scene had been or when the film had been developed originally.

Kane leaned around the corner. "You coming?"

Peeling her eyes from the faded image of a boy with his hands in a bag of flour and a girl beside him, both covered in white powder, Malin turned. Her mouth went dry. Caught, like she was doing something she shouldn't have. In Kane's questioning gaze, she saw that mischievous little boy from the photo. Now, he had too many lines on his face for someone so young—lines of worry and scars from fights. There was something else about him too. Something shadowy and heavy gnawing at him, and he wore it in the expanse of his broad shoulders, the set of his jaw, and the way he almost constantly curled his hands into fists.

"Well?" he prompted again.

Malin peeled her dry tongue from the roof of her mouth to speak. "I . . . er . . . yes."

Inside the sitting room, Kane took the seat on the couch

next to Beatha. "Mama, Malin knew Kiera in high school." He stared into Malin's eyes, his gaze confused and searching. "She needed . . ."

Malin scurried over to the chair on Beatha's other side and scooped up the woman's hand. She locked eyes with Kane as she said, "Mrs. Macleod, I am so sorry we worried you. My house is in a cellular dead zone"—fortunately, she'd had many years of practice with that particular lie—"or Kiera would have called you. Since it has been so long, Kane thought it would be best if we came in person."

Slowly, Beatha placed a hand on Malin's. "Well now, that's very thoughtful of my son." She half smiled, but the woman's drawl told Malin it wasn't like the son she knew.

"Yes, it is," Malin said, emphasizing the words and focusing her gaze on Kane.

His expression eased, eyes sending silent gratitude. No longer having to come up with lies on his own, he mouthed, "Thank you."

"The thing is," Malin continued, "my mother fell and hit her head. The doctors sent her home from the clinic with instructions to wake her every hour." *A bit of truth in every lie works best*, Malin thought. "But I had to work, and I'm terrible with anything medical. I had an anxiety attack right there in front of the doctor and Kiera, so your daughter volunteered to stay with my mother until she is out of the woods." She took a deep breath and waited for a response, preparing to launch into her next lie when the time came. And sooner or later, the lies always came.

CHAPTER 14

*E*VER SINCE LEAVING HIS MOTHER'S house, Kane had been itchy, his heels had been bouncing like they did just before a fight, or he'd been rubbing his neck. In other words, he had been fidgeting like a crackhead who just dealt to a plain-clothed DEA agent. The imagined bugs crawling under his skin lasted for the entire rail ride back to the West Side of Wickney, but Malin seemed lost in her own worries. He was grateful for the silence though because the fight had been building inside, and he feared the energy—or worse, The Rage itself—might break through in another unpredictable way. Just like it had with Kiera. He would take the silence if it meant being with Malin, and as much as he wanted to ask what her worries were, he didn't wish to speak about his own.

Perhaps silence was better in that moment as they tried to figure everything out. He couldn't fathom what Malin thought of his mother and didn't want to ask. At some point, his mother would make it clear what she thought about Malin, and that would sure leave him in an awkward situation.

They stepped off the train into the mostly empty station and walked the platform shoulder to shoulder. The only sounds were some Elton John song playing over a crackling PA system and the train whirring off into the night. At the street, Kane turned right. This route was routine for him, but Malin stuck to his side like they'd walked this path together for years. Did she use magic to anticipate his moves? Or was she just pulled to him like a magnet?

Or was it something else entirely?

Fate?

The Rage growled inside. Kane balled his fists and released them over and over as he hulked toward EMT, where he would have to face his trainer and answer for missing the day's workout. He needed that workout and to spar. That was the only way he kept his beast tamed. Just before turning the corner onto Becker Street and the Muay Thai club, they passed a building with a covered entryway, shadows looming in the corner. Kane looped his hand through Malin's arm and backed into the shadow. She followed without a sound, but her lips pursed in question.

Kane growled as the smell of her overpowered him, and he reached for her. Something in the back of his mind warned him: *the dragan.*

Fuck the dragan, he retorted to his inner guardian angel. *And fuck the consequences of whatever I'm about to do.*

He thrust his hands into the back of Malin's hair, watching her eyes intently, and pulled her to him. He kissed—no, he stole another kiss. Her lips were soft but firm and sweet like the sweet rolls he imagined when he smelled her. She moaned into his mouth, bringing him back and preventing him from pouring his tangled nerves, thankfulness, confusion, and Rage into her. He released her and growled again—an anxious instinct he couldn't control. In truth, he wasn't sure he wanted to control it.

"What"—she breathed heavily—"was that?"

"Sorry," he blurted with a curt shake of his head. Kane ran a hand over his skull cut. "Shit! I'm doin' a whole lot of sorrys lately, but I'm so fucking so—"

"Don't!" Malin cupped her palm over his mouth, and the skin of her hand was as soft as her lips, except for a few callouses he recognized from fighting. "No more sorrys."

She reached both hands up, grasped his face, and kissed

him this time. Hers wasn't as hard, but it was every-fucking-bit as demanding. With her lips and tongue, she told him she didn't mind. That she had desires too. Her body molded to his, causing him to harden, cock pulsing with need. It was like his own dragan. But she kept on, pushing her body forward. He felt the cloak, but her dragan seemed absent. Probably only hidden. Still, he didn't dare move his hands toward her body, and that took all the restraint he had within him.

This kiss dulled the urge to punch but made him want to do something far, far more reckless. With her tongue and lips, Malin warned him to stop being weird about it. After leaving the townhouse, she had told him things had changed, that she had learned something. But what? What could she have possibly gained from the short time with his mother?

Suddenly, she pushed away from him, leaving him wanting and throbbing. And cold in the humidity of July. "Now, why did you pull me aside for this? I'm not complaining. I'm not asking for effin apologies, but you best start talking."

Kane turned into a guppy, his lips working wordlessly until he just pressed them into a tight line. The Rage started to return, and he swallowed hard. *No. Not here. Not now,* he begged, and he hoped he wasn't wrong to beg.

"I need to fight," he finally said. "When we get to EMT, I need to spar."

That had to sound strange to her, but there it was. He needed to let the beast loose, to pound out the confusion that had been building over the last few days. He needed to hit something to erase the guilt over Kiera and the lies he'd just told his mother. And he didn't want Malin to be the one on the receiving end of his flying fists.

Although, she appeared much less on edge since leaving his mother's house—quiet but more calm. Now, she hesitated, her brows lowered. The uncertain look was one he never wanted to see on her face. Why had she been so confident when she kissed him back but confused over why he needed a fight?

Kane hooked his forefinger and lifted her chin with his knuckle until she looked into his eyes. He leaned forward, about to uncontrollably seize her mouth again, but wondered, *Why?*

So many whys. Why did he believe a kiss would ease her? Why did he want to taste her so bad? Why had he, of all the worthy people in Wickney, been the fortunate fucker to get a glimpse into her world? *Wait, fortunate? Really, man?* But he didn't care at the moment as his mouth watered for hers.

Gently this time, he pressed his lips to hers. Their lips danced together until he sensed her releasing her worry, then he pulled back.

Malin nodded.

"Sor—"

"No." She pivoted and stepped out of the shadow. "Don't you effin apologize. Let's go."

From the deeper shadows, Kane watched Malin strut away for a dozen or so steps. He cursed the cloak hiding both her dragan as well as the shape of her body. His imagination of how well his hands fit in the valleys above the swell of her hips sent lava flowing through his veins to the tune of the bass drum in his ears. His imagination and her lips didn't stop the throbbing of his cock that rubbed so uncomfortably against the seam of his sweatpants. He thought he was going to burst. He told himself to think of anything else, but only Malin flooded back.

He took a breath and skipped into a jog. "Left here," he said, catching up to her at the corner.

When they walked into EMT, the lights burned at first even with the contacts, and he couldn't make out details through the glare. As Kane's eyes adjusted, a dozen or so fighters took form on the mats: some sparring, some at the bags, and others warming up or doing cardio.

The door closed behind him and Malin, sounding a chime—something Kane had never quite understood. Why wouldn't it have sounded when the door opened? Regardless, Broc perked up, a toothpick hanging from his mouth. He appeared confused, as if he didn't know whether to smile and welcome Kane with open arms or make him run ten miles for not showing up on time. Broc had been working with another fighter but stopped. He motioned to one of his junior trainers and crossed the mats to the entrance. Toward Kane.

Kane said to Malin, "You can wait in the chairs there or hit the treadmills. If you'd like." The politeness sounded sore and wrong in this mouth, but he couldn't handle fighting two people he cared about at the same time. He didn't have the energy.

She narrowed her eyes at the approaching trainer then turned to the bank of treadmills. "I'll hop on that one at the far end. Shadows and all, ya know?" She shrugged as if he would find it the normal response.

Kane pretended to understand with a shrug of his own.

Broc watched her go. "A little bland for you, don-cha think?"

Kane smirked. If only he knew how incredibly not bland that woman was. And being from Wisconsin, Kane knew a lot about bland women—and food. Well, except the cheese. Sconny had the best cheese. Kane gave his head a small shake. *Cheese? What the fuck's wrong with me?*

His trainer balled a fist and lightly punched Kane on the shoulder. "Guess that answers the where ya been question then." The man tongued the toothpick to the other side of his mouth. "I'as about to send someone over to your flat to round ya up. Hope you worked out whatever you had doin' there 'cause you need to hit the bags. Don't want a little piece of ass to distract you from the prize."

"'S not like that, man." Kane started shifting his weight between the balls of his feet. Just being in the gym amped up his need to hit something, and he preferred a person rather than a bag. "Anyone here worth sparring with tonight?"

Broc scanned the gym and scratched at his stubbled cheek. "You fought Smalls before, right?"

"Yeah. He'll do." Kane's bouncing quickened. His stomach knotted in anticipation, and he salivated like a dog about to get a meaty snack.

His trainer nodded once, still appraising him skeptically. "Get changed and warm up."

"Sure thing," Kane answered, skipping toward the locker room.

Good thing Broc had laundry service at EMT that collected

the dirty clothes for the regulars along with the towels. The laundry service washed them up and sorted out the gym shorts to each of the lockers at EMT. Big perk to Broc's club. Kept Kane from having to pack up every time he needed to spar.

Changed, Kane jumped on the treadmill next to Malin, who watched the happenings with a keen eye but surprisingly kept quiet. He wanted to ask her what was wrong, but he didn't need the extra baggage when he was about to go into the ring. He needed a clear mind—and the lurking Rage. He jogged a mile then went to the bags for another five minutes to prepare his arms. He glanced over his shoulder to see if Malin was watching, but she was running on the treadmill with her head facing forward. By the time he finished, he had worked up a nice cleansing sweat. Kane nodded to Malin and was greeted by her narrowed gaze. She then returned the nod, so he went to the ring.

"Ready," he yelled to Broc.

Broc wrapped his hands and helped him into the gloves and headgear, then shooed Kane into the ring. Smalls stepped between the ropes on the other side. EMT didn't have a cage, so they used standard boxing rings for sparring. It didn't matter as long as Kane got what he wanted in the end.

The man, Smalls, was anything but small. He matched every bit of Kane's size and probably a few pounds more. If Kane recalled, the man usually went on a crash diet just before weigh-in to stay in the heavyweight class rather than bumping up to the next level. Kane had never had that problem. He had started in the middleweight class and worked diligently to put on enough muscle to make heavyweight. He ate a strict diet for many reasons, foremost because he needed to stay at peak performance if he was going to win the money in Vegas and quit.

"You know the dealio, right, Kane?" Broc held up the mouthguard a little distance from Kane's mouth. His eyes warned Kane as he said, "No TKOs in my club."

"No promises," answered Kane. He lowered his voice and leaned closer to his trainer. "Pull me off if it looks bad. I know your rules, but I can't control The Rage, and you know it."

Broc pursed his lips and gave a singular nod, then let Kane

bite the guard from his grip, and waved a couple of his junior trainers over. Standard protocol when Kane was in the ring. Embarrassment colored Kane's cheeks that only he had such an issue. The other fighters could control themselves, but when The Rage came out, Kane ceased to exist. All hell broke loose until the vision of the coach was chased back to the depths within Kane's soul. The cage was the only place that could keep The Rage in check when Kane was fighting, not this stringy boxing ring with holes for days.

The old-school bell sounded, that kind that sounds like a fork striking a tin pie plate. Kane met Smalls at center ring so Broc could give them both the rundown before the go-bell rang.

"Smalls, Kane needs to be in tip-top shape, so no low blows," he said. "And Kane, well, we'll deal." He shook his head with his hands on his hips. "To your corners."

The second bell rang, and both men came out swinging. It felt good—right—to be trading punches. The light through the contacts was bright but hazed with a pink-lavender color. And the details were so much more crisp. He'd always had good eyesight, but this was like he saw things in slow motion. Kane measured his pace. With each jab, he felt more at ease about the "Darkness," as Malin kept calling it. With each blow he took, he grunted but accepted it. Welcomed it even and considered it recompense for what he'd done to Kiera. Yes. The ring was where he belonged—beating and taking a beating. It fit him and was all he was fit for.

He and Smalls were evenly matched. They both connected with feet and fists, and both bounced back time and time again until the bell sounded. Kane danced back to his corner, relishing the sweat running from his bare chest.

He looked over to the last treadmill in the row. Normally, he couldn't make out details if anyone used that particular machine, but he could see everything about Malin: her cloak, the way the waves of her maple syrup–brown hair bounced with each slow step she took, the look of serious concentration on her face as she watched. A thrill ran through him at having her eyes so intensely trained on him while he performed. He thought the fight might banish some of the desire he felt coursing through his blood for her, but it didn't. If anything, he felt her pull more. He would stumble out of this ring like a lovesick puppy to get to her.

"Kane!" Broc shouted. "You there?"

Kane blinked. He had to focus. How many times had his trainer called his name? Kane spit the mouthguard into Broc's waiting hand.

"Man, you gotta snap out of whatever's doin' with you." Broc washed the mouthguard, squirted water in Kane's mouth, and offered the guard again.

Kane knew he should focus. So badly he knew. But what he should do and what he wanted to do were entirely different things. Kane spat and bit down on the silicone just in time for the bell to ring again.

*H*OLY *EFFIN-SHIT,* MALIN THOUGHT. *THE man is a work of art in the ring.* Kane's punches were precise, none wasted—unlike his opponent, whose arms and legs just seemed to flail. When Kane went for a kick, it seemed like the other fighter opened up the way for Kane's heel or the top of his foot to connect. Malin hadn't seen fighting talent this strong since . . . damn, she couldn't name anyone who had that much raw talent.

She'd set the treadmill to two and took exaggerated, slow steps, observing every one of Kane's moves and wondering if he made love with as much intensity as the way he fought. In her dream he had, but in reality? She licked her lips, pressed her thighs together, and kept walking. She had to stop thinking about him like that. His moves would be a great addition to their fighters, but she couldn't get that kiss in the shadowed doorway or the potential for sex with Kane Macleod off the brain.

Kane threw a right punch and a left hook, then grabbed on to the man's neck, slamming his head down to meet Kane's knee. The man stumbled backward, blinking and clearly dizzy from the blow. The trainer-ref moved between the two men and held out both hands, keeping the fighters apart. He took a couple steps closer to Kane's opponent, lifting three fingers. The opponent said something Malin couldn't hear from the distance, but apparently, it was the right answer because the ref motioned for the fight to proceed.

Something changed in Kane. His fists were half relaxed at his sides, and it looked like he wanted the man to close in on him. Wanted the abuse. The opponent didn't wait for a full-blown invitation before he went in swinging. Kane took a left, then a right, then another left, rolling with the punches, then he danced around to the other side where Malin could see his face. His trainer, Broc, leaned in, waving two other trainers closer. Kane's expression was hard, but his eyes weren't on the fight in front of him. They were staring into space somewhere. The man went in for another sequence, but Kane didn't block. Instead, he bared his teeth and growled. When the opponent pulled back, Kane's shoulders heaved and spittle flew from his lips where he breathed through gritted teeth. Kane's eyes suddenly looked like deep black pools, and then he launched into an attack.

Malin placed her feet on the side platforms, the treadmill rolling between her legs. The air thrummed, concussed around her, like the sound of wings from the legendary giant dragans beating the air. "Ho-ly-shit," she muttered. Her heart nearly stopped.

*T*HE CURTAIN IN KANE'S LINE of sight had closed and reopened to a pinhole.

The coach faced him from the other side of the ring. *Just you and me here, kid.*

Kane roared and launched at Smalls. No thinking, only punching. One-two-three, reverse. Kick, grab, push, pull, thrust.

Kill, the beast roared inside his skull. The thing before him wasn't a fighter; it was a predator in horn-rimmed glasses with a receding hairline. Kane could do nothing else. He gave himself over to the urge. Despite whatever he had been before, he became nothing more than . . .

Rage.

CHAPTER 15

$\mathcal{M}$ALIN INHALED AS STEAMY CURLS rose from the surface of the honey-colored tea in Kane's brand-new Walmart-sourced teacups. Malin wrapped her hands around the pottery mug and let the rising heat carry cinnamon-vanilla aromas to her senses. She blew on the tea and sipped. All the while, she stood with her back to the counter in Kane's small, sparsely furnished flat and suspiciously kept her eyes on the fighter. He decorated as much as she did. Her sister had done most of the furnishing and found most of the artwork that now hung in the coven house. Myla had had an eye for such things.

Malin put those thoughts away and looked over at Kane.

He held his own cup in one hand over the sink and tipped the teapot. *Classic rookie faux-pas,* she thought as the kettle-top popped open, and yup, there it was . . .

"Ow. Fuck!" Kane jerked his hand back, hissing as the tea flowed over the cup and burned his hands. He dropped the cup; it tinked and clattered against the porcelain sink. Grimacing, slowly hissing on an inhale and blowing through O-shaped lips on the exhale, the larger-than-life fighter shook his hand.

Malin glanced at the cup lying in the sink—good thing they had opted for the heavier, sturdier mugs so it didn't shatter. Or perhaps Walmart knew how rough their customers could be on dainty things.

Malin set her cup on the counter and took Kane's hand. She intoned, *"Fuar,"* from the magic-invoking ancient Gaelic tongue, sending a cooling spell into his skin. He looked curiously at her, but she only shrugged. "Nothing special. The same effect as cold water. Only quicker. Here, let me." She reached for the teapot, retrieved his fallen cup, and righted it on the counter. "Always hold the lid while you pour." She taught him what she believed he would already know from pouring any hot liquid, but apparently, he had gone thirty years of his human life without such a moment.

He clenched and released his hand, turning it over to inspect the back side and the palm alike. "I know that now," he muttered through gritted teeth.

Breyze hissed softly, no more than a rustling-of-wind sound, under Malin's cloak: her reminder that the night was running out. But she never wanted the night to end, not when standing next to Kane.

Malin handed Kane his tea and ran a hand over her dragan's scales. "May I use your cloakroom?"

Kane squinted. "Use my what?" He paused, then with widening eyes said, "Oh, my bathroom? Never heard it called that. Yeah. Over there." He tipped his head as if the cloakroom was hard to miss.

But Malin was already headed that way. His flat wasn't much beyond a combined kitchen and living area, bedroom, and, oh yes, *bathroom.* She had to remember to use the modern words. She circled the black leather couch—the only furniture aside from the flat-screen television mounted on the wall—entered and closed the door behind her. Scanning the tiny room with a toilet, baby blue tub and tile, a simple white plastic shower curtain, and a pedestal sink, she breathed in relief that they wouldn't have to rush back to the Fold before sunup. Now, all she had to do was convince Breyze.

She turned the lights off, and the strain behind her eyes immediately loosened. Soon, the shadows deepened, and texture reentered her sight, the distinctive blue-violet haze accompanying the darkvision. It looked almost like what the cowans called "black lights," but true Darkness didn't cause lighter colors to glow unnaturally. Malin shed her cloak and draped it from the solitary towel bar. She clicked her tongue against the roof of her mouth three times, and Breyze slithered from around her waist.

She removed his goggles. "I need to speak with Kane. You'll be fine here." *Even if we have to wait for the next darkfall,* she didn't add, but Breyze understood. Their bond allowed it.

Breyze spread his wings and lowered his snout directly in front of her face. He was the one who always made sure she crossed the Fold before daylight, and the scorn in his scowl was palpable. Staying would put him at risk, and by extension, she would be too. But all the signs she'd had thus far told her this was important; she should stay. They would be safe.

Ignoring his admonishment, Malin added, "I'll make sure we're sheltered from the light, and if not, we'll go. Promise."

Her dragan lowered his snout—reluctant acceptance. The best that could be given.

"Water?" she asked.

Breyze chirped at the offer and lowered himself into the tub. Malin turned on the cold-water faucet, and by the time she finished using the toilet and washing up, Breyze was rolling around and splashing. Dragankind loved the cool water and spent most of their time frolicking or relaxing in the springs and trickling falls in their cavern-home back in the Penumbra.

"I'll return to you soon." She exited and pulled the door closed behind her.

"Did you need a towel?" Kane's booming voice made Malin jump.

She whirled around to find him leaning one shoulder against the wall with a smirk on his face and a towel in one hand. She exhaled. "Ahhh, no. I was just—no matter. After the gym and the stroll to the twenty-four-hour Walmart, it's getting too close to daybreak." She was never so unfocused, but these events with Kane had her priorities all twisted. Damn her responsibility. She had never wanted to stay in the Daylight Realm so long.

Kane furrowed his brow.

"We should be returning to the Awen," she added, "and crossing so that the Darkness within the Penumbra can protect my dragan from the daylight."

"Oh." He lowered the hand holding the towel and let his eyes drift down her body. "Where *is* your—"

"If I stay," she blurted, "I'll need to remain here until dark. Can Breyze stay in there? He'll be safe as long as we don't let in the daylight. Filtered daylight won't harm me the same way as it does our familiars, but it nearly blinds me after so long living in the dark."

Kane's furrowed brow eased. In fact, his whole body seemed more relaxed after his berserker-style fight at his gym. For some reason, that fight drew her even closer to him. The mere memory made Malin's fingertips itch to touch him now, to grab on to his thick biceps, to press her body against his and kiss him, to . . . She squeezed her eyes and opened them wide.

"And, uh," she continued, denying temptation, "we should, um, chat." Her voice squeaked like a mouse's, and she cleared her throat.

Malin pushed past Kane, anything to get out of touching and kissing proximity. For her self-preservation. For his safety. But the air between them was so thick with his scent and tension it almost choked her. They truly did need to discuss his situation. At the counter, she grabbed the mug and gulped the now-lukewarm tea. It tasted nearly stale on her tongue when she had hoped for something refreshing.

Swallowing hard, she felt static energy at her back—Kane's energy. Recalling that stolen kiss in the archway, her insides liquified. *No, Malin. Talk. Remember?*

"Chat about what?" he asked.

Malin turned, pressed her back against the counter, and looked up into his fierce eyes. *Berserk*, she thought, and for an instant, she recalled the legend of the Old Norse warriors who fought in a trance-like state. That was how Kane had fought at the gym, his eyes icy-blue and focused on something only he could see. Blue-tipped daggers, they seemed, held Malin captive even now. But berserkers were just a legend, right? She blinked hard several times, dismissing the idiotic thoughts and the notion that Kane could possess the bloodlines of some ancient warrior.

Desperate to get control of herself, she blurted, "Your mother." There. That should turn down the heat a notch. Her mother would work too, but he thankfully hadn't met her.

Yes, thank the All Mother! It worked. Kane recoiled, looking at her askance. "My mother?"

Malin pressed her lips together and nodded. "She's blind." She swallowed, her eyes dropping as she re-envisioned his mother's milky eyes as clear with remnants of the blue in Kane's.

"Yeah, and?" His words sounded like the snarl of a wolf.

Nonsense, Malin. Focus. She heaved a sigh. "Do you recall what I told you about the nimh?"

"That strange gland you say I have? Yeah. Still not so sure I believe you." He folded corded arms over his chest.

Bringing up his mother had shut down his advances, *Thank Aodh*, and now he was closing himself off.

She couldn't let that happen. "Your mother hasn't always been blind, right?"

Kane pressed his lips together and shook his head. His eyes went blank for a split second, the way people's did when a memory was unexpectedly called forth from the deepest recesses within their minds. She knew that feeling too well.

Malin lowered her voice. "She's been touched by Darkness, Kane." When he didn't reply, she added, "Your mother has the gland too."

The man before her was frozen, not a muscle moving in his body. His breathing too—nonexistent.

Running a hand through her hair, she snagged her fingers on a knot at the ends. She ripped through, wincing slightly. "To be perfectly honest, I'm surprised none of the Cailleach found her before it progressed far enough to cause blindness. Ours is not the only coven in the Penumbra."

Kane's expression sank into a frown, and his arms fell to his sides, slowly as if they were restrained by marionette cords. "What"—he balled his fists—"the"—his brows pressed together—"actual"—and into a V—"fuck?"

Malin's fingers tingled again. She rubbed them with her thumbs. Her touch had calmed him before, but to touch him now was to play with fire—a searing blue flame that would surely burn through her skin and bones all the way to her soul. He took a step backward. Was he turning now? Going into that trance?

Damn. She didn't have a choice. She certainly couldn't calm him once the legendary berserker's rage surfaced. She sucked in a breath. To hell with the consequences; she reached for him, grabbing on to both his arms.

*T*HIS IS INSANE! KANE SHOOK his head jerkily, twitching as if his neck muscles spasmed. *The doctors said Mama had macular degeneration.*

No, no, no, his inner beast railed against the thought.

Mom's blindness could have been prevented?! No fucking way!

But when he opened his mouth, the disbelief and questions jumbled somewhere between his brain and his throat. It choked him. He couldn't get enough air, and the dark room was getting darker.

Malin's hands, small but strong, latched on to his upper arms. Did what she was saying mean his mother's blindness could be cured if she went into that dark place too? Truly, his mother never should have went blind in the first place? He needed to speak. To ask these questions. This news could have meant they never had to move to Wickney from the farm? That Dad—

NO! I won't go there!

Kane took a step away, his feet somehow knowing he needed to back away from the exotic woman before him before he harmed her too. Just like Kiera. He took another step, his shoulders raising and lowering with his heavy breathing. Oxygen didn't help. His vision narrowed. Darkening.

Malin whispered, "Kane." She was moving with him.

He shook his head faster, held up his hands to push her away. He couldn't risk hurting Malin like he'd done with Kiera. But her voice stalled his retreat. Her touch pressed pause on the narrowing focal point before him. She held his arms with unreal strength, kept him teetering on a razor's edge between everyday normal and his dangerous state of pure Rage.

She stepped closer, squeezing his biceps above the elbows. No. He needed to get away. To move. To hit. But that urge seeped slowly away. She hadn't said any of her strange words, but cool power eased through his veins and the tunnel vanished entirely. She was bringing him back little by little. But how?

Kane looked down at one of her hands, at the other, then he squinted, searching for answers within her violet eyes. His labored breathing slowed. "H-how do you do that?"

Malin pinched her lips and shrugged. "No clue," she said confidently, then added in a softer voice, "but I feel it too. Maybe it's the Darkness, perhaps Aodh, or it could be something entirely different. I can't explain, but . . ." Her breath caught in her throat, and she swallowed down whatever she truly wanted to say.

He wanted to hear it. Desperately.

Kane leaned closer, his eyes dropping to her pouty bottom lip, and his tongue darted out, wetting his own lips. His throat remained tight, but his mouth watered as they each searched for answers in the other's face. A heavy weight pulled at him south of the elastic waistband in his sweats. He held steady, not closing the distance this time, denying his body what it so desperately wanted.

After what seemed like minutes, his stomach growled. In the silence, it might have been a lion roaring. Malin giggled and turned away; she twisted her head and rubbed the muscles in her neck.

"I'm so sorry, Kane," she said with her back to him. "About your mother. We—I mean someone from my world—should have found her. Her blindness could have been prevented. You have every right to be angry."

Deathly quietness hovered between them, and Kane watched her shoulders round. The larger-than-life woman curled in on herself as a ray of daylight streamed through the slit between the curtains. Although anger had been his first reaction, he could no longer muster The Rage. He moved sideways to the window and overlapped the material, never taking his eyes off Malin. This situation troubled her too, but *why?* Regardless, the sun had risen, and she had stayed. She'd removed her cloak and her dragan. That meant something, right?

Kane reached out a hand, keeping it mere inches from her shoulder, then he thought, *Fuck it,* closed the distance, wrapped his arms around her waist, and buried his face in her neck. She needed comfort and so did he. He allowed the smell of warm cinnamon to take him away from the moment's worries.

FOR A SECOND, SHE LIFTED her arms, shocked at the sudden strong embrace from behind. After her surprise passed, she lay her arms over his and melted into a sense of safety. Into him because she fit so perfectly. Perhaps she would be damned tomorrow, but Malin's entire being relaxed in the protective circle of Kane's arms. Chills crawled upward into her hairline from her neck where his hot, moist breath caressed the delicate skin beneath her ear. Then the tingling traveled down her spine and legs until every part of her body shivered with anticipation. Her knees quaked, and she thought she might fall. He would catch her.

Kane had backed off the edge of his berserker rage and held her like she was a lifeline. Into her neck, he murmured, "Did you know of my mother or her condition before tonight?"

"No," Malin breathed, "but—"

"No buts." His voice lowered to a growl. "No apologies." Kane sprinkled kisses from her earlobe down to where her neck met her shoulder. "Not now."

Malin's logical side told her to squirm. To run far away until she couldn't run any farther and then run more if the thoughts of Kane followed. She should explain to him that it was *her* responsibility as a coven leader to find people with the nimh before they suffered the consequences. But then and there, her lonely side won. Every piece of evidence she had led to the conclusion that this man and his family were meant to be in her world—that there was Darkness within Kane reflecting and matching her own. She couldn't pinpoint the source of his, but she didn't feel like fighting it today.

She'd been strong for so long, bent on vengeance since the awful day Godric had the life-changing, gruesome package delivered. With Kane wrapped around her, she could put those memories in a box and tuck them away for a time. Desire thrummed through her veins, twisting her insides, tempting and enticing her. And Kane surprisingly helped her feel stronger and safer, as if they could face anything together. And she felt closer to the truth than she had in a long, long time. This was an ember—like the vision of her sister and mother had told her— glowing within her chest, ready to ignite this tension between them. It told her this situation with Kane would be okay, right even. She could rest for a while and put aside thoughts of her sister, revenge, and her duties for one day. And yes, she could. Right?

Malin turned in Kane's arms so their bodies were pressed together, and oh yes, the heat burned hotter. She felt his heavy cock pressed against her lower belly and gasped, then her lips spread into a small smile.

"I should thank you for closing out the light." She made small talk as she reached for the zipper on his hooded sweatshirt. The annoying garment between them was half-undone already, so she finished the job and ran her hands over the ridges on his abdomen. His skin warmed her hands and arms as she reached around his waist until she caressed the bunching muscles in his lower back.

Kane pulled her closer, and a rumble erupted from his chest. Was it a "you're welcome"? or a "shut the fuck up and kiss me"? She couldn't tell, but she didn't really care. She just wanted him, his hands on her, their bodies touching with no accursed clothes separating them.

He cupped her cheek lightly before sliding his hand into the hair at the back of her neck. Malin leaned into the touch and groaned when he wrapped his fingers in the strands and gently pulled. It exposed her neck to him, and he didn't waste time. Kane immediately lowered his head and mouth to her collarbone, peppering her neck with small kisses then running his tongue from her throat's hollow up to her chin. This man, his movements, his strong body, the way he was already reading her desires, became her entire world for a time. There had been electricity between them since they first met, and it was building to the point it would have no choice but to erupt into a bolt of blinding light.

With her arms still wrapped around his waist beneath his shirt, he backed them into the bedroom. Their mouths warred with one another as they fumbled their way through the doorway. Malin caught glimpses of another undecorated room with a huge bed in the center and crisp white sheets. Of course he would have a huge bed; Kane Macleod was bigger than most men, in more ways than one. And her desire for him, for her dream about him to become reality, pooled in her lower belly. The wet heat between her legs became almost painful.

What are you doing, Mal? her inner monologue chided.

"Shut up!" Malin said aloud.

"What?" Kane pulled back.

"Nothing. Don't stop!" Malin grabbed his face and kissed him hard.

So far, he had shown her that his kisses could be demanding, desperate, and sweet. But she didn't want sweet right now. She wanted to take him and for him to take her in return. She told him that with her lips and tongue. This was going to happen; *they* weren't turning back now. And it was going to be some of the most epic, animalistic sex she'd ever had; she could feel it in her bones.

She severed the kiss and stepped back, a gleam in her eye. With both hands on Kane's abs, she pushed him backward onto the bed. Whatever happened now didn't have to mean they were a couple, but they were stuck together in this apartment for the next dozen hours. Sex, then sleep, and maybe some food when they woke up around twilight. And, if they woke before darkfall, perhaps there would be a round two. She was already thinking about it, and they hadn't had round one. But the anticipation was just as well. A man like him couldn't be bad in bed.

Chapter 16

KANE LANDED ON THE BED with a bounce, propped himself up on his elbows, and looked up at Malin. Her eyes shone with raw emotion—desire, definitely, but perhaps also an all-too-familiar obsession. Hidden anger. Repressed pain. Hot focus on something else. The way this was going, it wasn't going to be an act of connection. No, this was exactly what he did in the cage. And he didn't want that beast anywhere near him and Malin. *If* there was a "him and Malin." His beast had retreated, but she had one too. And hers was here, front and center.

What the fuck is wrong with you, Kane? he asked himself, his beast threatening to take his body over for entirely different reasons than normal.

But really, what *was* wrong with him? He had a gorgeous woman crawling up his body from the foot of his bed, and he was about to—

Her hands caressed his cock through his sweats. The bastard jumped. Kane threw his head back against the bed, bit down hard, and grunted. Where the hell had this good-guy vibe come from? He'd never had this kind of hesitation when taking a woman to bed. No, he was usually just the opposite. Get down to business, get his rocks off, and get the chick out of his house so he could sleep like a baby. Why was he having such a hard time doing that now?

Good guy, he thought again. But was he truly being a good guy? *Nah*, he thought. He just didn't want her to use him to vanquish her demons like he used the other MMA fighters.

Kane grabbed her wrists and pulled them wide apart. In doing so, he pulled Malin's body up his, her body slithering across his body. A grind of her breasts against his abs. Her ribs rubbed against his throbbing cock.

Shit, that didn't help!

"Mmmm," he uttered, but he didn't open his eyes, didn't lift his head. He needed to extinguish his desire. Damn his newfound conscience. That'd never plagued him before, and he cursed himself harder.

"Hrmmm," Malin replied, and it was the sexiest sound he thought he'd ever heard, an adorable little lilt at the end. It sent a jolt through his body and his mind; he wondered what other sounds she could make with her perfect mouth.

Breathe, man. Just breathe.

Malin kissed his shoulder. Her mouth was heavenly-sweet against his skin. He pulled harder at her wrists. With a moan, she ground her hips into his. "Ahhh, yesss," she hissed.

"Damnit, Malin. Stop," he ground out through clenched teeth.

She squirmed. His entire body locked up, fighting the tease against his cock.

"I said stop!"

Finally, blessedly, she stilled. Her body was firm, like a marble statue against him, only it burned with her heat. The combined hardness and smoothness of her made her seem like something out of ancient Greece. Who was that goddess of beauty and physical pleasure he'd learned about in school?

Kane didn't open his eyes or lift his head. Though he could imagine the confusion written on her face, he couldn't look at her because that would surely tip him over the edge and send them into something they might both regret. He took slow cleansing breaths, like the counselor during his teenage years had taught him, counting . . . One. Two. Three . . .

He felt Malin's hair spill across his chest and imagined how erotic that must look. How soft her hair was. How he wanted to reach out and twirl it around his fingers, feel the silkiness, and give a tug.

No, Kane! Fuck, focus on something—anything—else!

He had it. *Kiera.* He thought about his sister sitting in darkness somewhere with her eyes bandaged. Thankfully, it worked, and his desire ebbed. He continued measuring his breathing, desperately trying to get the blood back to his other head. He needed to think.

Malin started kissing his collarbone gently, tentatively, then moved up his neck. She made it impossible to think, and why was he thinking anyway? There were far better things to be doing.

Kane huffed. *Find the words, motherfucker. Move. Get her off you.* "Mal, we—ahhh, shit! Not okay. Not right—" He wasn't making any sense.

"Why?" Malin pulled at her arms again; this time, it wasn't playful. Her incredible strength ripped her wrist free from his grasp, and she rolled off him with a grunt and something muttered under her breath.

Was that anger? Damn it, he'd hurt her. That was the last thing he intended.

The bed bounced beside him, and he took one last breath before opening his eyes.

She sat cross-legged with her arms folded protectively over her chest. "You started this. And now you don't want it? I don't get you, Kane Macleod!" The only light in the room was from the dawn glowing at the top of his blackout curtains, but he could still see her face clearly. Her brows were heavy, her eyes dark.

Kane propped himself up on one shoulder and glared at her. It felt like he had sand in his throat when he said, "Let me be real fucking clear, Malin. I want this. I want you. But there's something wrong."

"Aodh help me, there is nothing wrong." She plunged both

hands into her hair and pulled it away from her face. He fought the urge to do it himself. "We've clearly been dancing around this. You're clearly ready; I felt that much. So what's the problem? What's *wrong*, as you put it?"

Malin pulled her hair over one shoulder, and they stared off for a good minute. There wasn't any goddamn way in heaven, hell, the Darkness, or on Earth he was about to tell her what he was feeling. That shit wasn't anything anyone needed to know about him. That some people knew—his counselor, the courts, and his mother—was bad enough. He didn't need to burden someone else with the mess inside. This thing between them, whatever it was, was definitely *not* going to work. But she couldn't go anywhere now, and he only had the one bed. They couldn't have sex because even though their connection sent off fireworks, there was something just not right. No sex. Nothing. Now or ever. He needed to figure out what this gland-thingy was, and he couldn't let Kiera go blind like his mom if she really had it too. Geez, it was starting to feel like a disease. He needed to focus on getting Kiera out of their realm and getting some real science to look into her concussion as well as whatever this *disease* was. Malin had said something about the heart being malformed. They would have to start there.

But then again, there was this sexy, sweet-smelling, tiny-but-curvy diva sitting in his bed. *No sex*, he reminded himself. But she was as broken as him; he just knew that somewhere deep inside. *No sex, Kane.* He never thought he would say that to himself.

She rolled her eyes and started to slide off his bed. Kane reached for her arm, latching on just above her elbow. She jerked, tried to pull away, reached for something to hold on to with her other hand, but came up empty. Yeah, he was a selfish bastard because even though he wasn't giving her what she wanted, he wasn't letting her run away from him either. He rose to both knees and reached for her with the other hand.

Malin was facing away from him, but struggling, twisting her shoulders and writhing with all her strength to get off his bed. "Effin-A, Kane, if we're not having sex, let me go! I need some distance."

"Not . . . a chance . . . in Darkness." He yanked her back into his chest, clasped his arms around her, and lowered them both onto the pillow. With one hand around her arms, he slid the other down to her waist and held her close to his body. Damn how he loved the way her small frame fit into his body. His raging hard-on wouldn't give in, but he'd gained enough control to ignore it for now.

Kane could tell something was breaking free inside her. Something was forming between them. This had been the strangest few days he'd experienced in his entire life, but he didn't want to let her go. He held on tight against her attempts to squirm away. He buried his face in her hair, breathing cinnamon, sugar, and vanilla.

"Just rest, Malin. Sleep. Be here with me. You're"—dare he say what he always wanted to hear back then?—"you're safe here." There it was, in the open.

She stilled and wrapped her arms over his. She curled tighter into herself, and he curled his body tighter around hers. Whatever demons she had, he was going to protect her too. He would do it at any cost. His life and body were hers to have. After a pause, Malin sniffled and took a deep breath. Those were the only signs she gave, but for some reason, she'd started to cry. Her tears were like a stream upon his skin.

Kane squeezed and hoped his bodily strength would ease her into sleep.

SOMETHING TOUCHED THE FRONT OF Malin's thigh, hot and strong, massaging. She was warm under only a sheet with a body—Kane's body—molded to her back. His cock, still rock solid, pushed up against her rear, but the rest of his body was just as hard. Had he gotten any relief while they slept? She hadn't thanks to her tears and dreams of Kane inside of her. Over her clothes, his hand moved upward, caressing the curve of her hip, dipping into the valley at her waist, then cupping her breast.

But he hadn't wanted this. Why would he be teasing her now if he still didn't want it? What had changed while she slept? She sighed. "I thought—"

"Shhh . . ." Kane hissed. His hot breath tickled the crook of her neck. His finger encircled her nipple.

Malin let out a small, whispered "oohhh." *Guess I thought wrong.* She arched her back, pressing her ass into his rigid cock. "Are you awake," she whispered, "or dreaming?"

Kane slid his arm from beneath her, eased Malin onto her back, and trapped her body beneath him. His delicious weight pressed her into the bed. "If I'm not fucking awake, I don't want this dream to end." His voice was little more than a lion's purr, and she wondered how his full-on roar would sound.

"What changed betwee—"

He seized her mouth, and his lips moved with soul-searing insistence. *Who the fuck cares?* it answered. *Less talking, more kissing*, it said. *Feel me now*, it demanded.

And yes, she felt every bit of him through the annoying clothes. She tried to keep her hands away, tried to respect what he'd told her before they'd slept, tried to keep from matching his movements, and desperately fought the desire warming her insides and dampening her panties. Then again, she had been the one who wanted sex before, so why should she worry about it now if he was willing? He, and his family, may have become her responsibility, but she wasn't his effin guardian angel. She was no one's angel. So yeah, she would take what he was offering.

She grasped on to his shoulders, her fingertips digging into the skin, kneading and pulling him closer. She lifted her hips to meet his and retreated when he pulled back. She kissed him with the fury she'd felt before she'd broken down in his arms.

Aodh, yes! It's been so long, and he's so much better than he was in my dream, so much stronger. Real, raw, and oh so deliciously demanding. Whatever ghosts either of us have, they can wait until this is done. Malin ran her hands down his back, tugging at his waistband when she reached his lower back. She wanted—hell, she *needed* skin on skin.

Kane raised up but didn't remove his sweats for the moment.

Instead, he lifted the hem of her shirt, pulled it over her head, and unlatched her front-clasping bra. Malin wriggled out of the straps and reached for Kane. He wasn't getting away from her this time. He answered her call, kissing her again, his chest warm against hers. The way his stubble scratched at her lips and chin heated her blood to near boiling. If he didn't touch her soon, she thought she'd explode.

By Dorcha, as soon as he did touch her, she would explode too. But that detonation was exactly what she needed—a release of pleasure and pain and all the tension she had pent up inside.

He settled between her legs and tilted to one side, his hand caressing her stomach and then her breast again. His fingertips scratched against her skin, but the texture felt so erotic. Malin moaned as they brushed over her nipple. Her back arched involuntarily, and she squirmed to get closer to him. If only that were possible.

Kane broke the kiss.

Malin gasped and released a long sigh as he moved down her neck. She shivered when his tongue ran down to the little spot beneath her ear, and he breathed heavily. He fluttered kisses along one collarbone then the other, then cupped both breasts and paused. Malin looked up at him, confused, and found him staring at her chest with awe, his eyes almost glowing blue in the dark.

"Perfection," he breathed.

She reached for his head and pulled him to her, squirming as his hot mouth latched on. The warm suckling sent a bolt of electricity straight to her core, and she mewled. She needed her Aodh-damned pants off—his too. Damn this teasing! She needed to come.

"Kane, please."

Against her breast, she felt his lips smile, his teeth still holding her nipple. He bit gently, then released her to move downward. She peered down her body into his eyes. He kept his gaze locked on to hers as he dragged his chin down her belly.

He reached for the button on her pants. "This?" he questioned teasingly.

"Mm-hmmm." Malin lifted her hips to help him slide the offensive clothing from her lower body.

Kane tossed them to the side, then scooped her legs over both his shoulders and lowered himself—so close to home. Eyes still alight, he quirked a brow. "And this?"

"Oh yesss."

He blew on her slit. Her muscles clenched in anticipation. Her knees jerked together, almost closing on his head, but his strong arms forced them apart. She urged them to stay apart and stay open. To allow her to feel every part of this.

Malin tried to squirm, but Kane grasped her hips and held her still.

"Aahhh—oh—ah." The restraint was such sweet torture.

Kane kissed the inside of one leg . . . then the other, and when his lips finally touched hers, she cried out, "Oh, effin, yes. YES!" and threw her head backward onto the pillow. She tried to push her clit up into his mouth, but he held her steady. Her body was climbing toward that sweet release. "I'm so close," she blurted, and so soon. More—she wanted more and all of it!

But Kane pulled away, holding her still.

Malin punched both hands into the sheets at her side and grunted. "No. Please . . ."

The sensation ebbed, and she peered desperately at him.

Kane smirked.

Ah, so a game, it is?

He blew on her again, then covered her with his mouth, maintaining eye contact like the predator that he was. Malin couldn't . . . Her eyes fluttered closed as her body drove toward orgasm. Her muscles trembled and she fisted the sheets in her hands.

And then the touch was gone again. Malin whined, took a deep breath. Without seeing him, she knew he was watching her, reading her body. And when the threatening apex receded, Kane lowered his mouth again. He licked from her core to the top of her clit. She jerked under his ministrations. A wave pulsed through her body, her legs, arms, and her head yanked up. Her hair fell out of place.

"You're so deliciously wet," Kane purred, then blew on her again. His hot breath was almost enough to send her shrieking again.

Damn! How was he holding out like this?

"I want to know exactly when you're going to come, Malin."

She almost did when he growled her name.

"Count for me. Ten means you're coming."

Malin couldn't do anything. Couldn't move. And couldn't talk. And he wanted her to . . . what exactly? It didn't seem possible.

He waited, and when she didn't speak, he growled, "Answer me, Malin."

She swallowed. "Yes. Anything." She did mean anything, her body and soul included.

With that, Kane returned to her core, licking.

"Seven," she managed.

Suckling . . .

"Eight," she whined.

Stroking her so—

"Nine!" she yelled, and the sheets in her hands ripped free from the corners of the bed.

And Kane was gone, then in a single move, he was on top of her, impaling her with his thick, hard, and impossibly big cock.

"TEN!" she screamed. Fireworks went off. "Ten," she chanted, lightning rolling through her clouded sky. "Ten!" Thunder rumbled through her body. "Ten," she wailed as her core clenched over and over and over again. She wrapped her arms around Kane's back and dug her nails into his skin.

Kane held utterly still and let out a groan as her orgasm stormed through her body. She clenched around his cock and effin felt the effects in her fingers, toes, and all the way to the ends of her hair. *Ho-ly Mother of Darkness is this a thousand times better than the dream!* And then a cooling sensation flooded through her body as her muscles went languid. Only then did she wonder when he had removed his sweats.

K ANE LET OUT A LONG, pleasure-filled groan as he thrust inside Malin.

God help me!

The feel of her pulsating around his cock—nirvana. The prickling of her nails in his back almost made him come there and then without a second stroke or thought. But he clamped down his muscles, arched his back, and held the urge at bay. He watched the pleasure twist Malin's mouth and wrinkle her forehead as her brows shot upward. She bit her lip, arching her breasts into his chest, and then, so very slowly, her body eased onto the bed, and she opened her violet star-filled eyes, so wide that they took up her whole face. The aftermath of her orgasm had them glossed over as her lips curled upward in a lazy smile.

Fuck! Everything about her was sticky-sweet to his eyes, a tonic to his soul, and a torch to his desire. They shouldn't be—no, he shouldn't be taking her this way—but after suffering for hours with her in his arms, he couldn't contain his Raging need. And the feel of her around his dick, well, her dark god or the god of light or whatever gods existed in this jacked-up world needed to help him now, because he never, ever wanted this moment to end.

Malin reached for him and pulled him to her, his mouth to hers. He had to hold still a little longer. Let her recover. It was the only gentlemanly thing to do. But then they kissed, and stroke after stroke, she thanked him for giving her the release. Then, her kisses grew more urgent, and she lifted her hips into his with surprising strength. He wasn't giving in that easily though, and he wasn't going to control this so completely. He wanted her to own him just as he had claimed her.

But one more time, he thought, pulled back, and thrust forward into her—*home*—again. He shot her a half grin, then rolled them over in a single move. Malin's eyes went wide. She braced herself with her hands, and she giggled. An actual giggle. A sound he never expected from her, but it was also a sound he wanted to hear again and again.

Kane reached up to her face, sliding his hands into the hair at the back of her neck and running a thumb along her jaw. She leaned into his touch. *There is something different about this, special.* His cock jumped at the thought.

Malin inhaled sharply, then a devious look overtook her. What was she planning? Was she going to try to pay him back for the edge-play, tease him then retreat? She couldn't know, but he was likely too close to his own explosion for that to work. He had to hold on. He wanted her to have another climax, preferably at the same time he did. So he planned to watch her ride them both into ecstasy.

She leaned down and kissed him softly, then deeper, then she bit his lower lip and pulled away. He moaned, wishing those lips and teeth were wrapped around his cock. But that wasn't happening this time.

Control, Kane.

But why was control so damn hard?

Malin sat up, bracing herself with her hands on his pecs. Kane slid his hands down her shoulders, tiny waist, and settled them just above her hip bones. She started rocking. He kept his eyes on her face. Back and forth, she kept a steady, almost musical rhythm. Every so often she bit her lip again or her eyes rolled back in her head. He met her movements, pushing upward into her sweet heat.

Control.

He bit the inside of his lip, concentrating.

Malin slowed her back-and-forth motion and raised up high on her knees, pulling away almost enough for him to slide out, but then she lowered herself in an agonizingly long stroke. She repeated, letting out little high-pitched moans as he filled her, as she took all of him in inch by inch. Again, she pulled away and sank back upon him until she consumed everything he had to offer.

"Malin," Kane uttered between his teeth, "come for me again." He couldn't hold out much longer, and he wanted them to do this together.

"Mmmm," she answered and lowered herself. She resumed the rocking motion, curling into it, her hands on his stomach now.

"Oh . . ." he panted, "yeeeess."

She quickened, seemingly almost there now. She started with the most adorable little noises that mimicked her fighting grunts, and with each one, he came so much closer, closer, nearing. Again, again, and again.

Malin threw her head back and sighed loudly, her long hair falling over his balls. A soft caress. A tickle that made his body scream.

Kane thrust up into her one more time, coming harder than he ever had in his life, sitting and hugging her tightly to him, his face buried in her chest the same way his cock was buried to the hilt in her heavenly heat. He spilled himself into her, emptying his cum and his soul into this amazing, mysterious woman.

CHAPTER 17

ODRIC LAFERTY, IN THE MIDDLE of supervising the training regimen, turned to the sound of a door opening. Daniel and another soldier by the name of James or Jamie or Jonas—whatever—strode across the training room's floor toward where Godric watched over the new Semaphor recruits. If he were being honest, they were a disappointment. The worst he had ever seen. There used to be greatness within who the Light provided, but these weren't any kind of dazzling.

"She didn't go back through last night," J-whatever whispered, stepping to Godric's side.

Godric squeezed his fist, spilling half the contents of his full can of Monster Energy onto the floor. "How is that fucking possible? Cailleachs don't stay in the Daylight Realm after sunup." They didn't have safe houses in this realm either, thanks largely to his own efforts in ferreting them out and eradicating them one by one. His ex had to have someone on this side sheltering her. He threw the drink at the nearby garbage can, and blue liquid dribbled onto the floor. "Hey. You. Number three, clean that up. You two"—he glared back at Daniel and J-whatever—"outside."

Godric pivoted on a heel and left the dozen new recruits to their training under Jill, one of his seasoned soldiers. Outside the double doors where the newbs couldn't listen in, Godric stood with his back to his two soldiers. "You followed her, right? Where'd she go?"

"I had reports that she was at Infinity last night with a m-man," J-whatever answered.

Godric whirled on him and narrowed his eyes. "What?" He paused, waiting.

Daniel raised his brows at the other, clearly a warning, and rightly so.

"What are you hiding from me?" Godric demanded, fighting the urge to slam J-whatever into the wall for his lack of respect. Didn't he train his soldiers to be more prompt than this?

Daniel took a deep breath. "John and his team lost her and the man at the train station."

Godric glanced at Daniel, his second in command, then back at John. Enunciating each word, he asked, "Is that so?" and slid out his dagger of Light from the sheath at his belt.

John's lower jaw started trembling then moving like he had something to say but suddenly found himself mute. And dumb. Real dumb.

Godric channeled the Maker's Light into the dagger and slashed it across John's throat. The Semaphor lifted both hands to his throat. His mouth moved; shock stretched his eyes wide. He brought his hands away to see if there was blood, but the Maker's blades weren't that gory. The blade sealed up the wounds on contact, like those cauterizing knives surgeons used. Only these didn't have to be plugged in. Godric smirked and watched the light dim in the lackey's eyes. Death from asphyxiation and lack of blood to the brain at the hands of the Maker's prime servant. John crumpled to the floor.

"Put that scum back in the pool. Maybe when he's reborn, he'll be of better service to his Maker." Godric returned the dagger to his belt. "You know better than to disappoint me, right, Daniel? Lest the Light take you too."

Daniel bowed his head. "Well then, perhaps I should tell you a little more of what I learned from John's team. The one who likely shelters your target is Wickney's own prizefighter."

Did this imbecile think Godric spent time watching fighting matches? "Who exactly would that be?" he asked, cocking his head.

Daniel stood at a military parade rest, his eyes still downcast. "The MMA fighter bound for the national title. His name is Kane Macleod."

"And that should scare me for what reason?"

"The rumor is that he fights with some unnatural drive. Like he thoroughly enjoys taking a beating, and then he snaps and almost always takes out his opponent. Eight out of the last ten fights have been knockouts. I saw one of the matches, and I swear his eyes glowed when he snapped into whatever was driving him."

"You think he's god-touched? Aodh or Danu?" Godric folded his arms over his chest, wheels whirling in his head.

"I don't know much about such things, sir. All I know is the Maker's hand, and it's certainly not that."

Godric lifted his chin toward the training room. "Go supervise that. I need to do some research." The door swished open and closed in his wake as his boot heels clomped on the floor. He climbed the stairs to his rooms, slammed the door behind him, and fell onto his bed with his iPad. Opening the browser, he typed in "Wickney fighter." Loads of news articles populated. That reporter Amy Jennings from the *Wickney Weekly* must have had some fascination with this person.

He scrolled through the headlines until he came to the YouTube listings and clicked on the first one, a fight from only a week or so before. Kane Macleod was fighting who looked like Andy from Raggedy Ann and Andy. "Kane Macleod vs. Ian Ramm," the ticker at the bottom of the video read. It must have been a no-bones day for him. But Macleod pummeled the poor bastard, and within seconds, Ramm fell. Ramm's medic crouched over him while the ref counted, pounding on the mat. Meanwhile, behind the knockout, Macleod was being restrained by two other refs and his manager—a glow in his eyes subsiding.

"Damn," said Godric in awe, "Daniel was right."

Over the PA system, the emcee's voice echoed. "And that's

another TKO for Kane Macleod! Our local hero is moving on to the finals. Kane will be heading to Vegas for the UFC Heavyweight title match!"

That fighter was certainly haunted, and Godric wondered how he would do as a part of the Semaphors. He returned to the search bar and navigated to the dark side of the web. Time to do a little digging. After about five minutes of searching, he found all the details necessary. Macleod's father had left the family before he was ten, and his mother, Beatha Macleod, moved to Wickney shortly thereafter with Kane and his sister, Kiera. Godric found a reference to the Wisconsin state services for blindness and poked around in the state's database for a while. Sure as shit, Beatha Macleod was blind as a bat. Onset as an adult.

Godric leaned his head back against the wall. Malin had found another family of witches to bolster their strength, and he couldn't allow that. Daniel had said that they were lost at the rail station. So, maybe . . . He returned to the web, searched Beatha Macleod's address, and traced it to the nearest station. Could he be this lucky?

Once he pulled up the train station's camera, he hacked into the video and watched, fast-forwarding to each time a train arrived and searching the faces of everyone who exited. He likely wouldn't recognize Malin given her magic, but he could pick out Macleod and a plain-looking woman.

"By all that is holy," he drawled, freezing the footage.

Godric tossed the iPad, still displaying the still shot of Macleod with someone who looked like an anonymous woman, onto his bed and glanced out the window—still daylight. He swiped his phone from the nightstand and found Malin's number. He tapped the camera on the text message screen, snapped a photo of the image on the iPad, and tapped the little airplane-shaped button.

CHAPTER 18

IN THE AFTERGLOW OF TWO orgasms that outranked every one Malin had ever experienced, she fell forward onto Kane's chest. She lay there with her whole body delightfully exhausted yet tingling with new and strange energy. Her core throbbed warmly, clenching and unclenching. Kane, beneath her and still inside her, was lazily running a hand up and down her arm. Their breathing rose and fell like the ocean's waves.

Suddenly, he stilled and wrapped his strong hand around Malin's upper arm. She raised her head. What had changed? She watched his face as his satisfaction slid into a frown and then a scowl. Her brow grew heavy. "What?"

He jerked underneath her, and a jolt ran through her body again. She was spent but was ready to go again if he was. His eyes, though, were darting upward, away from hers. "We . . . ahem . . . didn't um . . ." He squinted, but his brows shot upward as he grumbled, "Yeah, fuck. We didn't wrap it up."

Malin laughed.

"And you're fucking laughing?" Kane looked appalled.

"You have much to learn about my world." She rolled to his side, draping one leg over his. She settled onto his chest and propped her chin on her hand. "It's been so long since I've introduced anyone to the Darkness." She lowered her gaze to Kane's chest and traced circles across the smooth skin with her forefinger. His nipples were as hard as diamonds. "I'm kinda doing a shitty job of explaining the whole thing to you."

His breathing came shallower, more punctuated than the peaceful rolling waves from before. "Maybe you can start with telling me if there's some kind of magical morning-after pill."

Malin chuckled again. "There won't be a baby. At least not until I wish to become pregnant."

"How the fuck does that work?" he blurted. His eyes were harder than she expected, like the deepest blue sapphires.

She winced.

Kane took a deep breath. "Sorry, but that's just not normal. You can simply control it?"

"Something like that."

He didn't need to know all the ins and outs of the All Mother's blessings on her dark witches. After all, she suspected some of that knowledge was what turned Godric to the Light—not Danu's Light, but the corrupt Light from the fallen god Semar the Semaphors called their Maker. No, Malin had already bent Kane's mind enough with everything she had shared. Time to drive the conversation to a different subject.

She continued, "And disease-wise, I'm clean. I haven't been with anyone in a really long time."

"Oh," was all he said as his body settled. But he didn't reply to her disease comment. *Strange.* Malin had been under the impression that diseases spread through sex were on everyone's mind in these modern times. The cowans had it written on billboards around downtown as well as on the advertising plaques in restrooms right next to meds to treat various forms of impotence. Obviously, the latter wasn't a problem for Kane. He had been rock solid until she came, and now, against her leg, she felt him starting to stir again.

Beep—beep—beep.

Kane uncurled his arm from Malin's shoulders and slammed

it down on the offensive alarm clock. He let out a long groan. "Training."

Malin glanced over at the clock. 5:01. A couple of daylight hours remained.

"I have a sorta big fight coming up. Need to hit the mats every day." Kane sighed again. "I should shower first."

But he didn't move to get up just yet. Instead, he pulled her up his body, grasped on to her face, and pressed his mouth to hers. His lips demanded an answer, and Malin responded. Their lips moved together, tongues dancing. The taste of him sent cool waves through her body. The feel of him warmed her skin. His strong arms cocooned her. His broad chest . . .

She was getting too comfortable, forgetting herself. Forgetting Myla. Her eyes burned suddenly, and she pushed him away. They both panted as she tore her gaze away, then her body. "Let me get Breyze so you can shower."

Curse me with Danu's Light, the sex and connection with Kane was good. Too good. The best, even. Malin strode out of the bedroom on sex-weakened legs and to the bathroom door with a singular purpose: to cut this off. *A fling, that's all it is, Mal. Nothing more,* she reminded herself.

She paused at the bathroom door, leaning her forehead against the frame, cool from the air conditioner, and gathering herself. The towel Kane had offered sat on the floor beside the bathroom's entrance. She squatted down, grabbed the towel, and went into the small, dark space where her dragan had spent the day.

Breyze chattered away in the water.

"It's okay, sweet boy. Darkfall approaches, but we have to stay a while longer." Malin held the towel out, beckoning Breyze to come to her. "Kane needs a shower."

Her dragan clicked and squealed in a higher pitch.

"Don't worry. His chambers are well protected against daylight. If you remain under my cloak or a blanket, you'll be safe."

With a few more grumbles, Breyze flew into the waiting

towel, leaning into her touch and pets. Malin dried him off, pulled the plug in the tub, then reached for her cloak. Wrapped in the dark-magical material, she felt the weight of her phone in the right inner pocket. Wings spread and creating a breeze in the small room, Breyze circled her as he waited. Malin reached inside, pulled out the phone, and swiped away the lock screen.

Every muscle in her body seized up as if wrapping around a knife in her back when she read the text notification.

CAREFUL TO LEAVE THE ROOM in darkness, Kane pulled on his sweats, grabbed a towel from the freestanding closet next to his bedroom door, and went to the bathroom door to wait. Obviously, he wouldn't push through, even though they had shared some mind-blowing intimacy. Something Kane hadn't known he was capable of. Rather than a quick slam-bam-goodbye, he actually wanted her to stay curled up in his bed. They fit like a jigsaw puzzle while sleeping—and a lock and key while having sex.

He winced. *Having sex* sounded so clinical in his brain. But he couldn't call it fucking, and he wasn't about to call it making the L-word. He didn't even use the word with his sister, so he sure wasn't using it in reference to Malin.

Yet, his inner beast added.

Kane rolled his eyes and slumped against the wall. "Everything all right in there?"

The door flew open, slamming against the tile wall with a clatter, and Malin appeared. "All yours," she barked and tried to push right past him. She was already dressed in her cloak and street clothes, and Kane's heart raced. He liked her in his apartment and didn't want her to go yet.

"Whoa!" He latched on to her elbow, not whirling her around but waiting for her to face him.

She first stared at his hand on her arm, then lifted her eyes to meet his. They were glassed over. Sadness? Anger? Either way, it hurt him to see her like this. Was it something he did? Or had something happened in the bathroom? No, it had to be him. What else could it be?

"What's doin'?" he asked, trying his damnedest to keep his tone casual.

Malin clenched her teeth, and Breyze jutted his head from beneath her cloak and hissed. She pulled away but didn't retreat far. Her face slowly eased, and she shushed her little dragan. Once Breyze was tucked back inside her cloak, she stepped closer to Kane and rested a hand on his bare chest. Her hand was right above his thundering heart, and he wondered if she felt it. Did she know what she could do to him?

"I just received a somewhat disturbing message. You should get ready and go to the gym. When darkfall comes, I have a stop to make, then I'll meet you at your gym later. 'Kay?"

He pinched his lips together but didn't know what to say or do. He couldn't keep her there against her will. *She's a big girl, man,* he told himself. And if their coupling earlier felt as right to her as it did to him, this thing was far from over. He gave her a nod and watched as she stalked into his bedroom.

With a sigh, he went to shower. He needed to get her off the brain for a while. Focus on toning his body and get the upcoming fight in hand. After washing, dressing, and grabbing his bag, he leaned over the bed where Malin was sitting and scrolling through her phone. "See you soon?"

"Soon," she echoed without looking up.

Another pang squeezed his chest. They weren't a couple, but he wanted her to look up at him. He wanted to check her eyes. He needed her to say something because, while he tried to speak, his tongue was heavy and dry in his mouth, a tightness gripping him around the neck until he choked. Clearing his throat, he gave Malin a chaste kiss, denying the kick his cock gave. "Lock is a code, so nothing needs to be done to lock up when you leave." With that, he left her in his bed, unsure of when he would see her again but trusting that he would. He would have to.

Strange how Kane couldn't trust anyone before, but something in his gut said she was different. And after all, he wasn't only trusting he would see her again; he was trusting her with one of the two only people in the world who mattered to him: Kiera.

THE DOOR SNICKED SHUT, AND Malin breathed a sigh of relief that Kane would be out of her hair for this. The last thing she could handle was to introduce Kane to Godric in any way, shape, form, or fashion. And the fact that the bastard had footage of Kane and her magically disguised image leaving the train station near Beatha's house absolutely terrified her. She felt sick, and her heart rattled her rib cage. Somehow, she needed to expedite getting all the Macleods into the Penumbra for good and keeping them there until Godric was only a bad memory of her sister's death.

Finally, she found the name she was looking for in her phone. She had forgotten about the numbers Morgana included in her name. She tapped the contact "M0RG4N4" and typed.

MALIN: "NEED HELP."

Her finger hovered for a second before she hit send.

Malin's old covenmate—and family she didn't want to acknowledge—replied,

M0RG4N4: "WTF?"

Three little dots scrolled across the bottom of the texting window. Then . . .

M0RG4N4: "U'RE IN DAYLIGHT?"

MALIN: "SHELTERED, BUT YA."

M0RG4N4: "WHADDA YA PINGING ME FOR?"

MALIN: "I NEED A TRACE."

Yeah, Morgana had told Malin when she left that she was done. The incessant killing on both sides had eaten her alive. Once the bond with her dragan Pysae had been severed, that'd been the final straw. Morgana had grown up in the Penumbra, but she lived in the Daylight Realm now. Malin didn't know where or how, but she suspected that with Morgana's technical know-how she would be more than capable of maintaining near-darkness wherever she went.

However, now that Godric had sent Malin a message, there was surely an electronic trail, and Malin knew that if anyone could trace it, Morgana could.

She typed, "Morgana, I need you to help me find Godric. I have a tex—" Malin backspaced furiously and changed the message.

Malin waited. Her stomach flipped and flopped.

And waited.

Effin-great. Morgana had gone dark. Malin needed a hacker for this, and Morgana was the only witch-hacker she knew. Trusting any old cowan hacker could bring down the human law, and that was the last thing any of them needed. *How the hell am I going to do this without her? I don't know jack-shit about computers or electronics or how these messages move through thin air.* She had a lead with this, but it was dying on the vine as she waited, watched the phone, and hoped Morgana would help.

Malin slumped, allowing the phone to drop to the bed beside her. Then it chirped. Whipping the phone back into her line of sight, she swiped away the lock screen and read:

CHAPTER 19

Sweat splattered onto the mat as Kane's head snapped to the side with Smalls's left hook. The man hit like a wrecking ball. Despite how much of a beating he took, Kane couldn't access The Rage. He couldn't think about his haunted past, couldn't encourage his mind to focus on the negatives after such a thrilling time that afternoon with Malin. Every time he tried to bring the coach into existence, a vision of her breasts hovering above him flashed into his mind, and the feeling of her riding his cock . . . *Shit! Focus, man!*

Ding!

The bell sounded, and Smalls danced away to his corner. Kane turned, glancing toward the windows at the front of his gym. EMT was fairly dead that evening; only one other fighter was working the bags at the moment. And outside, it was dark. Kane wondered if Malin had left his flat or if she was waiting. Waiting, he hoped. But as much as he wished for that, somewhere deep within, he knew better. She wasn't a woman who sat idly by.

"Macleod!" Broc called.

Kane blinked and turned slowly to face his trainer. "Oh, yeah. Wassup?" He bounced on the balls of his feet a few times. *Loosen up. Focus on the fight.* He had to get his head back in the game but wished his cock was still inside of her. His fingers wrapped in her hair. His nose in the crook of her collarbone.

Broc motioned him over, holding out his cupped hand. Kane spit the mouthguard into the waiting palm and tilted his head upward, mouth open to receive the water. As Kane spit blood-pinkened liquid into the pan his trainer held, Broc said, "What's happenin' in that head of yours? You're not moving like the Kane Macleod we all know."

Kane fought the urge to roll his eyes. No one *knew* Kane Macleod truly, though Broc might be the closest. He sighed. "Can't really say, man. Just distracted."

"That woman from last night?" Broc scowled and placed the pan on a table just outside the boxing ring.

Kane cocked a half smile, then forced his mouth into a tight line, refusing to give anything away.

But his trainer caught the look before he had time to squelch it. "You gotta pull your head out of *her* ass and tend to business. I'm counting on this payday." Broc's brows dropped, and he switched his attention to the door. "Thought it was your big dream too," he said absently.

Vaguely, Kane registered the little tinkle of the bell announcing someone's arrival. He followed Broc's line of sight, but unfortunately, he knew it wasn't Malin walking in. Not yet anyway.

The man strutting into EMT had to be the guy who carried Kiera into that inky black portal. Conrí, but he didn't look the same. Tonight, the man looked thinner and shorter than Kane recalled. Kane saw that he was dressed in a white T-shirt and ripped jeans. Strange, none of them had worn anything but black before. He must have been using a spell to mask his appearance like Malin had done the night before.

Broc's eyebrows were knitted together in confusion, not knowing this man, but Kane was sure. Conrí grinned at Kane and loped over. Yep. That smile was the one he recalled. Definitely the same man but projecting an entirely different, easy-going persona. Kane wondered if he had his dragan under the magical disguise. "How'd you know where to find me?" Kane asked, slightly concerned but more impressed.

"Ha!" Conrí laughed. "You're not exactly unheard of around Wickney, ya know. I could ask any local waiter or newspaper-stand salesperson where you'd be right now, and they'd point the way to EMT. Nice gym, BT-dubs."

"Macleod!" called Broc loudly from just a few feet away. "You fightin' or yappin'?"

Kane glanced over, hesitating, but Conrí let him off the hook.

"Your trainer, I presume?"

"First clue?" Kane shot back.

"Fair 'nuff. You finish up. I'll watch. After, gotta take you to your sister," Conrí said. "Or maybe I should change, and we can spar? That one doesn't look like he's much of a match."

Sizing up the apparently small witch-man before him, Kane considered, then said, "He's got fifty pounds on you, and he's a trained MMA fighter." Having seen Conrí fight with the others in the alley, Kane knew the man had pretty intense skills. But he also had magic. Would he know where to begin in a run-of-the-mill MMA match with no magic allowed?

A hand landed on Kane's shoulder and pulled him back. Broc stepped in front of him facing Conrí, who stood head and shoulders below Broc. Even in disguise, Kane suspected he would be taller than his trainer, but Broc used the height added by the ring to his advantage.

"Look, I got no clue who you are, but you'll need to wait over there." Broc pointed. "This man's got no need for more distraction." He turned his back on Conrí and pushed Kane toward his corner of the ring. Broc motioned Smalls to the center of the mat, then putting his nose almost right up to Kane's, Broc lowered his voice. "Gonna say it once: Vegas." His eyes were wide, impressing his meaning on Kane. And yes, that had been Kane's only purpose a few days ago—really? Only a few days?

Hell, it'd seemed like a month since he'd stumbled on Malin and coldcocked his own sister. In the distance, Conrí grabbed a newspaper from the table in the sitting area, opened it up, and seemed to be reading it intently.

Broc grabbed Kane's chin. "Focus. Only a couple of weeks, and you need to hone every last skill you can to face The Russian in the title match."

Yeah, The Russian. Kane took a deep breath and blew it out intently. If anyone could take on The Rage in the ring, it was going to be Demitri Vladimirovich. Kane ran his gloved hand over his skull cut. He had been telling himself to focus for the last two hours, but that self-pep talk hadn't worked in the least. Now Conrí had shown up to bring him to Kiera. And of course he needed to go. His sister needed him.

Kane started removing his gloves.

"Really?" Broc balked. "What's your malfunction?" He crossed his arms over his chest, standing with his feet wide.

"My sister's hurt. Concussion, I think." Didn't need to share that it was his goddamn fault, but he was aware. The Rage inside of him knew and pounded heavily in his chest, wanting to be released from its cage.

His trainer jutted his chin toward the couches. "And that little man's come here about her?"

Broc's calling someone else a "little man" made Kane chuckle under his breath. "Likely. Didn't get a chance to ask, but . . ."

"But you're all twisted up in knots?" Broc pursed his lips, then added, "You've never let family into the ring."

Kane scratched his jaw with the back of his gloved fist. "Fuck." He pinched his lips, sighed through his nose, and let his head fall backward. He had to go. Being here wasn't doing shit for his preparation for Vegas. "Listen, I've been at this for two hours, and I'm not feeling it."

Broc's brows shot up toward the stocking cap covering his receding hairline. "You're fuckin' joking, right? You've never pulled out of training. Ever."

"Well, Kiera's usually the one taking care of me. I can't just let her deal with it on her own." He didn't want to tell Broc what had happened, but the instinctive punch he threw was what put her there. His fault. And today, he'd just spent the whole of the day wrapped around Malin, fighting a hard-on, and then getting both their rocks off. Where the hell were his priorities?

He placed both hands on top of his head, needing to get out of here and out of his head. Nowhere was safe. His knees twitched with the urge to leap into a run.

"Fine," Broc finally said, pointing a finger at Kane. "You take tonight off. Better yet, take the weekend. Deal with your shit. Then get your ass back here on Monday and be ready to get in the best fightin' shape of your life. Both our futures depend on it." He walked away, looking at Smalls and swiping a hand across his throat in a cut motion.

Smalls dropped his fists, spat on the mat, and said to Kane, "Next time, fucker. I owe you for that bout last night."

Kane waved him off, ducked through the ropes, and jogged over to Conrí. "Is everything okay with my sis? You talk to Malin?" He fought the urge to slap his forehead with his palm. Apparently, the Malin thing was creeping in way too far. She was eating away at everything in his brain and popping up in everything he said. He backpedaled. "My . . . ah . . . yeah." He cleared his throat. "Kiera. How's she doing?"

KANE EASILY KEPT PACE WITH Conrí as he marched in the direction of Club Infinity.

"Drink up," said Conrí as he turned to the wall in the alley across from the club where Malin had previously opened up the entrance to the dark mirrored version of Wickney. Conrí began making some movements and the series of interlocking shadowy lines formed. The wall once again started to waver.

Kane's heart leaped like an antelope hurdling a hedge as he anticipated the feeling of total blindness . . . sight obliterated by the darkness. Was that what his mother felt like every day of her life? Her blindness caused by some weird body part that no one here knew about or could see? What the actual fuck? Kane held the vial of orangish liquid, knowing that he wouldn't be able to see when they entered that place if he didn't drink. What had

Malin called the dark side of Wickney? *Ah, yes. The Penumbra.* Kane definitely needed the nasty-tasting shot, because he didn't want to have to cling to Conrí like he had with Malin once they were inside.

He tossed it back, let out a pained sigh, and shivered from the top of his head to the tips of his toes. "Gah, that shit's nasty!"

Conrí laughed and inspected Kane for a moment. "Man, something's different about you."

Kane frowned. "Been hearing that too much lately." He shrugged and shifted his weight from foot to foot. Why had everyone been telling him that? Malin. Had to be. Her effect on him was the easiest answer.

Conrí snapped his fingers three times, his face lighting with understanding—or maybe an idea. "That's it." He pointed at Kane. "Malin didn't cross through the Fold before daylight. So she spent the hours in the Daylight Realm. With you." He smirked. "You know what? Nice work! A mite sneaky that you and Malin spent the whole fucking day together. And I'm guessing the agenda was filled with a bit of f—"

"Kiera," Kane barked. His time with Malin was none of this man's business. "Can we go to my sister now?"

"Hey. Just sayin' . . . Malin's been in a real funk since her sister."

Groaning, Kane started, "Can we—wait, what? Malin has a sister?" Why hadn't she told him that when they had been talking about family before? "Where is her sister now?"

Conrí bit down, looking like a kid who had just robbed the candy store. "Well, yeah, she had a sister, but that's not my story to tell. Sorry I, uh . . . ah . . . Hey, your eyes adjusted yet?"

Kane blinked repeatedly, then peered up at a streetlight. The light, although dim and yellow, burned. "Yep. Think so."

Conrí nodded and stepped through the wall. Even though he'd seen it before and done it once himself, Kane gasped at the sight. It wasn't every day people walked through walls.

Inside, the purple haze settled over everything, but the shape of the city was still the same.

The magical disguise Conrí had before was gone. He appeared taller than, and almost as broad as, Kane now, and he wore the same style of cloak as Malin did. "So, are you wearing your dragan too?" asked Kane.

Conrí chuckled and pulled his cloak to the side. "This is Rezei, The Calm."

A small baby-blue dragan slithered out, and Kane stumbled backward. He'd seen Malin's dragan before—a deep pinkish-purple color—but at least she had kept hers tucked away for the most part. But Kane decided that if he was tied to this world somehow, he best get more accustomed to them. Slowly, he extended a hand for the small snakelike creature.

Rezei turned his head, the membranes around his face flared, and he hissed, pink tongue pulsating out and flicking at the end.

"Whoa, now." Conrí reached out and stroked Rezei's belly.

Rezei accepted the belly rub like a dog. If he had legs, Kane felt certain the back one would be twitching with pleasure over the scratches.

"Where'd he get the name 'The Calm'?" asked Kane.

"Oh, he's all good," Conrí said, but Kane couldn't tell if he was soothing the dragan or him. He cooed, "That man didn't mean to frighten you there."

So, the dragan? Hm. And it didn't seem like Kane was going to get an answer to his question.

Rezei circled around Conrí's arm in a clear caress and then hovered just above their heads. With his eyes on his dragan, Conrí said to Kane, "He's a little shy on the right side. A Semaphor clocked him a good one about five years back and he never regained all his sight on that side."

"They don't normally lash out like that, right?"

"Nah. You just reached for his blind side. Anywhosit, ready to fly?" The witch tilted his head with a small smirk.

"Ah, no. But yeah, I guess if we have to."

"A little boost, Rezei?" Conrí said, presenting his bare wrist to the dragan.

When the dragan sank his fangs, Conrí breathed in deeply as if he could gulp the sensation deep into his gut. Kane watched in horror, but Conrí seemed in ecstasy with the experience. When the exchange was done, Kane couldn't make out a mark on the guy's wrist as the witch extended both hands. Gone—as if the bite never truly happened.

A thought fluttered around his mind about the insanity of this whole thing, but he had to let it go. He'd gotten himself neck-deep into this underworld.

Soon, Conrí was guiding them as they soared over the dark version of Wickney toward the square. Kane's stomach churned, and he was glad he hadn't eaten yet. Riding—or flying?—with Conrí was more turbulent than with Malin.

When they touched down, Kane stumbled away from the man with a wary look over his shoulder. "Why don't you guys fly on brooms like normal witches?"

Conrí lifted a brow.

"Yeah, yeah. I get the stupidity of that particular question. Let's just go inside." He pivoted toward the door where he and Malin had entered before.

The dark version of Wickney's courthouse resembled something from an age forgotten with huge Gothic spires, steeply angled gables, and intricate sculptures decorating the facade. Kane hadn't looked at the dragan statues in the square, and he tried not to think about the alternate version of Wickney's government building as they went inside.

Just a hospital, he told himself.

Kiera smiled broadly to greet him, and when he reached her bedside, she clasped on to his hand. "Kane." Her voice sounded weak but relieved to have him there with her. This place must be even stranger for her than it was for him. At least *he* had a tour guide. Though Malin probably wouldn't have liked that particular title. She wasn't a woman of titles.

"Things are so very weird here." She lifted her baby-blue eyes to look at him, a feature that had always been in stark contrast with her honey-colored skin and dark red hair. He always believed his were less striking because of how he kept his hair close to the scalp.

Kiera's gaze wandered then settled back on him, eyes narrowing. "You look well, dear brother. You're not as hollow. How's that?" She tilted her head, seeming sweet and curious and confused.

It reminded him of when they were kids in Shawano and how she used to beg him to give her piggyback rides. But now, her voice was also light, flighty, distant in some way. In high school, college, and adulthood, Kiera had always been the grounded one.

Kane couldn't talk past his closed throat; could he have possibly changed her with that blow? He coughed. "What do you mean by less hollow?"

Kiera shook her head, then immediately raised a hand to her forehead. Kane reached for her, but she said, "No. No, I'm fine. This is just—or I feel *strange*." She gulped.

The doctor, Emrys, entered the room.

Kiera continued musing, "Why is this hospital so dim? Most are bright with fluorescent lights. Where are we? I've never seen a place like this in Wickney." And she would be one to know. She had worked at most of them.

Emrys studied papers on a clipboard, absently answering, "We call it the Haven."

"How did I get here?" Kiera tried to sit up but began to fall back onto the pillow.

This time, Kane caught her in a cradle before she crumpled. "Kiera, you're not ready to get up yet. Just rest. Emrys here has been taking good care of you." He eyed the doctor, who didn't seem to notice Kiera's condition or Kane's concern. "You'll be back to yourself in no time. Right?" he said louder to grab Emrys's attention.

With a placating smile, the doctor leaned over the other side of the bed as Kane eased his sister back onto the pillow. Kiera whimpered, smacked her lips, and closed her eyes sleepily.

"Kiera's improving well enough. This is simply her brain shutting down again to heal." Emrys opened her eye and waved a hand before it. Didn't they usually use a light for that? The doctor continued, "She's been awake for a while now, so we should probably let her rest."

Kane looked from his sister to the doctor. "Did you give her that see-in-the-dark concoction?"

The doctor reached up to a bag of liquid connected to Kiera's arm. Kane traced the tube from the bag to her arm, but then looked away when the room began to spin. The door swished open—blessed diversion. *Thank you, Conrí!*

But the person who stepped inside wasn't Conrí. Malin stood holding the door. An excited jolt hammered through Kane, and he lurched forward, just barely holding himself back. How could he explain that he was so excited to see her? That he missed her? When was the last time they had seen each other? Time was odd here, but still, it felt like too long.

"A word, Emrys?" She tilted her head toward the hall, seeming to ignore Kane's presence altogether.

Emrys put the clipboard in the slot at the head of Kiera's bed and adjusted something on one of the tubes. "She's healing, but she should sleep for a while now. I'll check on her every hour or two."

The doc crossed to the door, passing Malin as he exited the room, and Malin finally made eye contact with Kane. He stood with the intent of join them, but her expression seemed drawn and all business. Her look was loaded with a whole shit-ton of *Sorry. But* . . . She gritted her teeth.

But what? Kane wondered.

Malin shook her head. "Stay with her. She needs you. I'll be back." Tucking her chin, she stepped outside, and the door swooshed shut behind her.

Kane gaped. After the day at his apartment, was that really all they would talk about? He sank into the chair beside Kiera's bed. A rock settled into his throat, another in his gut, and his sinuses stung. *What the fuck's that?* He hadn't had that sensation since right after . . . *No, not touching that topic.*

He took his sister's lifeless hand in his and chuckled. "So, sis. Do you remember when we used to pretend we went to another place? When Dad came home, and we didn't want to be there anymore? We thought it was like Narnia, only dark. Well, I've got some news for you when you're feeling up to it."

OUTSIDE KIERA'S ROOM, MALIN TOOK a deep breath. Damn her to the Light, why did telling Kane to stay feel so wrong? It was the right thing to do, but it went against every feeling she had in her heart. She couldn't bring Kane into this fight with Godric. No, she couldn't risk losing him the way she lost Myla. She had to protect him at all costs. Her heart included.

It's for the best, Mal, she told herself and then asked Emrys, "How is she?"

The healer answered, "Recovering, but she has a long way to go."

Malin crossed her arms and wondered what had to be taking so long. Had Kiera been that close to death when she was brought here? "You tested her for a nimh?"

Emrys nodded. "And yeah, she's of the Dark."

"I assumed as much." Running a hand through her hair, Malin searched the hallway for anyone who might be listening. Her fingers snagged, and her hair felt heavy. She really needed a shower. *After this,* she told herself. "Their mother is too. Blind."

Emrys gasped and paused for a second, wide-eyed. "You must bring her through the Fold. If she stays in the Daylight Realm, she will start losing other abilities."

"Yeah. I'm aware. How long? Do you know?" Malin didn't mean to come across as rude, but everything was forced. Falling through the cracks.

"How long has she been blind?"

Malin chewed the inside of her lip. "Dunno. I'll have to figure that one out, somehow."

"You could just ask Kane." Emrys motioned to the door.

Shaking her head, Malin said, "Yeah. I'll do that. Shit's just a little awkward with him right now." That might've been her own fault.

Emrys eyed her sideways, knowingly.

"No lectures." She held up a hand to forestall his warning. "Perhaps I should visit another coven and see if they have time to deal with the Macleods. Closest is in the Twin Cities."

Malin checked the time—still three hours before she needed to meet Morgana. She could make it there and back, but there definitely wasn't enough time to discuss the situation. Plus, given it was nighttime in the Daylight Realm, they might not even be in the Penumbra at the moment.

"I assume you gave Kiera the elixir?" asked Malin.

"I did."

"And Kane has obviously had a dose tonight too. We can't keep giving them that." Malin paced with her heart racing about what the effects could be on him. "Any recommendations?"

Emrys wrung his hands. "It isn't my place to give such advice."

"Damn your place, Emrys! I asked for it."

"Well, if their mother is already blind, you're on the clock with these two. You don't want to let that deterioration start with the siblings, or it could be irreversible. And, true about the elixir. We've seen that lead to some mental disturbances."

I effin know that much! Malin wanted to say. Instead, she kept it nice. "You're giving me old info. And you can say insanity. I'm aware of the side effects."

"It seems like you have two options. Three if you go to the Twin Cities and successfully petition the coven leader to adopt this family. But that is assuming the cowan man in there will go." Emrys looked skeptical.

"Shit. I knew you'd say that." She paced some more, twisting her hair around one finger. "Cailleach or pháirtí," she mused aloud.

Kiera was younger than her brother, so she had more time.

But Malin needed to figure out what to do with Kane, and damn her to Danu's Light, she wasn't ready to undertake the All Mother's sacred mating rituals. That decided it. She was going to have to find Kane a dragan to bond with.

"I can't commit to anyone at the moment, so he'll have to become one of the Dragan Gardaí. Breyze, anyone in your nest a match?"

Her dragan slithered from under her cloak and chittered, then flew down the hallway toward the exit.

Not knowing exactly what he said and after his rapid exit, Malin assumed that was a yes. She called after him, "We'll meet you at the nest!" Breyze would come through; she had complete faith.

Emrys bowed his head. "If you'll excuse me, I've other matters to attend to."

"Of course. Thank you."

Though what she thanked him for wasn't quite clear. Perhaps just taking care of Kane's sister? Perhaps being honest with her about her choices? She didn't need smoke blown up her ass at the moment. Sex was fine, but again, mating was definitely the last thing she wanted to think about.

Malin pushed the doors to Kiera's room wide and stood there with her arms propping them open. When Kane turned to face her, she said, "Come with me."

Kane lowered his brows, his forehead wrinkling. "Where?" His voice was rough.

"I'm going to take care of—uh, both our problems."

He stood. "And what fucking *problem* is that? Up until you showed up here, I didn't think we had problems."

She threw her hands in the air with a huff. "Haven't you put this all together yet? Your mother. Blind. Your sister and you have the gland. Blindness is your fate, and your sister's before long. And we need to bring your mother into the Penumbra too. I can stop the progression, but I need you to come with me now. Then we'll take care of your family."

He hesitated, looking down at Kiera then back at Malin.

His brows had eased, but he clearly still hesitated.

"You're going to need a familiar. You're older than your sister, so your time is more limited. Breyze went to the nest to find you one."

Kane held up both hands. "Wait a hot fucking minute. No way am I tying myself to one of those dragans!"

Malin recoiled. "Why?" she asked honestly and was taken aback by his vehemence. Breyze was the only one who truly knew her. Wouldn't Kane want that connection too?

"That drink is nasty, but I'll stick with it if those are my choices. Neither your dragan nor Conrí's liked me much. And the whole biting thing? What makes you think I'd want one?"

She sighed. If that was all he worried over, it was easily solved. "Breyze and Rezei are bonded. An unbonded dragan is less territorial. Your familiar will become just as protective over you. It gives us the magic we need to fight the Semaphors and protect our way of life."

"No." Kane walked slowly around the foot of Kiera's bed. "I have commitments. A fight in two weeks. Gotta get this shit off my mind and focus." In three more steps, he stood within her reach.

Malin's heart hammered in her chest. More quietly, she argued, "You can't keep drinking that elixir. It'll drive you crazy. Literally." She hoped he would understand and wouldn't have to experience it for himself, but he seemed like a guy who had to learn things the hard way.

"Kiera took it too, right? We're both okay," he countered.

"Yeah, but it's her first dose. You're on number three. And she's younger." Malin breathed, trying desperately to keep her body under control. "You have less time." Damn, she sounded like a broken record.

"The only thing driving me crazy right now is you." He stepped closer and lifted her cloak to look inside, but Breyze wasn't there. Kane slid a hand under her cloak and around her waist.

She felt his touch through her clothes and her body

responded with an anticipatory gush of desire. *Effin-A.* She couldn't succumb to his charm again. Her mind needed to focus, but her body had other intentions.

Leaning in near her ear, he continued, "The smell of you drives me mad. I can still smell us together from earlier today. I think I drove you a little crazy too, right?"

Suddenly, she felt like she'd eaten a handful of dry crackers. No words. All the moisture in her body pooled between her legs. *Mal . . . gotta stop this.*

Kane slid his hand down her hip and around to cup her ass. He drew her body up to his. "What I want to do right now is find somewhere we won't be seen."

Me too. Malin squeezed her eyes shut. *Godric. Morgana. Myla. Quit thinking about getting laid, Mal. Focus.* She placed both hands on his chest and checked her watch for the time again. Only a few minutes had passed, but it somehow seemed like an hour. She had time, and damn was she tempted!

"Malin," whispered Kane, hot breath tickling her skin and sending a flush down her body. "Once Kiera is well, she can make her own decision. But this dragan thing isn't me. I have three days to get my shit together and back to training. A pet dragan won't help me at all."

"It's not a pet," Malin grumbled.

"Got it. Not a pet. Regardless, this fight's my life. After, I'm retiring. We'll find another way for me then."

That other way was precisely what worried her.

CHAPTER 20

THE HOT WATER POURED OVER Malin's shoulders, warming her from the outside in. She should have taken a shower before she'd left Kane's place, but at the time, she figured she would be heading directly back to the coven's house, washing up, and returning through the Fold to the Daylight Realm to meet Morgana. Malin grabbed the loofah—a fantastic invention in modern times—and lathered it up under the running water. It had been quite the progressive move when Morgana had figured out a way to channel water from the Daylight Realm into the Penumbra.

Damn, Malin missed that witch and her heavy-duty knowledge of all things mechanical, technical, and computer-y. Malin wondered how her dragan Pysae had adapted to their separation. She hadn't seen him since Morgana left him here at the nest. At least Morgana had agreed to meet. Despite having to visit the faeries' number-one hangout in Wickney, she was thrilled to see Morgana.

Regardless of the chosen venue, this was the first time since Myla's death that Godric had been careless enough to contact Malin, and she couldn't let it pass. Now, she just had to avoid Kane Macleod long enough to get to the Local at 1:00 a.m.

Good thing she had Conrí babysitting him for a while. Yet the thought of that man, his berserk fighting style, and their tryst earlier in the day made her guts turn to liquid.

No, Malin, don't forget what you need to get done tonight, she told herself.

But that didn't stop her from sliding her hand down her soapy body and looking for a bit of relief. Unfortunately, the relief she could get wasn't as good as Kane. It wasn't anything like what Kane could do to her body. Or what she wanted Kane to do to her body. Over and over and over again.

Leaning over the table, Kane rested one hand on the green felt and placed the cue stick in the valley between his thumb and forefinger. His nose itched from the smell, and he twitched and twisted it back and forth. He couldn't escape the stench.

"Would you shoot already?" said Conrí.

Not moving, Kane rolled his eyes to look up at the man who had become his apparent babysitter for the moment. "Nose itches, asshole." Others might have loved the smell of old books, but they just made Kane want to sneeze. But he was in the home of witches, so he should have expected such a room. "Don't you guys have TV?"

Conrí just gave him a sour look.

Kane took the shot. Balls clanked, but only the solid white one sank into a hole. "I've never been one for this shit." He leaned against the doorjamb just behind him. Might as well get comfortable, because if the last three games were any indication, his opponent was about to run the table.

Conrí chalked the tip of his cue and lined up to take his next shot. "TV requires electricity, man," he said and then struck the ball with the stick. He hit two striped balls, and both went into the opposite corner pockets.

"What about music? Too quiet around here." Kane's heel bounced with nervous energy. It gave him some distraction from his head, which raced with thoughts . . . of Malin.

"Same dealio."

Kane leaned his head back and rolled it to the side to peer into the foyer of the huge house. Malin had excused herself too quickly, and he wanted—no, he needed to extract himself from this torturous game of billiards and find her. She'd climbed the stairs, but he wasn't certain where she had gone after that.

"Ah hell!" Conrí said. "Thought I had that one for sure. Your go."

He had cleared all but two of the stripes, yet all Kane's solids were still on the table. "Know what? Nah." Kane tossed the cue stick on the table.

"What? C'mon. No one else around here will play with me," Conrí whined, throwing his head back.

"Of course not, you run the table." Kane marched out the door.

"Wait. Where you off to?" Conrí asked, his voice growing louder as he followed.

"I'm not fucking here to play games. Only in this place for two women. The other's my sister." He climbed the steps two at a time.

"Riiight," Conrí drawled. "You're looking for the last door on the right then."

Kane waved a hand—a quick thanks. He hesitated at the door and listened, unable to control the urge to find Malin. Not much he could hear through what appeared to be solid wood. Cracking it open, he heard the constant sound of running water, but sheMalin was nowhere in sight. He slipped inside and closed the door quietly behind him. The entire room smelled like her, and he gulped the scent through his nose as if it were the only source of air he'd had in the last ten minutes. The clothes she had been wearing were slung over the side of a basket near the only other door in the room, and the mirror visible beyond the opening was clouded over with steam.

I may be a motherfucker, Kane thought as he slipped off his shoes, unzipped and removed his sweatshirt, and dropped the basketball shorts he'd put on after the gym. His cock was already heavy at the thought of her naked and soapy in the shower. He didn't even need to work for it; the demanding thing was already leaking precum off the tip.

She was all into me . . . the sex . . . us before. I just need to give her a little reminder now.

He left his shoes by the door and padded into the bathroom, dropping his clothes on top of hers in the basket. Inside, the sound of rushing water grew louder, the humidity warmed his skin, and he heard her humming from the other side of a tiled wall dividing the toilet, sink, and counter from the shower. Kane stepped around the corner and took a moment to appreciate the shape of this woman. Hell, even the steam seemed unable to resist the glistening curves rounding downward from her narrow waist into long, muscular legs. She had a fighter's build—slender but stacked with hard muscle. That alone reeled him in like the little sunnies he caught as a kid at the lake. Clean water washed suds over her shoulders, and she ran her hands over her breasts and stomach, hugging herself until her fingers peeked out on the opposite sides of her body.

Kane took a step closer, stretching his hand forward. But then he stalled and stepped back to the corner of the enormous shower. He choked out, "Mal . . ."

Malin jumped, whirled around, and hugged herself tighter. One arm covered her nipples, but the rest was clearly visible and shiny wet. Kane's cock kicked. A series of emotions and thoughts ripped across her face, but then her features eased. She put a finger between her teeth and scanned his naked body from toe to head and back down again. Kane stared at the tip of her finger, wishing it was his cock. But then he studied her eyes. Something was happening in that sharp-witted brain of hers, and he wished he was privy to that information. He waited.

Standing there naked and at full attention, Kane held himself back. She had to choose this now because he wouldn't ever press himself on someone who didn't want the same thing. But she held him in suspense for what seemed like an eternity.

Then a smile spread from the corners of her mouth. She sauntered closer, water dripping from the tips of her breasts. Malin reached for Kane's wrist, pulled him under the water, and turned him so his back took the brunt of the water falling. He gasped when the hot droplets prickled on the back of his neck, but when she put her hands on his chest, he forgot all about that heat and focused on the heat between them.

Malin grabbed the bar of soap and washed his body. He'd showered before leaving EMT, so he didn't need the bath, but he wasn't about to turn away her touch. She slid soapy hands over his shoulders, his pecs, his abs, and around his back. She turned him to face the wall and placed both his hands on the tile. "Stay," she commanded.

And damn him, he was going to do every little thing she asked in that moment. He watched her over his shoulder as she lathered up again and began washing his legs, then his butt, and his balls. Kane groaned, started to take his hands from the wall.

"No, no," she chided.

"Aahhh," Kane uttered. "You're killing me here."

"Am I?" she asked in a syrupy-sweet voice. "I've never heard of anyone dying from pleasure."

"Mmm. What changed your mind?" Kane asked, strained.

"Ha," she laughed, but it was forced. Not the playfulness of before. "Would you be quiet?"

"Mm . . . hmm."

Malin continued washing his legs, circling around to the front of his body, then she took his cock in her soapy hands and stroked. Kane had to clench his teeth and try hard to keep his hands on the wall while she touched him. He desperately wanted to pull her up against his body and kiss her for all she was worth. Then, if he had his way, he would brace her against the shower wall, wrap her legs around his waist, and fuck her into next week. Instead, he did as she asked and held as still as humanly possible under the circumstances.

"Obviously," Malin said, "you sensed where my thoughts had drifted here in this shower."

Kane asked through gritted teeth, "Did I?" He was getting too close, needed her to stop.

And thank the fates, she did. She stood back against the wall and between where his hands were planted. "You must have. I was thinking about you earlier and touching myself like this." She ran her fingers around her nipples. "And then like this." Malin slid one hand down the line of defined muscle marking the center of her stomach and over her smooth mound, sliding her middle finger between her folds. Her hips bucked, her skin touching his for a second. "And ooh, I'm still a bit sensitive there."

Kane growled, so primal and deep it rumbled his chest and cock. Where that came from, he couldn't say, but it sounded like a lion's roar in his ears.

Malin *tsked*. "I think it's my turn to have a little fun with you." She placed her hands on Kane's chest and ran them down over his abs, squatting onto her heels as she went. She kept eye contact as she moved. "I want you to watch."

She grasped on to his shaft and put the head into her mouth. Her tongue swirled around the lower side—the most sensitive spot. Kane tried in vain to grip on to the wall, anything to hold him in place.

"Mal," he breathed. "This is going too fast. I'm . . ." She slid him into her mouth halfway, and he rolled his eyes backward, allowing his head to fall back too.

She released his cock then and ticked her tongue on the roof of her mouth. "I told you to watch."

"Ya. Okay." Kane panted, breathing out in a huff through O-shaped lips. Then he looked down at her again.

She took his head back into her mouth and slid her hands down to the base of his shaft. Her eyes peered up at him as she took the length of him into her throat.

"Holy fuck, Mal!" he breathed, his hips starting to rock in sync to her movements. She kept a perfect rhythm, and the pressure started to build. "I'm gonna—oh." He pushed forward again. Mal met his thrust. He could barely keep his eyes on her. The sight was the most erotic thing he'd ever seen. His balls clenched. "I—ah—oh."

She pushed down onto his cock, putting the head at the back of her throat just as his body seized up and jerked uncontrollably. In wave after wave, he emptied himself into her, and she swallowed every last drop.

When he was spent, she stood, grabbed him around the back of the neck, and kissed him viciously. He tasted his seed on her lips, and without even a ten-second break, his cock started to stir again.

*I*F IT WASN'T FOR THE running water in the shower, Malin would be standing in a puddle from how wet she was while sucking Kane to orgasm.

"Am I free to move now?" Kane asked, looking down at her, his eyes bluer and brighter than they'd been a moment before.

Would the berserker come out for sex? Malin mused. Did she want it to come out? Could she control him enough to see his beast come? And would he destroy her the same way he destroyed his opponents in the ring? With a small smile, she answered, "Mm-hmmm."

In a single movement, Kane released his hands from the wall, grabbed her around the waist, lifted her, and buried his cock hilt-deep inside her. Malin cried out in pure, perfect ecstasy. Heck, she shouldn't be doing this; she had other things to attend to tonight. But what were they? This felt so effin amazing, she couldn't recall what she'd had on the agenda.

At the moment, *she* felt so deliciously full. Kane Macleod filled her in ways she didn't want to acknowledge—couldn't let herself acknowledge. When they came together, their bodies made magic.

She had nearly come when Kane emptied himself into her throat, and it tasted so delicious on her tongue. And that searing kiss afterward. She wanted to share with him exactly how much sucking him to his release had turned her on. And now, she nearly came from being impaled. He didn't move, letting her adjust to his remarkable size. It surprised her she could take in all of him, stretching for his girth. She tried desperately to hold her orgasm at bay, but with her legs wrapped around his waist and him buried so deeply inside, her kitten was purring and massaging Kane's cock like a scratching post.

Okay, morbid comparison, but oh-effin-well. Her inner walls pulsated relentlessly. She mewled and panted and bit her lip so viciously she might have drawn blood—hard to tell with the water running over their naked bodies.

Kane started to pull back, but she dug her nails into his shoulders. "Hold on," she uttered. "Just a sec. Don't. Ahhh."

"Baby doll, I can't stay still much longer." His voice was hoarse, struggling to growl out those words, but *baby doll?* Yeah, that was going to do the trick.

Wait, Mal. Not yet. The building pleasure slowed as she adjusted. "Okay," she finally uttered, preparing herself for what promised to be a brutal and beautiful ride. "Go!" she commanded.

Kane pulled out and thrust back inside her—deeper, if at all possible. Together they cried out. He retreated again. And together, they sighed. He pounded into her. They grunted. Retreat, return, retreat. He set an excruciating rhythm.

With each thrust, Malin's back climbed the wall, but Kane held her hips with death's grip. When his hips withdrew, she slid down. Up. Down. Faster. Faster. Up, down, up . . .

"Ah . . . harder," she breathed. Her fingernails dug in.

He obeyed, and she adored having him answer to her every whim. Her orgasm built to the music of their ohs and ahs.

He pumped faster, and Malin's vision went entirely dark. Harder, and pinpricks of light began flickering. Were her eyes closed or open? She hadn't a clue. And then, her body locked down on his cock. But Kane kept punishing her, and she came over and over and over again. She rode her high like hills, crest and vale, crest and vale. She lost her voice but held on to his shoulders for all she was worth.

And suddenly, Kane pushed deep inside with a roar that shook her world, and she swore he detonated within her throbbing sheath. Time stopped. And for that moment, Malin could no longer tell where Kane Macleod ended and she began.

Minutes later, it seemed, the water showering them ran cold. Malin jerked, her eyes flying wide open. She slapped Kane on the shoulder. "Shit. What time is it?"

"Who the fuck cares?" he said, lazily pulling away from her and setting her on her feet.

Shivering, Malin washed up quickly, shut off the water, and grabbed a towel. "I have to get back through the Fold to meet someone." She darted around the tiled wall bound for her closet. If she missed Morgana, she might not get another chance.

When dressed, she grabbed her weapons belt and looked up to see Kane leaning on the bathroom doorjamb, a towel slung around his waist. She saw his V easily, and if the towel would just dip a tiny bit lower . . . She had to look away or regret the choice later. He was watching her curiously, like something was on his mind. But she didn't have time at the moment. She lowered her head and pivoted toward the door.

Just as she reached for the knob, Kane cut her off with a hand holding the door closed. "Ah, before you go, can I, um . . ."

Malin checked her watch. Half past midnight. She raised her brows, careful to keep her eyes from looking down at his body again. He was too close, and she caught his musky scent. "Can you what?"

"Date." Kane coughed. "Uh, can I take you on a date tomorrow at dark?"

A laugh exploded from her chest. After their tryst earlier and just now in the shower, he was asking her on a date? Could it be that innocent? Like two teenagers going to a movie and dinner? She couldn't remember the last time she went on a date.

"Yeah. Of course," she said breathlessly. She couldn't think about it more or she would get bogged down in the details. "But I really gotta run now."

Chapter 21

Exhaustion made Kane's limbs heavy, but a new energy thrummed through his veins. Too many things to process had transpired, and he wanted to sleep for a week. He flashed back on the afternoon with Malin and then the shower, again musing over how well they matched one another's movements. It seemed absolutely unreal. And the thought made him hot, his ab muscles tightening and mouth running dry like sand.

Now that Malin was gone, he stood in her room alone. What did that say about how much she trusted him? Or maybe there wasn't anything here to trust him with. Regardless, he wouldn't go snooping for fear of betraying her trust. He sucked at trust. In fact, he'd only ever asked a woman on a date once before. And that had turned out badly, the same way the rest of his teenage years had gone to shit the week before that homecoming dance that was supposed to be his first real date.

For this date, he didn't want to let any time pass, didn't want anything to rip him from their date. The idea he had was perfection, and he couldn't wait to escort Malin to the festivities that would kick off the Wickney Renaissance Festival.

But what should he do in the meantime? Stay here? Sleep? Tired as he was, he wasn't certain he *could* fall asleep. Not with all that was happening and the feel of Malin still on his lips, the feel of those sinful lips wrapped around his cock. No. He had to get out.

He could go back to Dark Haven and wait at Kiera's bedside, but what was the point? None, really. Pool with Conrí? Kane rolled his eyes. Absolutely not. And he didn't know how to get through the Fold without help from one of the witches.

He let the towel around his waist fall and walked over to Malin's bed. Still doubting his ability to sleep, he lay down. The feel of Malin's satiny sheets on his back was reminiscent of her more gentle touches. Damn he adored how her hands ran over his shoulders and back. He considered what he had to wear for the date, and soon his eyes drifted closed. Maybe he would snooze for a wh—

Kane awoke, still alone. He pulled back on his shorts and sweatshirt and poked around the top of Malin's dresser. He found a pen first, but the closest thing to a piece of paper he could find was a small napkin. On it, he scrawled as neatly as possible, "Half an hour past dark. Wickney Festival Grounds. Eve of Renaissance." It wasn't easy to write on the napkin and without a hard surface, and his handwriting looked like a third-grader's. As long as the point got across, hopefully, his penmanship wouldn't matter.

He laid the note on Malin's pillow and went to find Conrí. He had some prep-work to do before he met her tomorrow evening.

MALIN HAD TRAVELED BETWEEN THE realms countless times, but the feeling never changed. Walking, or moving in general, through the Fold between the Penumbra and the Daylight Realm felt like swimming through peanut butter. The magical division between dimensions or worlds—whatever the various creatures chose to call them—wasn't ever a simple thing. Tonight, Malin was headed to see someone she hadn't seen in ages, and though Morgana was one of the Cailleach—one actually born in the Penumbra—unlike Malin and Myla, she had chosen a faerie gathering place for their rendezvous. That simple happenstance had Malin contemplating how creatures from each culture viewed such things. In truth, she was preparing herself to come face to face with some of Danu's creatures: the Fae. She always started thinking about how the diverse creatures behaved when she had to be around them.

In the thickness of the Fold, she watched her boots as her muscles worked, moving her forcefully through the black mists. She had been to Faerie once—through their Veil, as they called their portal between worlds. Her visit had been an age before she had become a witch and member of the Dragan Gardaí. In that time, humans believed more readily in the creatures from other worlds: hers, Tír na nÓg, Zion, Irkalla, Olympus, Valhalla, or any of the other dwellings of gods. Now, people seemed more apt to shove those beliefs aside, and as a result, most of the creatures didn't mingle in the Daylight Realm or any of the others. The Semaphors, contrary to the gods—well, they were a creation of the fallen god Semar, a corrupt sibling of Danu who had been stripped of his ability to maintain his own realm. He had launched a personal crusade against Aodh's children.

Malin stumbled upon reaching the other side of the Awen. *Seriously, Mal. This is all too much to think about.* She needed to focus, but focus seemed harder and harder by the second.

The alley near Club Infinity was empty, but the night felt cool against Malin's cheeks. She inhaled deeply, slid her wrist up Breyze's body, and tapped him just behind his right horn—a silent request. Breyze sank his fangs into her vein, and the blessed venom flooded through her body. With the magic of Darkness flowing, she cast the seeing spell upon herself. *"Féach."* When the Darkness took effect, she not only could see more intensely with her eyes, but she could also sense the presence of nearby beings. She extended her senses to the mouth and the depths of the alley, and only sensing a family of mice in their nest behind the dumpster, she said, *"Gaoth,"* and levitated into the air, arms wide as she welcomed flight.

Above the buildings by twenty feet or so, she circled, scanning the humans departing in stumbling herds from the club.

Closing time for most of the nightclubs and bars in Wickney approached, so the exodus was natural at this hour. Only the Local downtown had an exception to the city's ordinance dictating a 1:00 a.m. bar close. Malin had never bothered to learn how the exception had been granted, but she had always assumed Fae magic was involved. Those effin tricksters had the authorities under their belts at every turn, and the owner of the Local, Maximus Linardi, had two faerie thugs in his service. *Ugh*, Malin couldn't understand why Morgana had chosen Faerieville. Maybe to discourage someone from Aodh's realm—Malin or other coven members—from showing.

But Malin wouldn't let that stop her tonight. She had one need, and this appointment was simply a means to that end.

"*Gaoth*," she said again, this time calling the wind to carry her to Wickney's city center. She soared over Wickney University and then the Arboretum.

To her magically enhanced sight, the faerie mound pulsed with a bluish light and rang like an old note struck too loudly on a harp. She shivered and looked away, up the hill, and toward her destination. Soon, Morgana could take her phone and trace the text from Godric. She could destroy the thing afterward if it meant Malin didn't have to go back into Faerieville to meet her again.

Malin spotted a shadowed area on the theater's rooftop at a diagonal from the Local and descended. As soon as her feet touched the ground, she looked at her watch—five 'til one. She hopped into a jog and scurried down the fire escape stairs on the back side of the building, cloaked herself with a quick spell, and ran to the Local. Under the bar's sign, she released the cloaking spell and murmured, "*Chumasci*," to blend in with the crowd. She blew past the coat check, but the girl with pink pigtails behind the counter called out to ask if she would like to check her coat. What a ridiculous question. Malin ignored her and descended the stairs. On the last three steps, her phone buzzed.

M0R64N4: BOOTH IN FARTHEST CORNER.

Malin rolled her eyes. She doubted the timing of the text was coincidence. She would never understand Morgana's seemingly omniscient abilities: knowing exactly who was where and when.

Yet the text eased her worry over missing their scheduled time, and Malin slowed her steps. The other witch wouldn't leave, knowing Malin was already on the premises.

Music blared, bodies cavorted near the stage, and the lead singer for a grunge-style band growled into the mic. Thanks to her spell, Malin easily made her way through the throngs of faeries and humans toward the back of the underground level until she spotted Morgana with her head hung over the table. Darkness deeper than that in the Penumbra always shadowed the witch. Malin had to remove her dark glasses as she sat in the empty bench seat.

"Why couldn't you just come to the Awen?" Malin asked.

When Morgana looked up from the table, the stark white skin, aqua-colored scar, and mismatched stare sent electric shockwaves all the way to Malin's bones, as if she'd been stuck with a thousand tiny needles. All Morgana said was, "No point. I don't belong."

"But you do." Malin reached forward but stopped as both the black and the near-colorless eye fell on her hand. She curled her fingers slowly into a fist and shoved both hands under the table, adding, "More than me." This was the first time she could remember coming face to face with the hacker since well before Myla's death. Did Morgana even care for what they'd lost?

"Listen," the other witch spat, then she snarled, "big sis. Not gonna happen. Ever."

So rare that someone caused such a sense of a barren winter to settle into Malin, but Morgana did so like no nightmare could, not even Godric. How and why did she fear her younger sister so much?

"But Mother—"

"For fuck's sake, Malin, don't mention the evil witch in my presence."

Malin rolled her shoulders back. "I just don't understand."

"Ask Minerva about that shit. Or Aodh. She'd know too. I'm done with the gods and goddesses. This is the most godless realm, and that's where I'm staying." Morgana lifted a glass of amber liquid on ice and guzzled the half remaining liquid. A spirit of some sort, and a strong one too. She hissed in through her teeth, slammed the glass on the table, and demanded, "The phone."

"What about Pysae?"

Morgana's gloved fingers squeezed tightly around the glass. "I can't reach Pysae. He's in your realm."

"It's your realm too."

Her brow arched toward her hairline.

As if on cue, the music halted then blared louder and lights strobed throughout the club. Malin squinted and threw a hand up to shield her eyes. Morgana didn't flinch as Malin whispered, "*Dubh.*" Then she looked at her sister's long black hair, the thick locks hiding her white birthmark streak at her right temple. "Don't the lights bother you?"

"You simply don't understand, do you?"

Malin stared at her blankly.

"I've existed in the mortal realm for more than a century. No dragan. I'm as good as a human but imprisoned in this near-immortal body." Morgana pulled out a cell phone, swiped up, and started typing on it furiously.

Malin opened her mouth to speak, but Morgana held up a hand to stop her. "Shh." She kept typing while Malin tried to swallow her next question. What in Darkness was her sister doing?

Morgana seemed to finish whatever she'd been doing, then turned the phone screen-down on the table and slid it across to Malin. "New phone for you. Same number." She wiggled her gloved fingers in a come-here motion. "Just give me the one he texted. And leave."

Malin's eyes darted between the phone on the table and Morgana. She couldn't just let things be like this. Clasping her hands under the table to keep them from shaking, Malin gritted her teeth and spat out, "No."

"Fine." Morgana started to stand.

Malin sat back and reached under her cloak, brushing a

hand over Breyze's scales. Her dragan responded to her wordless need, giving her the Darkness, and Malin uttered, "*Bhac.*"

A wall of Darkness, an invisible magical force, blocked Morgana from standing. Still facing the unseen barrier so that Malin could only see her nose beyond the curtain of black hair, her sister said, "I'm changed, Malin, and there's no return. This is the last favor I'm doing for one of our kind, so just give me your phone and let me be."

Morgana wasn't a little woman, taller by a head than Malin was, or Myla had been. She was built differently too, wider at the shoulders than the twins and fewer curves. When Malin had known her well, she'd always seemed larger than life. Now, she seemed defeated. The sadness in her sister's voice and her curved posture cut deep into Malin's heart. All that Malin had endured clearly couldn't compare to whatever life her younger sister had led.

Malin finally took the phone from the front pocket of her jeans and slid it across the table, replacing it with the new phone her sister had given her. Her mind drifted back to the happiness she'd left earlier with Kane.

Morgana swiped it across the table, down, and out of sight, then waited in silence.

"Is there at least someone you can rely on?" Malin asked.

No immediate answer came, but Morgana's body quivered, as if her leg bounced nervously where it was hidden. She then cut a glance over. "I don't know. And I stopped searching decades ago. Humans are no good for me either. They die from stupid shit like cancer."

Looking down, Malin answered quietly, "Or become pháirtí." The words were more to herself than to her sister, and she released the barrier.

"Not for a banished witch, Mal." Morgana stood. "I'll drop you all the info in a day or so." She walked away.

Malin sat in the booth alone for a long, long time, considering her own bitterness and need for revenge. Yeah, she still needed to rid the world of Godric Laferty, but she also needed to avoid ending up like her sister. She hadn't been close to her younger sister since before they'd left Ireland, and she wondered now how much she'd missed.

For another hour, maybe two, everyone in the club either didn't see or ignored Malin, and when last call was announced over the PA system, she slid out of the booth and marched out the club's back door. Into the night. She suddenly wanted nothing more than to run back into Kane's arms.

MALIN RETURNED ON FOOT TO the alley where she could open the window into the Fold. Four in the morning and the streets at the West End of Wickney were dead. The quietness that hovered in the city seemed unnatural to Malin even after all the years she had spent in the Wickney area—both the Daylight and the Penumbra versions. Sometimes, she longed for the times with open fields where corncrakes croaked amid the grasses and tawny owls hooted the nights away. The city was a far cry from the grass-roofed hut where she had spent her fleeting childhood amid rolling hills and miles from the nearest neighboring village farm. It had certainly been a simpler life.

The dragan familiars to the village's witches had made their nests in the sea cliffs far from the reaches of most humans. When it was time for a witch to make the familiar bond with their dragan, they had to hike for days and descend steep rock faces, for they didn't have venom coursing through their veins or the knowledge to cast the flight or levitation spells.

She sighed when she reached the alley's entrance. Perhaps hunting would be better than returning to the coven house, but she could use some tea and approximately a whole week's worth of sleep. At the spot on the wall she knew so well, Malin lifted her hand and drew the Awen to open the Fold. As with most doors between the realms, entering was less of an ordeal than exiting. Once inside the Penumbra, Malin levitated and soared to the nest several city blocks to the north, and before parting, Breyze punctured her wrist. He shared the Darkness with her again—enough to fuel her flight home and some small spells afterward—then licked the wound closed and left her on the street.

"Enjoy your rest, dear friend," Malin said and watched him wind his way toward the aerie before she flew back to the coven's house.

In the foyer, she shed her cloak and startled at Tierney's amused voice. "What stories you must have." Sarcasm dripped from the words. Her arms were crossed over her chest, and her hair was pulled back, the blonde ponytail falling off to the side.

"For another day." Malin stepped past her friend into the kitchen. Chamomile called her name.

Tierney followed. "He left, you know? Earlier."

"Mmmm?" Malin hadn't expected Kane to wait for her return. "With his sister, I assume?"

Her covenmate shrugged. "Not sure."

Panic pulsated through Malin. Kane was gone, and not with his sister, but where else would he be? She shook her head to clear her thoughts.

Tierney sat at the small table and leaned toward Malin. "So what happened?"

"Nothing," Malin snapped.

"The color of your cheeks doesn't say 'nothing.'"

"Well, *I* say nothing. Now, drop it."

The teapot whistled like a scream in her ears. Her cheeks heated, and she wished she could relieve the pressure in her head like the teapot released the steam. Malin took the whole thing, her canister of chamomile, and a cup, and left Tierney at the table.

"Mal?" her friend's voice followed.

"Another time, T. Swear." Malin took the stairs two at a time, ducked into her room, and heaved a breath of relief.

While pouring her tea, she noticed a napkin on her pillow that hadn't been there before. She left the tea to steep on her dresser and picked it up. Her eyes scraped against the paper, and her mind took a moment to understand. Kane really was gone, left, and panic bubbled up in her for a moment before receding. He left a note, but it didn't feel the same.

"Renaissance?" she mused. *That could be fun.* A smile spread across her face.

CHAPTER 22

With the Wickney Festival Grounds in sight, Malin released her hold on the dark magic spell and descended into a small copse of trees near the entrance. Breyze, who'd been at her side with the wind in his face, tucked himself back into the cloak's concealed inner pockets. Malin held her layered skirts up as her toes reached the ground. When she released the material, it flared and billowed to the ground below her. She ran her hands down the bodice and sighed. Tierney had been right that it was good to return to the ancient dress from time to time. The last occasion they'd had to retrieve the occasion gowns from the wardrobe had been when Queen Maeve had married Alil mac Máta. Malin shook out her arms; the sleeves made of midnight blue velvet fell heavily in large bells from her wrists. Finally, she checked the jeweled circlet topping her head and the pile of braids and curls Tierney had crafted. It seemed they withstood the wind with magical grace, and Malin wondered if Tierney had indeed cast a spell to ensure their hold.

It didn't matter, she decided as she took her first steps toward the entrance to the festival grounds. "Thank the Darkness for practical shoes," Malin said aloud to no one except the trees. How wonderful it was that the shoes of the olden days were made for trekking or, in this case, dancing about one of the bonfires in the fields.

In the distance, the fiddles already wailed on the wind. Malin smiled at the thought of the ceili dances around a blazing fire. Surely, there were some to be had this evening. But she lost all matter of thought when she spotted Kane Macleod near the ticketing building.

She had yet to see him in clothes other than athletic gear or naked, but the sight of him dressed in the traditional fashions from her homeland literally stole her ability to command basic bodily movements. Her feet grew roots, and her throat had sealed itself off. The man standing there was definitely Kane, but his attire was authentic, unlike the partygoers passing him by with curious glances. She wondered who'd dressed him.

Kane wouldn't make eye contact with any of the gawkers. Instead, he continuously scanned the crowd forming a line toward the parking area.

Looking for me? To her own surprise, Malin did hope. She actually hoped his search was all in anticipation of her arrival. When was the last time she looked forward to seeing someone or wanted someone to be just as eager to see her?

Kane dropped his gaze to the ground, shoving his hands into the pockets of his cóta mór and kicking at a rock.

When he lifted his head, he peered over the heads of the crowd and directly at Malin where she watched him from beneath a beech tree. Both smiled as their glances met and retreated like children being coy with one another on the playground. How was it possible that after centuries of existence she'd become a lass admiring the lad from afar? This was like the high school dances she had seen in the 1980s rom-coms. Then again, this was a first date. They had had sex, but this was a first rite of courtship, perhaps? Maybe this could work.

Malin closed her eyes, needing to clear her head. When she opened them, Kane was taking the final steps to meet her under the shelter of the beech.

"Milady." Kane bowed deeply. The motion with one hand wrapped around the front of his waist and the other proffered toward Malin looked a little awkward on the muscular fighter, but he didn't falter. And she was frozen, wondering if she was meant to curtsy to him. The old ways dictated she should, but she didn't bow to men anymore, unless she was aiming for one's cock.

He asked, "Won't you join me for the Eve of Renaissance?"

As he returned to his full height, Malin smiled and placed her hand in his. "It would be my honor, my lord." Her lips twitched, refusing to keep a straight face while addressing him with such a formal and ancient greeting. His lips spread in a smile too.

Together, they broke into laughter.

Looping her hand into the crook of his arm, Kane led Malin toward the gates. "I worried you might not come. And I would look like a fool in this." He motioned to the clothes Conrí had insisted were the epitome of fashion from the Renaissance era in Ireland—Malin's home, he had also noted.

Kane preened as Malin looked him over while they meandered into the festival grounds.

Peering up at him, she said, "I like how you wear a léine and cóta mór."

The rise and fall of her words brought this festival to life. While Malin spoke in the contemporary fashion for the most part, she slid into clearly old habits at times. Kane had no clue what *léine* and *cóta mór* meant, but her lilting voice hearkened back to an era long ago.

"Don't get used to it. I feel like I'm walking around in my gram's nightgown." She snickered, another sound that didn't fit the persona he had seen thus far.

Kane wanted more of it though. This side of her—free from the constant weight he sensed on her shoulders—was cute. They walked past groups of people huddled waiting in line for mead, leather-working shops, and a vendor hocking oversized dill pickles. He held one up to Kane. "What do you call a pickled deer?"

Kane and Malin exchanged dumbfounded glances.

"A dill doe!" the vendor drawled and waved the paper-wrapped pickle toward them both. "A little dill doe for you both?"

"Not tonight." Kane moved them beyond the stand. And when they passed a clothing shop, Kane raised a brow, regarding the differences in their wares and Malin's costume. "Your dress seems heavy?" He wanted to reach out and hold it in his hands—hold her in his hands, and better yet, remove the dress from her body.

"Because it's authentic. It was quite cool in Ireland. Even in the height of summer, nights were brisk. The gúna kept women warm. This one is lightweight." A fiddle started playing some distance ahead, and Malin's face lit with anticipation, her brows wagging. A broad smile crossed her face, and Kane was nearly blinded. "C'mon. The Circassian Circle."

Kane was pulled along before he could ask what the hell she was talking about. As they jogged, the music got louder, a soft drumbeat joining in with the fiddle. They rounded the shops at the end of the row to find people gathering around a small band in a circle and latching hands. The circle moved toward the center then back.

Kane stopped, standing rigidly in place. She wouldn't make him dance, would she? She wouldn't be that cruel. Pinkness flushed his cheeks, and no matter how hard she pulled, he bolted himself in place.

Malin turned. "Let's join?"

"I, ah, don't dance." It was one of the many rules in his life, but he stood by this rule no matter what.

"I've seen you dance in the ring. You're perfectly capable of this. It's simple."

He glanced at the dancing couples. It didn't seem too complicated, but dancing? He narrowed his eyes on Malin. He wanted to keep up the stubbornness and say no, but looking at her, he knew he would do anything for her. He had proved that, and he would prove it again. For the rest of his life. Whatever she wanted, he was her puppet. All she needed to do was pull the strings.

She tugged on his hand. "I'll teach you."

One more look at the dancing people, and then he grumbled, "Fine."

They didn't join the others in the dance proper but stood several paces behind while Malin walked Kane through the steps. They moved forward and backward together, then took turns repeating the same move.

"Now you go forward and turn."

When he went to turn, he stumbled, catching his balance just before he tumbled both of them to the ground. "See, not a good idea." His feet were too large and not quick enough. This definitely wasn't like the cage.

Malin laughed aloud, boisterously and carefree, a sound Kane wanted to hear every day. Music to his ears, it made him want to dance and twirl. Hell, anything to hear that sound again.

"You're doing great," she said. "Just think of it as tracking your opponent in a match."

When they tried again, they moved perfectly together.

She reached both hands toward him. "Now we cross hands and spin."

Amid all the people, Kane only saw Malin; the festival simply provided the background and passed in a blur as they revolved around one another. The band paused, and they came together, both breathless and . . . laughing. The sound exploded like the sun on a clear dawn within his chest.

Kane lifted a hand and slid it along her chin and into the hair behind her ear. "Thank you for meeting me tonight." The words felt raspy in his throat, implying sentiments he had never expressed to anyone. He wanted to say more, but words to express feelings were as foreign as the names of the clothes she had spoken earlier.

Malin's eyes lowered, seeming as if she had lost words too.

He leaned in to softly brush his lips against hers, and she

wrapped her arms around his neck. He was about to throw all caution into the night and kiss her like he truly desired—

"Shit!" Malin jumped backward, fumbling in the pouch she had strapped at her waist.

Belatedly, Kane heard the distinctive buzz of a cell phone. He dropped his head back and groaned.

"They wouldn't call if it wasn't critical." She swiped across the screen and lifted it to her ear. "Yeah?" Her eyes darted back and forth as she listened. Then she slid the phone back into her pouch and looked up at him. Regret and urgency warred with one another in her stare. "I'm sorry." She hopped as if she were about to dart away.

Kane caught her arm. "Where are you going?"

"Semaph—uh, I mean emergency with Conrí and Tierney."

"What emergency?"

She inhaled and shook her head. "Light-wielders. Semaphors. The slime we were fighting when we met."

Realization dawning on him, Kane's eyes popped wide open. The reason Kiera was . . . "I'm coming too." He could help her or . . . whatever.

Malin grabbed on to both his arms and mumbled something. Weight seeped into Kane's feet and legs like he was encased in concrete as Malin added, "I'm sorry, Kane."

He stood, forcefully riveted to the ground, while she jogged away then simply dissipated somewhere in the crowd.

MALIN FLEW FROM THE SOUTHERN borders of Wickney toward the club downtown where the Fae gathered. Not where she wanted to be but where Conrí had told her the fight was going down. Things were brighter and busier near the Local up the street from Wickney University and the Arboretum, so their chances of being seen were too high for her tastes. When she arrived, the streetlamps normally lighting the parking lot behind the Local were dark. At least her coven had taken care of that. Near the dumpsters, flashes of light strobed through the night.

Donning her dark glasses, Malin touched down on the concrete landing outside the back door and ran a hand over the handle. "*Séala*," she whispered. The metal plate around the handle pulsed with the blue hint of Darkness then dimmed. The last time someone had stumbled into one of their battles, she ended up meeting Kane—and he had proven too much of a distraction already.

Malin had taken her eye off her goals, and . . .

A sharp cry pierced the night—Tierney's voice. Shit. Malin ripped away her skirts and hopped over the railing. Thank Aodh, she had worn leggings underneath. Landing, she fell into a crouch, and as she launched toward the dumpsters, she pulled her weapons free.

"Breyze, now," she commanded as she walked toward the battle.

Her dragan's teeth sank into her just below the collarbone and more Darkness filled her body. Breyze freed himself from her cloak and flew at eye level beside her. She called forth her S-blades then and paused just long enough to assess the battle. Tierney, she assumed, lay on the ground. Only one of her legs could be seen clearly. The other seemed broken, twisting away awkwardly from her body. Conrí and Brogan battled two Semaphors each, their dragans striking occasionally, but those weren't good odds for banishing them for good or capturing one to find out where Godric was hiding.

Malin twirled her blades of Darkness as she marched straight for the one Conrí was fighting. Breyze went for Conrí's second. Two were disposable, and then they could focus on the two others. Malin crouched and leaped, revolving with her S-blade and severing the head of her target. It rolled onto the concrete with a thud, then a whoosh-pop as the body steamed away. Breyze latched on to the second's back, sinking his fangs into the slime's neck while Rezei attacked him from the front. Conrí stepped back and skewered it then. Another whoosh-pop, and they were left with two Light-wielders.

"Trap them," Malin uttered to Conrí and glanced over to where Tierney rested on the ground—not conscious at least. Hopefully not worse than that. Fear clogged her throat, but Tierney always ended up all right. She'd pull out of this too. Malin focused on the last two Semaphors.

Tierney's dragan, Ommi, The White, coiled beside her head, at the ready to protect her. His wings were spread as he scanned the action. In the next blink, he struck at Tierney's collar then returned to his vigil. Malin's chest squeezed tightly around her heart. It seemed Ommi was keeping his bonded witch alive with infusions of Darkness.

Brogan blocked one sword of Light, then the other's staff, all the while grinning like a madman.

Conrí leaned into Malin, pointing. "I'll nab the fucker from behind. You remove the poison capsule."

Malin shivered, not wanting to stick her hand in the Semaphor's mouth, but she nodded. They needed to get Tierney to Dark Haven, but Malin had been working for this opportunity for years. If Ommi could keep Tierney safe for a little longer, perhaps they could capture one and finally rid the world of the bastards who had twisted light into something so hateful.

Conrí crouched then sprang at the Semaphor's back. The Semaphor dropped his staff.

"Mal, now." Conrí twisted the thing around to face her, and Malin shoved two fingers inside the slime's mouth, sweeping out an inch-long capsule from between the teeth and cheek. She moaned her disgust, tossed it on the ground, and crushed it with her boot.

"Hold him." She grabbed the other with both arms under the shoulders, locking him in a headlock. "Bro, the pill."

Brogan tossed his weapons to the ground and reached inside, but the Semaphor in Malin's arms started convulsing. Too effin late. She slung the body to the ground with a disgusted grunt. *Whoosh-pop!* And it was gone.

The slime in Conrí's grasp writhed but remained absolutely silent. Malin had never heard any of them except for Godric speak to her and wondered if they could. Or if they were allowed. Maybe they didn't because of the capsule they held tenuously in their mouths. Malin pushed her dark blade into the Semaphor's throat, and it stopped writhing. If it still had blood, it would probably be gushing over the blade. Its eyes went wide with terror.

She held the position for a long time while peering over at her fallen covenmate. "What happened?" Malin finally demanded.

Conrí, still holding the Semaphor, spoke, "One of the Light staffs slashed across her on the back and she crumpled."

Brogan crouched and placed two fingers to the side of Tierney's neck. "Pulse's strong."

"Can we move her?" asked Malin.

Conrí grunted and muscled the Semaphor into submission again. "Maybe we can stabilize her spine with a spell, but it'd be best if we had a litter to carry her."

"Shit!" Malin clenched her fists tighter around the hilts of her blades. "Shit-shit-shit!" She had finally captured one alive, but she had something far more important to deal with.

CHAPTER 23

GODRIC STARED AT THE SCREENS in front of him while his fingers curled slowly until his nails dug into his palms and his fists shook. His knuckles protruded from his skin, taut and white, and he almost shoved his hand into his mouth to stop himself from screaming. *No, Godric told himself, not that way.*

Flexing his fingers, he settled back in the chair and stared back at the screens. Two more dots had disappeared. Two more Semaphors. Two more of the Light-wielders, and all because of that bitch Malin . . . it had to be. Who else? Her other covenmates were fools with dark swords, and if anyone would know, Godric would. He'd trained beside them until he'd returned to the Light himself. They may have had skills, but they were nothing without Malin.

But two more? No, there had been four of his soldiers out there. Then there were none. Disappearing from his screens like they were never there, and even if Godric went to the spot behind the Local, there would be no bodies. Poof! Gone, taken back to the Maker.

Godric was ready to scream again, but then he took a deep breath. And another. And one more for good measure. This was a backward step, but this wasn't the end. There were more lemmings, weaklings he could convert to Semaphors. He would make more. The Maker demanded it. More and more by the day, people were seeing the Light. And if they didn't, Godric had his ways.

Picking up his teacup, he took a long drink. Reveling in the taste. He wished he had coffee, but no, tea was calming. Tea was meant to reduce his stress, and stress seemed to be around every corner. Just as Malin was. The fury returned, but before he could set down the teacup, he crushed it like the dainty thing was made of paper and not porcelain. It balled up into his hand, and the shards clattered to the tile floor with high-pitched pings.

When he released his fingers, blood oozed to the floor, starting off as lazy inklings before blooming into a stream. His blood ran off his hand and leaked like a faucet. Drip. Drop. Drip. He turned over his shoulder, lips peeled back to give an order, but there was no one there. Where was Daniel?

He got up and wrapped his hand in a bandage. Then he stared at his screens again, planning his next move. After several long minutes, he picked up his phone, dialed, and waited for an answer.

"Yeah, boss?" said Daniel.

"Meet me at the church."

CHAPTER 24

KANE'S DAILY ROUTINE—THE PUNCHING BAGS, the treadmills, the shadowboxing—seemed mundane now. Kane hadn't thought about that before because training had been his life. He lived at the gym, and he fought. The same schedule, day in and day out. He knew the route he would jog to EMT as well as what to eat and when to eat, all while thinking about nothing and no one except his next opponent. He would count the days remaining until his next fight, and he would stare at pictures of his opponent, ready to let the beast out of the cage and tear them apart, limb by limb.

That was before he had something else to thrive on. Before Malin.

He rocked back on his heels and looked around EMT. Another normal day. Another boring day. Another day when Malin wasn't beside him where she belonged. She fit so perfectly, like a puzzle piece. He thought about how perfect she was, maybe not for everyone, but for him. He remembered every curve of her body. Her hair wrapped around his fingers. Her body pressed against his own.

"Kane!"

He pulled his head back, giving it a small shake. He hadn't

even realized he had stopped throwing punches at the red punching bag, and he'd spent so long standing there that the bag had stopped swinging.

"Kane!" Broc appeared at his side, something the older man couldn't usually do, as he didn't walk very quickly. Apparently, Broc had been calling him for a while, but Kane couldn't get his head out of his ass long enough to notice. Or Malin's curls.

His cock grew heavy just thinking about it.

"Kane!" Broc called again and Kane blinked out of his daze. The man stood there with his hands crossed over his chest and eyes wide.

Kane heaved a deep breath. "I didn't hear you." He threw his fist forward again, but the heavy bag barely swayed with such a half-assed punch. Kane didn't even feel the jolt run up his bones. It was weak, and he knew it.

"You didn't hear me?" asked Broc with a mocking look. "How didn't you hear me? The whole building heard me. The whole street heard me! The whole of Wickney—"

Kane whipped around to Broc, red flashing across his gaze, but then Kane shook his head again. "I got it."

"Do you?"

"Yes."

"Really? Because I think what you got is that girl in your head. She's messing with your game."

"She's not." But Kane's lie was barely above a whisper.

Broc leaned forward, the man small compared to Kane's height and lean, compared to Kane's girth.

Like a twig to be snapped, whispered the beast in Kane's head.

Before Kane could pull back, Broc reached up, locking his hand around the back of Kane's neck, forcing Kane to look deeply into Broc's eyes. "Listen to me, Kane. Get out of your head. You got one goal. Hear me? Vegas. Money. Remember that? Lose the chick and focus. It's the only way you're getting out of Wickney and out of this life."

The words pushed through Kane's brain fog without him

quite understanding, but suddenly, they stirred something in him. Deep and dark and so low came a growl, like a monster in the shadows that he thought had been there as a child. The beast beat against his stomach, and blood rushed past his ears, sounding like waves against a shore.

"That girl is good for nothing. She's a waste of your time and energy. She might be a good fuck, but you can't let it take your eye off the prize."

Kane wondered if Broc even heard himself. Broc had never spoken this way—or had he and Kane never noticed? Broc sounded like a monster, suggesting he use a woman and throw her away. But hadn't Kane done that in the past? Tossing women aside after he got what he wanted, never to speak to them again, and forgetting their names and faces?

Rage built in him, and Kane latched on to Broc like his trainer had latched on to him. They were intertwined, but Broc didn't fit like Malin did. How Broc spoke about her like she was a piece of trash. Broc talked about her as a passing phase instead of the soul that now kept Kane's heart beating.

Then again, Malin hadn't texted Kane back. It had been days since she'd left him standing in the middle of the Renaissance Festival alone . . . on their first real date. Gruesome, long, and lonely days followed without her, and she hadn't returned. After all that talk about him and his family becoming like them, she left him here in Wickney! She left him alone! He couldn't get back into the Penumbra without her, or back to Kiera, even though he had gone to the wall every night, waiting hours for her to step through. He had waited until morning light. Yet she never came.

She had abandoned him. Just like his father had.

"Do you hear me, Kane?" asked Broc, pupils enlarged until they took up his whole irises. "Are you listening to me? Drop the chick. She's only causing you pain. She'll cost you everything soon."

"No!" roared Kane, pushing Broc away. The older man stumbled, but Kane was there to grab him. Kane's massive hands grabbed Broc's skinny, flabby arms, and his fingers curled just below his twig-like shoulders.

"Kane!"

That wasn't his name.

Tunnel vision blocked out the bright fluorescent lights. His eyes narrowed on Broc, who wailed in protest at the top of his lungs. His mouth swallowed his face, eyes darting outward. Kane felt hands on him, not Broc's flimsy hands but strong hands.

Malin?

He turned, but it wasn't Malin. It was Smalls, the huge man with the oxymoronic name. But at the moment, just like his name, Smalls was *small* to Kane. Tiny. No more than an ant to be squished under Kane's boot. And Kane could do just that with The Rage's help.

Smalls kept pulling at Kane, yelling something unclear with hot breath pulsating on Kane's skin. What a rancid scent that oozed from his mouth. Kane's nostrils twitched. The Rage rattled Kane's rib cage, like a gorilla attacking the bars of his prison. It couldn't be contained, yet Smalls attacked Kane again.

Snap!

So quick. So easy.

"Kane!"

Kane dropped the twigs within his grasp, and then he turned to Smalls, who was backing away quite sheepishly for a fighter. His feet dragged against the ground; his bare hands pushed forward to ward Kane away. Smalls backed away. Smart man, yet not so smart to have confronted the boiling Rage. Kane laughed, and he didn't recognize the laugh that echoed out from his mouth. It sounded hollow. Evil. Flowing past his ears, it sounded so wrong.

The beast? The Rage?

More alive inside him than it had ever been. It wanted Kane to know that it was growing, preparing to swallow him alive. Kane's other self—the one who turned his saliva to acid. His sight darkened and hazed over in red like blood running over his eyes. It rattled his ribs, pounding his heart until his chest felt ready to explode. His mind switched to automatic mode with one thought chanting in his mind.

Fight. Fight. Fight.

Suddenly, Kane stumbled back, heels dragging against the floor, and then he fell to the ground, landing with a splat like a raw egg. His shell cracked, armor broken and chipping off piece by piece. He stared up at the ceiling with his heart thundering in his chest, and the dark tunnels closed off his vision until he was blinded.

He was back in the real world after being somewhere else. Not the Penumbra, but somewhere darker, if that was possible. What could be darker and drenched in blood? The buzzing stopped, and he was left with the dull echo in his head—and Smalls yelling, "What the fuck, Kane? What is wrong with you?"

Slowly, Kane pushed himself into a sitting position, and he thought he was going to be sick. Bile clogged his throat, coated his tongue with acid. He looked around, but the keening sound came from behind him. Turning around, Kane was struck with horror and frozen in a kneeling position.

Broc lay on the floor of EMT, groaning and rolling around. His arms tangled like elderly tree roots. The man was red in the face and quaking with pain. Beside him, Smalls was kneeling with his cell phone in his hand and yelling into the phone, demanding, "Get here now. We need an ambulance. Please. Help."

Kane stared, his mind was slow and body slower. What had happened? Deep in Kane's gut, he knew it had been him. "What happened?" he mumbled.

Smalls glared. It was the most anger Kane had ever seen in Smalls, and Kane had sparred with the man a hundred times. Smalls's hand patted Broc's balding head like a parent would do to a child in pain. Broc cried, tears running down his face like streams, and his face was a deep crimson, as if all the blood had flooded to it.

Kane fought the stirring Rage inside. The sick thing that lived inside him, that was part of him, wanted to come out at the thought of blood.

The beast wanted to taste the blood.

Kane's vision blurred, and he swore as the red cloud passed his eyes again, flooding his head. The Rage was taking over. The heat built up in his chest, spreading across his neck and arms like wildfire. Kane was ready to start swinging.

And when Kane blinked, he saw the coach lying on the floor, writhing in pain like the beast wanted. Like Kane and The Rage wanted. To have revenge and finally take back his life from the coach, who so wrongfully stole it from Kane when he was a boy. Kane couldn't fight back then and hadn't known what was happening until he was too late—but he was frozen. Couldn't do anything. He had to prove he was a man by doing what the coach said. He always did what the coach said, and—

Kane fell back, landing on his ass with a grunt, and the beast disappeared like a puff of smoke. It released from his lungs with a deep breath of air, stale with sweat. Kane focused on Broc again—his trainer, the only one who understood and who had been there for him.

And Kane had hurt him. Like he had hurt Kiera. Kane would hurt Malin too, if given the chance. He didn't want to, but it was only a matter of time. Kane hurt everyone around him. It was the only thing he was good at.

THE STERILE SCENT BURNED KANE'S nostrils and fried his brain. He scrunched his nose and sniffled, taking in the smell, but it did little to clear his thoughts. His nose only ran more. His eyes teared, scorching hot, and he rubbed the tears away. A few dribbled off the tip of his nose. His eyes blurred, the white screen of his cell phone obscured, and he blinked the tears away again, looking up to clear his head.

When he looked down again, he focused on Malin's cell phone number. The nine digits were seared into his mind. He would know her number for the rest of his life, like it was tattooed upon his skin or a song that was stuck in his head. The cell phone, though, held the digits for him to stare at, which he had been doing since arriving at Wickney General Hospital after Broc had been taken there via ambulance. This was where Kiera should've gone, but no, she was in the Penumbra. Taken there, gone from his normal life, and he couldn't get to her without Malin.

Leaning his head back, he hit the cool wall with a thud. He felt a jolt of pain run across his skull, but he deserved it. He deserved the pain after what he had done. He deserved to be blind and forever alone. He had hurt the one person who had pulled him from the streets. And how had Kane thanked him? Two. Fucking. Broken arms.

Broc was the one who had always been there for him, and the only one Kane could always trust. Kane should've been in jail, but no police had come for him. And Kane sat freely in one of the white-walled hospital waiting rooms with people coming and going. Nurses in scrubs came to get family, taking them to see their loved ones. Kane waited to be taken to Broc; he needed to apologize and explain.

But what could he say? What words did Kane have to say? Sorry wasn't enough, and would an explanation be any better? The whole story would sound crazy.

Yeah, Broc, so Malin is this dark witch, and she took me to this dark other world, and she has Kiera, and I can't get back there, and I'm fucking gone over her. There's all this magic shit, and I can't pronounce half of it. But Malin has me wrapped around her finger and—

Kane dropped his head into his hands. He wouldn't believe such a tale from Broc if the roles were reversed.

Oh yeah, Broc, and my mother, who is blind, and my sister are both all those things too.

Broc would cut his losses. He'd been banking on Kane's big fight, but the trainer still had EMT, so he'd be fine, financially. But Kane would never fight again.

And really, should Kane fight again? He balled his hands into fists, knuckles poking from his skin, and the phone shook in his hand. He waited for a crack. His Rage craved it, the beast in him coiling around his gut and squeezing it like Kane squeezed the phone. Waiting for something to break.

To go crazy and let The Rage take over his life, which would happen if he returned to the Penumbra, or to let the blindness overtake his life, which was what happened to his mother? The latter was better after what happened to Kiera. Kane shouldn't have let it get far enough to hurt Broc. He shouldn't have gotten out of hand with Kiera! What else would he do? Who else would he hurt? Would his mother be next? Would he kill someone on the street who looked at him the wrong way? What about Malin?

His finger hovered over Malin's cell number. He should delete it and erase it from his mind. But he couldn't. Kiera was still in the Penumbra. It was his fault that she was there, and he had to get her out. No matter how much space he should put between himself and Malin, he couldn't. Not yet.

ONLY FAMILY MEMBERS WERE ALLOWED in the room, so Kane left with a deflated heart and self-hatred racing through his veins. When he got back to his apartment, he fought the urge to drive his fist into his bedroom mirror. He caught sight of himself then. The monster that he was. The beast lurked below, in the depths of his eyes, and soon, the beast would take over. It clawed at the surface. He tore himself away from the mirror.

In the kitchen, he pulled out a bottle of whiskey that he had been given after one of his wins. A thin layer of dust coated the glass bottle, transferring to Kane's fingertips, and he stared at it for a pregnant moment with his tongue heavy as lead and stomach churning. He didn't drink, only a Sazerac every now and then after a win. It was part of his training, but his training had only taken him so far. To destruction. And his thoughts wanted to destroy him and everything around him. The beast purred, a slither like a serpent's tongue reaching up through his throat, and he drowned the serpent with the whiskey. It seared his throat and settled into his belly, making him flinch at the taste. He heaved a breath.

Kane thought he was going to be sick, but then he felt the whiskey's effects, sending him swaying where he stood. He took another gulp straight from the bottleneck and then placed the bottle down on the kitchen counter, leaving it there as he staggered over to his bed. Without changing out of his clothes, Kane fell into the blankets.

They smelled of Malin, and when he pulled a blanket over him, he pretended she was wrapped around him. He remembered her pressed against him. Her hair lying against his face. Her hand touching him. Before he knew it, his hand was sliding down his body, underneath his tented gym shorts, and grabbing his member. It throbbed with a heartbeat that seemed all its own.

He leaned back into the bed and shut his eyes, rocking back and forth as he imagined Malin on top of him, riding him like he was a stallion. He remembered the perkiness of her breasts, her nipples as hard as diamonds, and he ran a thumb over his own nipple. His hands were too calloused for it to feel right, but he gritted his teeth when he imagined her touch. He imagined how tight she was and how she took a hold of him, her folds accommodating his girth, and he rubbed harder. His asscheeks flexed as his hips jerked, and he reached to the ceiling as he imagined her there. Right there, and he was driving himself into her. Impaling her. It wasn't enough, but it could be. So he rubbed himself harder—and there!

He let out a grunt as dark spots blotted his vision. Exhaustion itched at his chest, clawing at his neck and making his eyelids heavy. He grabbed a tissue off his nightstand, cleaning up his hot cum, and then threw the tissue off the side of the bed. Not wanting the feeling to end, he rolled over and imagined his cock still buried between Malin's thighs. He fell asleep with a smile upon his face.

SLEEP WAS SHORT-LIVED, AND WHEN he awoke, he felt more tired than before. He skimmed a hand across the bed, hopeful, but it was empty. And cold. Even in the July humidity, it was icy cold. Rolling onto his back, he stared up at the popcorn ceiling and forced himself to move. If he stayed here, then there was a chance he would never get up again.

After he showered and changed, night was beginning to descend over Wickney, so Kane headed to the West End. There was a line waiting to get past the bouncer at Club Infinity, but Kane's star power allowed him to cut the line. He hadn't tried to hide himself, wanting Malin to be able to easily find him. Although, if Malin *was* looking for him, which seemed doubtful at this point, she wouldn't have any trouble. She knew where he lived, where he trained, and even where his family lived. No. She wasn't looking for him anymore.

Kane hulked his shoulders forward as fans pushed in on him, asking for photos and autographs, saying that they were going to tag him. Another guy wanted to fight, but Kane stepped away, letting the black-clad bouncers deal with it. Men always wanted to fight him, thinking they were the next hot shit, but as the hottest shit, Kane could wipe the floor with the untrained men. It wouldn't even require The Rage.

At the bar, the bartender Quinn set down his favored, amber-colored spirit in front of him, but Kane didn't pick it up. He hadn't won a fight and shouldn't be drinking. But did he have cause to care now? His eyes scanned the crowd. In the darkness with flashing neon lights, bodies ground against each other, slick with sweat and loud with screams. Glasses in the air reflected the light, blinding him. Kane turned his head away, but once the moment passed, he turned back.

What had Malin called them? Semaphors? Could he spot them too? If he hunted what Malin hunted, maybe he'd find her too. But none of the men here seemed to fit. Men pushed toward him. Perhaps they just wanted to get to the bar, but it felt like they were looking for a fight. Were they insane enough to nominate themselves as tribute to his Rage?

Kane ignored the teeming crowd and searched. Whatever was special about the Semaphors, Kane didn't see it. He couldn't tell if any were here or who might not be human. It didn't stop him from looking. For them or for Malin.

CHAPTER 25

LEAVING TIERNEY'S SIDE PHYSICALLY HURT. For the last few days—since Tierney's injury—Malin hadn't left her friend's side. This was Malin's fault. She should've been there! Instead, she had been gallivanting with Kane. She had allowed herself to be distracted. And for what? *A few good effs*. No, *good* wasn't the right word—they were amazing. Lustful. Ecstatic. Orgasms that sent her soaring into the sky.

But it had to come to an end. Tierney wouldn't have been hurt if Malin had been there like she was supposed to be. She wasn't supposed to be distracted. And because Tierney was hurt, there would be no hunting until she was better. That saved time for Malin to have sex with Kane, but she shook her head. Those thoughts would get her killed. Or worse, others killed. Tierney was lucky, but Emrys wasn't sure when Tierney would wake up or get better. Myla's death weighed on her shoulders, and Malin had been telling herself not to get distracted. She knew how she much she had failed.

Again.

She stood at the window to the Fold, hand raised toward the Awen, but she hesitated to go through. Suddenly, Breyze appeared beside her, ready to snake under her cloak, but she shook her head, fingers running over her dragan's head. "Wait here," she said as Breyze leaned into her touch.

Breyze gave a shake of his head, like a toddler having a tantrum over being left behind.

"Yes," she said. "I'll be back soon. I'm not hunting."

Breyze's eyes slit, staring at her, measuring her, and she rolled back her shoulders and sighed. Finally, he seemed to believe her and flew back a few steps. He would stay behind, but she wished he wouldn't. She wished for him to dive through the window with her, but at what cost? The cost weighed on her mind, her shoulders, until her feet dragged her through the Fold. Then she stepped out on the other side.

After a moment, her eyes adjusted to the Daylight Realm. The thunder of music pumped out of Infinity, rattling the concrete street underneath her feet. The brick of the buildings seemed to chatter like teeth in the cold. She stayed close to the Awen, almost like she was about to turn back, but then she felt the buzzing in her pocket, an onslaught humming against her thigh. She reached into her pocket and pulled out her cell phone.

Sliding up the screen, at least a dozen messages lit up the display, backlogged because the cell phone didn't work in the Penumbra. They were all from Kane.

"Hey. Can we talk?"

"I know ur probs busy, but I really need to speak to you."

"It's about Kiera. I'm worried about her. I haven't heard about it."

"Malin, are you there?"

She slid her finger up, scrolling past those messages, but there were more. Shorter. Longer. Typed-out messages that she couldn't allow herself to read now. If she did, she might lose all of her courage. Closing out of the messages, she opened her GPS tracker and found his phone nearby. It was almost too easy. Like he was waiting for her.

Slipping the phone back into her pocket, Malin raised her

head and took in a breath. She would need all the strength she had for these next moments.

Inside Infinity, bodies brushed up against Malin, and she did her best not to jerk back. The place was packed, brimming with cowans. Her eyes scanned the surroundings, looking for Semaphors like this was any other night and she was on a hunt, but then she reared back her head. She only had eyes for one man tonight: Kane. Her small stature didn't allow her to see over the wave of heads, so she pushed her way through the crowd and over to the bar.

The long counter took up the back wall of Infinity with the other half of the club used for dancing. Booths sat on along the far wall, and shadows hung over the booths like dark clouds. She saddled up at the bar, trying to blend in with the cowans around her. A man brushed up against her, but she didn't move for him. Her fingers flexed for her weapon, especially as the man pushed against her, but no, cowans were rather weak. And she wasn't staying long.

Down the bar, Malin spotted Kane's large body leaned back against the counter, elbows on the bar, and his head peeking over the crowd. An amber-colored drink sat off to the side, filled to the brim, with an orange slice for garnish. Kane's head turned, and Malin ducked her head, turning away with her hair acting as a curtain. When she popped her head up again, Kane's head was turned away. She sighed and reached into her pocket. She was a coward, she knew, but couldn't do anything about it. Just looking at him made her core heat, her knees quake, and her mouth run dry. Was that sweat upon her upper lip? She grew hungry for him, and her lips parted.

Her cell phone was a brick in her hand, weighing her down. Bright lights flashed on the screen, and she squinted, waiting for her eyes to adjust. Her fingers slid over the screen. Autocorrect was her friend when it finished her thought as her vision blurred, tears clawing at her eyes. She read it once more, heart thundering and her stomach clenching. Almost every part of her didn't want to do this, heart reaching for Kane as her eyes glanced toward him and her body ached for him, but her mind kept her to the task. Her thumb hit the send button, and then she was gone, pushing out of the crowd and into the night air.

She gulped it down. The heat upon her skin was like wildfire, and she stumbled over to the brick wall, holding herself up. Her chest was ready to collapse in on itself. Like she lost Myla, she was losing Kane, but this time it was her choice.

KANE BLINKED AT THE CELL phone again, rereading the message because the first few times didn't make sense.

MALIN: "KIERA'S NOT AWAKE YET. SOMEONE WILL CONTACT YOU ON THIS PHONE WHEN IT'S SAFE TO BRING HER THROUGH. EMRYS THINKS IT'LL ONLY BE A COUPLE OF DAYS. I'M SORRY, BUT I CAN'T CONTINUE THIS THING WITH YOU. M."

Then he was gone in a flash. Cash down on the counter and running out of Infinity. Was Malin here? She had to be. Where else? He pushed through the crowd with others yelling, "Hey!" The people were like feathers against his strength as his muscles strained against their confines. He burst from Infinity and turned to the alleyway. In a few steps, he was shrouded in darkness.

"Malin?" Kane's tongue was heavy in his mouth. He squinted. "Malin?"

Deathly silence filled the alleyway, sending goosebumps over his skin. The darkness was unnatural, with the orange hue from the streetlamps polluting the darkness. Wickney was never this dark. He stepped further into the alleyway, his hand balling into fists, and he turned his head, listening. The blood rushed past his ears, but his heartbeat seemed to slow. The adrenaline pumped through him.

The Rage lurked in the depths, stirring and chomping at the bit to be released. The beast was hungry.

Were there Semaphors here? No—there weren't any light flashes cutting through the darkness. Was he in danger? Was Malin?

There was a change in the air, and before he thought, he punched out his fist, landing a blow into someone's chest. A crunch—almost. His heartbeat picked up, a drum in his head, brain rattling in his skull. He was pulling back his fist when his other pushed forward, but he was only met with air. Another whoosh of air tingled along his arms and legs, so quick. A cold brush in the humidity.

"Ka—"

The beast ordered, *Fight!* Red, hot Rage flooded Kane's veins, drumming through with every quickened heartbeat.

That was all Kane could do. He couldn't see through the murky darkness. It was like he was back in the Penumbra for the first time, before the potion that allowed him to see through the darkness. He wished he had that drink now. The beast was hungry for it.

He threw another punch forward, and his hand tangled in hair. Caught in a ponytail. While he considered pulling it, the other fighter used their hair as a weapon. He was pulled toward them, and the other fighter kicked. The blow landed on Kane's stomach, and a puff of air escaped his lips. He had tensed his muscles, like he did in every fight, but that kick had serious weight to it. It almost hurt, but he couldn't feel it through the adrenaline pumping through his system.

The leg had pulled back, and he prepared himself for the next blow. The darkness affected him more than whoever was around him, and the beast roared inside of him with a wave of blood rushing to his head. When the next kick came, he was ready, grabbing a hold of the small calf in his hands and gripping it so tight that he could snap it in half.

Like twigs, growled the beast.

Kane startled, his hands releasing. He had snapped Broc's

arms like twigs; the memory of that sickening crack made his stomach hurt now.

The firm and petite leg was pulled from his grasp. A whoosh of air as it tilted and spun away from him. A tickle upon his skin from hair. He reached out to grasp it, then grabbed the whole head that was attached. The person was smaller than he imagined. Skin softer than he thought as he wrapped his other hand around their frail neck, wanting to hear that *snap!*

The beast wanted it, calling up The Rage with the coach mocking him and telling him to stop being a pussy.

"Kane!" a female voice called. "Stop! Kane!"

The person had the heartbeat of a frightened rabbit, so quick. And their hot breath was upon his skin, leaving goosebumps in its wake.

"Kane!" The voice was music to his ears.

His heartbeat slowed, no longer a drum but a steady thrum in his veins. The darkness covered his eyes, but it seemed to clear ever so slightly. He could make out the outline around the person in front of him. While the rest of him slowed, his mind clearing, his hands still stuck around the person's neck, ready to snap. The beast wanted to hear the crunch.

A change in the air, and a hand slapped across his face. Kane stumbled back, heels dragging against the concrete. His face burned, and the tension began to fill his body again, like a snake coiled around his chest and across the muscles of his back— and he swore something was on his back. When he reached, he found nothing there. The beast growled deep inside him—what was on his back?—but he shook off The Rage. Though it clung with its nails digging in and wanting the taste of blood.

"Kane." The voice was soft, a brush against his ears, echoing out from the darkness hanging around. "Kane . . . is that you?"

He said nothing, unsure if he could.

A hushed whisper in a language he didn't know, but the word was almost familiar. With all the magic that Malin had been performing on him. The darkness seeped away like water running into drains. It fell to the ground and rushed away into the corners of his vision. He wanted to watch it—to understand it—but then his eyes found Malin with the cloak around her body. Her hair haphazardly fallen from her bun. Her breathing was heavy, a flush on her cheeks and working down her neck. He wanted to see what was hidden beneath her collar, though he had seen before. He couldn't ever see enough. Ever touch enough.

"Kane." Malin stayed there with her hands up, palms raised like she was trying to calm a wild animal.

Him. He was the wild animal.

Something low in his body pulled, pants tight against his crotch, and he wondered why he was getting a hard-on during a fight. That had never happened before. But he couldn't stop the blood rushing from his head to his cock, and it wanted to spring to attention.

Kane sprung forward, his hands aimed at her throat again. Malin jumped back, quick like a dancer, but he was prepared. Just like he would be when going in for an attack when in the cage. He locked his hands around her neck, fingers intertwining in her hair, and pulled her up until her body was smashed against his. He held her there as he kissed her deeply, forcing his tongue into her mouth, parting her lips and her clenched teeth until they finally released. His thumb pressed into the frantic pulse on her neck, and she grunted, trying to push him away. He kissed her deeper. Harder. Only breathing enough to speak one word.

"Malin."

CHAPTER 26

MALIN'S NAME SOUNDED PRIMAL ON Kane's lips, and it melted her inside—hot lava flowing through her veins and making her forget why she had come to the Daylight Realm. What was it? *Oh, yes.* She needed to break it off. But she needed this right now more, if only a way to escape from the shit that had her all twisted up inside.

"How do you effin do this to me?"

His beast—the berserker, she was now certain—answered to her touch, turning away from frenzied hysteria as her kiss brought him back from the brink of insanity.

Still kissing her with the savagery of a wild bear, he backed her against the wall, but she didn't care. In fact, it made her wetter for him—only him. His hands fell to the buckles at her belt, working it loose, then they reached inside her waistband and popped the button. He growled in her ear, and Malin had a flicker of reasonable thought.

She put both palms against his chest and pushed away. The kiss broke, and both their chests heaved as they tried to breathe.

"Kane, I . . . can't."

"Can't what?" He dipped his head to her neck and bit the

sensitive skin below her earlobe. She moaned, chills racing all over her skin. She wanted it—*him*—despite herself.

"No!" She pushed him harder, but he was unmovable. Like a ton of boulders, his skin as smooth as marble, his abs chiseled like something out of a Greek museum. Then, he lifted his head, eyes glassed over.

Malin panted. "I can't do this. Too much is on the line."

His eyes flared with electric blue intensity.

Kane's face twisted, his gaze losing all connection to the here and now. He bared his teeth, and his body went rigid as if he were about to fly into the berserkergang, the state she had witnessed at EMT—surely the reason he had earned the name Kane "The Rage" Macleod.

She watched. Torn. Her body ached for him, throbbed to feel his touch, and he could light her on fire. However, her mind told her to stop. Push him away and kick his ass if necessary. She needed to focus. This wasn't good for her or the mission, but what was the mission without Kane? What was life?

"Effin-A!" Malin grabbed his hoodie and pulled him to her, crashing their mouths together. She had no choice left to get out of this situation. Her inner walls contracted with the need for him to be inside her, stretching her so deliciously. She hated it, but she couldn't stop if she wanted to. If she ran now, she would fall into an abyss and Kane would be lost to his Rage.

The legends said this was the only way when in the throes of berserkergang. It was sex or destruction for both.

In their case, she wondered if it would be destruction by sex.

Their hands roamed, and Kane pushed her pants down around her ankles where they stopped because of her boots. He didn't bother with those but stepped into the circle created by her legs and pants, hooked the material with his heel, slid his hands under her ass, and lifted her until her legs surrounded him. His cock met her entrance and pressed into her just by the tip.

Aodh, she prayed, *I love the feel of him. I love—NO! I effin can't! Sex, Mal. Only sex.*

"So wet," Kane hissed in her ear. "Dripping all over me."

The girth of him pressed deeper into her and she gasped, clutching his shoulders. "Wait. Slow down." She felt certain he would rip her in two if he kept that pace.

He paused and gritted his teeth, his look that of intolerable pain. His shoulders expanded with his breath, contracted, and expanded again. "Mal, I can't hold on any longer. It's fuck or fight," he said through clenched teeth.

Malin bit her bottom lip until she tasted the metallic tang of blood. She then reached around his neck and took his hood in both fists. "Fuck, then."

She pulled his mouth to hers as he slammed into her, erasing everything, stretching her with his girth to the very limits. Destroying her in the best possible way. Fireflies started flittering in the dark edges of her vision, and she was flying—or falling. She couldn't tell which. Her body locked, her inner walls spasming uncontrollably. She was burning alive, but then the cool wave of her release flooded her veins, soothing the scorch from the inside out.

And Kane kept pushing her faster—harder.

*M*INE! KANE'S BEAST ROARED AS Malin's body seized around his cock.

Her backed up against the building was one of the best damn sights he had ever experienced, but Malin's orgasms drove him absolutely insane with heightened need for her. She was still locked around him, milking him, helpless to her pleasure, and it was the best damn thing in this world or her world or whatever worlds existed that he knew nothing about.

Not. Letting. Go. Ever, The Rage insisted.

Kane pounded into her with all the fury and passion that had been building over the days he hadn't seen her. If she wouldn't talk to him, let their bodies fucking talk because they knew each other's language.

Her hands held on to him in a death grip, and his body worked, punishing her. He took her. Claimed her. Marked her as his.

"Mine!" Kane growled aloud.

She mewled and fell into him at last, spent, but he was having none of that. He thrusted and retreated and thrust forward again until she quickened once more and began to match his rhythm.

Faster. And she let out the most exotic, erotic noises. She whispered something, but he couldn't think enough to hear what. His ears rang a little, but he pushed with more fury.

Harder. Their bodies met and repelled like magnets.

More. His lower belly clenched.

She cried out.

He grabbed on to her hips, moving into her lightning fast as fire coursed through his veins, ready to—

He pushed once more, exploding in ecstasy as she screamed with her own pleasure.

"Miiiiiiiiiiiiiiiiiiiiiiiine!" he yelled, but at the same time, his beast inside purred with a satisfied *Yooouuuurs.*

Kane was too overloaded to consider that as his hands caught his weight on the brick wall behind Malin. He buried his head in her neck and quivered with the aftershocks. And she leaned into him, fitting like a perfect puzzle piece into his body. With her back still against the wall, his entire body shielded her, and she clung to him with legs around his waist and arms encircling his neck.

He moved a hand under one thigh and slid another under her thick hair. She was so small, yet so strong. Kane tilted her head back. Her hair fell over his arm, and he took in a deep breath of her scent. Now mingled with sex and sweat. An orgasmic sweetness.

"Kane," she said, her voice sounding like wind howling through a graveyard. Hollow. "Put me down."

Kane looked down at how she was still tied around him, pants still binding her ankles behind his back. His body was spent, and his beast soothed, so he did as she asked, refusing to think about the implications in her tone.

They both dressed hastily, then she came forward and placed a hand on his chest, her hair swept over one shoulder and still exposing the length of her neck. Quickened heartbeats passed, and then she wrenched herself free of him. She marched five paces away with her back turned to him, and he caught sight of his handprint on her skin, five red splotches on her neck like tattoos. Or stains. Her arms were marked too with his large prints, red marks where his fingers had dug in. He bet his same handprints covered her thighs and hips and everywhere he had gripped her.

He had claimed her as his own, but at what cost for her skin to be marred? For her hair to be pulled, strands still within his grasp. He held up his hand, letting the dark threads fall to the cobblestones at his feet. She wouldn't even look at him.

Kane leaned against the wall for support but wished he could fall into the bricks and be buried alive with the humiliation that he felt. The beast had taken over, The Rage clawing its way out and claiming what it wanted. Kane had lost control. Just like he had done when he snapped Broc like a twig, but Malin hadn't snapped . . . right?

No, he thought. He was very wrong. He had broken her. Just like Coach Robbins had done to him. Hurt Kane and made him feel like a weakling. Nothing. And Kane couldn't fight back then, because if he did, it only got worse. No one would've believed Kane, and no one wanted to believe Kane. Coach Robbins had been creating heroes in high school, getting kids scholarships into colleges and getting them out of Wickney. Coach Robbins was everything a coach should've been: supportive, respected, responsible. But the coach was everything he was not supposed to be too. Now, as an adult, Kane knew what happened to him was wrong, but at the time, the coach wanted to make Kane a man. Said he wanted Kane to be the best wrestler he could be. The coach made Kane a fighter.

A survivor.

Kane reached his hand forward, wanting to take Malin's shoulder and whip her around. Force her to look at him, though he couldn't look at himself.

What he had done to her . . . what The Rage had done to her. Was it just like what the coach had done? Was Kane no better than Coach Robbins? Would he haunt Malin like the coach haunted him?

With a blow of deep and hot breath, he spun around and ground his forehead into the brick wall of Club Infinity, the music still thumping inside. He couldn't face Malin, and he wouldn't. Where was the darkness when he needed it?

MALIN SHOULD HAVE HATED THE primal thing that had taken Kane over. She certainly hated herself for it. Even knowing what was happening to him, she didn't stop it. The berserker had come out—*The Rage,* it seemed to be called. Instead of calming him, she had gone with it. She couldn't face him after letting that happen. Some part of her wanted to see how far it could be pushed. How far Kane would go. What could happen. All she knew about it was what she had read in books. Was it wrong to want to see it with her own eyes?

Yes, she answered herself because he wasn't in control. *Because instead of helping him, I used him.*

How was she supposed to face him after that? After using his body to pleasure herself. Her core still throbbed. The heat was fire across her skin, starting between her thighs and moving up her bones until she felt electrified. She had jerked like in a seizure, all while the flames built, transferring between their bodies.

She knew about pleasure. And pain. She had done this before, and she should have learned her lesson from her time with Godric and from the pleasure and pain he had brought into her life.

Godric . . . a name that brought a different kind of heat into her soul. A different kind of blindness. It made her want to throw a fist into the brick wall and scream to the heavens above. This was on her; she had gotten distracted yet again. With Godric, Myla had been the one to pay—with her life and the life of her dragan. Malin had been obsessed with Godric and what he did to her body, but she could no longer remember his smile because, looking back, it had never seemed genuine. He always had these sayings that were now stale in her mind. He didn't seem lifelike, like he was an actor trying to be a bigger name than his talent justified. Yet she had fallen hard and fast for him, so Malin had herself to blame for her sister's death.

With Godric still alive, she needed to focus. He was her one and only true pleasure and pain, and she couldn't stop until she experienced the pleasure of taking his life, of watching him gasp for his last breath. And only then—maybe—could she allow herself to find happiness again. These specks of happiness with Kane were fleeting moments haunted by Godric. Would she still be haunted by Godric after she ended him? Now too, did she have to add what she had done to Kane as a mark on her soul?

"Malin."

Her name from Kane's lips was like a breath of chilled air against her exposed skin, cooling the flames that threatened to gobble her up whole. But she tilted her head back as if she could lean into his breath. As if she could feel his touch again. His body pressed against hers and him buried deeply inside her.

Snapping out of it, she gave a hard jerk of her head and spun around, facing him and what she had done head-on. She nearly crumbled when she saw tears in his eyes, water oozing from the corners and running off the tip of his nose. While he faced her, he wouldn't look at her. His eyes cast downward. The large man had curled in on himself, looking more like a scared boy than the fighter that she had grown to know.

What had she done?

"I'm sorry," Kane said, voice cracking like shattering glass, and he turned his face away, his neck craning impossibly. His whole body trembled.

"What?" she asked, unsure if she heard him right. She didn't understand. How? What? Why would he be apologizing to her?

He sniffed, clearing his throat, and after a few seconds, he turned back to her, looking straight into her eyes. She wasn't sure if she could survive the pain that she saw in the depths. "I'm sorry," he repeated.

Malin took a step forward, reaching out her hand, but he turned his face away. She dropped her hand to the side, feeling like she had been slapped. Tears sprung into her eyes, but she blinked them away, hiding in the curtain of her hair. This wasn't the time for her to be crying after what she had done.

"I didn't even ask," he said, choking on his words that clogged his throat. "I'm sorry. I shouldn't have. I didn't mean to. I just attacked you."

She looked back at him. "Attacked?"

The word made him flinch, and he turned his body away from her.

This time, she didn't hesitate. She grabbed Kane's hand and pulled him back to her. He wasn't easy to turn. He may have had height and weight on her, but she had enough strength. She made his body face hers, even if his face pointed down the alleyway, toward the exit and onto the street. Would he run from her? She wouldn't allow it until they spoke.

"You don't have a reason to apologize," she said. "I wasn't attacked."

"But I—"

"No," Malin snapped, anger bubbling in her gut and threatening to ignite. She was gasoline fueled; one spark and she might explode. "What? You don't think I can defend myself? That I couldn't take you?"

He sputtered, "I didn't say that." He blinked rapidly, eyelashes like a flutter of wings. "I mean, could you? That fight—"

"I was trying to stop you," she said. "I could've beat you. Easily. You wouldn't be able to get back on your feet. You would be going to one of your cowan doctors. You would be—" She cut herself off and took a deep breath. "That was sex. The best sex I've had in years." He raised his head while she thought, *The only sex I've had in years.*

"Sex?" he repeated, like he was hearing the word for the first time.

"Yes!" she burst out. What else could it be? No, she didn't want to think about that. She didn't want to answer that. But if she did . . . she gave a jerk of her head and said, "It was sex! Consensual. And that's all it can be."

"Sex?"

"I can't give anything else. I turned my back for a moment, and Tierney was injured. I have to stay on task."

She turned her head away, wanting to offer more but unable. If she opened herself up as much as she had with Godric, there would be a repeat of what happened with Myla. Tierney was almost the repeat, because where had Malin been when Tierney was injured? With Kane. If this thing between them continued, where would Malin find herself the next time her covenmates needed her? With Kane. She had to put a stop to it, but the sex . . . she grew warm thinking about it. She licked her bottom lip, still tasting him.

He nodded. "I think we need to talk." He sounded serious, so deadly serious, but just as exhausted and hurt. His lips pursed, and he stared at the ground, his shoe kicking at a can in the alleyway. Then he slid down the brick wall, his head falling into his hands with a slap. Skin slapping skin.

A shiver ran up her spine as the throbbing between her thighs reignited at the sound, but then she shook her head. Something was wrong. With her . . . and maybe him? Definitely both of them.

"I understand," Kane said, words muffled by his hands.

She didn't know what he could possibly understand about this whole thing. About the Penumbra. About the dark witches. About the Darkness and the Semaphors and all that came along with it. These were the things he should've known, but she didn't want to teach him. Maybe he understood but she didn't. She should have turned her back, ignored and deflected, but instead, she was here in the Daylight Realm after having rough sex with him and wanting nothing more than another taste.

KANE SWALLOWED AND THEN SWALLOWED again. It was to get the bad taste out of his mouth— metallic-tasting blood— and to bide his time and tamp down the beast that wiggled around in his belly. The beast wasn't done yet—far from done. It had gotten a taste of action and craved more. It would've done anything for more. He swallowed, but the beast fought back, and he coughed.

Malin's head jerked up, her hair falling around her shoulders, and he couldn't explain just how beautiful she was as she looked down at him. The tinge of pink on her cheeks, her eyes narrowed on him intently but seemingly taking up her whole face. She crouched down opposite of him, making them the same eye level.

He turned his gaze away, telling himself not to get distracted. The beast ate up the sight of Malin, and it licked its chops for more. Kane ran his tongue over his teeth, almost ready to take a bite out of her, but no—he pushed back against the wall with his heels, feeling the scrape of brick on his back. He had no further escape. Not just from Malin but from The Rage that wanted to devour all.

"How long—" He cleared his throat. The question sounded too childish. Too unlike the strong fighter he projected. He wanted to be brave. "How long do I have until I go blind?" He peeked under his eyelashes to watch Malin shift uncomfortably.

"It depends."

"On what?"

"How strong the Darkness is inside of you. Stronger equals sooner."

His heart nearly stopped in his chest, and to restart it, he took a deep breath, spitting, "Fine," through his clenched teeth. It certainly wasn't fine, but how could he argue? What was Malin hiding from him?

"Twice today," he said, "I've lost control."

She stilled, her eyes growing large enough to resemble moons shining through the night at him.

"Twice today, I've shown my evil side—"

She interrupted, "You're not evil."

Kane wasn't so sure after what had happened today: first with Broc and then with Malin, even if she claimed the only thing between them was sex. What would Broc call Kane's assault when they finally spoke again? Nothing good because Broc didn't mince his words. That was another thing Kane would have to deal with.

"I've made enough money that I can leave the cage," he said, "so I'm leaving. I'll fight alone. Away from where I might hurt—" His throat felt suddenly tighter, and he couldn't continue with those thoughts. "I'll wait until I get the call from you about Kiera so I can take her home to Mom." He needed to focus on righting his wrongs instead of having his mind wrapped around Malin like her legs had been around his body. Her hands on his skin. He pinched the bridge of his nose and inhaled. "Then I won't bother you again. I'm sorry."

Kane started to climb to his feet, but his knees quaked, body rocked unsteadily, mind swayed. He bit his tongue so he wouldn't say anything else, or worse yet, go back on what he already agreed to.

Using the wall as a brace, he waited there longer than was wise. He should have run away, but he just wanted her to say something. Tell him no? What words did he want to hear? What words *should* he hear from her?

"Yes."

One simple word: breathy, resigned, and hanging in the air as if there were more terrible things she needed to say. Kane wanted to ram his head into the wall.

"That's probably for the best." She jumped to her feet—*too eagerly,* he thought—and it almost hurt him. "I can't be distracted right now. I have to eradicate our enemies." Her lips pursed, as though she would say something more about the Semaphors, but she changed the subject instead. "When Kiera is better, someone will bring her through and contact you." She started to move past him, lifting her hand toward the wall.

He stepped out of the way, holding himself back from

reaching to seize her outstretched hand and bring it to his face. He wanted to feel her again. He retreated further, no longer towering over her small stature. A stature that could kill him, if Malin so desired. A stature he would allow to kill him and rid the world of the beast he had bound to his soul. Maybe after he'd returned Kiera . . .

He latched his hands behind his back as Malin traced the lines of the Awen. The inky black pool wavered and separated— the parting of dark seas—and the Penumbra appeared on the other side. She turned her head, and he waited for her to say something, holding his breath until he felt like he might pass out. She gave a nod and slipped through the window, the ink folding in around her and solidifying into brick.

Kane collapsed against the wall, hands bracing against the brick, and he felt the stone cut into his palm, drawing blood. He couldn't care less. About anything. Nothing at all! Not with Malin gone, and the life he could have had with her. He lost everything today, and he didn't know where to go next.

CHAPTER 27

*I*N THE SHADOWS OF THE alleyway outside Club Infinity, Daniel lurked with his body pressed against the thumping brick outer wall. He kept eyes on the prominent MMA fighter Kane "The Rage" Macleod—*what a ridiculous name!*

He had watched the scene before him play out: Malin of the Dragan Gardaí versus The Rage. How strange that a fight ended up with Kane buried in the dark witch. It was enough for Daniel to get a hard-on, and he hated himself for that. For the Maker's sake, he had gotten aroused watching his sworn enemy having sex—angry sex at that. He'd have to repent, perhaps wear his cilice vest as an homage to the Light of the Maker. He crossed himself.

While The Rage and the Dragan Gardaí hadn't seemed like enemies throughout, they also hadn't left things on good terms. The silent aftermath made it easier for Daniel to slip away unnoticed, leaving the fighter with his head resting on the brick. The same way the dark witch had done.

When Daniel returned to the warehouse, he had a pep in his step. The car ride had been just long enough for him to shuffle through ideas, picking out the best one to impress Godric with. Daniel had been walking on eggshells since John's death, so really, he didn't want to disappoint. He always needed to show his loyalty and to prove his worth in order to survive Godric's wrath. But when Daniel stepped in front of Godric, all those plans to come off suave and intelligent went out the window, and he vomited every detail of what he had seen and heard between the two.

Godric's lips turned up at one side of his mouth. Not enough to be a smile because it never reached his eyes, but at least Daniel didn't get stabbed.

Godric turned to his screens that tracked the soldiers, and then he leaned over the controllers, hands braced shoulder-width apart. "This is . . ."

Daniel held his breath.

"Very, very good," Godric finished.

Daniel, who had been wringing his hands nervously behind his back, suddenly straightened, taken aback by the first kind words his boss had ever said to him. "What will you do, boss?" squeaked Daniel, taking a step forward. "I can help. However you like. I'll be there. I'm your guy."

Godric chuckled hollowly, sending Daniel's stomach into knots. "Isn't life funny sometimes?"

"I don't know, sir. I guess?"

"It is. It's ironic." Godric turned and leaned against the controllers, crossing his arms over his chest. "That was me once, and now Malin has a new guy. History repeats itself. Or it shall." His head tilted as he thought. "I killed one twin, so if anything, I'm being—shall we say—courteous by killing the other. And she will make such a fine offering to the Maker."

Daniel swallowed but nodded his head, hanging on Godric's every word as if his leader were the Maker himself. "What will you do, sir?"

"Find out whatever you can about this Kane-guy. His home, parents, friends—everything. Leave no stone unturned." For once in the time Daniel had known Godric, the man actually smiled, showing his whole crooked, toothy grin. Godric continued, "If we can lure him to us, then it could be the end of the Dragan Gardaí. We can eradicate the serpents and the Darkness all at once."

CHAPTER 28

SOME THINGS HAD NEVER MADE sense to Godric Laferty, and over the years, he'd grown convinced it was a problem with the so-called social norms in today's society. Who was insane and who was sane? And why did some people get to make that decision but not others? What made one person a coward and another a hero? Godric didn't often struggle with this kind of question and certainly didn't want to now as he smoothed down his white suit, adjusting the golden cufflinks and plucking off a single black hair. He flicked it away with a curl of his lip. Where had that come from?

Disgusting, he thought and then focused forward again. He adjusted his nametag on his left lapel, right above his heart, and he plunged into the infested pond that was the Wickney Prison. Concrete walls created a dingy white maze and the repugnant scent of body odor and urine leaked down the concrete flooring toward a drain encircled with mold. The once-silver bars rusted, the metal losing its shine, as the prison had lost its government funding due to budget cutbacks.

Who truly cared for the prisoners here? These men who had broken laws and hurt others to feed something horrible, something dark in their souls. Well, the answer to these prisoners' rehabilitation needs was Faith Prison Ministries, of which Godric was a member, and he had a better solution than most. Thanks to the Maker.

Prisons were good recruiting grounds, if one could call them that, for new members of the Semaphors. The Maker believed in second chances and shedding Light on those who wanted to make a difference in their community, those who had long been cast in shadow and wanted to feel the grace of the Light upon their skin. Also, if they died, usually no one missed them, especially their victims. The men in prison were usually meaty with a lust for life after being locked up with only an hour of outside time a day.

The prison guard led Godric toward the meeting area. The man wore ironed khakis and had a stain dribbling down the side of his shirt, like an unhappy prisoner had spat on him that morning. He swiped his badge to unlock a door to the meeting room and smiled at Godric. Over the loud buzzing sound, he said, "After you. This one is the worst of the worst." His eyes trailed down Godric's pristine white suit as a click sounded: the metal door opening. The hinges squealed, and the guard followed Godric inside. The guard wouldn't leave him alone with a prisoner, no matter how much money Godric waved in front of his face or what favors he offered. He had tried.

A prisoner was already seated at the metal table, which was bolted into the floor, along with the chairs. One of which, Godric slipped into. The prison guard waited by the door with his hands behind his back and legs shoulder-width apart, looking more like a soldier than some measly prison guard. If only Godric could recruit him too, but alas, no, Godric was stuck with the prisoners. Specifically, the one in front of him now.

"I heard you're seeking the Light," Godric began, measuring the prisoner's weaselly face, receding hairline, and wire-framed spectacles. Cheap glasses. All that nerdiness paired with the broad chest and arms held away from his torso due to his overinflated lats. This man had clearly spent his time in prison bulking up, but he'd probably been pretty fit before.

"Yes," answered the prisoner and pursed his lips.

There was no reason to believe a man who was being paroled

in a matter of hours. The man just needed somewhere to land, and he couldn't go home after his wife had kicked him out and he had lost all his money in the court proceedings. And given his previous career, of course he had no job to go back to.

"Your file says that you used to be a teacher and a wrestling coach at Wickney High School," said Godric. "Would that be correct?"

The man shifted in his seat, lifting his thick arms, wrists still cuffed, and resting them on the table. "Yes."

Godric fought the urge to smile. A high school was a perfect hunting ground for a sick predator like Coach Robbins. "Well, I think I've heard all that I need to hear. You want the Light, I can give you the Light. But you'll have to be baptized first."

GODRIC TRANSPORTED HIS LATEST RECRUIT back to his warehouse made sanctuary, parked in the bay adjacent to his latest warehouse renovations, and led the coach inside to his office. Coach Robbins carried all he owned in a single plastic bag. Most parolees at least had a cardboard box, but this one hadn't accumulated that much since the day he was incarcerated.

No one had come to see Coach Robbins. No one had written to him. He was forgotten like a piece of shit in a dumpster. He wore the clothes he had most likely been wearing when he was picked up. The shirt stretched across his chest, now too tight, and he sported his Wickney High School jacket and matching baseball cap. Pleated shorts rode high on his thighs, white knee-high socks, white tennis shoes, and an undershirt that smelled of sweat and cigarettes. He carried the bag close to his chest with the money, dead cell phone, his expired driver's license, and a few receipts he had in his pocket that day. Years later, it told the story of his life before prison.

"Drink this." Godric shoved a tumbler into the coach's hands and stepped away. The prison scent lingered in the air, wafting off the coach's skin and greasy hair and lingering on Godric's white suit. He threw the name tag into a desk drawer until next time. The war was far from over, so there would be a next time. Godric wasn't giving up until the Darkness was gone forever.

The coach drank hesitantly, prison having taught him wariness. Like the many Godric had saved before, this man would clearly never be able to trust again.

Good, thought Godric. *That'll keep him on his toes.*

"I read in your file that Kane Macleod was one of yours," said Godric nonchalantly, settling on a chair opposite the coach. He studied the man, waiting for some sort of tick or acknowledgement or some claim to innocence. The coach had pleaded not guilty to all crimes, making his victims relive those moments on the stand, and in front of many others who would go on to gossip about it. However, Kane had never testified. *Interesting.*

Robbins glared at Godric, which Godric met with a steady and unflappable gaze. He wasn't scared of this man. Robbins set the tumbler aside. "Will you take me to the Light or what?"

"Yes." Godric hopped up from his chair. "I think the other recruits are here now." Godric led the way through the warehouse, which was sectioned off by man-made walls to give some sort of privacy. Apart from Godric's private suite though, all things here could be heard. The grunts of recruits training for battle, the squeals of doors opening and slamming shut, and heavy footsteps on the floor.

With Coach Robbins behind him, Godric stopped and motioned for the coach to join two more recruits, brought in by Daniel. They were both expendable. Neither of them had come from the prison, both from the local county jail with rashes clawing up the sides of their necks and track marks in their veins on their bare arms. They shivered but not from the cold. The two looked to Daniel, like he had promised them something. He probably had. That's what addicts needed, after all. No worries, though, the Light would show them the path.

Godric clapped his hands together. "Welcome. You have been chosen by the Maker to join the Light and fight the Darkness that plagues this realm and others."

The recruits looked between each other in jerky motions, but Godric ignored the questions written on their faces and continued, "You shall join the rest of the community who have been touched by the Light, and your lives shall finally have purpose."

The three new recruits stared as Godric held out his hands, his head tilted up to view them over the tip of his nose, waiting for thunderous applause. Of course not. He'd get none of that because he was dealing with idiots.

Godric dropped his hands to his sides. "Daniel."

His loyal number two pushed the two drug addicts toward one of the rooms, and Coach Robbins followed with his hands at his sides. At least, the coach understood what needed to happen to be cleansed of the Darkness. While Daniel was doing that, Godric grabbed the Light staff and held it in his grasp, feeling the Maker's magic pulse in him, giving him the strength to continue. A splash. Then the screams started, high-pitched cries like small children calling for their mothers. He took the staff with him as he followed the sound into the back room, slamming the door shut behind him.

The three of them were in a large vat, sunken into the ground where the concrete warehouse floor had once been. The pool was twenty feet deep with no way to climb out. The room was dark, so the three hadn't seen what they were walking into until it was too late. With a flip of the light switch, Godric turned on the overhead fluorescent lights, and they flickered to life with a deep buzzing that sounded like an attack of bees. The Maker needed to see his new soldiers being made, but darkness was necessary for this one purpose: to lure people to their deaths. Godric knew because he tried other ways. Some of this process over the years had been trial and error, but only those who truly wanted the Light would survive.

"Go ahead," said Godric as he leaned against the wall.

Daniel flipped a switch and electrical shocks coursed through the water, frying the three men where they treaded water. More screams followed, collected by the waves lapping against the sides of the pool. Bursts of light followed—proof of the Maker's need. Then Daniel turned off the switch, and the three bodies floated there, bobbing with the waves of the pool.

With a sigh, Godric motioned them up. "Let's get a move on."

Daniel was quick to jump into action, and Godric took note of how hard Daniel worked. It made Godric wonder what he did to inspire such loyalty. Godric hadn't seen any other men like him; those who'd come before Daniel were sluggish, lazy, and easily killed, but Daniel was proving otherwise. He fished the three bodies out of the pool with a long pole and laid them out on the concrete warehouse floor, their eyes open and staring up at the ceiling. Into the Light.

Godric hovered over the first body, Coach Robbins. The man looked half melted, body charred with blackened marks running up the skin. The head and feet were the worst, but the water, at least, made most of the damage even. Another soldier dead in Godric's quest to eradicate the Darkness, and the sacrifice was worth it.

Holding the Maker's staff within his hands, Godric felt the power flood him, and his eyes turned up toward the fluorescent lights. The Maker's grace. Then he slammed the staff into the coach's chest. Another electrical shock ran through the coach's body, and he seized like a fish on dry land, slapping around to save his life, and only when light flared in Coach Robbins's eyes did Godric pull back the staff.

The coach took a deep breath.

"Welcome back to the living," said Godric. "You have been saved by the Light. You will now serve it. Kill for it. And die for it."

CHAPTER 29

THE NIGHT PASSED IN A blur as Kane tossed and turned in his bed, reaching out for Malin, who wasn't there. The bed was more empty without her than he had ever known. He rolled over and stared at the darkened ceiling, tracing the ridges as if they were mountains in the distance. He used to do the same when he was a child, stare at them and dream about climbing them someday. He dreamed about being somebody important too. Now that he could technically be called "a somebody," he wished he wasn't. What had gotten him to this point was only trauma, violence, and The Rage that'd been born at the hands of the coach. Even now, in the dead of night, The Rage slithered in his belly, hungry for more.

Kane flopped over to his stomach and buried his head into the pillow, letting out a strangled scream. Tears burned his eyes, but he blinked them away. He couldn't cry now—not after all these years and all that had happened. Not after the pain he had caused.

Why couldn't he put his past behind him and move on? Kane wasn't the only victim, and some of those guys were married and had kids. They even held successful jobs that didn't involve beating someone to a pulp. Why could they do it and not him?

What was wrong with him?

Flopping onto his back, he pushed that question away. It was too large and nebulous. He couldn't grasp his feelings in his hands, though random things sprung to his mind: Not worthy. Not a man. Weak. Beast. Savage.

Dawn peeked through his curtains and lightened the bedroom. It almost blinded him, and he shied away from the light. He couldn't remember if he had avoided the light before, but he had never been one to greet the light of a new day or bask in the sun. Usually, he wasn't awake for it. Not after his late-night fights and a drink afterward to bring him down from the high and to squash the bloodthirst the beast always ignited within him. Had those truly been simpler times? *Nah*, he decided, *I just didn't know I needed Malin or the Darkness in my life.*

Not being able to pretend to sleep any longer, Kane pushed himself out of bed and took a long shower with cold water rushing over his body. A chill cut to his bones, making his teeth chatter, but the beast inside drew back. It couldn't feed off the cold, avoided the iciness, and maybe that was the reason Kane could never truly leave Wickney. Unless he went further north. He hated the cold, but the beast loved the heat more, thriving on it and coming alive in it. Kane never got this angry or out of control in winter.

Stepping out of the shower, he dried himself off and looked at himself in the mirror. He hated who he saw. The face staring back at him wasn't his own, especially the feral eyes lit with an electric blue. He threw his fist into the glass of the mirror, not feeling the prick of pain, and the glass along with his reflection shattered, falling into large shards over the sink and counter. And when the noise ceased, he could hear the splash of red, hot blood flowing from his hand and splattering against the bathroom tile.

The blood was quick, rushing like a waterfall coming off a mountainside, and it turned into a pool at his feet before he finally found the energy to pick up a towel and wrap his hand up. The blood was quick to bleed through the white towel. It wouldn't stop flowing until he got stitches. Worse, he would probably need shards of glass removed from his hand. This wasn't the first time he punched a hole inside, though it was perhaps the most destructive. A wall would have been a better choice. He'd done that a hundred times before, and only come away with broken knuckles once.

In his gut, the beast was laughing, like nails against a chalkboard, and Kane buried his ears toward his shoulder blades in an attempt not to listen. The sound only became louder, mixed with his heartbeat thumping in his ears like a bass drum.

Grabbing another towel, Kane wrapped his hand again. Broc was going to be pissed when he saw what Kane had done, but it wasn't the worst injury Kane had brought on himself. It wouldn't keep him out of the cage. But Broc would tell him to keep it wrapped up and have it looked at by a doctor before it got infected. That would mean Kane would be on his ass for a week or two. Not a chance that was happening with Vegas coming up. He needed stitches at least though.

When Kane got to Wickney General Hospital, there was a line for the emergency room. The front desk nurse took one look at Kane, decided he wasn't dying, handed him some forms to fill out, and told him someone would call his number soon. People sat in hard plastic chairs that looked straight out of the '80s, heads in hands. Some coughed loudly. Others held their hurt limbs or stomachs. Hushed whispers passed between patients and their loved ones, and a baby cried in the distance from one of the exam rooms.

The doors whooshed open, bringing in a breeze and humidity that both Kane and the beast leaned into, as two EMTs brought in a gurney with a patient rolled up in a blanket. The doors closed behind them.

There were open chairs in the waiting room, but Kane preferred to stand, rolling up from his heels to the balls of his feet and back down. He couldn't stay stationary for long in any case, especially when Broc was in the same hospital. Maybe Kane would try to see him again after his hand was fixed up? Maybe Kane could lie and say he was Broc's kid or nephew or something? Hell, why hadn't he thought of that before?

He turned to the paperwork on the clipboard and pen. It was really hard to fill out these forms when his hand was in such shape, but that was his own damn fault. Now, he had to deal with the consequences—always dealing with consequences, it seemed.

The news was on in the waiting room, loud enough for the words to be made out but with the closed captions rolling underneath in a black block with white writing. "Are you ready for some fighting?" asked the anchor, sounding more like an announcer than a journalist. "Well, Kane 'The Rage' Macleod is. He'll be taking on 'The Russian,' Demitri Vladimirovich, in Las Vegas in the upcoming weeks."

Kane tried to keep his head down, but he felt the eyes turning toward him. He didn't need to raise his head to know the pictures that flashed upon the screen, probably one of the pictures taken from his weigh-in or some action shots of him punching an opponent in the face. The newscasters' favorites were when Kane—or more precisely, The Rage—got out TKO.

The news anchor continued, "Kane, a hometown Wickney boy, has one of the best records in the UFC right now, winning nine out of the ten fights so far this year. If he wins in Vegas, he's expected to rake in over fifteen million dollars. He'll be one popular guy if he wins that." That was the end of the news story, commercials flooding the waiting lobby, but Kane didn't lift his head. *Yeah, fuckers. There's lots of money in being bat-shit crazy and nearly killing the other guy every time I get in the cage!*

Eyes burned into his scalp. His shoulders. His chest. His arms. His hastily wrapped towel around his bleeding hand. He glanced down to make sure no blood had dripped to the floor. He found one spot, but he couldn't tell if it was his blood or someone else's.

"Kane."

No, he wasn't doing this now. He wasn't taking pictures with fans or signing autographs in the waiting area of a hospital. He moved with his feet carrying him away and taking the paperwork with him. The last thing he needed was a crazed fan grabbing a hold of it.

"Kane!"

There weren't many places to go in a hospital, which was pretty much in lockdown, so Kane stepped outside. The humidity clung to his skin like hands, wrapped around his body and pulled him close. He couldn't take a breath without his lungs filling with the steamy heat, and the beast in his belly woke up, tasting the air and thriving off Kane's anger that some innocent person recognized him. It wasn't like he tried to hide himself here. He didn't even wear a sweatshirt and pull the hoodie up around his face.

He collapsed against the wall near the ambulance bay and ER doors and breathed in deeply. The air smelled of cigarettes and gasoline, which lingered without any wind movement to push it away. The ambulance was running with two medics inside, and it idled, huffing out puffs of exhaust like a smoker.

"You!"

Before he knew it, Kane was thrown into the wall outside the hospital with his head snapping back against the sandstone. Taken off guard, but not again. The Rage boiled in him, shooting up his arms and spine. He raised his hands like he would in a fight, but a hand connected with his jaw first. He fell, just barely catching himself with his hands before he face-planted into the pavement. A jolt ran up his arms, and he started to feel the pain radiating out of his hand. Kane was about to whip around—the beast ready to explode—when a voice said, "That's the least of what you deserve, Macleod."

Kane couldn't argue, but he paused, the beast thrashing inside of him. He breathed deeply, needing to keep control. Not only because he did deserve that and more, but because he thought he recognized the voice. He turned his head. "Smalls?"

Smalls shook his head, putting his hands on his hips as if that would keep his fists from flying. "Come on. I didn't hit you that hard." There wasn't a joking tone in his voice. "Would you get to your feet? I don't like killing a man when he's on his hands and knees."

Kane pushed up to kneeling, but he wasn't sure he wanted to be on his feet. With the state his hand was in, he wasn't sure he could protect himself. It wouldn't be a fair fight, but then again, when was it ever a fair fight with Smalls? The guy had weight and height on Kane, but Kane had the skill. And his beast.

"Will you, or won't you?" demanded Smalls, face closing in

on Kane's.

Kane swallowed. Unsure what to say and unsure what to do.

"Broc is dead, motherfucker."

Kane blanched, heart stopping in his chest and breath catching in his throat. It only started up again when his body went into automatic preservation mode. Still, he was frozen, staring at Smalls with his ear turned toward his opponent and teammate like he didn't quite hear correctly.

"What?" A single word was all Kane could push out of his lips, and he sounded like an inconsiderate idiot.

"He threw a blood clot and died," said Smalls.

"Threw a blood clot?" repeated Kane. "He died? Broken arms."

Smalls pulled back his head. "I didn't hit you that hard, man. What the fuck is wrong with you?"

Using the wall to balance himself, Kane staggered to his feet and dropped his hands to his sides. He was ready if Smalls decided to kill him now. Kane would've taken it because he killed Broc, the only person who had truly ever helped Kane. Made Kane better. Made Kane into the champion that he was to this day. Broc had seen all the bad parts of Kane and still decided to help him, even though others would've walked away. Others *had* walked away.

"My fault," murmured Kane.

"I didn't say that, man."

Kane's eyes flashed up. "But you were thinking it."

"Yeah." Smalls ran his hand through his hair. "I have to go. I said I would help his wife with the funeral arrangements." And then he was gone in a blink of an eye.

Kane stared at where Smalls had been.

Kiera was the first person Kane had hurt. And he still hadn't heard anything about her. She could be dead for all he knew. Had Kane killed his own sister? And then Broc? It wasn't even the first time the beast had escaped the cage, but it was the first time it had killed someone. Who would be next? Malin?

Of course, it would be Malin. Who else could he care about and hurt? Well, his mother, but he stayed away from her, because he had been afraid of what he could do for a long time. He never wanted her to meet The Rage again. It was the main reason he never allowed her to come to his prizefights.

Ever since Coach Robbins first touched Kane and Kane came home and had to take it out on someone. His mother was the easy target, and while he never touched her, he wanted so badly to hurt her or anyone around him that night. The Rage craved hurting someone, anyone, like he had been hurt.

His mother was supposed to protect him, but she couldn't even protect herself because she was blind! Instead, he had punched his hand through the wall for the first time, and the hole was still there in his mother's townhouse . . . a sick reminder of what he could do. Now a picture hung over it. Kiera's work, he was sure.

Family, friends, and love—none of those things could happen, not when Kane had a beast inside of him. Not when he couldn't control his Rage. Not when he was a monster! Broc had tried to rebuild and reteach, but Kane couldn't unlearn what made him tick, the one thing that made him deadly in the cage.

Thanks, Coach Robbins, all I'll ever fucking do is destroy.

CHAPTER 30

Malin slashed her blade forward, and it whistled through the air. She worked outside, feeling the cool caress against the heat building up in her body. Sweat slicked her skin and wet the back of her hair, curling the wispy baby hairs at the nape of her neck. She circled the blade through the air again, her body spinning to follow it as she practiced her standard warm-up sequence. By now, the routine had been ingrained into her muscle memory. She could do it with her eyes closed—*had* done it before with her eyes closed in case she ever had to fight without her sight. But now, things were different.

She stilled and poised herself for an attack, wishing the target in front of her was a real foe. Someone she could eviscerate just to work out her frustration. She needed her eyes open now and her focus on the dummy, because every time she so much as blinked, Kane flashed into her mind. His intense blue gaze pinned her against that wall again, and she wanted to run back to the Awen and forget everything she'd worked so long and hard for.

Shaking her head, she went in for another blow. The blade smacked wood, echoing off with a sickening crack. She licked the sweat off her top lip and panted. She couldn't breathe fast enough, her lungs burning for more air, as she drove the sword forward again and again. Then she backed off, repositioning herself to begin the moves again.

Malin slashed then stilled, blinking as she saw Kane's face. She swore she could feel his hands upon her body, gripping her hips and kneading her breasts. She spun away from the dummy, inhaling sharply and running from Kane's invisible hands. She walked in a large circle, and when she finally returned to the dummy, the feeling of Kane was gone.

Her blade hit the dummy with a whack, reverberating up her bones and rattling her jaw. It almost hurt. She struck again, a quick and easy blow, then she went into a series of strikes until the inanimate thing fell over onto the dirt. But her assault didn't stop there. She slammed the blade against the dummy again, wood chips flying.

In her sparring, she normally pictured Godric. He was the one who needed to die, the one who had betrayed her trust. He had killed Myla and Aemro. He led the Semaphors, recruited new ones. That extremist would do anything to hurt her, and she was the only one determined enough to hunt him. The only one committed enough to give up what she wanted most.

I will stop him, Malin vowed again. She had to because no one else could. She was the coven leader, whether by default or choice, and everyone was counting on her. She'd let them down by not being there for Tierney. Had she been a part of that fight, perhaps her friend wouldn't be unconscious in Dark Haven now. She would never allow herself to do that again.

No more distractions. No more Kane. Just the end of Godric. The continuation of the dark witches. Survival. A future. An end to Semar's Light-wielders. And then what?

The blade slid from Malin's sweat-slickened hands on her backswing. The long blade went flying off into the grass, and she stared at what remained of the dummy. The wood had mostly been chipped into mulch. No more fighting now. But her heartbeat still thundered in her head, her pulse erratic. She sucked in a deep breath. Another. Then one more. None of it calmed her heart or filled the void in her chest. She gasped for air, but it wasn't enough.

It was never enough.

AFTER A COLD SHOWER AND a change of clothes, Malin visited Tierney and Kiera. She walked with her hands latched behind her back and wished Breyze was with her. But Breyze rarely spent time with her in the Penumbra. He had a family back at the nest, just like she had her coven. And Malin had no need for the venom now, though she craved the confidence and focus her familiar dragan gave her.

"Hello, Emrys," greeted Malin.

The healer sat at his desk, studying. A thick textbook with pictures of the human spine lay open, and his computer—black screen with white text—had a bulleted list showing on the screen.

Malin swallowed down other thoughts that threatened to fly from her mouth. She wasn't an overly conversational woman, and she sure as the Light didn't want to share much about her feelings. So what had happened that she now wanted to talk about it all? There was one . . . and only one . . . highly obvious answer.

She bit down to squelch all thoughts of Kane.

Emrys studied her for a few pregnant seconds and then said, "Mistress." He seemed to know that she was hiding something.

Malin ignored the implied question. "How is Tierney?"

"Not well."

She blanched. "I thought she was doing better."

"She was, but . . ." Emrys released a deep breath. "Her injuries were extensive, and unfortunately, nothing we have done is helping."

Her eyes burned, but she blinked the tears away. "What will we do next?"

Emrys moved past her. "I am working on a few things, mistress, but I don't have complete hope."

"You have to save Tierney." Malin looked away quickly, blinking away the burning sensation behind her eyes. She would not cry.

"I am trying," he said softly.

"I know." Malin balled her hands into fists, and she bit back another demand—one that seemed more like a tongue-lashing. But Emrys didn't deserve that. He was a gentle soul. It was what had drawn Myla to him, and Malin knew he was doing everything he could to save Tierney. She breathed deeply then turned back to look at the darkling. "What are her chances of survival?"

Emrys cut a glance at her and then turned back to his desk. "Spinal injuries are difficult. Ommi is with her now, feeding her the Darkness. It's keeping her stable. I don't think she'd be alive without it. I also think that she was hit with a staff of Semar's making, and it might be poisoning her. A back injury is just physical. It would mean she might not walk again, but it doesn't account for her lack of consciousness." He hung his head and his shoulders heaved. "I'm working on it, mistress. That is all I can say for now."

She turned her back too, eyes brimming with tears, and she took a deep breath. This wasn't the news she wanted to hear. She'd been clinging on to the notion that Tierney would bounce back as she always seemed to. She needed Tierney to fight alongside her, to help seek revenge on Godric. Kill him. Eradicate the Semaphors. But it seemed Malin would be doing this alone.

Clearing her throat, she asked, "And the other . . ." she searched for the name in her head but only came up with Kane. All she could see was Kane's face in front of her.

"Kiera." Emrys filled in the blank. "She is doing well, but she's sleeping a great deal. It is partly the Darkness. Her mind doesn't know when to wake up. But her brain swelling is going down. She'll make a full recovery."

And then what? Tierney's voice asked in Malin's mind—only a ghost of Tierney, but it was exactly what her friend would ask.

And then Conrí would add, *The coven needs new blood, Mal.*

Malin plunged her hands into her hair and paced. She had left Kane in the Daylight Realm, but what about Kiera? What would the fighter's sister want? Kiera had more time before she lost her eyesight or went crazy, so would she want to return to the cowans and continue her nursing work? What about Kane's mother? These thoughts swirled around, and Tierney would question them all, help Malin work through the right path to take, and probably have answers. Malin really needed Tierney right now. And always. In the absence of Myla and even Morgana, Tierney had become her sister. She absolutely couldn't bear losing a third person who was so very close to her.

"Thank you," said Malin to Emrys.

"Yes, mistress." Emrys had his head bent over the large book, already back to work.

Before she left, Malin stopped outside of Tierney's room. Pushing through the door, she stepped to Tierney's bedside. Ommi, resting in a coil on the bed at her shoulder, lifted his head when Malin approached.

She ran a hand down the dragan's spine. "We'll figure out a way to save her," she said, soothing Ommi's, as well as her own, worries. Tierney rested in a death-like pose. A blanket was pulled up to her armpits, and her head pointed up at the ceiling. Malin brushed back Tierney's light blonde hair, feeling the radiating warmth off her forehead. Too warm.

"You need to get better," whispered Malin. "I can't do this without you. I know I've been distracted, but I will be better. For you. For Myla. For our coven and our realm." Her voice cracked, and she balled her hands into fists again. She wanted to be training again, chipping away at that dummy with her blade and then burning it to the ground. Like she planned to do with Godric.

Malin kissed Tierney's head, lips lingering there for a moment. She didn't know if she was drawing her strength from Tierney or if Tierney was taking strength from her. Either way, they both needed it. They both needed to survive. The Cailleach, Aodh's children, were dying far too often, numbers dwindling, and without them, the dragans would cease to exist, whether or not Godric or another fiend managed their slaughter.

"I'll fix this. Just hold on."

Malin was wasting time here. She needed to be doing something.

Godric had to die. Now. And then, Malin needed to rebuild her coven.

CHAPTER 31

*I*T FELT WEIRD FOR KANE to have people in his apartment. He had his asscheeks pressed against his kitchen counter, staying out of the way as the movers brought a treadmill into his apartment. Kane could've done it himself. In fact, he was larger and likely stronger than the hired movers who struggled with the box, jiggling it to either side to get it through the door, sweat dripping down their faces. They grunted, annoying sounds like they might birth a baby. But Kane didn't have a car, so he had to use the shipping and movers offered by the sporting goods store. At least they were free because he spent a small fortune on his new equipment.

"Where do you want this set up, sir?" asked one of the movers. Sweat stained the man's armpits, the crack of his back, and his shirt collar. The humidity outside in July didn't help. The mover used the back of his hand to wipe away the moisture on his glistening bald head. The other mover was doing better, his dreadlocks tied behind his back, and he wore shorts—a strange-looking combo with the steel-toed boots.

"No, I got it from here," said Kane.

"Are you sure, sir?"

"Yeah." Kane didn't want these people in his apartment any

longer, especially not with the smell of their sweat wafting off into the air and covering Malin's lingering scent.

"Okie dokie, sir. We'll get the last piece of equipment." The two movers rushed out, leaving the apartment door open.

Kane could've gone down himself and grabbed the last piece of equipment. That would mean the men wouldn't have to climb the steps and come back inside, but he was hesitant to do so with how unstable his temper had been. He didn't even want to leave his perch from the counter, where he had stayed since allowing the movers in. He had put space between him and them, but it didn't feel like enough. He couldn't trust himself not to harm them with the stifling heat and the beast slithering in his belly. The Rage drank in the hot air and blew out smoke, growing constantly stronger. As soon as these movers got the hell out of his space, he'd crank up the AC and try to keep his beast on a tight leash.

Kane checked his cell phone again, but there were no more messages. He opened a few apps, spending his time with his mind somewhere else instead of what was really happening. He didn't want to think about his reality.

A knock resounded on the open apartment door, and Kane waved his hand. "Put it anywhere. I'll take care of it."

"Um, Kane? I got nothing for you."

Kane's eyes flickered up, and then he swallowed. The Rage in him started to boil, building after a reminder of what happened last time he came face to face with Smalls. That was a few days ago, and Kane had a bruise on his cheekbone to prove it. Thankfully, Kane didn't have any more mirrors in his house. Still, the beast felt the pain and wanted to return it.

Smalls leaned against the doorway like a vampire banned from a home until invited inside.

And Kane wasn't about to extend that invitation. "Shouldn't you be planning Broc's funeral?" His voice caught in his throat, and he looked down at his phone again. Anything to keep from making eye contact or allowing The Rage to see something more threatening. The last thing Kane needed was to allow his beast out to attack Smalls.

"His wife's got it for now. His kids are flying in from out east."

Kane gritted his teeth. He hadn't even known Broc had children because he never spoke about them. He barely knew Broc had a wife, except for when Broc would complain about his wife nagging him. Sometimes, Broc brought muffins she had made to EMT, but Kane had never tasted one. It would've broken his strict diet.

He nodded and set his phone on the counter. "Listen, man, I'm busy right now."

Smalls raised his eyebrows. "I can see. You're having exercise equipment delivered."

"Yeah." Kane looked over Smalls's shoulder. "Speaking of . . . where're those two with my punching bag?" Just speaking the word caused his hands to curl into fists.

"I saw the movers struggling with it on the street."

"You didn't think to help?"

"No, it's their job." Smalls peeked over his shoulder, following Kane's gaze down the empty hall. "Why are you here, man? You should be training at the gym."

"Nah." Kane shook his head fervently. "I'm done. Broc's dead, and it's my fault."

"No, it isn't."

"You said it was the other day."

Smalls rolled his eyes. "I say a lot of things, and you've never listened to me before. Why start now?" He waited for an answer, but Kane had none to give. "Do you want an apology? Will that make you feel better? *I'm sorry, man, of accusing you of murder. The police aren't counting it as such.* You got to get your shit together. You've got a fight coming up in Vegas."

"No."

"No?"

"No!" Kane roared, the beast rearing up for an attack, and Kane's hand latched on to the kitchen counter, holding himself back. Holding the beast at bay, though for how long? He tried to think about what Malin had said. Would he go crazy or go blind if he didn't become one of *them*? The beast in his gut said otherwise.

Smalls raised an eyebrow. "Are you finished throwing your tantrum?"

"I'm not—"

"Yeah, you are. Like a toddler."

Kane shook his head. "You don't get it. And you won't get it. I'm not safe, and I can't be out on the streets. I'm too dangerous. I've already hurt people, and others will get hurt sooner or later too."

If possible, Smalls's eyebrows raised higher, nearly touching his hair, and then he started to laugh. "You take yourself way too seriously. Man, this life's a fight. You're either in it or not. I don't know what's going on with you, but have you tried therapy? Talking about your feelings? Holing up in here's gotta make it worse."

Feet thudded against the floor outside of Kane's apartment. Then a thunderous thump as the punching bag fell against the floor, walls of his cheap and shitty apartment rattling. Kane could afford somewhere else, but he didn't need the space, and this had been close to the gym. Not that that mattered anymore. Smalls stepped into the hallway to let the two movers pass. They seemed to struggle more with the punching bag than the treadmill. In fact, it looked ready to fall again, and they huffed as they finally dropped it in the corner and stumbled. The bald one placed a hand in the small of his back.

"Anything else, sir?" asked the one with dreadlocks, recovering more quickly.

"No," said Kane.

"Please sign here." The mover held out an electronic pad, and Kane used his pointer finger to scribble his name. "Thank you, sir. Have a good day."

"Yeah," Kane breathed. *Good day, my ass.*

Kane was marching over to slam the door behind them when Smalls stepped back into the frame. "Don't do this, man.

Seriously. You'll regret it. Whatever is happening with you, it'll only get worse unless you get help."

"Close the door on the way out!" yelled Kane, but it was too late.

Smalls was already treading after the movers, and the door hung open. Kane crossed over and slammed the door, hearing it rattle on its hinges, and the beast laughed at such an outburst. The Rage jumped into his throat, but Kane swallowed it down.

"No," he told the beast, but it coiled in his belly, ready to pounce. "No." And he sent his fist into the boxing bag. It wheezed in pain, a hiss escaping from the small hole in the vinyl.

"No," he repeated.

*A*REAL FIGHT FELT SO MUCH better to Malin than training. She worked arcs and twists, thrusts and slashes with the S-blades in either hand. As she drove the blade forward, her heart pumped energy through her veins, making her move all that much faster. The Semaphor fell forward as she pulled the blade out, reaching toward his non-bloody wound. He was no longer human, having been morphed into something else. His pale arms were covered in track marks, and Malin wondered just how deep into the trenches of society Godric was reaching for these people. The Semaphor disappeared into steam.

His partner backed away with his eyes wide and hands fallen to his sides. He didn't look to be breathing. All that fear meant little to Malin, and as she lurched for him, he turned and ran. One less of the slime-ridden bastards and one step closer to Godric.

Buzzzzzz, and she jerked away, hand already reaching for her cell phone. Apparently realizing her distraction, the remaining Semaphor slowed and then raced back toward her, but Breyze jumped off her back and attacked the slime with his open jaw, teeth sinking in, injecting venom. Death in serpent form.

"Good job, Breyze," she said, and her dragan chittered back. She checked her cell phone.

CONRÍ: "KIERA IS AWAKE."

Malin bit the inside of her cheek as she watched the Semaphor writhe and evaporate. Two bodies down and none left over. None remaining to take out her frustration. Thank Aodh the normal cowans couldn't see them on the street, or someone would've called the police. And she really didn't want to use the Darkness or spells to wash any cowan's mind in order to keep their war under wraps. She turned back to the screen and typed a message.

MALIN: "CALL KANE. YOU HAVE THE NUMBER."

She hit send and was about to slide the phone back in her pocket when she felt it buzz again.

CONRÍ: "DID THAT. NO ANSWER. CAN'T FIND HIM ON GPS."

She rolled her eyes. Did she have to do everything? Especially when she was trying to avoid Kane altogether. She typed again.

MALIN: "WTF? I'M OMW. TEXT HIM AND MEET ME IN 2 HOURS AT INFINITY WITH KIERA."

With a jerk of her head, she signaled to Breyze, and he jumped on her back again as she started down the street.

MALIN HATED HOW ANXIOUS SHE was, pacing back and forth beside Club Infinity with her hands on her hips and head down. She kicked an amber beer bottle that still dribbled a tan-colored ale. The alleyway smelled like stale beer and piss, and she tried to breathe through her mouth. How much time had passed? She checked the last message she'd received on her cell phone.

CONRÍ: "HE'LL MEET US THERE AT 3."

There was still some time left. The air changed suddenly, and Malin turned her head to the wall. No, it was just a passing car that had sent the ground rumbling.

Breyze peeked out from under her cloak, his forked tongue hissing, then he purred, leaning his head against her shoulder blade. Of course, he felt how anxious she was. How impatient. How much she wanted this to be over. And while sometimes he could help, it wouldn't be enough now.

Her stomach roiled, and the urine scent that hovered in the alleyway like a cloud only made it worse. Her knees shook, and her hands felt clammy. She wasn't sure she could hold an S-blade with how much her hands sweated. Maybe she should take some of the venom Breyze offered. The familiar Darkness would surely help her calm down, but then she was suddenly bathed in bright lights from the mouth of the alley. She threw a hand over her eyes—the contacts only shielding her so much from the blinding pain. "*Dubh*," she snapped to bring on complete darkness as she lowered herself into position for an attack.

But it wasn't necessary; the car backed out and reversed direction.

Get out of your head, Malin, she told herself. *You're going to get yourself killed . . . or worse, someone else.* That was easier said than done because the thoughts needled at her, crashed against her soul like angry waves on Ireland's cliff-faced shores. Aodh, how simple her life had been then, before they'd come to this new world.

A hand grabbed her shoulder, and she whipped out of the touch, pulling out her S-blade and readying to plunge it into her assailant. She stopped an inch before slicing into Kane's neck. Kane's hand was still on her arm, his fingers digging in, and his eyes were large and dark with even darker shadows hanging below them. They darted between the blade and her, but she didn't remove it yet. *Why?* she wondered, but her hands had begun to shake, arms locked up, and nervous energy pumped through her. The blood roared past her ears. If it were a Semaphor before her, then she wouldn't hesitate. She had killed so many of them that it had become routine. Muscle memory. But Kane . . . he represented a different kind of muscle memory. A warmth spread over her, her heart quickened, and her tongue ran dry.

His throat bobbed, nearly nicking the tip of her blade. "Are you going to kill me?" Strange how his voice sounded completely devoid of emotion, as if he craved that result.

Kane's words snapped her out of the trance, and she shook her head, dropping her blade. An apology was on her tongue, but she swallowed it back. "Don't sneak up on me," she said instead.

"I didn't. Was calling your name."

Malin looked down the alleyway, but there was no one else. Cowans passed, not that they heard or saw her. She slipped the blade back under her cloak, but her hand remained firm on the handle. She wasn't sure why, but she felt like she needed to protect herself. Especially alone in this alley with Kane. She could still feel the grain of the brick against her skin, his hands gripping her hips, and his cock driving into her throbbing core. At the reminder, her core clenched and flooded her panties. She stepped away from Kane, needing to put enough distance between them to not feel his presence so keenly. She took a deep breath, now relishing the piss-scented alley and how it stifled the cravings inside.

Kane took a step back too, his broad arms crossing over his chest. He looked down at his feet, as if unable to meet her gaze. She too jerked her gaze away from him, focusing on that beer bottle. She could break it, shatter it into a hundred pieces, or she could pick it up and throw it away.

"Guessing that Kiera and Conrí haven't come through yet," said Kane.

She knew him too well and could picture his stance: hands stuffed into his pockets and rocking back on the heels of his feet. When he wasn't in a fighting stance, he was always trying to back himself away, put himself into a box.

"Not yet." She looked to the brick wall, just waiting for Conrí to emerge with Kiera. And then, this insanity would be over between Kane and her. For good.

Then, she could focus again—fully—on Godric and ridding the Daylight Realm of Semar's minions. She wouldn't allow herself to be distracted again, no matter how much she craved the man waiting with her.

"Listen," began Kane.

She held up her hand. "No."

"Please."

He stepped closer, and she fought the urge to pull out her S-blade again. It was for his and her protection alike, and to keep the distance between them they so desperately needed. But his hot breath coaxed goosebumps to rise on her skin, and she shuddered under the heat. She couldn't look at him, knowing the blue depths she would find. The eyes she wanted to find staring back at her.

But eyes were too close to lips, and she knew exactly what delicious devilry he could perform with those lips. On her skin. Between her legs. The thought of those lips was enough to make her wetter. The wettest.

"No!" She looked up at him with hard eyes.

Kane stepped back, mouth dropping open. He had rocked forward, and he had freed his hands from his pockets. One had already come to a fist in front of him—fighter mode.

But she would meet his fight with her own. "I have duties, Kane. And too much damage to fall for someone." *Like I already have . . . but I can't admit it. Not with so much on the line.* Her heart shattered within her chest, like her boot striking the bottle. She almost heard the glass fracturing into a hundred pieces as her heart scattered within her rib cage. She couldn't collect them. She had to embrace the hollow void remaining, and simply remember the whole heart her ribs once embraced.

"Malin, me t—"

Then, the Awen opened with the marks searingly carved upon the brick wall. A pool of ink spread and parted, revealing a darker version of this mortal realm. Malin stepped toward the wall and away from Kane. She needed to escape his scent that lingered too close to her. His musk filled her nostrils, muddling her mind when she needed it clear. A few seconds later, Conrí, with Kiera in his arms, stepped through. Kiera leaned against Conrí's chest, and Kane jerked forward protectively. Malin simply watched her covenmate set Kiera down. She had been so wrapped up in her head and Kane that she missed what had been happening around her. Was it truly the case that Kiera had only recently healed enough up to cross the Fold between realms? Or could Conrí simply no longer come up with a reasonable explanation for her to stay in the Penumbra?

"Kiera." Kane wrapped his arms around his sister, but she was hesitant to return the gesture, her fingers still entwined with Conrí's.

Malin cut a look to Conrí, but he gazed at the tip of his nose, down at his feet, instead. He wouldn't face her. But she would have time with him later, and she would get the truth.

"I'm so, so sorry," said Kane.

"I know," said Kiera. "You didn't mean it. And Conrí explained some things to me."

Conrí squeezed her hand, and Malin stiffened, drawing in a deep breath. Conrí must've noticed because he dropped Kiera's hand.

"How's Mom?" asked Kiera. "Have you talked to her? Gone to visit her?"

"We'll go see her now," Kane promised. His eyes settled on Malin, and she returned the look, giving a small nod of her head. It seemed like too much because they were nothing. Couldn't be.

Clearing her throat, Malin said, "Conrí and I should return to the Penumbra."

Conrí looked ready to argue, but she pushed him through the Awen, leaving Kane and Kiera behind.

WAITING IN LINE OUTSIDE OF Club Infinity, Daniel had his back against the brick wall and pretended to check his phone. His head tilted to the side, listening to the conversation between the four of them. *Malin and Kane, almost cute*, he thought, and it made his job that much easier.

A moment later, Kane exited the alleyway with a woman who was not Malin, his large body standing between her and the crowd, and Daniel narrowed his gaze on the back of Kane's neck. The fighter whipped around as if he could feel it, but Daniel had returned to scrolling on his phone, pretending to be minding his business. Humans surrounded him, none yet reborn in the Maker's Light. Most of them were also on their phones and either drunk or high. Save for the fact that he couldn't get drunk anymore—or drink, for that matter—all the phone-surfers made it easy to blend in. The small woman with dark red hair pulled on Kane's arm, and he trailed after her. In the murky light, Daniel followed them down the street with his eyes, deciding the two looked too much alike to be lovers.

That must be his sister, thought Daniel. He had done his research and knew all about Kane, including his sister Kiera. Even enough to be a considered a super fan. The only thing he didn't have was the life-sized cardboard cutout he'd seen online. But that was okay. Soon, they would have the real thing.

"Kiera." Daniel tasted her name on his tongue, and it tasted pure. Perfect.

When Daniel pushed off the wall, the siblings were far enough down the street it wouldn't seem like he was tailing them. Keeping a block back, he became a predator after his prey.

CHAPTER 32

KANE DIDN'T HAVE MUCH TO say besides, "I'm sorry," and Kiera remained silent the whole way to their mother's townhouse. Every conversation he thought to start was thick on his tongue, heavy like molasses sliding down his throat. He coughed, trying to clear his throat as they rode the late-night train, but nothing of substance came out of his mouth. He swallowed another apology because Kiera had made it clear that she didn't want to hear it. That she didn't blame him.

She should blame me, he thought—the only thing that popped into his mind. And damnit, it made him want to apologize again. The beast in his belly had slithered away, hiding in the shadows, but he felt the weight of it like a boulder in his stomach. A reminder of The Rage that could escape at any time.

Kiera was a survivor.

Broc hadn't been so lucky.

The train jerked, lurching forward, and Kane braced himself with a grip on one of the gross chrome poles, grimacing at the fingerprints and smudges of shit only the gods could identify. The beast in him gurgled with the movement, awakening and thirsting for blood. The monster would take any blood, and Kane's eyes fell onto Kiera sitting opposite of him. Sensing

Kane's awareness of how he'd hurt his sister, the beast cowered again, begrudgingly hiding in the shadows. Kiera had healed. Well, there were bruises still on her skin, but they were fading. No permanent damage, he hoped. If so, he believed Malin or Conrí would have mentioned something.

"Kiera." Kane cleared his throat. "I'm so—"

"Nope." She held up her hand, cutting him off.

"Please," he said.

"No." She glared at him and then crossed her arms over her chest, and she pushed out her small chest as if she was a fighter too, ready to weigh in before a prizefight. She had never fought like him—she probably didn't need to. He didn't want her to, but she knew how to act like she was. Even small and trained as a nurse, his sister was strong enough to do some damage too if she wanted.

"Kiera—"

She hissed, "No," eyes flashing over to the one other person in the train car.

They were curled up into a ball with a green army jacket wrapped around them, head pressed against the glass of the window. They hadn't moved since Kane and Kiera had gotten on the train, riding the seat like it was a wave, not even lurching with the train car.

Kane pulled his eyes away from the obviously homeless person. Having used the late-night train many times, Kane had grown accustomed to homeless people using the train to keep out of the elements of the night—that was, until the cops did their early-morning sweeps before the corporate types boarded on their way to whatever boring desk job they had downtown. In the summer, there were fewer train squatters, but in winter the cars were usually packed with people. He found himself wondering if Malin's realm had a homeless population, but probably not. He'd never seen that many people in the Penumbra, so he doubted it. Besides, he wasn't part of that world. This place was his life and his reality. He needed to forget.

Leaning down, he braced his elbows on his knees, his head closer to Kiera's, and with a huff, she mirrored his position. Her hair fell in front of her face, but she didn't push it back. It covered her bruises. He laced his fingers, holding himself in place. Then he met her gaze, and she was glaring at him, eyebrows raised halfway to her hairline.

"I swear if you apologize again," she began but didn't finish. She didn't need to finish. He didn't know exactly what she would do, but he trusted that she would find some way to make him pay. No violence included.

Or well, maybe, Kiera could punch him in the face and knock him out cold. That would make him feel better? What was that old saying? An eye for an eye. Yeah, if she coldcocked him, that would only be fair. The beast in his belly slithered out of the shadows, hungry at the thought, but Kane swallowed it down. His fingers tightened until he felt the bite of pain, the stitches in his right hand pulling against the skin from when he had sent his fist through the mirror.

"Kane?" Her hand touched his own, and he jerked away, the blood pumping in his body and The Rage boiling in his blood. It was enough for her to flinch, though he saw her trying to fight it. No, what he had done to her would haunt her for the rest of her life, no matter how much she tried to brush it aside.

"It's fine." He drew his hands further back. "I'm fine."

"I don't believe you."

"We need to get our stories straight for Mom."

Kiera blanched, her eyebrows climbing further toward her hairline. "We're going to tell her the truth."

He shook his head. "No."

"Yes."

"We can't."

"And why the hell not?" she asked, leaning forward again and her eyes darting to the person on the train. "She needs to know the truth. What we are. What *she* is."

"And what do you know about that?" he hissed, and he fought the beast rising in his chest, warming his skin. He balled his hands into fists and shoved them in his pockets. It was getting worse, he knew, and the beast had awoken again when he saw Malin, like she accidentally coaxed it out. Perhaps it craved Malin too. No, he couldn't think about that possibility now.

"Conrí told me a lot."

"How much?"

Her eyes narrowed on him. "Why? How much did Malin tell you?"

Kane bit his tongue. Enough. Malin had told him enough. Her realm was something else—fascinating and scary—but when he had seen Malin and got lost in the sound of her voice, everything melted away. He felt whole, and he could only focus on her. He should've been paying more attention to the Penumbra itself, but it was too late now. All of it was gone.

"I just don't think it would be helpful," he claimed. "Why overload her? Neither of us are going back. We're done."

Her eyebrows knitted together. "No, we're not."

"Well, I am." He sat back in his seat, crossing his broad arms over his chest again. "Nothing good comes from that place." *Except Malin.* He sighed.

She rolled her eyes. "You can be a real ass, you know that?"

The brakes on the train squealed, and Kane fought the momentum sending him forward. He was up before the train came to a stop, out through the doors as they hissed open. The humidity in the air lingered, and he drank it in. The beast breathed it too, reveling in the heat even in the night. No, that wasn't what he wanted. The control was seeping from his grasp.

Kiera stepped off the train and was already walking down the platform to the stairs. He pulled up his hoodie and followed after her, calling, "Maybe we should come back in the morning."

"No." She didn't turn around. "I have to see Mom now. And no offense, but I don't trust you to see her alone or tell her what's going on." She headed down the steps.

"She's probably asleep."

Kiera didn't respond, and he rushed to keep up with her.

Kiera was a flash of lightning, never slowing or stopping, not that there were many cars on the street. When they got to the townhouse, Kiera drove her key into the lock and entered the house, calling, "Mom! It's me! Are you here?"

Kane paused outside the door. He rocked back on his heels, sighed, and headed inside, keeping his head down.

Kiera was already moving up the stairs. "Mom!" Her voice echoed off the plaster and antique furniture. The furniture hadn't meant to be antique, but his mother never updated. Didn't have the means and didn't care how it looked. As long as the furniture was usable, it served her just fine. Although most of it wasn't made for anyone Kane's size.

Walking into the kitchen, he flipped on the lights, which didn't immediately burst to life. The buzzing began but then hushed. He flipped the switch again, and the lights flickered before coming on strong. He stumbled back, holding up his hand to cover his eyes. The beast inside lurched forward, preparing for an attack, and he doubled over, protecting his eyes. A migraine burst in his head like fireworks, cracking against his ears and rattling his skull. He hissed in a breath, and the beast gurgled, belching it back up Kane's throat. He pulled his eyes up, dark dots dancing across his vision—and saw his mother on the floor.

Seconds passed. A beat in his chest. A thundering drum that rushed past his ears. "Mom!" Two steps, and he dropped beside her. "Kiera! In the kitchen!" His hands hovered beside her face and crumpled body. She lay in a heap on the linoleum floor. Her gray hair tattered around her face. "Kiera!" His voice was strangled in his throat, calling for his sister. She could fix this.

He couldn't. He only destroyed. He only hurt. He would do it again.

His mother already looked broken. Not shattered but also not whole. Pieces of her splayed awkwardly. Her legs and arms tangled like roots of old tree. Her long and spindly fingers seemed like frail twigs. Was she breathing? He couldn't tell. He didn't see her chest moving, not through the tears brimming in his eyes.

He couldn't hear her, not over the rushing of blood past his ears.

"Kiera!"

"I'm here." She dropped down beside him, her hand outreached toward their mother. "Mom! Can you hear me? Mom!" She ran a hand under her nose. "She's breathing. Call an ambulance. Now! Mom!"

He scrambled to his feet, his knees turning in awkward directions like he was a newborn giraffe instead of an MMA fighter. He accidentally knocked over a chair, which clattered to the floor with a smack. The wood splintered and the arm went flying like a dagger for a vampire—*do vampires exist if witches exist?* He shook his head; he didn't have time to think about this now. Or ever.

God, what the fuck happened to his logic?

"No," groaned a weak voice from behind him as he reached for his phone.

"Mom, you have to lean back," said Kiera.

She groaned, "No." Kane turned to his mother and gripped his cell phone, but she yelled, "No! Would you just listen to me? I said no. This my house, and I won't leave it."

"Mom," said Kiera, her voice patient but strangled, but his mother's order had left Kane frozen, thumb hovering over the nine. "Mom, we found you unconscious. We need to take you to the hospital. To get you checked out. Sit back."

"No." She pushed herself to her knees, managing to get up faster than Kane, but she was sturdy. She was leaning off to the side, and Kiera caught her. At the same time, Kane dropped his phone on the counter and grabbed a useable chair for his mother to sit down. Thankfully, she did, landing with a thud and huff. "I'm fine," continued their mom. "I was just tired and decided to lie down—"

Kiera interrupted, "Mom."

"No. Listen to me, Kiera. I mean it because I won't repeat myself." Spit wobbled off her bottom lip. She reached up and touched Kiera's face, thumb running over Kiera's quivering bottom lip. "Kiera, where have you been?"

Kiera shared a look with Kane, and he gritted his teeth, hoping she would remain quiet. Kiera was too truthful with their mother, but maybe he was too much of a liar? He had been lying to his mother since he was a child. Since his father left. And when they moved to Wickney, he lied about what exactly Coach Robbins was doing to him too. He had to protect her because no one else was going to.

Kiera turned away. "It doesn't matter, Mom. I'm back now."

He felt sick to his stomach, for many reasons, and he took a step back, looking down at his feet. After a few seconds, he raised his head and watched Kiera with his mother. She was always better than him at handling her. Or anyone, for that matter.

Kiera started, "Mom, are you sure—"

"Yes. This is my home. I won't . . ." Her voice caught in her throat, and she coughed, sounding more like a hack as phlegm speckled her lips like watery snowflakes. Her thin lips pulled back, revealing her gums, yellowed teeth, and red tongue. She coughed, and some blood oozed out.

"Mom." Kane leaned in, keeping his distance, and his stomach dropped like a stone, weighing his steps and gluing him in place. What was happening? She hadn't been this bad before, had she? Had he not noticed? Of course, he wouldn't notice. He wasn't Kiera, and he had been so wrapped up in his head when he had showed up here last time. Since she was blind, he never usually bothered to turn on the lights anyway, and he tried to make his visits as quick as possible, sometimes never even stopping by her townhouse.

"Mom." Kiera's voice was soft like a feather, a hand resting on their mother's knee. "What is happening?"

Several gravid moments passed, each met with a thundering heartbeat inside of Kane's chest, blood rushing past his ears.

"I'm dying."

Kane stared at his mother, wondering if he heard her right. But no, that wasn't possible. His mother wasn't dying. She was blind, but she was as healthy as a horse . . . or so he thought. Or so she had been telling him and showing him. He turned to Kiera, wondering if she knew. She was a nurse, so she had to know. If anyone would have known, it would have been her!

Kiera was still, like a statue. No, like a caught criminal under a bare and swinging lightbulb in an interrogation room. Slowly, her hand began to rub her mother's knee, and Kiera raised her head, turning to him.

So she did know. How long had she known? How long did they keep this from him?

"Kane," began their mother.

He took a step backward, the backs of his thighs bumping into the kitchen counter.

She placed a hand on his sister's shoulder. "Kiera, go to your brother. I can't hear him breathing."

He wasn't breathing. His breath was caught in his throat, and his lungs ached—burned—for air. But he couldn't breathe. His mind wouldn't start up his lungs again.

"Kane." Kiera placed a hand on his face, forcing him to look down at her. "Kane, look at me. Breathe." She took a deep breath and released it, forcing him to follow along with her breathing. "Good, just like that. Deep breaths."

As he inhaled, the beast breathed too. The air was stale, a sterilized smell that scorched his nostrils like they had been at the hospital. The beast took in the scent, living off it and the humidity clogging up the house. Kane felt betrayed, and the beast fed off it. Why hadn't they told him? How long did she have left? How much time had he missed? The Rage built in him, throwing him into a tidal wave that knocked him away, out of Kiera's grasp. The hurricane wind picked up in him, and he braced himself, feet shoulder-width apart. He balled his hands into fists, wanting to throw one forward.

Kiera.

Bruises still blemished the side of her face. From him. From what his Rage had done.

What his Rage wanted to do again.

It skimmed the surface. A shark with its fins cutting through the waves. The beast smelled blood, and it was coming in hot and fast, jaw wide and teeth sharp.

Kane stumbled back another step, further away, and Kiera stepped toward him. "Stay back," he ordered, his voice a rumble of thunder.

She stayed where she was, stationary. Out of the corner of his eye, he watched Kiera look toward his mother.

Is she scared for herself? Or of what I could do to my mom? he wondered. *Kiera, of all people, knows exactly what I can do.*

"Kane," said his mother, "sit down. Kiera, make your brother something to drink. Honey, do you want something to eat?"

"No." He stayed standing, eyes peeling toward the back door of the townhouse. It was his quickest escape.

Kiera had a glass in her hand and was filling it up with tap water from the faucet. She tried to hand it to him, but he wouldn't take it. She was too close. So she put it on the counter, and after a few long seconds, he picked it up and drank it. The water was like acid down his throat, and the beast jerked its head back, hiding once again in the shadows. He wanted more if it kept the beast at bay.

"Are you feeling better?" asked his mother. "Kane?"

He wasn't sure if he could answer. He didn't trust his own voice. His answer wouldn't be true. He wasn't better, only worse without the beast to distract him. Without The Rage to give him life. Now, he felt empty and sad, and his shoulders fell forward. The rest of his body swayed, wanting to do the same. He caught himself on the counter.

"How long . . ." The words caught in Kane's throat, and he couldn't spit them out through his clenched teeth.

His mom said, "We were going to tell you after Vegas. We know how important that fight is for you. We didn't want to distract you."

Tears sprang into his eyes, and he blinked them away before they leaked from the corners. That wasn't what he wanted to know, but maybe it was what he needed to know. "How long"— he cleared his throat—"do you have left?"

"It's hard to say," answered his mother, and Kiera looked

over at her.

He shook his head. "That's not how it works." In movies and TV shows and even the stupid books he had to read in school, there was always a timeline! Six months? A year? It was never long. Just long enough to get everything in order and spend all the money and live for one last time.

Kiera stepped in between. "I've been taking Mom to her appointments. The doctors don't know what's wrong. Only that she's dying."

Kane raised his head to meet his mother's gaze, and he hated how defeated she looked. Like she had given up. But it also made him realize how much he had been missing. Or purposefully ignoring. He saw the changes but decided that they weren't important. It was age or something. He didn't realize, or ever consider, that she could be dying. That he would be losing his mother like water through his fingers.

"Mom," said Kiera, "let's get you to bed."

"That would be nice, dear." She slowly got up, Kiera beside her to catch her, where Kane should be. His fingers curled into the cheap kitchen counter, feeling the fake stone mold like Silly Putty in his grasp. The two of them walked out of the kitchen together, and then Kane heard their slow progress on the stairs. Taking one step at the time, as Kiera said, "Step up," and the stairs groaned under the weight. Kane turned his head to the door, thinking that he should run. And keep running because he was a worthless piece of shit.

But he waited in the kitchen, unable to move and lost in his thoughts again by the time Kiera came back down. She had pulled her hair back into a ponytail, and she walked over to the sink for her own glass of water. She chugged it down and refilled it. Then she said, "Conrí thinks that it has something to do with the Darkness."

Kane raised his eyebrows. "How would Conrí know?"

"I spoke to him about it."

The beast roared inside him, rushing past his ears. "You would tell a stranger but not your own brother?"

"Sometimes, telling strangers is easier." She shrugged. "And he isn't much of a stranger anymore. Conrí was there, basically, every time I woke up."

Kane's heart ached. He should've been there every time she woke up. But no, he had been distracted by Malin.

She continued, "You know, Mom just wants you to be happy. That's all we've ever wanted."

He cut her a look. "And you thought lying to me was making me happy?"

"Protecting you was what we thought would make you happy."

He scoffed. "I haven't been happy for a long time."

"Trust me, we're aware. Mom more than most." She sipped on her water and then turned around, back pressed against the counter, and she leveled a look at him. "Listen, Kane. This has something to do with the Dark Realm or whatever it is called—"

"The Penumbra."

"Yeah, that."

"Malin said it only made us blind," he said but didn't add anything about the sweet seeing potion possibly making them crazy.

"I don't think she knows everything."

He cut Kiera another look, and the beast answered with a hiss. "Don't talk about her like that."

"While I'm happy you really like her, you need to take a step back."

Kane shook his head. "I don't really like her."

She snorted and rolled her eyes. "You could've fooled me."

"Can we stay on topic here? You know—the fact that our mother is dying," he said. "You seem pretty passive about it."

"I've had time to grow used to it."

"Fuck!" yelled Kane.

"Keep your voice down," she whispered. "You'll upset her."

"She should be upset."

"She isn't, Kane. She knows she's dying, and she's grown used to the idea. Now, we just need to keep her comfortable and happy. That's why she wants to see you so much. Touch you while she can."

He shook his head. "You know, you could've just told me. Then I would be here all the time."

"And what about Vegas?" asked Kiera.

"What about Vegas?" he retorted.

"You would just give it up? Your career and the life you're making for yourself. What kind of life would that be?"

"I would just give it up," said Kane. "Of course, I would. I don't even want to go to Vegas anymore."

She groaned, "Kane, that is exactly what Mom didn't want to happen."

"It isn't about Mom—fully. I've been thinking about it for a while." He kicked at the linoleum that was curling up from the floor and sticking to his feet.

"What caused that?" she asked.

He didn't say anything, grinding his teeth together, and when she reached for him, he backed away.

"Kane," said his younger sister, her voice as soft as a feather, and it sent a shiver down his spine.

"I need to get out of here." He was already backing toward the door.

"Kane, please stay. Don't go."

He opened the door.

"Kane!"

Then he was out the door and running toward the train station, heart pounding in his chest. The beast inside of him wanted to take flight, and it nearly carried him away. He pounded the pavement to keep himself grounded. The hoodie fell away from his face as he felt like he was flying down the Wickney street. The smell of gasoline and cigarettes leaked into the air. A car honked at him, nearly missing him, and he couldn't even care if he got hit. Why didn't he get hurt? Why not him after all that he had done?

CHAPTER 33

KANE ABANDONED THE TRAIN STATION and walked around Wickney for a long time with his hands stuffed into his pockets, shoulders hunched, and his hoodie pulled up over her head. Morning light brought the stampede of people onto the street, and he finally turned toward home. His phone had gone dead, not like he wanted to use it, but Kiera had been calling and texting all night. Inside of his apartment, he took a shower and tried to fall asleep in his bed, but even after walking around all night, he wasn't tired.

Well, he *was* tired. But it was the kind of tired that came after he drank five energy drinks within ten minutes. His heartbeat fluttered in his chest, and when he blinked, he saw flashes before his eyes. When he stared at the ceiling, his mind played tricks, shadows crossing over the chalky popcorn ceiling. He curled his hands into the blanket as he lay on top, his skin straining over his knuckles. His muscles tensed, coiled and ready for attack.

The beast wanted to attack.

Jumping off the bed, Kane crossed his bedroom and walked out into the living room. His lackluster furniture had been pushed aside for the exercise equipment. The only nice thing he had was the sound system with big subwoofers and massive speakers. In the middle of the day, most of his neighbors should be at work, so he turned up the music until it was screaming in his head, rattling his windows and doors, and making the floor shake as if an earthquake rippled the Midwest.

He needed the sound, especially as the beast growled in his belly.

The Rage groaned, building up in him, and he tilted his head, jerking it in a vain effort to get the beast out. He turned up the music until it filled his ears, screamed in his brain, and sent his blood pounding to the beat.

After wrapping up his fists, Kane stood in front of his punching bag, staring it down like he would stare down an opponent, and then he drove his fist forward. A jolt ran up his bones with the impact, but he sent his other hand forward. Again. And again. And again. He ran through his training, sweat beginning to bead on his body, and he licked it off his top lip.

Yes, the beast hissed in his belly. *Give in to it.*

He did, fists pumping forward and only seeing red. The red of the punching bag and the red crossing his vision, of his blood pumping and running through his body, coursing through his veins from his toes to his head, down again.

"No," he ordered and drove his fist forward.

Kane threw punches again and again into the bag. The red burned, and he blinked away images that flooded his head. Coach Robbins behind him, on his body, having him bent over while Kane tried to jerk out of his grasp. Kane punched the bag harder, like he had wanted to punch the coach back in high school but never did. And then the coach had gone to prison and Kane had never gotten the chance. Kane would never get the chance. He punched until he saw the coach bathed in red, bloodied and dying, but he still had that stupid half smirk on his face and still chuckled under his breath.

Kane drove his hand forward again. Pain spiraled up his bone, a zing across his skin, a burn in his muscles. If that pain wasn't enough, there was the cold sweat of being alone after he'd finally found warmth next to Malin. Her strong hands upon his body. The feel of her skin against his own. The tickle of her hair . . . and then his hands wrapped in her hair, wrenching back her head until it nearly snapped.

The beast laughed, echoing in Kane's head.

He swung his fist again, hitting the bag with a smack. Then again. Harder and faster, throwing his whole body forward, hips bucking like a wave running down his skeleton. Harder. Faster. The pain rolled up his arms until he thought his bones would shatter.

Like how he shattered Broc's bones. How he snapped Broc's arms like twigs. Like how he had killed the one person who brought him back from ruin.

The punching slowed, one . . . after . . . another. Caught in automatic training mode. It was the same workout he had done for years—until it had been interrupted by Malin's arrival in his life. The thought of her was a beacon turning on in his head, leading him into a darkness that seemed more right than the darkness that weighed on him.

Was she the only chance he had to save himself from blindness? Or from insanity? Death? Did he have to go crazy in the process? He felt nuts right now with the beast coiled in his belly like her dragan curled around her body. But while her creature helped her, all he got was hurt—and Rage.

Malin was the hope he never dared to feel, the only good choice in his sea of terrible choices.

Kane threw his fist into the punching bag. Over—and over—and over—and over again. He didn't even feel the bite of pain but saw the blood leaking out from his right hand, the stitches probably torn away. More blood started to flow, and the beast ate it up. The Rage sucked in the scent, heat coursing through Kane's veins and turning his vision to red. He beat the punching bag until it fell from the ceiling and spurted white stuffing across the floor, opening up like a body, and he stood over it. The creature who wanted to eat its guts and suck the bones dry until there was nothing left but a hollowed-out shell. He bellowed like a crazy animal, screaming over the music, and all the while, the beast egged him on in his head.

Over—and over—and over—again!

More! screeched the beast. *More!*

Warm liquid splattered across his face, dripping into his

eyes, blurring his vision, and he blinked away the blood. Yet he didn't stop plummeting his fist into the warmth, fingers pulling out slick sludge and discarding it next to the shell. His fist went in again.

More! The Rage urged. *Give me more!*

Kane yelled, "More!"

He tasted blood in his mouth. He knew the metallic taste from how many times he had been punched and his teeth had rattled, a few falling from the holes. He knew the taste of blood, and the ravenous beast licked it off his lips. Wanting the salty, metallic tang that mixed with his sweat.

"More!"

Something hit him in the head, and he whipped around, hunched over for an attack. His fists had turned into hammers, his finger turned into talons, and he would rip into a body for more. And there were more bodies.

The Rage licked his lips, someone else's blood coating his mouth.

"Again."

He lunged forward, following the voice through his black-tunneled vision that was covered in a red haze.

Something hit him in the chest. Like a prick of a needle. He looked down to see something sticking out. So small. Puny. And they thought they could take down the beast. It was almost laughable.

The Rage lurched forward, taking a step, but his knee was like Jell-O, jiggling, and then he fell to the ground with a loud smack of his face against the floor.

Kane blinked the redness from his eyes, only for it to be replaced by black.

DANIEL THOUGHT HE WAS GOING to be sick, and he turned his nose up and away, pointing to the ceiling. One of the only surfaces that wasn't covered in red blood from one of the Maker's newest soldiers.

Semaphors weren't supposed to die like that. Daniel had seen several die at the tip of one of the S-blades, but those were imbued with Aodh's Darkness. And when stabbed with that, they simply evaporated, their essence returning to the Maker to be reborn in another. Once baptized though, the Semaphors weren't supposed to have their bodies splayed open by someone's hands, their limbs nearly torn off, heads lolling to one side like a gash that made him look nearly headless. But that was what Kane "The Rage" Macleod had done.

No wonder they called him that, he thought, peeking out of the corner of his eye. That was a bad choice because Daniel stumbled forward, heading to the sink before spilling his guts out. That splattered like blood too, and he wretched harder.

"Daniel," asked one of the other Semaphors, "what do you want us to do?"

"Grab Kane," ordered Daniel, wiping his mouth. They only had one job, and he was not letting down Godric. Though, he hoped Godric would understand when he brought back one less soldier than had gone out on this mission. But Godric had been right. They needed to rid the world of this man. Kane had left this place a mess. He was every bit a beast they needed to cage.

"What about our guy?"

"Leave him."

"But—"

"Leave him!" Daniel cleared his throat and blinked tears from his eyes. He used the kitchen towel to wipe vomit from his face and shirt, then shut off the stereo. "Come on. We need to get out of here before one of his neighbors notices." As he stepped into the hallway, it was a surprise that no one had emerged from the other doors. Today just had to be Daniel's lucky day.

CHAPTER 34

HEAD HANGING, MALIN PICKED AT the dirt under her fingernails, flicking it onto the ground underneath her. She knelt, no longer having the strength to stand. It felt like all the breath had been swept from her lungs. Thoughts were like bees in her head without a place to call home, buzzing around and stinging. She tried to shake them from her mind, but the thought bees grew angry. Kane's image came back until he was all she could see in her vision.

"No," she groaned, voice echoing down the tunnels of the tombs. It broke the silence around her, and her own voice came back to slap her in the face, though it sounded jumbled, taken away by the wind and combined with the spirits around her. If she could believe the spirits were here . . . then she could believe that Myla's was still alive. Somewhere.

Reaching out a hand, Malin placed it against Myla's tombstone. It was cool to the touch, moist due to the dampness underground. The shudder of death waited on the inside and raised the tension until it was nearly unbearable. Malin swallowed it down, dread and guilt brimming in her until she couldn't breathe. A strangled cry escaped her lips, and she hung her head again. The sound was caught up in her chest, and she pulled her cloak tighter around her, meaning to comfort herself and hold back the sound.

"Myla," she whispered, "tell me what to do."

But there was no answer. Of course, there wouldn't be. There was never an answer. No matter how many times she came down to the tombs, every time hoping something would be different, she never found her sister. Only worms and cold, damp earth.

"I can't stop thinking about him," she whispered to Myla, like she had when they were young girls—teenagers just coming into their own, gossiping with each other about cute boys. They would whisper about all the hopes and dreams they had about boys long into the days, after their mother told them to go to sleep.

Myla had been the one to push Malin toward Godric after she had bonded with Emrys. Despite her better judgement, Malin had fallen into a relationship with him, and look how that turned out. That situation alone was a good enough reason not to get caught up in—Kane. Her mouth ran dry at the mere thought of his name.

"You would tell me I'm being ridiculous," continued Malin. "So would Tierney. She would shout it from the rooftops." Her voice cracked. Tierney was still unconscious, nearly dead after the Semaphor attack behind the Local.

These were all the reasons not to get distracted. Like Malin had with Kane. Her lower gut clenched. Well, apparently, she was still distracted and still lusting after Kane. She shook her head, trying to clear him away, but all the thoughts came back to that fighter. It wasn't lust because lust was too simple. If it was only lust, she wouldn't be thinking about him here. Now. Again.

His smile, something he didn't do often, was brilliant. It could bring life into the darkness if he would just allow it.

His laugh. It was rare, but it happened. More often when they were alone.

His eyes. She melted in them and saw herself reflected back. They were whole and perfect, alert.

It was hard to describe perfection, and maybe Kane wasn't perfect. She wasn't. No one was. But the way he held himself . . . the way he acted . . . he was perfect for her. He fit into the hole in her life like a puzzle piece, their jagged edges melting together, sliding into place. They were both broken pieces. But piece after piece. Layer after layer. Together, they fit.

"No." Malin whipped up her head. "No." She pressed her palm flat against Myla's stone, feeling the coolness. If only it could chill the rest of her. She pressed her head against the stone. "Talk to me. Tell me something."

Myla was silent, but she didn't need to speak.

Malin and her sister had spoken their whole lives—up to the point of Myla's death. Malin practically knew what Myla would say before Myla had said it, and often, they finished each other's sentences. Nothing could've torn them apart, not even Emrys or Godric when they entered the picture. The difference there was that Emrys hadn't tried, while Godric . . . well, Godric had stolen Myla from her in the worst possible way.

Still, Malin believed Myla's counsel would be unchanged: "Follow your heart, Malin. You think too much. You're in your head, and that only leads you down dark holes. Find the bright side of the Darkness. The joy."

Godric had become the effin Light *in the Darkness—and look where that got me.*

Malin's greatest failure of all.

To all of this, Myla would then say, "Don't hold yourself back, Malin. You're capable of more than you know. You've fallen once, so you won't do it again." Then Myla would laugh and dance away, almost singing, "You're the type of person that needs to learn a lesson twice."

But how true was that? Wasn't Kane the second lesson? Malin had to think so. Or was Kane different than Godric? A different lesson altogether, but with the same horrid results.

Tierney.

She sighed. The buzzing of her thoughts had dulled, but they came roaring back like the tide. She had to hold on or be caught up in them, rolling in the depths. Overtaken. Drawn into more thoughts of Kane. Everything was a thought about Kane.

His breath. Touch. Body.

The way he said her name.

As if he was behind her, she rocked back into his touch. Warmth spread through her, starting in her core—a throbbing she couldn't control, making her squeeze her thighs together. Heat spread up her veins. She nibbled on her bottom lip, wishing it were *his* teeth.

"Malin." A male voice was rough against her ears.

She wanted to lean into it.

"Malin!"

That wasn't Kane's voice.

Her eyes snapped open, and she remembered where she was. She stared at Myla's tombstone in front of her. The words engraved there—*Beloved daughter. Sister forever. Sleep in Darkness, dear child of Aodh*—could break her heart into a hundred pieces, but there was nothing but a hole in her chest where her heart should've been. She couldn't break if she couldn't love.

The thunder of footsteps neared, and she craned her neck to see Conrí running down the corridor. She jumped to her feet, her knees trembling, and she straightened herself by holding on to the cavern wall. The dampness transferred to her hand, and she rubbed off the dirt.

"Malin!"

"I'm here!" She went to meet with him. These halls belonged to the dead, and someday, her body would be added to it. She hoped that day was long off.

He skidded to a halt in front of her, out of breath. He gulped in air, getting his breathing under control. His brows were peaked and his eyes shifted, searching her face, and then Malin looked down. Her heart stopped with the memory: a simple letter, leading her to a box. Opening the white box. Gagging to find a dragan's husk, blacker than night and shriveled. And beside Aemro's remains, a bleeding heart. Myla's. Cut from her chest while she lived.

In Conrí's hands was another letter and a Semaphor dagger, one that wielded the Light.

Conrí wheezed. "I found these."

"In the Penumbra?" asked Malin, staring at the blade.

"No." He held out the letter, and she snatched it from her grasp. "I found it in the Daylight Realm . . . when I was looking for Kiera at—" He doubled over, falling to his hands and knees, and barfed.

She didn't need any more information. Where else would Conrí look for Kiera? She read the letter and knew Godric's handwriting from the damned letter he'd sent to draw her to the package. Even though it was short, she knew.

"I HAVE HIM."

No need to say who wrote it, and the bastard knew that. It slammed Malin in the gut and dropped her to her knees.

All those buzzing thoughts fell silent, replaced by images of the day Myla died. Godric had delivered a sweet message, disguised as a love letter, but tainted with his fanaticism. The box he'd lured her to had been anything but sweet. Myla's heart's blood was fresh, crimson, and wafting with life.

Now, Godric had left another letter. He didn't bother with the sweet words this time and didn't even take the time to write his name. Malin prayed to Aodh and then prayed to the other goddess who had once visited her. She flashed on a moment in the faerie fortune-teller's cart. Danu had come to her, warned her of a fight for Darkness. And this. This had to be it.

Please, Danu and Aodh, please don't let there be a box waiting on the other side. Give me the chance to fix this once and for all!

Malin shook her head. "Is this all you found?"

"The blade." He held it up like a prized gift, but she didn't take it. "And a dead Semaphor."

She furrowed her brows. "Dead?"

Conrí nodded. "Ripped to shreds. Blood everywhere."

She nodded. The berserker! There was hope.

"Let's go," she said, rushing past him. She glanced over her shoulder at Myla's tomb, hoping she wouldn't be putting someone else in there anytime soon.

CHAPTER 35

*S*o, *THIS IS WHAT IT'S* like to be in a cage and unable to get out? Kane thought, needing to focus on something. Normally, he could just leave the cage after a fight, but there was no escaping from this one. No ref to open the gate, and no crowd cheering his victory. Even with The Rage growling and hissing in his gut, he couldn't break the chains. What were they forged from, these links binding him to the wall and ceiling?

He didn't know how long he had been hanging like this, but the cuffs had dug into his wrists, and he no longer had feeling in his arms. And how long had it been since he'd been taken? His brain told him there should be pain, but the lack of blood movement had numbed him. Or maybe it was adrenaline constantly thrumming through his blood, ebbing and rushing again with every heartbeat.

When he had woken up here, he had tried to put the pieces into place in his mind, but there were holes. The last thing he knew, he'd been fighting, and there had been so much blood. But what did he know now? Better yet, what didn't he know? Who did this to him? Some sick fuck had clearly taken advantage of his snap. Of The Rage breaking free. But who? Anyone who might have a grudge against him would take it out in the cage, not tie him up and leave him hanging. There was no dignity in the unfair fight. And trained fighters weren't exactly known for their patience, so they sure as hell wouldn't take the time to carry him somewhere and tie him up.

So why was he here? And what did the asshole who brought him here want?

"Hey!" he called, but only silence answered. The same response as the last hundred times he'd called out.

What were they waiting for? Why not kill him and get it over with? Wouldn't be a huge loss to society. And now that Kiera was better and Malin was gone, why not? He didn't even need to fight for Broc.

Kane pulled on the chains again, and he felt pressure against his wrists. Blood dribbled down from where the metal chains bit into his skin, sliding down his forearms and eventually reaching his neck. It dropped onto the floor like water leaking from a faucet. *Drip. Drop. Drip.*

Eventually, the door swung open, and a man in a suit stepped inside. He adjusted his cufflinks, acting more like he was going to a suit-and-tie event than coming to get his prisoner. Somehow, Kane knew this guy was in charge. The one who'd ordered him captured. Maybe just by the way he swaggered in, checking his watch, and then walking over, halting ten feet away. Every last detail about this man said he had no conscience. The man's presence alone sent more chills down Kane's spine than if he'd been facing Coach Robbins.

"Excuse me if I don't come closer," said the man. "Your reputation precedes you. Not that it needs to. My associate showed me exactly what you did to one of my Light-bringers." He pursed his lips, though his eyes seemed amused. Almost as if he were stoically laughing inside at something so ridiculous and absurd about the situation.

Kane spat. "What do you want?"

"Hasty, aren't we?"

The beast growled, deep from Kane's gut.

"I'm Godric. Perhaps you know of me?"

Why did that name ring a bell? He tried to think, mind clinging on to answers but not quite getting it. Water falling through his fingers.

"Oh, yes. You've heard of me then," continued Godric, latching his hands behind his back. "From Malin, I expect."

Kane lurched forward. The chains clanked against each other violently, and it reminded him of a tiger at the circus his mother once took him too. When someone got too close to the cage, the tiger lunged but couldn't go far. Kane didn't know if it was The Rage or himself who lurched, his whole body advertently wanting to crash forward and take a bite of out Godric. Or snap his neck like a twig. Or rip his organs out from a hole in his chest. All of it and more if he'd hurt Malin—anything, as long as there was blood.

A half smile pulled at Godric's lips. The amused look was gone, replaced with something darkly sinister below. "So she's told you about me, yes? I'm surprised. Malin was never one to open up."

Kane couldn't remember Malin saying a damn thing about Godric, but he doubted it was anything good. Then, something clicked. "Semaphor?!"

"Now we're getting somewhere."

"You've no right to speak her name. Your kind . . . you're"— Kane yanked against the chains again, spittle flying from his lips—"a sick fuck."

Godric *tsked*, shaking his head. "No reason for that. I wouldn't want this to get ugly." He pulled out a whip from behind his back, his long and slim fingers sliding over the leather thong then down the fall.

Kane bit his tongue, stopping the assault that wanted to spring through his teeth. His eyes narrowed on the whip, and The Rage inside beat against Kane's ribs, wanting free. The only thing the beast would break would be Kane if he kept this up, so he swallowed, a silent message for the beast to calm. As Kane should calm. There was no reason for this to get uglier than it was, not that he wanted to agree with Godric, at least not until Kane was out of the chains. Then they would see how chains could really be used.

"My associate did tell me that you were hard to leash, so let this be your only warning: If you step out of line or hurt any of us, I will whip you until you scream. Bleed. Pass out. Even die," said Godric. "Is that understood?"

Kane glared.

"I'll have a response." He lashed the whip through the air, cracking it loudly a few feet from Kane's ear.

Kane didn't flinch, and through gritted teeth, he said, "Yes."

"*Sir.*" Godric tilted his head and smiled.

Kane stared straight ahead, imagining his hands wrapped around Godric's skinny neck and wringing the life straight out of him. He relished imagining the slime's heartbeat quicken and then fade under his fingertips; Godric's final and strangled breaths would pulsate from his lips as they went blue, and his tongue would loll to one side.

Godric coiled the whip around one hand. "Don't make me hurt you with it."

Kane didn't see how refusing to call this man "sir" would get him whipped. But that was stepping out of line, Kane supposed, and Godric was obviously crazier than even Kane's Rage.

"Say it."

The rational part of Kane pushed the stupid word up to the tip of his tongue. It was the smart thing to do. One word, no pain. The beast growled, *No. We bow to no one. We cower to no one. Not. Ever. Again.*

Shaking his head, Godric pulled back the whip and sent it snaking forward. The lash stung Kane's torso, the bite of pain spreading across his skin like wildfire. Warmth radiated out. The beast Raged in Kane's chest, and the rest of his body followed suit, pulling against the chains that held him in place and trying to reach the Semaphor. Godric pulled back the whip, angled his body, and held the handle poised just behind him. Ready to send it snaking toward Kane again.

But he held the pose rather than lashing out. His voice remained cool when he said, "I didn't want it to come to this." As if torturing Kane was nothing but a business deal.

Bullshit! He didn't *have* to whip Kane. No one *made* him

abduct Kane. Yet he acted like God Himself had forced his hand and he was dealing divine justice. Godric's body tensed, muscles coiling for the attack, as a sly smile tugged up at his lips.

Then the door squeaked open, and another man appeared. Kane's eyes burrowed into him, and the beast took a deep breath, sniffing at the man. Familiar. The light in Kane's dungeon was dim, but the outline of him and the smell of him. Kane had met him before, but where? He searched his mind—not the most reliable thing at the moment—and swore he saw an image of Coach Robbins staring at him with a gaping mouth. A sneer upon his lips. Kane's eyes snapped back to the new man, who whispered in Godric's ear.

"Thank you, Daniel," said Godric.

Daniel paused, staring at Kane like he was a monster.

"You may go," Godric commanded this Daniel person.

He didn't budge. Must be more cracked than Kane to want to remain in this room. "But sir, he's dangerous."

Godric wrapped the whip around his hand. "He's not as tough as he looks while in chains. I've got him."

Daniel still hesitated, and for a split second, Kane wondered if Daniel could help him. Maybe Daniel felt bad about this? Someone had to know this was wrong. But then Daniel ducked his head and left through the door. Kane caught the flash of another person outside before the door closed, and he was alone with Godric again.

"Right?" asked Godric. "Your bark is worse than my little friend's bite." He let the length of the whip fall to the floor, stroking the thong all the way to the popper at the end.

"My bite is pretty vicious," growled Kane.

Godric laughed, but it sounded forced and as hollow as the walls around them. "I'll let you get away with that one because I have good news. Malin is on her way."

Kane's heart stopped.

"We couldn't just let her not know you went missing. That might've taken too long, and frankly, you don't have that much time." He tilted his head, eyes raking over Kane, and licked his lips.

A shiver ran down Kane's spine; his whole body recoiled from Godric. He wanted to run to Malin. Warn her not to come. Protect her with everything he had.

"Yeah, a little birdy mentioned something about you and the witch. Such sinful creatures those dark witches, and their little dragans too."

Kane was pushing himself away. Further back. As far as he could go. But neither the chains nor the wall would let him run. He couldn't get far enough back.

"Daniel will keep me up to date with the witches, especially Malin." The whip curled further around Godric's hand like a viper ready to strike.

"No," said Kane, voice low and rough as gravel.

"No?" mocked Godric, then he let out a singular sardonic laugh. "Daniel is loyal to the Maker's cause. One of my best."

"No to Malin."

"Ahhh, but she's already on her way. It would be a shame to exclude her from our little party." He paced slowly, keeping his eyes trained on Kane the entire time.

No! The beast inside roared, the sound cutting through Kane's lips. "No!"

Godric jumped back a step and flung out the flimsy whip. As if that could hold back Kane and The Rage. Even the chains trembled. It wouldn't be long until he could tear them from the wall, and then he would break them into pieces like they were glass. He would tear down these concrete walls and turn this building into dust. He pulled and pulled and pulled—and Godric took another step back, no longer able to keep the traces of fear from his face. The beast inside Kane Raged, and it was only a matter of time.

Stifling the fear, Godric slung the whip out, slicing a gash across Kane's chest.

Kane didn't feel the pain. Not with his body so tensed, coiled and ready to tear Godric limb from limb and bathe this room in blood. And definitely not with Malin coming for him.

She would be in danger, and it would be his fault.

Kane should've defended himself better. He knew how, but he had failed, giving in to the beast within for no good reason. Whatever happened in his apartment while he was blinded by his failures, his beast, The Rage . . . however he had been captured was careless of him. Kane was a fighter and a victor, and after failing everyone around him, he had failed himself too. Not again. Not anymore. Not for Malin. He wasn't worth saving. If he couldn't free himself, then there was no point for him to live. A fighter who lost was no fighter at all. For him, it was no life at all.

For Malin, though, he had to fight. Fight to save her, fight for her Darkness, and fight to save himself because . . . what was the feeling stirring in his chest? It wasn't The Rage. No, it was something warmer flowing through his veins. Yet The Rage was louder too, rattling his rib cage. He closed his eyes and tried to calm the beast. He wanted to feel the warmth again. Not the heat that scorched him from the inside out but the warmth that calmed him. Under his closed eyelids, he found Malin, the only person who had ever settled his Rage.

The whip cracked against Kane's skin, and his eyes flashed open. He saw blood. Felt it running down his skin where he had been slashed. The Rage felt it too, bellowing, and Kane pulled on the chains again.

"Does she like this savagery in you?" taunted Godric. "Perhaps that's where I failed to keep her satisfied."

Kane roared. The thought of this slimy fucker touching what was his had him pulling on the chains again.

"Ah now, none of that." Godric tsked. "But honestly, I never realized she wanted a man so primal. So . . . primitive." His nose scrunched, obviously disgusted. "If my childhood friend, Emrys, hadn't already bonded with Myla, perhaps I should've gone for her. She was the lighthearted twin. But I wasn't thinking at the time. I was so engrossed, tempted by the wretched Darkness. Drawn into their sinful ways." He glanced upward, as if seeking absolution. "By the time I found the Maker's Light, I knew what needed to be done." He pulled the whip back, the leather slithering across the floor, pulling pink-tinged water away from the drain.

Was that a clump of hair? What had happened in here?

Godric took a long, deep breath and let it out on a sigh, checking his watch. "Malin will be along soon enough, so I guess I should share you." He chuckled. "Although, she may not be in a sharing kind of mood."

Kane gritted his teeth. Vomit bubbled in his stomach, not from the pain but from what his eyes had seen. *Let it be a trick. Let this all be a nightmare. Don't be real.*

"I brought an old friend to say hello."

The door creaked open, and another man stepped into the room. A jolt of recognition ran through Kane's body, and he seethed inside. Years in prison hadn't been kind to Coach Robbins, but worse, he hadn't changed much. He wore the same old tracksuit in black and gold, the Wickney High School colors, and he had the same glasses sitting on the tip of his nose like he was always looking down on people. Kane had been taller than him in high school, but by the way the man acted alone, he had seemed like a giant. And prison bulked his arms, and his once thin and lithe legs now resembled tree trunks. The coach ran his tongue over his yellow teeth.

"Hello, Kane," the coach purred.

His name on the sick fuck's lips sent shivers down Kane's spine, and a whimper clogged his throat. The beast refused to release the knot and receded deeper into Kane, crawling back into the shadows. Fear overtook the beast like it had overtaken Kane when he was a teenager. Years had passed, and nothing had changed. Weren't people supposed to grow and heal? Kane thought he would with the coach locked up. Kane thought The Rage had been his way of overcoming all that he'd been through. But now, staring at the coach, he knew. He hadn't healed or coped or even fully acknowledged what happened. He quaked in his clothes, a cold sweat breaking out across his skin, and his teeth chattered.

"It's been a long time," said the coach. He kept his distance, back plastered to the door.

Godric smiled. "Come now . . . You're good friends, yes?

Go meet your *student*, wasn't it, Coach Robbins?" He pushed the man forward and then stood several feet back, leaning against the wall with his arms crossed over his chest.

Coach Robbins stood five feet away, and Kane swore he smelled the coach's cologne, so overpowering it strangled him, burned his nostrils, and hurt his lungs. Kane couldn't breathe, as if the smell were poison to his system. The smell used to keep Kane up at night after he had come home from practice with the smell on his clothes and in his hair. No matter how many showers Kane took, he couldn't wash the stench away. No matter how many times Kane wished he could forget, he couldn't. Even now, he felt the coach's hands touching his body, his cigarette breath whispering in Kane's ear.

He closed his eyes and tried to think of the warmth. He wanted to shake the coach off. *Please,* he begged. *Please, no. Not him.* And for once, his mind complied, replacing the coach with Malin. *Yes, Malin.* He breathed, knowing her scent too, more recently than the other, fouler odor. It replaced the coach's cologne and the murkiness of this dungeon.

Malin would be close.

Don't come, Malin. Please. Save yourself, he begged soundlessly. Before, he'd been happy to die here to save Malin, but the coach was here. Now, he wanted to be saved. Kane couldn't save himself back then, and he didn't know if he could save himself now with his beast hiding too.

Peeking out from under his eyelashes, he saw the coach was still there. Kane hadn't woken up from his nightmare turned reality. He wanted to fall back into his dream of Malin.

She was enough for him. More than enough—more than he deserved, especially after all that happened to him and all that he had done to others. He was a monster, created by the monster in front of him, built to be a Frankenstein, a creature who only knew how to be a monster. But didn't a monster deserve love too? Malin had already given him more than he thought he would ever have. Would she come? Save him? Give him more? Could he give it in return?

Yes! he and The Rage roared at the same time.

His heart fluttered in his chest, his stomach churning as the warmth he craved spread through him. He loved her, and he would love her until the end of his days, whether that be today or far in the future. He hoped for the latter. He needed to get back to her to tell her. And he needed it to be anywhere but here.

Strengthened by these sudden warm emotions, Kane opened his eyes to find Coach Robbins staring at him exactly the same way he had when Kane was a teenager. Weren't pedophiles supposed to have an age limit or something?

Kane heard the coach's words in his mind, the ones that always came before Coach Robbins took him. *Just you and me here, kid.* It sent shivers up and down Kane's spine. He would repeat it like a mantra every time he'd asked Kane to stay after practice. And afterward, he would clean up and turn to Kane, who lay on a mat, curled into a ball, trembling from the cold and splitting pain, and he would say, "I'm just a man, kid. Desires and all. And I'll make you into a man too." And every time, minutes feeling like eons passed before the coach had tapped him on the back and said, "Take a shower. I'll see you at practice tomorrow." Then another eon before the door of the gym squeaked closed, telling Kane he'd gone.

"You're looking good, Kane," said Coach Robbins. "I've been following you. Since in prison."

Through clenched teeth, he spat, "And why aren't you in there now?"

"Good behavior. Overcrowding. I saw the Light." He tilted his head back to Godric, who gave a small nod. An acknowledgment.

That slimy bastard knows what this predator has done, thought Kane, *and they are working together.* He would kill them both for it.

"I've been keeping an eye on you," continued the coach. "From prison. You're a very good fighter. I suppose I can take some credit for that."

Bile burned its way up Kane's throat, and he swallowed. Hard.

"Heard my protégé was headed for Vegas. Wouldn't want to

take your old coach, would you?" he shrugged. "You know . . . for old times' sake."

Kane leaned against his chains, closing in on the coach. "Fuck off."

Suddenly, the whip cracked against his skin. The sound bounced off the concrete walls and floor, and the coach stumbled back a step, looking back at Godric from where he stood near the door. He wore a sneer on his face. For all the things the coach had done to Kane, he had never beat Kane. Not one punch or kick or anything of the sort. The term the coach had used in court was "loving caresses." There was nothing loving about it. However, the slap against Kane's skin, blood oozing out from marks across his body, stunned the coach, who froze where he stood, eyes wide and darting between Godric and Kane.

"No," growled Godric, already wrapping the whip up again. Readying for another attack. "No talking back. And no swearing!"

Kane's eyes narrowed on Godric. "Fuck you!"

Godric sent the whip spiraling forward again, and it slapped against the sensitive skin covering Kane's ribs. He barely felt it. Not with the years of training, taking punches. Scrapes and cuts were all part of the job. Godric thought a whip would hurt him? Kane had been far more hurt in his life. A whip against his body was nothing against the years of endured torture by Coach Robbins.

Kane returned his gaze to the coach, who hovered five feet away, looking more like a concerned parent than the monster who started this all. "And fuck you! I hope you burn in hell! I hope you die the most painful and worst death ever. And as soon as I'm free, I *will* kill you!"

The whip slapped Kane again, this one glancing off his body. A numb heat had settled over his skin, starting to smolder like embers. Movement started in his belly, the beast climbing out of its darkened cage. Rising from the fire. It would protect him now like it had protected Kane his whole life. It was the worst and best part of him. Soon, he would ignite, and everyone would die.

Godric was rearing back the whip for another strike when his phone rang—a high-pitched screech in Kane's ears, and he flinched away from the sound. His eyes cut back over to Godric. The coach had stepped toward the door with his shoulders drawing up to his ears. Godric smirked, the corner of his mouth upturned.

"Hello, Malin," he drawled.

"No!" Kane bellowed, thrashing against his chains yet again. And yet again, to no avail.

Godric scowled at him, and in a flash, he sent the whip forward. The tail wrapped around Kane's neck, and Godric pulled, tightening the grip. It drew Kane forward, tighter against the chains cutting into his wrists. Into the bone. Blood ran down his arms and splattered against the floor. The whip tightened like a boa constrictor around his neck until he couldn't breathe.

"Yes," Godric was saying into the phone. "Now Malin, that would be far too easy, wouldn't it? You can do better than that, especially for love."

Blood rushed past Kane's ears, making it hard for him to hear. But did Godric say *love*? Did Malin feel the same as he did about her?

Godric said, "Let's meet."

"No." Kane's voice wheezed. He coughed as dark dots burst in his vision, starting to blanket him as the whip tightened. "No."

"Yes, that will work nicely," said Godric into the phone. "I'll send you the location after I've had a little more fun."

Black splotches narrowed in, this time not because he was giving himself over to The Rage. Kane was losing, sinking, falling into the . . . Godric added something else Kane couldn't follow as darkness overtook him.

CHAPTER 36

WHAT IN THE NAME OF *Darkness did he meant by "having more fun"?* Malin wondered as she paced back and forth and nibbled on her bottom lip. *At least it means Kane is still alive.* But for how long? From the last time Godric messaged her, she had saved his number, and as soon as she made it into the Daylight Realm, she had called. But Morgana was still having trouble tracing it.

Malin's hands were balled into fists, held to her sides to stop her from picking at her nails. Even then, her thumbnail was flicking at dead skin. She balled her hands tighter until her fingernails dug into her palms. She knew she would have crescents branded into her palms afterward but couldn't care less. Not while Godric had Kane.

"Anything?" she asked, continuing her pacing. Her head pulled up, glancing at the clock, then the door. They were running out of time.

"Not since you asked me a minute ago," snapped Morgana. "Now shut up! You're giving me a headache."

"Oh, *I'm* giving *you* a headache?" Malin rolled her eyes. "You were supposed to have tracked the first message down days ago! Had you finished the trace then, we wouldn't be in this situation."

Morgana's shoulders expanded and then she rolled them back. "Do you want me to explain how many measures that fucker took to prevent my tracing that message? Or do you want me to find him now?"

Malin bit her lip.

Morgana's voice low, she asked, "Will someone remove her before I remove her myself?"

Brogan left Morgana's side to join Malin. She stepped around him when he tried to block her path, and he caught her arm.

She whipped around to stare up at her covenmate. "I'm not leaving here until we get some answers."

Brogan said, "You're the problem. Not her." Short-winded as ever, but he was right. Malin knew it but couldn't control her panic. She tried to control herself, because Morgana was doing everything she could, and Malin's little sister was the best hacker there was.

She slammed her hands into Brogan's chest, shifting her anger to him. "How am I the problem?"

"Hovering," Morgana called out. "Making me anxious." She had three screens all pointed at her, and she typed on one keyboard while focusing on one computer monitor. Another screen was broken up into sixteen cameras that flashed based on movement of Wickney. The last screen had some sort of jumbled text scrolling up the screen. Malin didn't know enough about hacking to know if this was a thing or not, but she had to trust Morgana. And she had trusted Morgana in the past.

"You should have an anxiety," said Malin. "We all should. Kane is missing. In Godric's hands. Who knows what he is doing to Kane?"

"Brogan," snapped Morgana without looking over from her screens.

His hand latched on to Malin's arm and steered her away. "Let's get some air."

"What I need is Kane found." Her chest tightened, and she couldn't explain the flip-flops of her stomach. She thought she was going to be sick, but no, she couldn't do that now. Brogan gave her a look with his eyebrows raised, eyes narrowed, and head tilted slightly. Malin relented. "Okay, let's get some air." She even let him steer her out of Morgana's basement apartment and onto the city street.

Wickney's high buildings popped up around her, reaching toward the night sky. The worst part was that they blocked the view, and the bright city lights clouded the stars, making the sky a deep bruise of purple without any definition. The moon was an orb of white, but even then, it was obscured by the lights of cars passing by and skyscrapers. She hated the Daylight Realm. They didn't know true beauty.

Brogan leaned up against the wall. "You gonna talk about it?" He crossed his arms over his chest.

"I don't know what you mean." She pressed a hand to her stomach to keep it from churning. It didn't work. The pressure wasn't enough. Only Kane with her again, alive and safe, would calm it.

"Come on." He rolled his eyes. "It's just us here."

Conrí had gone to keep Kiera and her mother safe. Tierney was still passed out, so yeah, they were the only two fighters left. Another problem with Aodh only knew how many Semaphors they'd face once they went in to save Kane.

"Malin?" Brogan drawled.

"My fault."

He cleared his throat but said nothing, which made her assume that he agreed. And of course, he would. They all should. This was her fault. She had let down her guard. She wasn't focused. Tierney was nearly dead because Malin should've been at her side. Their numbers were low, because Malin chose a vigilante mission over recruiting new members for their coven. Godric abducted Kane because Malin should've been protecting him and should've taken him back to the Penumbra.

Conrí now had to protect Kiera and their mother because they should've been in the Penumbra too. And Godric—most of all him! He was her fault because she should've killed him when she had that queasy feeling back when they were dating.

She'd had many chances with him in her bed. She shouldn't have let him get so close. She shouldn't have let him take Myla and Aemro. Her crimes were adding up. She shouldn't have been the leader. She should be the one dead. Myla should be the one alive.

"Not what I meant," continued Brogan, "but you need to check yourself."

Her head snapped over. "What?"

"It's not all about you."

"I know that."

"Good." He nodded. "Can you put it into action?"

"Wh—? Of course I can. This is all my fault, and I'll fix it."

"There." He pointed at her. "Again, all about you."

"But it is my fault."

"Who says that?"

Malin opened her mouth, ready to list who, but no one had. Then she opened her mouth wider, ready to list all that had happened because of her. Then she closed it.

Brogan took a deep, deep breath, and for the first time Malin could recall, he spewed more than a handful of words. "Look, Malin, I've known you for a very long time. Really, your whole life. And you take everything hard. You did when you were a kid. Myla got hurt falling off a log in the river—you blamed yourself. Myla stole a sweet from the village shop—you stepped up and took the blame. You're a gods-be-damned martyr. I'm surprised you haven't gotten yourself killed trying to protect everyone but yourself."

She scowled, her mouth hanging open.

Brogan took another gulp of air. "Ah, you were just thinking that, weren't you? Of course, you were. You were thinking it would be better off if you were dead and your sister was alive."

She planted her fists on her hips. "It would be."

"No, it wouldn't."

"Yes."

"Are you sure?" he asked, closing in on her, eyes narrowed.

"I don't think so. You're the best fighter we have. A good leader. Dedicated. Understanding. Kind. Generous."

"But people were killed on my watch."

"That's what our lives are." He swallowed and touched her hand. "We all chose this. No one is forcing us. We are protectors. Of the Penumbra, *our* realm. For the dragan. Our friends, family. You're not holding us against our will." He grabbed and squeezed her hand, and she looked down at it, wishing it were Kane's hand on her own. "But you're denying yourself."

She snapped her head up. "What?"

"Like I said, Malin, it's just us." He wiggled his eyebrows. "So, tell me more about Kane. What's he like? How's he in bed?"

"Eff off." She pushed away from him, but he held on, laughing.

"That good, eh?"

She rolled her eyes. "Girl talk, Bro? Really?"

"No time like now. Especially for a martyr like you."

Malin prepared a retort, ready to slam him back into his place, when her phone buzzed. She whipped it out, the screen flashing bright, and she stalled when she saw the name upon the screen. But so did Brogan.

"That's not Morgana," he said slowly. "Malin, why is Godric texting you a location? Have you been in contact with him?"

"Yeah. That's what Morgana's tracing. He wants to meet." Malin furrowed her brows. "To do an exchange."

His eyes went wide, illuminated by the phone. "Let me call Conrí and get him here."

"No. Godric wants me in exchange for Kane."

"That's insane."

"What can I say?" She looked up at him. "I'm a martyr." She took a step toward him, feeling Breyze upon her back, and she watched as his dragan Aemyn—brother to Aemro, Myla's bonded dragan—poked up from under his cloak. The dragans could smell a fight coming from a mile away. She didn't want it to be bloody, but she needed this over with.

To get to Kane. To save him. And if she survived, to love him.

No, she needed to focus, to kill Godric and be done with this once and for all. To avenge Myla and her dragan. For the Dark Realm—all realms—to be safer.

"Malin," Brogan said, but he was already locked in her grasp.

She touched Breyze with her other hand, and her dragan bit her. The venom rushed her veins, and she leaned into the Darkness. "I'm sorry, Brogan. *Cadal.*"

"Malin, wait. Let me help," he groaned, and Aemyn bared his teeth, ready to plunge them into Brogan or fight off Malin.

Malin pressed her fingers into Brogan's neck, feeling his quickened pulse as he tried to fight the sleep spell, but his pulse was already slowing as he fell into a comatose state. Her arms reached out around him and lowered him to the ground so he wouldn't hit his head. Aemyn continued to hiss, his breath icy as it reached Malin's skin. Aemyn Icebreath indeed. His forked tongue slithered from his mouth and aimed at her.

"I mean no harm to him," she said to Aemyn. "He'll wake up soon. Tell him I'm sorry." Then she was running, taking off into the night with Breyze on her back.

To save and to kill.

To live or to die.

CHAPTER 37

GUILT GURGLED IN MALIN'S STOMACH for what she had done to Brogan, but she couldn't have him hold her back and she couldn't risk his life too. He may be right, but she'd deal with that after she saved the man she loved. She ran, glancing toward the sky as the light began to illuminate. Sunrise was coming. Breyze curled tightly around her, hiding under her cloak. She reached down to make sure he was wearing his goggles and found them securely in place.

"Hold on," she told Breyze through her shallow breaths. "Hold on." That last one may have been to Kane, as if he could hear her. She turned her face forward and pushed her body harder, dodging through the cowans emerging after their deep slumbers and still groggy because they hadn't had their morning coffees.

"Come on," she urged herself, zigzagging around planters to miss the crowds. There were too many people. They were slowing her down. She was getting closer yet farther away. "I'm coming, Kane."

KANE SHIVERED AS COACH ROBBINS stared at him with those dopey but narrowed eyes. The kind of look that seemed empathetic at first glance, but was hungry beneath the surface, like a dog who dug through trash, got sick from it, then did it again. Coach Robbins was no better than a dog. In truth, he was worse. It would be praise to call him a dog. Coach Robbins should've long been in the ground, food for the worms. Kane should've done it when he was a teenager—fought back and killed him. And if not Kane, someone else. Why hadn't one of the prisoners killed Coach Robbins? Weren't they supposed to hate child molesters?

"Oh, good." Godric pulled back the whip that was slick with blood. It slithered on the ground, leaving crimson marks.

Kane's own blood pooled underneath his feet, making his toes slick against the ground. He had awoken again but could so easily fall into the pain that rampaged in his body. It wanted him to spiral. It wanted him to wallow and feel it until he couldn't feel anything else. But he focused on Coach Robbins, and his Rage numbed the pain. The same way it happened in a fight. The pain would come later, but for now, with adrenaline pumping through his veins and lighting his blood on fire, he was alive. He was numb. He was ready to fight.

"Malin is on her way," added Godric.

Her name almost brought Kane back to reality, and he felt the heat on his skin, like flames eating up his limbs. His blood boiled, and he could've screamed in pain. *No!* The pain could kill him, make him pass out so the coach could take what he wanted. What he always wanted! Kane focused on Coach Robbins. His torture. His death.

Godric sang, "Almost here, it seems. Since she accessed the pin I dropped for her, I can watch her come. Good technology, don't you think? Dark witches are always bad with technology because technology and magic are at constant odds. How unnatural the Darkness, as they call it, is."

The words rushed past Kane's ears, as if they were underwater.

Clogged and disoriented. The message ricocheted from him. The beast didn't let it stick.

The Rage licked his lips, tasting sweat and blood. It wasn't the first time. Kane's beast knew what it wanted: Coach Robbins. The question was how it was going to free itself to reach the bastard. Somewhere deep inside, Kane wondered if revenge was enough. How bittersweet it would be, and it would take a lifetime for Coach Robbins to feel what Kane felt. Years of torment and hate and guilt and pain and more—and even then, it wouldn't be enough. Coach Robbins's death shouldn't be quick, but how much time did they have? Once freed from these chains, the beast wouldn't let Coach Robbins escape this time.

Never again.

Not once more.

No one else would be his victim.

Ever.

Godric stepped into Kane's vision, and it seemed to snap The Rage. Pain exploded in Kane, and he clenched his teeth, tears burning his eyes. He was on fire. He was dying! The whip was wrapped around Godric's hand, blood leaking onto the ground from the thong. It still drizzled from Kane too. *Drip-drop-drip-drop!* Adding to the pool that couldn't crawl down the drain fast enough. The edges of the pool were starting to brown, coagulate. The metallic tang combined with the coach's cologne lingered in the air, too much in Kane's nostrils, and he reared back. His whole body lashed out, the chains jiggling from the wall, and he thought he felt the pull. The give. Did he hear a crack? A chance for escape?

"Daniel wasn't kidding. You really are dangerous. A monster." Godric's eyebrows pulled together, then he turned to Coach Robbins. He held out the whip. "Do you want a chance? Exercise his demons like you have done your own."

The coach didn't raise his hand, eyes trained on Kane, and Kane returned the gaze, his lips pulling back. A threat that if Coach Robbins even thought about it, Kane would wrap that whip around Coach Robbins's neck and hang him—no, too quick. Too kind. The beast inside sneered, *Whip him! Touch him!*

Just as he did to you!

Kane rocketed forward again but was jerked backward by the chains. Another pull. He got further than before. And he would go further yet.

"Hmm." Godric threw the whip at the coach's feet. "I'll leave this with you then. I have Malin to deal with."

Her name.

It sent a shockwave through Kane's body. Pain exploded in him while the beast roared. A savage protective instinct. All and nothing. Someone and no one. Only her name drew him back, but he couldn't. Not now on his deathbed.

Forget her, hissed the beast. *Fight for survival.*

Was it really that easy?

Godric flashed a grin and then left the room, holding his cell phone like he was getting second-by-second updates on Malin.

She was coming . . . for Kane. That would be too innocent of a thought. No, she was coming for revenge—against Godric and what he had done to her and her family. Kane didn't know all the details surrounding Malin and Godric, but it was enough to know that it was as bad as the pain Coach Robbins had wrought on him. And now Kane was left alone with the coach. Chained.

Kane trembled, buried in the depths of his memories. Shaking and crying and telling the coach *No. It doesn't feel right. Stop. I don't want to.* The beast bellowed louder, devouring Kane's teenage cries.

Kane narrowed his eyes on the coach, the innocent young boy remaining in him praying the coach wouldn't take him again. All while the beast wished he would try. Another reason to hurt Coach Robbins. The Rage dared the coach to pick up the whip. Kane gritted his teeth, holding back both the boy's cries and the beast's bellows.

Slowly, Coach Robbins bent down and picked up the whip, turning it over in his hands. Kane's blood stained his palms. "I don't want to hurt you."

Kane spat, "You already have."

The coach raised his eyes. "Don't put that back on me. I was making you a man."

"You were grooming me. You were using me. You were making me the monster you are. Try me now. I've found a new beast, and he thirsts for your blood."

The coach pulled up a half smirk, but the other half of his face was stuck in time. Maybe he had been injured in prison? Or maybe it was a stroke? While he was still as bulky as always, his left leg dragged. That side of his body was a step behind. Lagging. A weakness in what was once the great and powerful Coach Robbins, the man who won state championships and took people to nationals, raising fighters through the ranks and sending them into the professionals. How many kids had he gotten into college on full-ride scholarships? His fall from grace once had been an unimaginable blow to so many people. Kane had never stepped forward, but a few had—the brave ones. Kane felt like as much of a coward now as he did then, shaking in the chains that bound him.

"They say *you're* the monster now," said the coach. "The Rage. I heard you killed your last coach. Broc, was it?"

Kane pulled against the chains, and they rattled, slapping against the concrete walls. He jerked and heard a groan that ran up the chains. The wall crumbled softly, pieces of dust falling down into Kane's bloody marks upon the floor. He felt the tickle of pain, and he gritted his teeth to hold off the screech that wanted to follow.

Coach Robbins turned over the whip in his hands. "Are you going to kill me?" His voice sounded as calm as if he were asking about Kane's grades.

"Release me from my chains and find out," grunted Kane.

That smile broadened, his dopey eyes enlarging. His pupils narrowed. "You would like that wouldn't you?"

"You always preached a fair fight. This is anything but. Hypocrite." Kane—or The Rage—snarled at the coach.

But Robbins maintained his poise. "So you have a girlfriend now, yeah? This . . . Malin."

Kane roared, "Keep her name out of your mouth!" He fought

his chains, and even more, they pulled. Inch by bloody inch. Closer. The smell of the coach's cologne haunting him, entering his lungs, and making his head dizzy. Or maybe that was blood loss? Blood lust? Or was it only the pain echoing through his body?

The coach chuckled. "I never thought you had it in you, kid."

"I'm not a kid."

"Don't I know it?" Coach Robbins stepped forward, tightening the whip around his hands. "I made you a man."

"No. You didn't."

"You would be nothing without me."

Kane jerked against his chains. An inch more. Was it the wall giving out or his wrists? "I made myself."

"And here you are acting like a rabid dog. You know, they made me go to therapy in prison. I had to read these stories about"—the coach gagged—"victims. But what they don't realize is that those 'perps' made the 'victims' who they are. Famous and wealthy. Strong. You are who you are, Kane, because of me. And what do I get out of it? Not even a thank-you."

"Fuck you."

The coach unwound the whip from around his hand, and the thong and fall slid to the floor with a thud. Kane braced himself for the next bite of pain, The Rage growling inside of him. The coach pulled back the whip, ready to snake it forward, and Kane felt the beast thrash in his body. An armor overtaking his skin. He focused on the coach and how he would sink his teeth into flesh.

The coach paused, dropped the whip to his side. "This isn't right. This isn't how I like it." He sneered. "Or how you like it."

STEPPING INTO THE SHADOWS OF the warehouse, Malin checked her surroundings. Breyze was curling further under her cloak with the threat of light on the horizon. Daylight was too close. "I know," Malin murmured to her dragan. "I know. We save Kane, and we go." And if Godric died in the process, all the better. She tiptoed to the door, reaching out and about to whip it open. An S-blade in her hand. She was ready for an attack.

An electric crackle vibrated above, and then a deep breath followed. Malin blinked, memories of that breath against her neck. Godric's breath. Was it weird to remember how someone breathed? Godric breathed through his mouth, like he was whistling or wheezing half the time. Kane breathed through his nose, his nostrils twitching. She opened her eyes.

"Welcome, Malin." Godric's voice crackled from an overhead PA system, and it echoed across the blacktop pavement and the concrete block walls. It sent a shiver through Malin. "We've been waiting for you."

Her eyes flickered up as a red dot blinked on the camera aiming toward her. A lens narrowed on her, reflecting her morphed features. That wasn't supposed to happen. The Darkness usually protected her from such techy things. She swallowed, so much for sneaking in.

"You're early," said Godric. "No worries. I had you on GPS, so I expected you. Come on in."

The door buzzed in front of her and then clicked, pushing open with a pulse of air. She gripped the door before it shut, eyeing the camera lens one more time.

"Don't be shy," said Godric. "We've waited a long time to see each other, Malin, and if I were you, I wouldn't wait so long for Kane." The feed cut, crackling static disappearing, and she plunged inside.

Light flooded the warehouse, not from the windows but from the bright fluorescent lights that hung over the white-painted concrete with glitter embedded to shine back. It was as bright as snow on a sunny day. The walls were the same. Malin stumbled back a step, struck by the light, and Breyze cowered beneath her cloak. She should turn back and run—save Breyze—but Kane, and all those who could ever be hurt by the Semaphors. For revenge of Myla and Aemro. Malin closed her eyes, whispering *"Dubh"* for darkness, then she forced her eyes forward. It only dimmed the space around her, so she stared at the dazzling and blinding floor, allowing it to burn into the backs of her eyes.

In the middle of the warehouse, the floor was a moat—she blinked, was that right? Yes, it was. Godric apparently had the means and know-how, but it was strange. It was twenty feet across with gurgling water that looked deep enough to easily drown. Malin could swim across, but it wouldn't be that easy. It was never that easy.

Godric stepped out on the far side and clapped his hands. "Hello, Malin. Come in. Come in." He stepped up to the edge of the moat, toes tipping over the side. "Don't be shy." He turned his head and listened, then he gave a tightlipped smirk. "Did you come for me or for Kane?"

She drew her other S-blade, both of them pointed at Godric. She clenched her teeth, ready to launch herself into battle. Swim the moat. Kill Godric. Save Kane. "Breyze," she murmured, trying to coax her dragan out from under her cloak, but he was buried in the folds.

Godric chuckled. "Is it too bright? This is what happens when you see the Light! You can feel the Light too." He clapped his hands, and a few seconds later, the moat filled with water, crackles with electricity running through it. A zap here and there. Sparks dancing.

Malin would be electrocuted if she tried to swim across, meaning she'd fail her dragan, Kane, and herself. "Breyze," she urged under her breath. She needed the venom—the Darkness—to fly across. She needed to sink her blades into Godric and kill him. This could be so easy if she could access the magic. Once and for all, this could be over.

"Maybe Kane would like to see the Light?" asked Godric, and she stilled, raising her head.

Through the doors, Kane was brought in with thick-gauge chains wrapped around his arms and legs. Shackled so he couldn't run off. Another chain connected his neck to his wrists and a rusted chain running down to his ankles. Even then, Godric had taken the precautions of having him escorted by several Semaphors, a staff in each of their hands ready to slam into Kane's body. His shirt was off, and he stood in his underwear.

Slashes marked his torso and blood splattered across his body, dribbling down. Most of it was his, it appeared, from the random lines across his skin. Some sort of a weapon. But what?

A middle-aged man stepped out from behind him. He had wiry glasses, a receding hairline, and wore a tracksuit. In his hands, a whip dripped with blood.

Kane's blood.

She could've screamed with all the anger rushing through her, but she was beat to the punch: Kane bellowed, sounding more like a monster than a man. Like the giant lizard from a movie that Godric had forced her to watch—the type that climbed buildings and destroyed cities. It wasn't Kane. It was the beast inside of him.

The berserker.

Malin tightened her fingers across the handles of her S-blades, feeling them slip from the sweat building on her hands. Dread washed over her, and it slowed her movements like she was trudging through thigh-deep snow with an icy wind pushing her back. Her heartbeat was slowing, and she couldn't remember how to breathe.

"So I was never your type, was I?" asked Godric. "Not that I wanted to exist in the Darkness and sin where you live. And you never would come to the Light."

Malin barely heard him, not when her eyes were on Kane.

What had they done to him? He seemed in far more than physical pain. It shouldn't have happened this way or this quickly. Had Kane gone crazy? His movements lacked their usual gracefulness, and he seemed more like a rabid animal foaming at the mouth with other predators circling around him.

Even when Kane's eyes landed on Malin, he didn't seem to recognize her. It was the same burning hatred in his blue eyes— signaling the beast lurking below.

"A bit primal. Not really who I am. Or ever was," continued Godric. "Yes, the Maker's Light is necessary."

The Semaphors pushed Kane to the edge of the moat, and the berserker bellowed again, thrashed in the chains.

"Breyze," begged Malin, "I can't lose him." She couldn't lose Breyze either. She wasn't strong enough to lose anyone. Not after all the loss and pain she'd experienced already. She reached her arm deep within her cloak. "Please. Help me."

Breyze sunk his fangs into the vein in her wrist. It was enough venom, just the tip of an iceberg, but Aodh's Darkness spread through her veins, fire thumping with every heartbeat. Breyze retreated back into the dark folds of her cloak. The magic was ready to take off.

"*Gaoth*," she commanded, and her feet lifted from the ground.

She wanted something stronger, to push off the warehouse floor and drive her S-blades through the Semaphors, but she was lifting like a balloon. The slime watched her in unison, even Godric, who halfheartedly smirked.

Malin reached the other side of the moat, and the Semaphors lifted their staffs defensively, as if they meant to knock her down. She had one man to save and one to slaughter. Which would she do first? What impulse would win out? Her head or heart? What would be the biggest win?

When she looked at Kane, she barely knew him anymore, but wasn't that her fault? His eyes were crazed. His body tattered. He had a monster bursting through the seams of his muscular torso, ready to break free. Then what would he be?

She glanced at Godric, and something inside her took over. She craved revenge. Hungered and thirsted for his blood. Godric had killed her sister—the one person who knew her better than she knew herself. The only person who would ever truly know her. Myla had been the heart that kept the Pemumbra beating. Myla was the world, and she had been ripped away when Godric ripped out her heart. From that point, everything had been sucked dry, like Aemro's husk. Godric had torn life from them, and Malin was going to tear him limb from limb.

She landed on the concrete floor, halfway between Godric and Kane. Still torn. Godric stood seemingly defenseless, not one Semaphor slime to protect him. And apparently, he knew it, because his fake smile dropped, fear flashed in his eyes, and his hands dropped heavily to his sides. He backed away, eyes wide and head shaking. Absolute terror and disbelief that she was here, on this side of his moat. Or that she'd used the Darkness in his place of Light. How could he not suspect that she would choose revenge?

But then she heard Kane bellow.

The berserker.

The beast lurking below the surface.

A monster breaking free.

That monster—The Rage—broke free.

Chains clattered from his body to the concrete. He pushed two of the six Semaphors into the electrocuted moat, and they screamed as they fried like food. The scent—burned flesh and hair—wasn't nearly as appetizing. He pushed the other four away, and then tossed the remaining chains away from him. His muscles rippled. Blood like a shower splashed to the floor.

Kane stared at the ceiling, hands curled into talons and shoulders hunched like they might sprout wings. For a few seconds, silence gathered while everyone held their breaths. Even Malin. She knew this was her chance to attack—to kill the Semaphors and Godric, but Kane . . . the pain in his voice. The anger. The sadness. He needed help. He needed *her*.

His head lowered. His eyes narrowed. Trained on one person.

Malin's breath caught in her throat.

The Rage had his sights on the man with the whip. And then he ran toward him, knocking everyone out of the way as he reached out his hands.

"Protect me!" screamed Godric, running away. Speaking to his followers or Semar—their accursed Maker? He reached for a door.

The four remaining Semaphors moved ungracefully. Two toward her. Two toward Godric.

Malin couldn't hold her position any longer. She had to decide.

But before she could make that choice, the two Semaphors descended on her with their staffs outstretched. They closed in, faster with every heartbeat, and she tightened her grip on her S-blades, imbued with Darkness. One staff snapped out and slapped against her back. Breyze was there, so she wasn't met with the full blow. Her dragan screamed in pain and she felt it to her soul. Malin twirled around, meeting the staff with her blade. She needed the two Semaphors in front of her.

She raised her swords and sliced them over her head, trying to move the Semaphors in front of her. They ducked and jumped back, and she couldn't quiet explain it, but they were faster. Was that possible? She couldn't ever remember fighting Semaphors in daylight, so was that the issue? Was it her or them? Was she slower? She glanced over her back for a brief second, checking Kane and how close she was to the moat. Now with the two in front of her, they were pushing her back, using their staffs as barricades and only slashing them out when she jumped out of line. She glanced toward the door that had since slammed shut, Godric and his two minions gone.

Effin-A, she thought, biting on her bottom lip. She glanced at Kane and tried to find the words to tell him to stop, but she was at a loss. Could he even comprehend words? The staff slapped against her body, and she hissed in pain. That was going to leave a mark, but if she managed to get away with only some bruises, at least she would be alive.

Kane loosed a scream, and it drew her attention. She couldn't fight the staff that cracked against her knees. The other staff hit upside her head, and ringing clanged through her head as blood began to rush from her nose. Breyze slunk out from under her cloak, fangs out, but then he screeched when the light touched his scales.

CHAPTER 38

HE RAGE WOULD TEAR COACH ROBBINS limb from limb until there was nothing left of him but shreds. The heat was wildfire across his host's skin, electricity—the same as what lurked in the water below. The water crackled with laughter, waves reaching up like hands, grabbing any life it could take by the neck and searing it to death. The Rage swung its eyes back over Coach Robbins, who he had already sent to the floor. The coach's body bloodied and bruised.

"Cry," snarled The Rage, voice echoing through the room. The Rage's voice sounded like gravel pulled from the depths of hell and he breathed ash. "Cry for me, Coach. *Just you and me here, kid.*"

The coach pulled back his thin lips, revealing bloodied teeth. One of the front teeth dangled by a slim piece of pink gum. The coach laughed, but it was forced and coarse. It didn't reach the coach's eyes.

Terror lived within. Deep inside those dopey eyes.

Coward. Always. He had tried to teach The Rage's human not to be a coward—to be a man—but in the end, the coach was a sniveling coward. Scared. Tears collected in the corners of his eyes, yet the coach still tried to laugh. The stringy gum finally snapped, and his tooth fell into the black abyss of his throat. Then he spat it back at The Rage's face, splattered it with spit and blood and a single yellow tooth.

The Rage turned a little and swiped it away in a smear.

The coach laughed, louder this time. A madman. He should've been locked up forever with the key thrown away. Somehow, he got out, but The Rage would fix that. There was only the dark. And darkness.

No one would save Kane except for The Rage, so he had taken over. The Rage was on the move, and ripping from Kane's skin, leading with its teeth and talons. The beast would keep Kane safe within his own mind and body. Protect him.

The Rage crashed forward onto the coach, fists raining down like heavy pelts, slicing into the coach's body and pulling up skin and muscle, then throwing it away.

Blood was on his tongue. The coach's. It ran deliciously down his throat, and he swallowed it like a vampire. The Rage was stronger than Kane and would protect his human. He threw Kane's fists, now transformed into his, into the coach's chest until there was a nasty crack below.

The Rage drove his thumbs into the coach's eyes, just so he would stop staring! He'd seen those eyes through Kane's memories too many times. Following him through the halls. Even after the coach was locked away, the eyes followed them, waking Kane up in a cold sweat at night. But the coach's eyes under The Rage's thumbs felt like wet and squishy soft-boiled eggs, just the insides. No shell to crunch.

Blood bubbled up and ran from his eyes like rivers.

The coach screamed, sounding like a small child. He no longer tried to fight off The Rage's attack. He only tried to peel The Rage's hands from his face, but The Rage drove Kane's thumbs down further until he hit something more solid and the skull between his fingers felt ready to collapse.

The coach screamed, and the high-pitched whining reverberated in The Rage's head. Letting go, The Rage plunged his hand into the coach's mouth, knocking out the remaining teeth. Then The Rage removed it and curled his fingers around the coach's tongue and pulled it like taffy.

The coach screamed, so The Rage wanted to plunge lower and rip out his throat, his heart, his guts. All of it. Everything.

It reared back with its fist.

KANE SCREAMED, THRASHING IN THE body that no longer was his own. The remains of the coach lay on the floor around him while Kane's body collapsed in on him. The pain radiating out until he couldn't take it anymore. He closed his eyes and writhed.

Monster. I'm a monster, he cried. *Look what I've done. Look what I* can *do.*

Kane finally won control and released his hand. The coach's heart fell from his grip, landing with a splat.

Kane fell into the blood, curling into a ball.

KANE'S SCREAMS BURST IN MALIN'S head, sending stars across her vision as she turned her head toward him. Her heart rattled her rib cage and her lungs heaved. A staff hit her on the side, and she crumpled to one leg. Another staff cracked against her skull. She fell to her hands and knees. Her S-blades skittered across the warehouse floor. Before she could reach for them, another staff rapped against her hand, and she cried out in pain, her wrist seeming to explode.

"Breyze," she begged.

Another staff slapped her head, and she fell to her stomach, gasping for breath. Dark dots blotted her vision. The darkness was seeping in around her, and she suddenly feared a different kind of darkness. One from which she might never wake.

She was dying. "No," she groaned. Not yet. She had so many things to do. She had people to save.

Kane screamed again.

It ricocheted in her head, mixing with her own yells. Her voice strangled, ripping from her throat.

"Help me," she begged. "Breyze."

Light shimmered down through the high windows, letting in the golden morning sun, and the white-painted floor and walls amplified it. Light was everywhere. So bright—too bright. Unsafe for Breyze or any other dragan. As much as Malin wanted to protect Breyze, she wanted to save herself—and Kane. Her dragan couldn't survive in the Daylight Realm without Malin. Malin had to save everyone.

"Please," whispered Malin, voice hoarse and raspy with shallow breaths. Her lungs couldn't get enough air, not with the staffs slapping her back.

Then she felt the bite of pain. Breyze groaned, sun blinding him and burning him. As quick as it was there, it was gone. And she felt Breyze slither back under the cloak, hiding from the daylight.

The venom coursed through her veins, spreading into her blood, and the hair on her arms rose. Then the rest of her began to rise. Bracing her hands on the floor, she lifted herself with a grunted scream. A staff hurdled toward her face, but her hand flashed out and grabbed the staff. She stared straight into the Semaphor's eyes, and she saw his terror take over. The eyes darted left and right, but she had already sensed the change in the air that meant the other Semaphor was on the move. She reached out, and her other hand grabbed the other's staff. She heard the gulps.

But this was where they would end.

"Run," she said, a smirk pulling at her lips.

The Semaphors didn't run, so their deaths would be their own fault. Her soul would be clear.

Using the staffs as her own weapons, she whipped them out,

and the Semaphors jerked off on either side, falling back a step. She threw the staffs into the electrified moat. If they wanted them, then they could get them. She plucked the S-blades from the ground and pointed them toward the Semaphors. Both ran forward, no weapon in hand. Malin killed one with ease. Its body crumbled and then poofed into steam. She spun around, ready to drive the blade into the Semaphor's chest but stopped a mere inch away.

"Where is Godric?" she demanded, eyes narrowed.

The Semaphor gulped.

Then another scream came from Kane's direction. She refused to look at him—she would get to him. Revenge first. It was so close—within her grasp! She could end this today. Godric would be dead, and Myla would be avenged. Kane screamed, and her eyes jerked away from the Semaphor.

"No," she ordered herself breathlessly. She stared at the Semaphor and demanded, "Tell me where Godric is. Where would he go? What is he doing? What's the plan? Why?" Her voice cracked.

Why Myla? Why not Malin? Why any of this?

Kane screamed, like his body was being ripped apart. She knew those screams so well because she had screamed like that before. After Myla had died and a part of her had died too.

Her head snapped over, eyes landing on Kane's withering body. No one attacked him. He lay in blood—his own? No, the body parts strewn about him. By Dorcha! Did he do that? That body wasn't even a body anymore but roadkill. Roadkill after a few days in the sun and with vultures pecking at it. And Kane screamed, curled up in a ball, and shrank in on himself. Marks across his skin. He was broken and probably felt like he was dying. His hands clutched at his head as if he could turn off whatever replayed inside.

No, Kane, no, she silently begged. *No.*

A kick, a thud, pressure on her stomach and at least one rib broken—and Malin fell back against the floor, head snapping back. A sickening crack followed, Breyze crying underneath her weight. Shadows exploded her vision again, dark clouds blotting out her sight.

And the Semaphor stood over her with a sneer on his face. "Godric is going to love me for this."

PAIN RADIATED THROUGH KANE'S BODY. All the slicing and burning pain he'd been ignoring as The Rage had taken control. He was bloodied and bruised, marks everywhere on his body from the whip.

He screamed.

"Kane!" A face hovered in front of his. Male. One that he recognized but couldn't name. "Kane, you all right?"

Kane groaned.

"Conrí, stay with him. I'll help Malin."

Wait? Malin's here?

"Sure thing, Brogan." Conrí dropped down beside Kane. "Dude!" He scanned Kane's body, then hardened his expression. "You'll be okay. We'll get out of here. Just hold on." He pressed a hand down on Kane's arm, and Kane reared back, roaring. Conrí fell back and held out his hands. "Whoa, man. It's just me. Hold on."

Kane slid away while keeping his eyes solely focused on Conrí.

"Do you know me?" Conrí asked him.

Kane couldn't find his voice, his tongue sliding around his mouth. His eyes caught the bloody and pink tongue lying on the floor, and his stomach heaved. Kane looked back at Conrí and nodded.

"Good." Conrí sighed. "Kiera is going to be so happy to see you. She's been super worried."

Suddenly, a yelp followed, and Kane whipped his head around, feeling a pull. His eyes narrowed as Malin was kicked off the side of the moat. Brogan lay on the floor, sprawled out, with his S-blade lying a few feet away. The dragan under his cloak slithered out and jerked back, leaving a wake of white steam.

"Stay here!" Conrí yelled, launching himself up with his S-blade drawn.

Still in a ball, Kane watched Conrí kick the Semaphor back. The two disappeared from his bleary vision, but he was more focused on where Malin had gone. He didn't see her. He didn't hear her screaming. Was that a good thing?

"Malin." His voice didn't leave his clenched teeth, holding back another scream that wanted to rip from his mouth. "Malin." His jaw dropped open. "MALIN!"

He was up, getting to his feet and fighting the swaying of his legs. Maybe it was his head. He stumbled a few feet forward, reaching out and slamming to the floor. Blood flushed over him—more until he felt like he was drowning—then he half crawled, half swam through the blood that lapped over the side and fell into the moat.

"Malin!"

His heart thundered in his chest as he searched the water below with blue cracks of lightning flashing through it. The loud buzz echoed out, deafening his ragged breaths.

"Kane?"

He snapped his head over. Malin just barely hung off the side of the floor, her fingers holding on—only one hand—with her legs curled up to her core so she didn't touch the water.

"Hold on," he said, already slithering along the floor until he grabbed her hand. "Give me your other hand."

"It's broken." But she lifted it anyway.

When he took her hand, he felt the wrist and it shuffled under her skin like a sack of pebbles. She yelped. But pain was better than death. He pulled her up and onto the floor, then slipped in the gore. He slammed backward onto the floor with her falling on top of him. Her hair had come undone from her ponytail and tickled his nose. He breathed in her scent, even if it was mixed with blood and sweat.

It was Malin.

She was in his hands.

Kane would never let her go again.

"Malin, Kane, you good?" asked Conrí.

Kane didn't look away, but Malin pulled back, taking her body and hair with her. Her heart. Her love. So he followed— would always follow her. Anywhere. Malin jumped to her feet, retrieving her blades, but Kane couldn't make it off his knees. Not when he saw all the blood on his skin. His and the coach's. He gagged.

Kane looked toward Coach Robbins's body, but Malin stepped in his way.

Conrí's blade was out, eyes scanning the surroundings. He hovered near Brogan, touching his head. "We need to get out of here."

"We need to get to Godric," argued Malin. She looked ready to lurch forward, so Kane took her hand. She looked down at him, and he realized just how small he was. She was a tower, and he was just some ant in the sand.

"We need to get the fuck out of here," said Conrí. "Now! Look at Brogan. Yourself. It isn't safe, and more Semaphors could be coming." He bent down and wrapped Brogan's arm over his shoulder. "Kane, are you good? Can you get Brogan's other side?"

Kane wasn't so sure, but he took a hesitant step up. The rest of his body followed. Malin had put away her blade and held on to him. He leaned on her, and she kept his balance. "Yeah." He wrapped Brogan's other arm around his shoulders and lifted.

Before they started moving, Conrí said, "Malin, I swear to all that is Dark, if you run off now, I won't follow you. You will die."

Kane turned to Malin, wondering if she would go, but she stood right beside him.

She promised, "I'll stay." Her fingers wrapped around his other hand.

"Then let's go." Conrí shot a look over his shoulder. "What

was with these Semaphors? Why were they so hard to kill? They weren't this hard before."

Kane didn't know what he meant. What any of these words meant. Looking at Malin, he saw her understanding. She chewed on her bottom lip, and her eyebrows knitted together. Semaphors. The Penumbra. Dark witches or whatever . . . No matter what happened next, Kane would be with Malin. It was the only thing he knew.

GODRIC STARED AT HIS CELL phone displaying his surveillance feed, watching the three dark witches stumble out of the warehouse with one human. The screen changed, following as two walked out into the sun. He leaned closer to his cell phone, studying how Malin wobbled and the blood dripping off Kane and the other two. What were their names again? They hesitated in the shadows before stepping out into the light. Godric smirked.

The car brakes shrieked, slamming to a halt, and Godric nearly flew forward, held back in his seat thanks to his seat belt. "What was that?" he demanded.

"Sorry, boss," said Daniel from the front seat. His fingers thrummed against the steering wheel, and Godric rolled his eyes.

"Do you mind?" he snapped.

Daniel stilled his hands on the steering wheel. "Sorry, boss."

The other Semaphor was in the front seat, quiet and staring straight forward. He was becoming Godric's favorite, but he was from the next batch. Apparently, he'd made some errors, though: Coach Robbins, as an example. But the coach shouldn't have been left alive either. He deserved to burn for his sins, and at the hands of Kane "The Rage" Macleod, the coach had suffered his own personal purgatory for the last few minutes of his life.

"Hey, boss." Daniel cleared his throat, eyes glancing back at Godric through the rearview mirror instead of staring at the red light in front of him. "Why didn't we kill them? We had the chance. Definitely with Kane. And kinda with Malin. So . . . like, why?"

Godric stared at the screen, but the four of them were officially off his property. He closed his cell phone screen and slipped his phone into his pocket. "It's not always about death, Daniel. That's too easy. This is about creating a better future. A Light future. This is only the beginning of us. We are the future."

CHAPTER 39

MALIN FELT LIKE SHE WAS running for her life, and she hated it. She wanted to pull away and turn back, go back to the warehouse, find Godric, and kill him. She couldn't stop; this wasn't over. Yet somehow, it was. They were retreating—with Kane and Conrí and now an injured Brogan, whose head lolled to one side. The Semaphor slime had strengthened somehow, and they needed to regroup. Still. It sucked.

"You take Brogan back to the Penumbra," said Kane with a grunt. "I'll stay here."

Malin turned to her head. "What? No. You're coming with us. You have to."

"I'll be fine. I'll just go home and be done."

"No, you won't!" Her heart jumped in her throat, and she stifled a cry. "You're injured and need help too." She didn't want to leave him.

"I'll go to the hospital."

"And tell them what?" she asked. "The police will show up, and they'll ask questions. That's not safe." She thought back to the warehouse, and when she glanced over her shoulder, she saw the trail of Kane's blood that led all the way back to the warehouse. Back to the body—the single body of . . . Malin didn't know who—and Kane would be found. The cowans could be smart when they wanted to be. They'd probably have him identified by tomorrow with all the new testing they had developed.

Whoever that body was, it was connected to Kane. The police would come for him. Take him away. Lock him in a cage like he had been for most of his life. But this one wouldn't be of his own making. He fought in many cages, letting out the monster in a controlled setting, but the monster had come loose now. The berserker had exploded from within Kane and consumed him.

This wasn't over. The berserker wouldn't just simper away. It would come back with bared teeth, extended claws, and a taste for blood. Who knew what would happen next? Who would be the next person he hurt or killed? Maybe Kane himself. He couldn't be trusted alone.

"Breyze." She hated to ask this of her dragan and knew that having one of the dragan's venom coursing through his veins would expedite Kane's decision to either stay in the Penumbra or lose his eyesight. While hidden in the shadows of the Daylight Realm, the sun was beating down. She felt it, but Breyze would feel it much more. She didn't have to speak further; her familiar understood her unspoken request.

Before Kane knew what was happening, Breyze sunk his fangs into Kane's neck, and Kane stumbled backward, hissing under his breath. Malin whispered, *"Féach,"* and Kane was ready to go through. They all were. Her dragan curled further into the folds under her cloak, nuzzling into the small of her back. He was in pain, seared by the Light and the daylight, and it nearly broke her heart.

"Thank you," she said to Breyze, her heart swelling in her chest, and then she turned to Kane. "Let's go." She squeezed his hand.

Back inside the Penumbra, Malin still dwelled on the risks she'd taken with herself and Breyze. The fact that Malin had risked her dragan's life set guilt on fire in her stomach. She thought she might be sick, but they were back now, and her dragan could return to the nest and regain his strength.

Conrí lifted Brogan up easily with the magic flooding his veins from Rezei's bite. Conrí hadn't asked for his dragan's help in the Daylight Realm. He hadn't needed his dragan to take the pain like Malin had.

With a single glance back at Malin and Kane, Conrí levitated himself and Brogan, then was gone, taking the injured fighter to Dark Haven where Emrys and Aodh's other darklings could care for him.

"Breyze," she said, and her dragan finally poked his head out from under the cloak. "Thank you." She petted his head, and he leaned into it. "Go rest. You deserve it." Rest sounded so good to her too.

Once they were alone, Kane turned to her faster than she thought possible in his current state, and he stared at her, something writhing in the depths of his eyes. Something she didn't recognize and didn't want to look at. He pulled back his lips, and she saw blood had coated his teeth.

"Kane?" she asked.

There was a twitch of recognition in his eyes, a flash of the blue depths she knew so well, but then it was replaced.

"It's just us now," he said, reaching toward her. Picking her up like she was feather and pulling her body roughly against his.

KANE SCREAMED INSIDE HIS OWN head, but he was only met with echoes. He watched in horror and screamed, *Malin, no! It isn't me! No!* He threw his fists forward, trying to fight his way out.

The Rage held Malin close. His fingers grappled tightly around Malin's arms, feeling her muscles and her bones. The Rage pictured snapping them, and Kane saw what The Rage wanted. What it was hungry for.

Malin, no! cried Kane. *No.*

Then Kane's lips, operated by The Rage, took Malin's lips in his own, pressing so close, sucking, and devouring her mouth. His tongue shoved down Malin's throat, and Kane thought he would be sick. Her taste was so good, yet this was wrong. So impossibly wrong.

Kane roared inside of his head, fighting against The Rage, but he couldn't break free. There was nothing Kane could do about what he witnessed from deep inside his own head.

Malin pulled back and smiled at him, and The Rage growled, low and deep, echoing through his chest. Could Malin hear it? Could Malin feel Kane inside? Did she know it wasn't him who kissed her? He tried desperately to fight it, screaming at the top of his lungs though his mental voice was hoarse. He, and his beast, had screamed too much today.

Her hand reached up, fingers brushing across his face. "Kane?" She waited. Gave him the chance to come back to her.

He screamed, *I'm here, Malin. I'm here!* He didn't say how scared he was. How terrified. He didn't know what was happening. He'd never lost total control before.

The Rage answered, "Yes?" and it sounded like a demon's voice.

"Kane," she repeated, eyes narrowing, and then she hit him across the face with her fist closed. The Rage wasn't able to rear back fast enough. Her fist was enough to throw him off balance, and he fell to the ground. The Rage was about to kick to his feet when she brought down her hand on his head again.

Shit went black.

And Kane was okay with that.

MALIN STARED DOWN AT KANE'S body face down in front of her, his breathing even. Blood seeped out of his nose, which she had just broken. Her own wrist screamed in pain; it was already broken and on its way to being permanently damaged if she kept this up. She hadn't meant to hit him, but she knew—looking into his eyes—that Kane was gone.

Or if he was in there, he wasn't in control now.

His berserker was. His ally and his enemy. His protector and his demon.

She didn't know much about the berserkers or berserkergang, only having read books on them, but now, she felt like she knew enough. That wasn't Kane.

"I'll save you," she promised, still keeping her distance in case the berserker rose again. "Kane, if you can hear me, I'm going to save you." She just didn't know how yet.

CHAPTER 40

WHEN MALIN BROUGHT KANE IN, Emrys was already tending to Brogan's wounds, and his eyes went wide. Not only had Kane been whipped and bruised, bleeding with scabs starting to crust over, he had fresh blood on his face from a broken nose and a new black eye forming from where Malin had hit him.

No, not him. Not Kane. The berserker inhabiting his body, taking over his life, and destroying Kane from the inside out.

Malin felt guilty again, because the healer already had his hands full with Tierney and Brogan. Tierney was still unconscious, but she had apparently come to for a short time while Malin and the others had been in the Daylight Realm. And now, Malin threw Kane into his mix. "Is there another darkling here to help? Branok or Jareth?" Malin asked.

"I sent Conrí to get Jareth, mistress." He bent over the bed to look at Kane. "What happened? And why wasn't he brought to me immediately?"

Malin bit on her bottom lip. Yes, Kane should've been brought to Emrys immediately with the damage done to him. She sighed. "It's not all his blood. The fight was, well, I guess you can see." She didn't want to go into the details of the cowan

Kane's berserker had eviscerated. And then how was she going to explain that she had to knock him out? Worst of all, she had to explain that she just wanted a moment alone with Kane as everything bubbled up in her until it felt ready to boil over. She had to tell Kane how she felt; she hadn't gotten the chance before, and she didn't know now if she would *ever* have the chance.

What if the berserker had taken over so much of his life that he would never be Kane again? The berserker would be loose, taking over Kane's life and doing what it wanted.

Malin hated it—she tried to fight it—but she started to cry.

Conrí returned with Jareth. At least that left two darklings to deal with Brogan's and Kane's injuries. And Brogan was starting to slowly wake, blinking back the crustiness on his eyelashes.

Conrí pulled Malin into a hug, and she fell into him. It wasn't who she wanted to hold her—that was Kane and only the true Kane—but Conrí had long been her friend. He would understand.

"It's okay." Conrí flattened down her hair. "It's all going to be okay."

No, it wasn't, but she could make it okay. She would make it okay. Pulling away from him, Malin released a deep breath. "The berserker has taken over Kane's body," she told Emrys, and somehow, his eyes went even wider. That wasn't what she wanted, not from him when he was supposed to have the answers. "Help Kane, and I'm going . . ." Where? Where was she going? She would help Kane too, but she didn't know how just yet.

"I'll do all that I can," said Emrys.

Once, those words would have comforted her, but that was before this fight with Godric. Before Kiera had been knocked out by Kane and unconscious for so long. Before Tierney had been injured. Before Brogan. Before Kane. But was it Emrys's fault she couldn't be comforted or her own? Malin only blamed herself.

"I'm going to go," she said, taking a step toward the door.

"Where?" asked Conrí. "If it's the Daylight Realm, then I should go with you. I should check on Kiera—in case Godric is going after her." His words were too rushed to be distant, and she was happy at least someone was finding happiness.

Brogan started to push himself up, and while Emrys looked ready to tell him no, Brogan leaped up from the bed. He swayed where he stood, using his hand to brace himself against the cot. Swelling bloated his face, which would become heavy with dark bruises until the whole of his face looked purple. She imagined she looked no better, but she was still standing. Brogan looked ready to keel over at any moment.

"No, I'll go myself," she said.

"Malin." Brogan stepped forward and nearly collapsed. That wouldn't stop him.

"Stay with Kane, please—and Tierney. Make sure they get better." If he had a purpose to stay, perhaps it wouldn't seem like he was left behind. She would need her coven in the fight to come, so she wanted him to heal along with the others. Her eyes met Emrys's briefly, and he gave a singular, solemn nod of understanding.

Then she was leaving through the door, heading out. And Conrí trailed two steps behind her. "If you want to go to the Daylight Realm for Kiera, I won't stop you," she said without looking over her shoulder. She wasn't sure she could face him or anyone without crying again. She just barely had it under control herself.

"I need to see her," he said, voice gravelly and almost out of control. She knew the feeling too well. "To make sure she's safe and cared for and . . ." His voice cracked, trailing off at words that he couldn't name just yet.

Spinning around, Malin stood in front of Conrí, and he was clearly surprised she had stopped. His chest puffed out and he stood at attention, his eyes wide but focused, and his mouth hanging open like he was going to say something.

She cut him off though. "I know I've made mistakes—"

"Malin," he interrupted.

She shook her head. "I've made mistakes. I've done things that no one should do. That no one should want to do." She thought about Brogan calling her a martyr, and he had been right. She had rushed into Godric's trap, willing to die if it meant saving Kane or anyone else. It was reckless and stupid, and what had she become? "But my biggest mistake . . . right now . . . is"—she choked—"is not saying, 'I love you.'"

His eyebrows went up, and he couldn't control the short burst of laughter. "I love you too?" he offered. "Like as a friend." He cracked a smile.

She punched him lightly on the arm with her good hand—she'd have the darklings look at her injured one when she returned. When others weren't dying in Dark Haven.

Conrí feigned injury.

Malin scoffed, rolling her eyes.

"Okay, okay" said Conrí, chuckling. "Wanna try that again?"

She let out a shaky breath. "I love Kane. And I need to find a way to save him." Tears pricked her eyes, and she blinked them away before they overflowed. "I'm going to find a way to save him. And our whole coven."

"You don't have to do it alone, Malin."

"I'm not alone." She knew that. The memory of Myla was with her every day. Tierney would be up soon and by her side again. And hopefully—no, not hopefully. Kane *would* be there too. "But you. Take the time you need with Kiera. We'll be here when you get back."

He grimaced. "And if she comes with me?"

Malin nodded. All she could do. One member of the Macleod family at a time was all she could deal with. She wasn't used to having that much family around anyway, not without Myla by her side. And her mother proved to be distant, no longer concerned with protecting the realm, and keeping her nose in books more often than not.

Conrí wrapped her in a hug again. "I'll be back soon," he promised, giving her a kiss on the cheek, and then he was gone, half running all the way back to the Daylight Realm. She didn't doubt he would sprint once he was out of eyesight, but good. At least one of them had something to hope for.

Now, it was Malin's turn.

THE RAGE FOUGHT AGAINST ITS bodily restraints in the form of Kane, and Kane tried to hold it back. He tried to reel it in, but Kane had lost all control of himself. His body was no longer his own, like it wasn't when he was fighting in the cage. Except his body was now the cage. And Kane was in the fight for his life.

A hand was on his head, a light probe under the crushing weight of water that Kane felt. Someone pulled his eyelid back. All The Rage saw was shadows, spreading out like the ocean at night, far from any city lights. The Rage slithered and hissed in Kane's body, ready to attack but unable to move. Unable to see. But Kane saw the outline of Emrys peering down. And someone was over his shoulder.

Brogan!

Help, Kane yelled. *Help!* They couldn't hear him, but it didn't stop him from asking, *Where's Malin?* What happened to her? Why wasn't she here too?

The Rage perked at her name, the memories of the kiss and then Kane's memories of her body running through its mind. It was hungry for more. It would take what they both craved.

No! Kane ordered The Rage, but it had no interest in listening.

It wanted Malin, and it wouldn't stop until it got her.

So Kane would have to save himself to save her. For so long, he had been fighting. Fighting the other opponents in the cage and fighting the coach who haunted his dreams, using The Rage to help fight them because Kane couldn't do it himself. He had needed The Rage in the cage to be a good fighter. He had thrived on that anger and that pain that came from The Rage, Kane's torment bottled up until it was ready to explode and given a name.

Kane "The Rage" Macleod.

And then, it *had* exploded when Coach Robbins died.

The Rage had taken over when Kane couldn't. The Rage had been Kane's protector since Kane was a kid, cowering and crying for the coach to stop. The Rage was where Kane retreated when the coach took what he wanted. Always. Any time he wanted it, and he never apologized. That was what The Rage was and what Kane was becoming.

No, ordered Kane to The Rage. It's over. *It's been enough.*

The Rage bared its teeth. It wouldn't easily let go. And should Kane be surprised by that? Why would it, when Kane had been giving it more and more freedom? That liberty must have tasted so very sweet to his beast. The Rage experience not only the anger and the fight to survive, but the love and passion that one could have. That Kane had. It wanted more. But so did Kane.

The beast bellowed, and Kane roared, lunging forward for his attack. His final fight—live or die, it was either him or The Rage who would wake from this battle.

IN THE COURTYARD AT THE center of Dark Haven, Malin found the Great Dark Tree. With its imposing millennium-old trunk stretching larger than any tree in the Daylight Realm, and its roots cutting through the cobblestone, it was one of the grandest features in the Penumbra. The branches spread wide and high. It was a tree that was hard to miss with its deep purple leaves and black gnarled trunk. Most trees thrived on sunlight, but this one grew tall and proud, drinking in Aodh's Darkness. When Malin had been a child and her mother brought her, Myla, and Morgana here, Myla used to say the grooves in the bark were faces of the dead watching over the Penumbra, the dragans, and the Dragan Gardaí. Malin could see it now, and she touched a hand to where the bark looked most like Myla's and bent down—well, she fell down. Her knees gave out, quaking from exhaustion and emotion, and her lungs trembled for breath she just couldn't catch.

"Please." The one word came in a rasp, breaking apart her lips and breaking the dam of tears that overflowed her eyes, ran down her cheeks, and splattered against the pavement like a harsh rainfall. "Please, Aodh. Or any god or goddess who may be listening. Save him—Kane." Let there be no mistake. "I'll do anything."

She had been saying that for years. She had been trying for years.

"I didn't know what I needed before. I didn't know what I wanted before. I didn't know how before." More words threatened to spill out, but she swallowed them back, swallowing her tears. Her words were spilling out in a jumble. Snot coated her lips and the inside of her mouth, and her tears yammered the words together.

"I will rebuild the coven," she went on. "We can do it now. We will have the numbers again. With Kane. And Kiera." Conrí would bring her back, maybe even Kane's mother. Who knew? "I will rebuild it. I won't go after revenge. I will not avenge my sister." That broke her heart the most because for so long, revenge had been all she wanted—all she thought she needed. The one thing to prove that she was worthy of the love Myla had given her in life.

She pressed her other hand to her heart, trying to calm the thundering. "We will protect the Penumbra at all costs. I won't let anyone else down." She was willing to give her own life, but her own life wasn't good enough. She had been trying to get rid of that for years.

Malin begged, "Please, just save Kane. Let the darklings heal him." She bowed her head. "Let him be okay."

The tree continued to stand as it had been, but she hadn't expected it to crack open or anything. Still, she waited for a lightning strike to come down and set something ablaze. She waited for Myla's head to poke out from the tree and say, "Yes." All the tree did was whistle in the breeze that came through the Penumbra, branches slapping against one another like a sad round of applause. A few of the leaves twirled around and pinwheeled toward the ground.

"Malin." Her name echoed.

She sniffled and lifted her head to the tree. Was this the answer?

"Malin!"

No, that was Brogan's voice. She spun around, launching to her feet, and saw him sprinting toward her. He held his head in his hands, and he was probably still in pain. She rushed to meet him.

"What is it? What's happening?"

"Kane."

That one word sent her heart into a frenzy and her mind racing with a million thoughts warring against one another for center stage. She stilled, and her stomach flipped and flopped.

Brogan caught his breath. "Something is happening to him. Emrys thinks it's the berserker." His eyes caught hers. "He thinks Kane is dying."

Malin was running before the thoughts even caught up to her.

THE BEAST REARED UP, FIGHTING against Kane's skin and breaking his bones further. Kane felt them snap, but he still pushed, hollering in his own primal form. *This is my life. This is my future. I choose it. Not you!*

The Rage lashed out, trying to hook Kane in the jaw, but Kane knew that move. How many times had he practiced it under the supervision of Broc? So when The Rage thumped forward again and Kane danced back, Kane was ready for the next blow. The Rage threw its fist forward, missing any sort of grace about it. Sloppy, just sloppy, and Broc would've been pissed if he had seen such a punch. Kane spun away from The Rage, tensing his body. He would have to take a blow to give a blow. And The Rage's blow came, sending a shockwave across Kane's torso. What was another bruise against the marks on his body? What was another pain after all that had happened?

No, Kane told himself. It was that kind of thinking that had allowed The Rage in in the first place. By telling himself he couldn't be hurt, by not letting himself feel the pain, he gave The Rage exactly what it needed. The Rage fed off pain. So Kane let his body uncoil and breathe.

The Rage landed another blow. Kane stumbled back, heels dragging against the ground, though he couldn't have said where. It was a black void with a white mat underneath, nothing like Broc's gym or the gym with Coach Robbins. This was Kane's head.

Kane's first instinct was to fight. And he wanted to fight for his life. It was his life! But he needed to feel the pain that he had so desperately put away and pretended didn't exist. He needed to know what it was, and he needed to overcome it, or it would eat him alive. As The Rage had done.

So when the next blow came from The Rage, Kane took it. Memories flashed into his mind of the musty old gym from Wickney High School and Coach Robbins pulling back on his pants, wearing a dopey smile and satiated eyes. He threw a towel at Kane and told him to clean himself up.

Another blow from The Rage, and Kane remembered his father, who first got him into wrestling. Told him it was a man's sport. How they used to watch Friday Night SmackDown, and Kane would practice those moves when no one was looking to impress his father. It didn't matter. Nothing impressed his father, and then dear old Daddy was gone, walking out one night without a word. And his mother had crumpled into pieces on the kitchen floor.

The Rage came again, and Kane took it with his arms open wide. The kids at school made fun of him because of hand-me-down clothes and his blind mother and having to live on state benefits. Gossip about how he was dirty, but his sister was hot.

Kane dropped his hands to his sides, and more anger came with each punch, calling back memories from the distant past and not so distant past until they were plummeting into him, making him double over and shriek with pain. He fell down.

And then The Rage was on top of him, his own face reflecting back with red eyes and mouth dangling open, spewing hate. Fist after fist sliced into Kane's chest.

Kane had knocked out Kiera when The Rage had taken over.

Kane had lost control, and The Rage had snapped Broc's arms like twigs. Another person he cared for falling to the ground and yelling in pain because of Kane and his Rage.

Malin in the alleyway when Kane lost control of The Rage.

Even . . . even hateful Coach Robbins, and the blood that stained Kane's skin. The Rage had turned the man into a pile of dead goop, a violent roadkill, a deer caught in headlights and then splattered across the road by a semi-truck.

Kane felt the pain of it all, and The Rage brought nothing but more.

MALIN STARED AT KANE AS he flopped around in the bed. He convulsed like shockwaves rolled through his body, all aimed at his chest. He was a fish out of water, legs slamming down and arms falling sideways. Emrys attempted to hold him down, calling back on his warrior training, but Kane kicked him off too.

"Help me!" ordered Emrys. "Hold him down!"

Brogan jumped into action, but it took a second for Malin to sputter and then join. She stood beside the floundering Kane, so scared to touch him.

"What's happening to him?" she asked, finally setting her hands on him. His muscles were tense underneath. His skin was like fire, and she bit back a hiss of pain that scorched her own hands. His face had puffed and turned red, and his cheeks filled with air. He fought underneath her, rolling away, but she pushed him back down.

"The berserker you mentioned. It's the only explanation

I have," answered Emrys, picking through his brews. "I need something to calm him down."

Brogan stood opposite of her, having the same difficult time keeping Kane down on the bed. They shared a look, but she didn't like what was reflected back in Brogan's eyes. She wasn't giving up. Not now and not ever.

"Here!" Emrys pulled out a vial of hot pink liquid.

"What is that?" she exclaimed.

"The Fae use it to relax."

"No." She shook her head. "We're not using any faerie dope on Kane."

"We may not have another choice. Brogan, hold open his mouth."

"There is always another choice." She looked down at Kane, his eyelids halfway open and his eyeballs rolled up into his skull, revealing only the whites. "Kane, if you can hear me, come back to me. Kane."

$\mathcal{M}$ALIN'S WORDS WERE MUSIC TO his ears. The Rage's hits kept on coming, pummeling him further down until the void almost overtook him. Each punch brought a new painful memory, some hidden so deep in his collection they felt like new experiences. But if The Rage felt them, he'd clearly filed them away in a box underneath his bed. He only pulled out these memories to call for The Rage in a fight, and now, The Rage threw them back at him, forcing Kane to remember.

And Kane did remember. Yes! Every single memory threatened to drown him.

Every emotion washed over him until he couldn't breathe. All the pain and sadness and anger were like harsh waves that he couldn't fight. He couldn't get to the surface. The abyss took over until it was nearly all black.

"Kane, come back to me," said Malin.

I'm coming, he promised.

The Rage screamed, throwing another blow into Kane, but Kane couldn't sink further. He had hit the bottom. The Rage had no more memories to use, and the blow was softer. A wave lapping against Kane's skin. Another attempted blow came across Kane's face, but it was just a tickle.

Screaming like a banshee, The Rage tried to bring its fists again, but the touch never came. It moved away, caught in the undertow. And then it was gone.

"Kane."

Yes, that was his name. He was Kane Macleod.

Kane kicked to the surface, gasping in a new breath and a new life.

Chapter 41

*T*HERE WAS A DULL ACHE in Kane's chest, a hollowness that was once filled by the Raging beast, but that was gone . . . for now. He couldn't say if the beast would stay away. Even Emrys and Malin, who called the beast a "berserker," didn't know for certain. Life wasn't filled with certainties, though it would certainly make everything so much simpler. All he knew was he was alive.

But then again, he held strong beliefs about a few important things.

One, he knew that he loved Malin with his whole heart and every fiber of his being, and he wanted to be with her. Through thick and thin and whatever fucking madness happened, he wanted to experience it with her. He would stay at her side. Not only would he love her, he would *allow* himself to love her. To feel that emotion and own up to who he truly was.

No longer a monster. Yes, a fighter. But also, a lover.

Two, he made a choice to stay in the Penumbra. After being officially released from Malin's version of a hospital—Dark Haven—he had been taken back to her place but given his own room. Brogan had been the one to explain, saying that she was busy doing other things to prepare the coven for the future. He didn't blame her. She was their leader, and everything seemed to be a wreck.

Malin had spent time with Kane in the hospital, but it hadn't felt like much time. Would all the time in the world ever be enough with Malin? Kane didn't know, but he wanted to find out.

Three, because he was staying with Malin and in the Penumbra, he would become . . . he couldn't remember the term. A dark witch? Anyway, he would be part of this. He would fight the Semaphors. He would do his part to bring peace to the Penumbra. He would give his life to Malin. For however long he would have left, he'd be hers.

Although, he didn't wish to think about death when he had recently been so close to it.

A soft knock rattled the wooden door of his bedroom, and Kane raised his head from what he had been holding in his hand. His thumbs continued to run over the dark satin robe that looked something straight out of a Hollywood movie instead of real life. He almost smiled at the thought that this was his real life.

"Kane, are you in there?"

"Yes." The word was immediate, making his voice squeak. He cleared his throat and dropped his voice an octave. "Come in." He didn't know if he should stand or stay where he was, so he continued to sit. His body still ached from the beating and whipping and the internal havoc The Rage had wreaked on him. So when Malin entered, he found himself out of breath, his heart racing.

Her hair was done for once, rolling along her shoulders and cascading down her back. She hovered in the doorway for a second before stepping in and closing the door behind her. She had a hard time meeting his gaze, whereas he just stared at her like she was a dream that he didn't want to wake up from. He was scared he might blink and she would be gone—a figment of his imagination going up in a puff of smoke.

"Can we talk?" she asked, swallowing down something else she was probably going to say.

"Yeah." He moved to give her room on the bed, but she

stayed five feet away. That distance felt like the Grand Canyon. It needed to be filled, before it spread until she was a mile away. He didn't push it, though he desperately wanted to close the distance and wrap his arms around her.

She leaned against the wall. "I want to apologize—"

"Not necessary."

"I should apologize."

"I should apologize to you."

"No," she said. "That's not . . . no." She cleared her throat. "We need to talk because you're staying here and joining us, and that's wonderful. But I want you to be prepared for joining us."

"Brogan has already taken me through the ritual. I know what to expect." Apparently, it would be painful, and a dragan would bite him and . . . he didn't really want to think about it. Though he would allow the pain to happen without protest. This time, he didn't fear the beast returning.

"Good, but that's not . . ." She looked away, squinting at his walls like they were artworks in need of deciphering. "Listen, I'm damaged goods."

His eyebrows rose, and he waited for more. "As am I."

"Not in the same way."

"You wouldn't want to be damaged in the way that I am," he said.

"Neither would you," she replied.

Kane stared at her, waiting for her to continue, but realized it might be too hard for her. "This is about your sister, yeah? Mia?"

"Myla," she corrected and then bit her bottom lip. "Yes, and yours is about that man, Coach Robbins?"

He stilled at the name, blood rushing past his ears, and when he blinked, he imagined the coach's blood on his hands, the squishiness of the body and eyeballs, and finally wiping that smile off the coach's fucking face. "Yes."

"I'm sorry. I didn't mean to bring it up."

"No," he said. "We should talk. How else will we get to know each other?"

"That's what I wanted to talk about, Kane."

Just her saying his name sent an electrical shock through his body and made him feel alive, but those other words scared him. He already knew what she was going to say because he had used the excuse so many times, so he said, "I know, Malin, that it's been hard. And you don't think you're deserving of love—but I love you."

She blanched at him, and he wondered if he had broken her more. She stared at him, so long and so hard he wondered if she was frozen where she stood, which made him want to reach for her that much more. Instead, he tucked his hands under his legs, holding himself back.

"I love you too." Her voice was soft. "I've never said it aloud."

Kane cracked a smile. "Me neither." Then his smile faltered when he remembered. "Coach Robbins was my high school wrestling coach, and he . . ." What word did he want to use? What word was his own that he could live up to? But his mouth ran dry, and his tongue slithered back. His whole body leaned back like he wanted to get away from the thought.

"You're a survivor," she supplied.

"Yes," he agreed because that was true. "I am a survivor." Not a monster. Not a fighter. A survivor. "And you are too."

She shook her head. "I'm not."

"Yes."

"Some people would call me a martyr. And vengeful."

"For what Godric did to your sister?"

"Yes."

He nodded. "That's a survivor in my mind, and we've both been fighting instead of healing. We need to heal now, so we can continue to fight. So we won't only be survivors for the rest of our lives. So we can live and love." Tears brimmed in his eyes, and instead of fighting them until his eyes burned, he let the tears fall, rolling down his face until they collected on the satin cloak on his lap. He didn't even hide his face, and when he looked at Malin, he saw that she didn't hide her tear-streaked face either.

MALIN WORE THE SAME DARK robes as the rest of her covenmates, though their numbers were small. Brogan stood to her right, then Conrí, and then Tierney, who leaned on a cane to keep her balance. Dark bags hung under her eyes, coloring her face oddly. But they were all odd-colored at the moment, wearing their bruises and beatings and marks upon their skin. They were fighters.

And survivors.

Since leaving Kane to get ready, his words had been running through Malin's head, and she was unable to shake them. Not that she wanted to. The words tattooed her heart and branded her mind, and she kept telling herself to keep them close and remember them. But could she live by them? That was tomorrow's problem.

Minerva stood at the head of the gathering behind an old stone table with purple vines crisscrossing around the legs. Her bare feet poked out from her dark cloak. She held a grimoire in her hands, setting it down with a nasty thump. A puff of dust flew off into the air. It had been too long, the book proved, since they had gone through this ritual. Although Malin didn't need it proven. She was well aware of another of her failures, but today was the beginning of a change. A chance. And she would take it and lead with it.

Minerva glanced over her shoulder, meeting Malin's gaze, and Malin was stuck in the hold of her mother. Malin thought back to what Tierney had said Minerva saw in the tea leaves: her and Kane. Now, look where they were—not bonding as one witch and one pháirtí, but agreeing to love one another still, both one of the Cailleach. Minerva turned away, and the promise ritual began.

Kane exited through the back door of the coven house. An army and a family, tied together by Darkness. He wore his cloak, but it was too short, stopping at his midcalf. Unlike Malin's, whose dragged against the ground. Kane's eyes darted over to Malin, and she fought the urge to call out for him or tell him it would be okay. Brogan had walked Kane through this and wouldn't have left out any of the details. Kane stopped before the stone table and before Minerva, and Malin curled her hands into fists inside her cloak, holding herself back.

Minerva was already speaking in low whispers, the old Celtic words sounding like a song that flowed from her mouth, and while Malin knew the ritual and the words, she focused on Kane. He bent down to his knees and drank from the goblet Minerva offered. Malin still remembered the bitter taste that coated her insides for weeks afterward and how she couldn't escape it. After Kane finished the gobletful, Minerva drew it back, and Kane thinned his lips together. Malin almost broke into a smile. The ritual was ancient and wouldn't change any time soon, but it was almost funny that the liquid still tasted like crap.

"Do you accept the blessing of the dragankind?" asked Minerva.

"I do." No hesitation, even though Kane had just handed over his life. Malin hadn't hesitated either, but she had always known what she would become.

Raising her hand, Minerva called forth a dragan, "Kane Macleod, this is Xirgo of the Gentle Mind, soon to be your bonded dragan. Are you prepared?"

Kane nodded once and met Malin's gaze. She returned it, wishing she could tell him it would be okay and that Breyze had chosen the right match for him. The gentle mind to tame the beast.

Malin tensed as Xirgo came closer. The first bite was always the worst. It would get better. All of it would get better. Though, it couldn't get worse than it had already been, could it? Xirgo flew in and landed on Kane's back, and the big man shuddered ever so slightly. The anticipation was the worst of it all, Malin recalled.

Minerva raised her hands to the sky, and she called down

another blessing—and then the dragan struck, sinking its fangs into Kane's neck.

He let out a scream, and Malin jerked forward, making her three covenmates all raise their eyebrows in identical warning stares. She would deal with them later. For now, she was focused on Kane, who bit back his scream and stared deep into her eyes.

You can do this, Kane, she told him silently, and as if he heard her, he nodded. Even though he swayed on his knees, he stayed upright despite the pain Malin knew was coursing through his veins. She knew the venom had entered his system and spread through his body like wildfire. Malin remembered the sensation, and the memories came flooding back to her. She felt the same heat. The hairs on her arms rose.

Then Xirgo released his bite but stayed on Kane's back. They were partners now. And forever.

Minerva dropped her hands and turned to face Kane. "Welcome to the coven, Kane. As you still draw breath, Aodh and the Darkness have accepted you."

EPILOGUE

THERE WAS A DINER IN Wickney that Kane's mother loved to take him and Kiera to when they had been kids. It had been years since Kane had eaten there. It was in the heart of the city, but whereas the city modernized, the diner stayed put in the 1950s with matching roller skates, poodle skirts, and cat-eyed glasses.

The menu was also from the '50s: greasy, fast, and terrible for health. It was just what he wanted. While he knew he would have to take up training again, it was nice to have a few days off, and during the time, he wanted to enjoy himself. He ate hot eggs with Sriracha on the side, bacon and sausage, and a heaping stack of pancakes.

"It's been a long time since you've eaten like that," commented Kiera with a smirk as she sucked down a chocolate malt from a metal straw. No judgment, just happiness. And she relaxed back into the red vinyl seat that groaned every time someone moved.

"Are you going to eat your cherry?" he asked.

She pushed the lid to her malt open, and he plucked it from the top of the whipped cream. That too had been their ritual once. He plopped the whole thing in his mouth, biting off the red cherry and swallowing it down, and then his tongue went to work. He spat out of the stem when it was wrapped into a knot.

Kiera laughed. "Does that impress the girls?"

"If I say it does?"

"I would ask about Malin." His sister arched a brow.

"I haven't shown her yet," he admitted, not that there were a lot of cherries in the Penumbra. He would have to ask about that. Traveling back to the Daylight Realm made him think of many questions, such as what was the best burger joint in the Penumbra? So far, he hadn't seen one. He doubted Malin had ever had a burger, and that was just a shame.

Kiera waited, fingers tapping against her glass. "Are you going to tell me what's going on?"

"I'm staying in the Penumbra. With Malin."

"That's great!" She shot her hand over the table like she meant to hug him, but of course, she couldn't reach. The thought counted. "So it's going well? Am I going to have a sister soon?"

"Um, well." He coughed, clearing his throat. "Actually, I wanted to talk to you about the Penumbra."

Her eyes narrowed.

"Would you want to come too? Malin mentioned that you have the same gland thingy as me, and it's only a matter of time before you go . . ." He couldn't say it, but he didn't need to: blind like their mother. And maybe nearly dead like their mother.

"I can't leave Mom," she said.

"Not even for Conrí?"

Her lips pursed, and she looked ready to hit him. "You know I can't leave Mom."

"I don't want you to leave Mom. I don't want to leave her either, but . . . she should come with us."

Kiera's eyes widened. "And how do we explain that to her?"

Kane zipped his mouth together. His first suggestion was that she was blind and maybe wouldn't notice, but his mother noticed everything. Well, most things. "We'll explain, and maybe they can help her too. If her illness is related, perhaps just being there will ease her symptoms."

"Did they say that?"

"We're working on it, Kiera. Malin said that there hasn't been a case like us before. Not recently. There are lots of things they don't know, but we'll figure it out together."

She nibbled on her bottom lip. "I don't know, Kane. It all seems like a lot. Mom didn't want to leave her home in the first place and—"

The diner door swung open, bell tolling above, and she looked up.

Conrí and Malin walked in, not that the cowans noticed. A worker ran and pulled the door shut, muttering about the crazy wind Wickney was getting. Conrí and Malin stood at the end of the table, and Kiera stared up at them. She could see them, which was more than when this started. The nimh was getting stronger, which meant that it was only a matter of time before she went blind. Kane had to save his sister from that fate if he could. In truth, he'd speak with their mother separately if Kiera outright refused.

"So." Conrí slid into the booth next to Kiera, his eyes solely on her. "You coming with us?"

Kiera's mouth opened and closed, eyelids blinking slowly like she was lost in a trance.

Kane looked over to Malin. Did he look like as big of a fool as Kiera did? But as he watched Malin, he knew the answer. And when she turned to him, he just about fainted with the air whooshing from his lungs.

Finally, Kiera found her voice. "I guess it's a family affair then." She put her hand on Kane's. "When do we leave?"

THE END

Read Conrí and Kiera's story in book two of the Wickney Witches series: *For the Love of Darkness.*

https://books2read.com/loveofdarkness

ABOUT THE AUTHORS

SUSAN STRADIOTTO IS PASSIONATE ABOUT the written word, whether it is in her own writing or her editing practice. She is an author of fantasy and romance and has professional editorial experience with genres such as romance, memoir, mystery/thriller, cozy mystery, fantasy, and women's fiction. She attended Capella University for her BS in Information Technology and the University of Chicago's Graham School for her professional editing certification. She lives in Eden Prairie with her husband, a hoard of Bernese Mountain Dogs, and one Miniature Dachshund.

Read more from Susan Stradiotto

https://books2read.com/rl/susanstradiotto
https://www.susanstradiotto.com

Join Susan's Newsletter

https://www.subscribepage.com/susansfantasycommunity

* * *

SOPHIA-ROSE JOHNSON, WHO HAS ALSO written under the pen name S. Johnson, is from Minnesota, USA, and she is a northerner by heart and accent. She graduated from the University of Wisconsin-Superior in 2018 with a writing degree, and she argues about commas constantly. While she first published in 2022, she's been writing since 2011. When not working at her day or night job, she enjoys reading, hanging out with family and friends, playing with her dogs, making sarcastic comments, being a fake blond, chugging energy drinks, and wearing high heels as a tall woman.

Read more from Sophia-Rose Johnson

https://www.sjohnsonbooks.com

List of Spells

Bhac - to block or create a barricade
Bhaile - means home; used within the Penumbra to return home
Cadal - sleep
Clúdach - cloaking spell
Dearmad - forget; memory eraser
Dubh - call a cloud of darkness
Dùin - close off the flow of magic
Fuar - cool something down
Féach - ability to see more clearly; almost sense things around oneself
Gaoth - call the wind to fly
Grá síoraí - means love eternal; part of the bonding ceremony
Lanna - Calls the s-blades into existence
Saor - lift darkness
Socair - calm someone down
Sruthán - burn
Séala - to seal, shut, or close something off

www.ingramcontent.com/pod-product-compliance
Lightning Source LLC
Chambersburg PA
CBHW072005190726
48293CB00001B/165